1814—1829:
The Epic Continues...

The Brands. Jeremy. Zebulon. Two brothers as different as Cain and Abel. Both fighting for their land, both bitter rivals for the love of the headstrong, passionate Rebecca.

But now their dynasty has grown. There's Circumstance, Jeremy's half-Indian daughter, struggling against the censure of Washington society. Suzannah, loving Jonathan, a frontiersman, a man her mother Rebecca abhors. And Gunning, cursed with his father Zebulon's notorious ways.

They would know all the power brokers of their day—Madison, Monroe, the suave Henry Clay, the magnificent Andrew Jackson—as they helped forge the new nation that in turn gave shape to their own lives...

FORGED IN FURY is their story, it is our story, and it is one of the greatest stories ever told....

By Evan H. Rhodes from Berkley

THE AMERICAN PALACE series

BOOK 1: *Bless This House*
BOOK 2: *Forged in Fury*

Preface

THE WHITE HOUSE . . . in the course of the centuries, it
has become the most visible and potent symbol of man's quest
for freedom.

When the Founding Fathers first laid the cornerstone in
October, 1792, they called it the Palace in the Forest, the Great
Castle, the Executive Mansion, and the American Palace. In
1810, the name "White House" first came into popular use.
But no matter what the building's name, it has always been
imbued with an almost mystical quality, for in this House of
the People resides the *one* man chosen by Americans to lead
them through times of war and peace, adversity and triumph.

Even as the blocks of sandstone were going up, fate and
fortune chose one American family to be intimately involved
with the White House: Two brothers, Jeremy Brand, the dreamer, the builder; Zebulon Brand, the adventurer, the opportunist;
and Rebecca, the woman they both loved, a woman whose
beauty was matched only by her intelligence and ambition.
Their lives, and the lives of all the generations of their children,
will forever be entwined with the American Palace, and with
the destinies of the men and women who forged this nation's
history.

Along with the Brands, we'll be caught up in the ceremonies, inaugurations, allegiances, treasons, and assassinations
surrounding the White House. And through the Brands, we'll
experience not only the greatness of our leaders, but also their
secret, human side. We'll learn the answers to these questions:

Which President had a war named after him?

Which First Lady came down with a severe case of "queen
fever" and was shunned by Washington society during her
husband's first term?

Which President was accused of having made a "corrupt bargain," promising a cabinet post to another candidate if he would throw his electoral votes to him?

Which President had a fearsome reputation as a sharpshooter and by the time he was elected had already killed a number of men in duels?

Which President's wife was convicted of being a bigamist, leading to a scandal so vitriolic that she died of a broken heart a month before her husband was to be inaugurated?

Which President defended a suspected adulteress, and in so doing almost wrecked his administration?

Which President was the first to marry while in the White House, and to a woman thirty years younger than he was?

Which President literally worked himself to death while in office?

Throughout America's tumultuous history, future generations of the Brand dynasty will continue to be caught up in the epic of the White House, as more secrets are revealed and more questions asked:

Which First Lady was accused of being a spy, forcing her husband to publicly defend her?

Which President became so popular that he had a toy named after him, a toy that every child knows?

Which President was a reprobate, whose henchmen defrauded the nation of millions of dollars?

Which President spent twelve to fourteen hours a day sleeping, yet is still one of the most quoted of all chief executives?

Which President won his first election for public office when the schoolhouse where contested votes were to be recounted burned down mysteriously, thus insuring his questionable victory?

Which First Lady admitted to being a drug user and an alcoholic, advocated free love for her unmarried daughter, yet still remains one of the most admired women in America?

What was the dread curse leveled against the White House, foretelling that every President elected in a year ending in zero would die in office? In 1840, 1860, 1880, 1900, 1920, 1940, and 1960, that prophecy has proven to be horribly accurate. Will that curse be visited on the President elected in 1980?

All this, and more, will be revealed in this book and in the subsequent books of the continuing saga of *The American Palace*.

And now Book Two begins where *Bless This House* ends, with the burning of Washington, as disaster strikes the capital, the White House, and the Brand family...

"Arise! . . . I call upon the sons and daughters of the heroes who fought at Valley Forge . . . of the heroes who won the day at Yorktown. We can win this *second* War For Independence if only we have the will, if only we are imbued with the spirit of our founding fathers, who believed that freedom was man's most precious gift. They forged our freedom in flame and fury. Are we to say that their dreams have all been in vain? I say: Never! Arise! Arise!"

"Rebel Thorne" *1814*

PART ONE

Chapter 1

"I MUST reach Washington, I must!" Jeremy Brand swore as he stumbled along the road from Bladensburg to the capital. Blood stained his shirt; he'd taken a bullet in the shoulder, and a piece of shrapnel had grazed his scalp, matting his thick blond hair with blood. His wounds would have felled a lesser man, but at thirty-two, Jeremy Brand was in the prime of his life. His lean body, honed to rock-hard litheness from years of working on the White House, now stood him in good stead. His mission was desperate and could well influence the outcome of this Second War for Independence against Great Britain.

The war had begun in June of 1812, primarily over Great Britain's confiscation of American ships and her impressment of American seamen. With Napoleon keeping Great Britain's army occupied on the Continent, the United States moved to conquer Canada, hoping for a quick victory. But that turned into an ignominious defeat. Aside from a few American naval victories, Great Britain was proving herself more than a match for the new nation. And then Napoleon was defeated and Great Britain was able to turn her full and formidable attention to the war in the New World.

In the summer of 1814, an enormous British invasion fleet— more than fifty warships and troop transports—sailed up the Chesapeake Bay and landed at the Upper Marlboro. The English army of more than five thousand men, under the joint command of General Ross and Rear Admiral Cockburn, started their invasion march. Their objective: the capture and destruction of Washington.

A hastily assembled and ill-equipped American militia engaged the redcoats just outside Bladensburg, a town ten miles north of the capital. Some of the American soldiers had no shoes; others had no rifles, and those who did often had no ammunition. The American battle strategy was further confounded by the ineptitude of General Winder, in charge of Washington's defense, and the countermanding orders of Secretary of War Armstrong, and of Secretary of State James

Monroe, and even of the Commander in Chief, little sickly pale James Madison, who'd taken the field to be with his army.

But in the face of the brilliant discipline and tactics of Wellington's Invincibles, and of the new secret British weapon, the rocket, the ragtag American militia broke and ran. Jeremy was then serving with Commodore Joshua Barney, a valorous hard-bitten old salt, and only his unit's delaying tactics prevented President Madison from being captured by the British. Then an exploding shell injured Jeremy and broke Commodore Barney's leg.

"The battle's lost," Barney said to Jeremy. "You must get to Washington and warn Captain Tingey to blow up the Navy Yard. If our naval stores fall into the hands of the British, they'll have enough supplies to continue fighting on our soil for years."

Jeremy refused to leave Barney at first, but when the Commodore gave him a direct order, he raced off amid the hail of bullets from the advancing British forces.

Dusk had deepened when Jeremy finally reached the capital. The streets were strangely silent, most of the houses shuttered and barred. The city had always looked sparsely settled because of the enormous distances between the government buildings. First established as the capital of the new nation in 1800, it was still little more than a village, with forests and swamps being cleared. Houses dotted the main avenues. The grand design of Pierre L'Enfant, who'd laid out the city, was still little more than a vision; the population numbered only about three thousand, and this evening, with the panicked citizenry fleeing, it looked like Bedlam.

It took all of Jeremy's strength for him to reach the Navy Yard, where he gasped out his message to Captain Tingey. "You've got to blow it all up. Nothing must fall into the hands of the British."

"Aye, we were just setting the charges," Captain Tingey said. "We heard of the rout at Bladensburg, but we were still hoping for a miracle."

"No miracle will happen this night," Jeremy whispered.

Captain Tingey glanced at the clock. "Eight-fifteen now. I'll give the order to light the fuses in five more minutes."

Jeremy had known Captain Tingey practically all his adult life. Not only had Tingey designed most of the naval facilities in 1800, but during his fourteen years as commander, he'd made the Washington Navy Yard the best in the nation.

"This must be a grim day for you, sir," Jeremy said.

"Aye, and old President John Adams will have a fit when he hears of it," Tingey said. "This Navy Yard was his idea."

"You'd better make yourself scarce when the British arrive," Jeremy said. Tingey had been born in England, and thus would have been charged with treason if captured.

With a final glance around, Tingey shouted, "All right, light the fuses!"

Jeremy watched as sailors raced to the buildings, throwing the lighted torches everywhere. The warehouse caught fire, then the sail lofts erupted. The flames leapt to the paint supplies and from there to the lumberyard and sawmill. When the fire reached the ammunition dump, a great explosion turned night into day and threw out shock waves that rocked the city.

Jeremy recoiled from the blast of heat as the orange-and-red fireball roared into the night sky. He stumbled away from the blazing depot. Now he could go find his daughter, Circumstance. She would be at his cabin, which stood at the edge of the White House grounds.

General Ross and Rear Admiral Cockburn rode into Washington at the head of their troops. "These American soldiers are so inept that we've hardly suffered any casualties," Cockburn said. "I've sent a platoon ahead to the Navy Yard, and—"

Suddenly a gigantic explosion sent a rush of air sweeping over them, and plumes of fire flared into the sky. Explosion after explosion tore the Navy Yard asunder. Cockburn's face hardened. "Damn! Well, the Yankees beat us to it. Now we'll have to make the best of it."

Sean Connaught, a captain in the British Intelligence Corps, came galloping up to the two leaders. Working with his Connaught relatives in America, Sean had infiltrated the capital, and he had pressed for its capture. His young cousin Marianne and his aging Great-Aunt Victoria had told him how vulnerable Washington was. Though General Ross had been fearful of extending his supply lines so far, almost fifty miles from the fleet anchored in the Upper Marlboro, Sean's insistence that they invade was about to bear fruit.

"Sir, the Capitol is that building straight ahead," Sean said. "My scouts have already been through it, and it's deserted."

The British officers rode closer and Ross squinted through the darkness at the two wings of the massive building, which were connected only by a wooden walkway. "It's not an unhandsome structure," he said.

"But what it symbolizes is anathema," Cockburn said.

"Absolutely," Sean agreed. "There is the law of an eye for an eye. When the Americans invaded Canada, the first thing *they* did was burn the Parliament Building at York. Can you imagine such barbarity?"

"If we allowed every colony to get away with rebellion, we would soon lose the Empire," Cockburn said. Then the admiral slapped his thigh and a grin spread across his voluptuous features. "General Ross, do you realize that we've just captured the enemy's capital?"

As they came within two hundred yards of the Capitol, a shot rang out. Ross's horse whinnied, then fell over, dead. More shots were fired and four British soldiers took fatal bullets.

"It came from that building," Sean shouted. Taking a detachment of soldiers, he rode hard for Tomlinson's Hotel.

Inside the hotel, Zebulon Brand and a platoon of militiamen had been hiding cartons of congressional records in the basement storerooms. But when Zebulon had seen the British approaching, his erratic, impulsive nature had gotten the best of him and he'd given the order to fire. Zebulon was Jeremy's half-brother, but other than sharing the seed of the same father, they were as unlike as any two men could be. Zebulon was dark, brutally handsome, with magnetic dark brown eyes and an overpowering sexuality that had gotten him into trouble all his life. At twenty, he'd had a wild affair with Elizabeth Connaught, young wife of Devroe Connaught, an English aristocrat of great wealth but flagging virility. When Devroe had discovered Elizabeth's infidelity, he'd cornered Zebulon on a marshy shore of the Potomac River. But just as he was about to shoot him before the horrified eyes of his wife and his four-year-old daughter Marianne, Devroe had stumbled into a nest of water moccasins. Death had been almost instantaneous, and it had driven his wife into a madness from which she had never recovered. It galvanized the rest of the Connaught clan, notably the spinster Victoria and Sean Connaught, into an unreasoned hatred of the Brands.

As Zebulon saw the British soldiers galloping toward Tomlinson's Hotel, he realized his tactical error. "They know we're here for sure," he said. "Everybody out of the hotel!" Just as the redcoats swarmed through the entrance, Zebulon and his men escaped through the rear door and scattered into the darkness.

Sean Connaught tramped through the building. Guns and ammunition were stored everywhere. "I want this place leveled!" he ordered, and his crew set fires on every floor.

Then Sean rejoined the rest of the British forces. The soldiers broke open the doors of the Capitol and methodically ransacked the building. One enterprising redcoat cut down the portraits of Louis XVI and Marie Antoinette that hung in the room adjoining the Senate chamber.

Cockburn studied the Capitol. "These walls are so sturdy that I believe the only way to demolish the place is to blow it up."

"We can't spare that much powder," General Ross said. "If we'd captured their Navy Yard, it would have been a different matter. We could have blown up the entire city, and good riddance."

Sean Connaught interrupted with a stiff salute, "Sir, if I may be permitted, I believe our demolition team can set fire to the building. With this quick wind coming up, I think we'll be able to provide a merry blaze for your amusement."

Cockburn nodded at him with a smile. "Carry on then, Captain."

"Attention!" Sean ordered and the demolition crew snapped to. "Chop all the woodwork into kindling, then pile the furniture in the center of the room and sprinkle it with gunpowder."

The crew quickly carried out his orders. With a glint of madness in his eyes, Sean said to Admiral Cockburn, "You have no idea how much pleasure this gives me. These Americans have been a thorn in my side since I can remember."

Admiral Cockburn, who knew of the bitter Connaught history in Washington, said, "Then you shall have the honor of lighting the first match."

"Done!" Sean lit the trail of powder, watched the spark race toward the center of the room and then mushroom into flame.

In the House of Representatives wing, other British soldiers were firing rockets into the roof, trying to set the rafters ablaze. "We can't seem to get it started," a discouraged midshipman told Sean.

"I saw them constructing the damned place," he said. "The roof is covered with sheet iron, and that's damping the fire." He had them repeat the procedure that had set the Senate ablaze.

Now both wings of the Capitol were afire, the flames increasingly more visible through the windows. Everything inside began burning. "The thick limestone walls are acting like an oven," Sean said. The secret journals of the House burned, as did the law library, and the 740 books purchased in 1802 by Thomas Jefferson as a start for the Library of Congress. Then the gilt eagle surmounting the clock over the Speaker of the House's chair erupted into flame like a phoenix. The hands of the clock stopped at 10 o'clock. Sean watched the flames roar through the broken windows and open doors, and then at last the sheet-iron roof melted and fell in fiery globules to the marble floor.

Borne on the increasingly strong winds, the sparks quickly ignited four other houses near the Capitol, including two that General Washington had built nearby as an expression of his faith in the city. Some of the records of the House of Representatives had been secreted in these two buildings; they also went up in flames.

"All right men, on to the President's Mansion," Admiral Cockburn said. "Or as these colonials call it, their White House. I promise you it won't be white for long!"

Whichever way Tanzy turned, she was confronted by burning buildings. She clutched Circumstance Brand to her and tried to think of a safe place to go. When Dolley Madison fled the White House in the face of the British advance, Tanzy and Circumstance had followed her party in another wagon, but it had overturned in the crush of people and they'd been separated from Dolley. Tanzy might have found safety if she were alone; Circumstance, being only eight years old, slowed her down considerably. But leaving her behind would have been unthinkable. She'd promised Jeremy that she'd watch out for his daughter. And she owed Jeremy so much. She had once been Zebulon Brand's slave, but when Jeremy bought her from Zebulon years ago, he immediately freed her. Circumstance was only a babe then. Never once in all those years had Jeremy forced his attentions on Tanzy. Though there were times when she might have wished . . . but then, his heart belonged to another. Tanzy had come to love Circumstance and, indeed, would have given her life for this strange enchanted creature with the sky-blue eyes.

"The British must have cut off all the roads out of the city," Tanzy said. "People are turning back everywhere."

Circumstance pointed to the waterfront, where the fire raged in the Navy Yard. "We can't go that way, either. I wish Papa were here. He'd know what to do."

Tanzy and Circumstance had been hurrying hither and yon for hours, and both of them were ready to drop from exhaustion. "We've got to find shelter somewhere," Tanzy said, and ran to a house and pounded on the door. No answer came from within. Then Circumstance saw British soldiers running through the streets, their bayonets at the ready. With Circumstance in hand, Tanzy ran to another house. This time the door was opened, but by a grinning redcoat.

"What have we here?" he shouted to his comrades. "A dusky beauty if I ever saw one." He grabbed for her, but Tanzy slipped from his grasp and fled. The soldier raced after her. Strong hands grabbed her and threw her to the ground.

The leering redcoat straddled her. Circumstance flung herself at the soldier, but with a backhand swipe he knocked her aside.

Tanzy screamed and raked for the man's eyes with her fingernails, but a sharp blow to her chin stunned her. "I swear I never saw a woman as beautiful as this," the soldier said, tearing at her clothes, his eyes devouring the tawny skin, and the oval face and full lips.

Circumstance sprang at the soldier again, pummeling at him with her tiny fists while he tried to loosen his belt. The delay was long enough for Tanzy to come to her senses. She struggled under the soldier's weight, and with a wrench, managed to free one of her hands. She drew her knife from under her skirts and with a sharp jab plunged it into the soldier's side. She scrambled out from under the wounded redcoat, grabbed Circumstance, and ran.

"Stop her, she stabbed me!" the soldier cried.

Other redcoats raced after Tanzy. This time there were too many to fight off. "Pray that the soldier lives," an officer said to Tanzy. "Otherwise, Admiral Cockburn will see that you hang. Take her to headquarters!" he shouted.

Chapter 2

"HURRY, GET those buckets up to the roof!" Rebecca Brand ordered her slaves. Eli, Letitia, and Letitia's ten-year-old son, Tadpole, carried the sloshing pails up through the attic. "That's it," Rebecca said, "pour the water over the shingles." She climbed onto the roof of the Brand house built on New York Avenue.

Sparks carried on the wind flew all about her. Some landed on the wet shingles, sputtered, and died. Rebecca's huge hazel eyes flinched from the blazing city before her. Flames leapt from the Capitol, drawing the air up into a fiery vortex. At the river's edge, occasional explosions still rocked the Navy Yard, and the night air reeked of turpentine and resin. Here and there a private home fell victim to the leaping conflagration. "Well, that won't happen to my house," Rebecca exclaimed resolutely. "Eli, keep wetting the roof down. Tadpole, go and get more water."

Thank God they'd built the house of brick, Rebecca thought. If the wind didn't shift, perhaps they'd be spared. But the wind was growing more intense; a storm was brewing. She went down to the children's room. Seven-year-old Suzannah ran to her and six-year-old Gunning clutched her skirts and whimpered.

"It's all right," she said soothingly. "Mamma's here, no harm's going to come to you." She noticed that her son kept sniveling, but Suzannah looked at her with her dark brown eyes, so like Zebulon's, and not a sound escaped her. "Good girl," she said, stroking Suzannah's silky dark brown hair. She had a momentary thought that the backbone in this family might have passed on through the female line, and this distressed her, for she had an unreasoned love for Gunning—perhaps because the boy looked so like her with his titian hair and hazel eyes flecked with gold.

At thirty-five, Rebecca Breech Brand was considered among the most beautiful women in Washington. Her flawless skin, the health that seemed to radiate from her ample body, were the envy of many a younger matron in Washington society. Her father, Mathias Breech, a lowly stone merchant, had grown wealthy supplying stone for the federal buildings when the government finally moved to Washington in 1800. In her youth, two men had courted her—Zebulon Brand, dynamic, sexual, with a consuming appetite for life, and his half-brother, Jeremy, as fair as his brother was dark, hair white-blond, with discerning blue eyes and a sympathetic heart. Zebulon was a man of the world, a trader, a doer. Jeremy was reflective, with golden hands, a man who could draw or build anything.

Ten years ago, though it seemed more like a hundred, Zebulon had gotten drunk one evening and tried to rape her. In the ensuing struggle, the Breech carriage house in Georgetown burned down. Zebulon fled, in part to escape Rebecca's wrath, but also because Sean Connaught had returned to the United States demanding satisfaction for his Uncle Devroe's death. Zebulon went off with Stephen Decatur, joined the Navy, and fought in the wars against the Tripoli pirates.

Believing that fate had shown her the way, Rebecca turned her full attention to Jeremy, only to discover that he'd accepted a commission to join Captain Meriwether Lewis and Captain William Clark in their Voyage of Northwest Discovery. Jeremy could capture the essence of anything he drew, and Lewis needed such a man along on the journey. Though Rebecca did everything she could to hold him in Washington, Jeremy insisted that he'd given his word to President Jefferson, and left on the expedition with Lewis and Clark.

For two long years Rebecca waited for Jeremy to return, and when the nation received no news of the expedition at all, she finally gave him up for dead. Meanwhile, Zebulon returned from the Mediterranean covered with glory, and once more pressed his suit. He seemed so contrite, so loving, that at last Rebecca agreed to marry him.

And then fate again showed its mocking disdain for her. Jeremy returned home from the unknown wilderness; Lewis and Clark had done what no white man had ever done before, they'd explored the land from sea to shining sea. But Jeremy had a secret. On the voyage, he'd met and fallen in love with a Shoshone Indian maiden named White Doe. She'd died in childbirth, but Jeremy had brought home his daughter, a half-breed he'd named Circumstance. Jeremy always insisted that he'd married White Doe, that Meriwether Lewis had performed the ceremony, but Rebecca never took this claim seriously. Neither did most of Washington, particularly when Lewis committed suicide shortly thereafter and couldn't substantiate Jeremy's tale. When Rebecca pressed Jeremy to give up the child—send her back to the wilderness with her people, or put her in an orphanage—Jeremy refused. In a mindless rage, Rebecca married Zebulon.

She came to regret her decision, for Zebulon was always in trouble, involved in one hare-brained scheme after another. First there were shipping ventures in the slave trade with her father. Then he joined Aaron Burr's plot to seize the western lands, conquer Mexico, and crown himself Emperor—a fiasco that resulted in a trial for treason. Only the bitter enmity between Chief Justice Marshall and President Jefferson, which resulted in a contest of wills between the Presidency and the Supreme Court, prevented them all from going to jail or being executed.

Rebecca could have countenanced Zebulon's rashness, but she could never forgive his transgressions with the mulatto slave he'd bought in the West Indies, a girl named Tanzy. When Rebecca married him, she had insisted that he sell her. Jeremy had bought the girl; she acted as housekeeper and nurse to Circumstance.

Now as Rebecca stared out into the street aglow with reflected firelight, she wondered which of the two brothers she cared for more.

She whirled suddenly as the door burst open and Zebulon stumbled into the room. His face was grimed with perspiration and dirt and his hands were trembling. "I've killed some soldiers," he gasped. "They may have followed me."

"The root cellar," she said without hesitation and opened the door to the basement. He scurried down the darkened steps and she closed and locked the door after him. Then she went to the window, edged the curtain aside, and peered out. Her heart sank when she saw the ranks of British soldiers, their red coats seemingly aflame in the reflected firelight. She picked up a spyglass and held it to her eye. Perhaps a hundred and fifty men followed an officer on a prancing white charger. He was decked out in the braid of an admiral and was wearing an admiral's hat, that much she could make out. "That must be Admiral Cockburn," she whispered to her maid, Letitia.

"Yes'm," Letitia said, terrified beyond the telling of it.

"What a fool Zebulon is, to lead them here and jeopardize the children!" Rebecca couldn't help thinking that Jeremy would never have done such a thing.

Rebecca held her breath and then slowly released it when the soldiers turned and marched to the north. Obviously, they were after something more important. She watched with sinking heart as the redcoats continued straight toward the White House.

Chapter 3

FALLING, LURCHING forward, and falling again, Jeremy finally made his way to his house. "Circumstance!" he shouted. "Tanzy!"

His only answer was the banging of a shutter in the wind. His head reeled with his exertions and he clutched his temples, trying to think of where they'd go. "Dolley Madison," he exclaimed. "She promised she'd watch out for them."

He climbed the low fence surrounding the President's grounds and staggered across the lawn to the White House. The pain in his arm became so intense that the walls seemed to waver in his vision. He must have passed out momentarily, for when he became aware again, he found himself lying on the front steps of the house.

He dragged his way through the open doors. The entrance hall looked barren, the drawing room strangely naked without its red velvet curtains. Yet in the dining room, the table was set, as if guests were expected momentarily. Again and again he shouted Circumstance's name, but all he got back was an echo. Dazed, he lit a candle and climbed the stairs to the second floor.

"Where is everybody?" he shouted.

The house remained silent, brooding, waiting. He searched the upper rooms; there wasn't a soul in the entire place. "Everybody's gone," he said. His words had a terrible effect on him; it seemed that this was the final proof that the war with Great Britain was lost. The house of the President of the people . . . abandoned.

Then he glanced out the window and saw redcoats below, led by a man on a white charger. Jeremy knew that he could still make it out the end door and escape across the lawn, but something held him rooted. His waves of faintness were interspersed with a thousand memories.

I've worked on this house for more than twenty years, he thought. I know every room, every nook and cranny. I've seen three Presidents live within these walls, broke bread with them

and shared their aspirations for the glory of this great nation.
In this house I greeted its first occupant, President John Adams.
In this house I promised President Jefferson that I would go
on the Lewis and Clark expedition.

And now the enemy in their red coats were coming to destroy
it.

He heard voices, distinct English accents, and then the sound
of footsteps on the stairway. Unless I hide, he thought, I'll be
captured for certain. Where? The roof? Then it came to him.
The inventive Thomas Jefferson, while President, had designed
a unique clothes closet and had Jeremy build it for him. The
clothes rack worked on a swivel so that only one section at a
time needed to be exposed, the one appropriate for the season;
the other section fit into a cedar-lined well. Jefferson's ingenuity might well save Jeremy's life this night.

Once Jeremy wedged his way into the double-gated clothes
well, the voices became muffled. But Jeremy could still tell
that there were many soldiers in the house, searching through
every room on the floor, including this one. He held his breath
and waited.

On the main floor, Admiral Cockburn, General Ross, and
Sean Connaught tramped through the rooms. "Will you look
at this?" Cockburn said to Sean. "This dining table is set for
scores of people." The wine bottles lay in coolers that had been
packed with ice; it had melted in the August heat.

"I expect that little Madison thought he'd be victorious at
Bladensburg," Sean chortled, "and that this was to be his celebration dinner."

Cockburn sampled a generous helping of cold cuts that a
soldier brought up from the kitchen. The officers poured themselves a round of Madeira. "I propose a toast," Cockburn said.
"To the health of the Prince Regent, and success to His Majesty's forces by land and sea."

"It's not every day that one captures the capital of the enemy," General Ross said, puffed with pride.

"We've got to crush them, make these Americans heel, the
way you train a dog," Sean said between his teeth.

"We must have some souvenirs to recall the occasion,"
Cockburn said, and began to forage through the rooms. The
soldiers cried out every time they found a treasure, but Sean

Connaught saw nothing in the way of booty that interested him.

"I won't need anything to remind me of this triumph," he whispered to himself. For more than ten years he'd worked with the British Intelligence, preparing for this moment, and now the moment had come.

His clothes were so sweat-stained that they clung to his back. "I'd like nothing better than some clean linen," he said to General Ross.

"Why, perhaps that little gnome the Americans have for a President will be glad to lend you some," Ross replied.

Whistling "God Save the King," Sean went upstairs to President Madison's bedroom.

Inside the closet, Jeremy drew his pistol. He might have to kill the man, for he heard him coming closer. The closet door creaked open and a razor-thin shaft of light cut the darkness. Jeremy saw a hand reach for a shirt. The groping fingers came so close that he could see the man's ring... with a family crest that looked familiar. He couldn't quite place it, yet he knew that he'd seen that seal before.

The man chose a shirt, stripped, and changed garments, leaving his dirty clothes behind. Then he was gone. Jeremy slumped with relief. But that relief didn't last long.

With the food eaten and the wine drunk, a redcoat swept the remaining silver and plate into a tablecloth and carried it off. In the Oval Room, considered by many to be the most beautiful room in the White House, if not in all America, Sean ordered his men to pile the furniture in the center of the floor.

"The preparations are complete, Admiral," he said.

"Then the honors are yours," Cockburn replied. "See if you can't give us as merry a blaze as you did with the Capitol."

Sean's gunmetal blue eyes narrowed. "I stood in this very room years ago, and swore that I would see this house destroyed, along with everything it represents. Truly, this does prove to me that there is a God."

Sean stove in a barrel of gunpowder with the butt of his pistol and sprinkled it on the heaped-up furniture. Then the demolition crew raced from room to room throwing lighted torches on the pyres.

Upstairs, Jeremy smelled smoke. He fought his way out of the closet and edged over to the staircase. Dense smoke began to curl up towards him. "They've set the house afire!" he gasped

in disbelief. These so-called civilized men were destroying the
house, this work of art, just for the sake of destroying! They're
no better than Vandals! he thought.

Somehow, Jeremy felt that he himself was being violated.
His rage grew and became so monumental that he knew he had
to do something or lose his mind. Something to let these Huns
know that there were Americans who would fight to the death
for their country, fight to the death for their belief in freedom.

He checked his pistols; loaded and ready.

The wound in his temple reopened and fresh blood coursed
down his face. He might have lost consciousness again save
that the pain in his arm kept prying him back to reality. The
seasoned wood paneling caught fire, the windows shattered
from the heat, and the air sucked in from the outside fanned
the flames into a roaring blaze. As the fire licked at the walls
and at the balustrade, Jeremy stole downstairs. He smelled the
acrid odor of hair burning and then realized that it was his own.
He slapped at the back of his head, blinked the sweat from his
eyes as the grand entrance foyer melted in his swimming vision.

Suddenly a voice called out, "Who's there?" Jeremy whirled
to see Sean Connaught confronting him at the foot of the staircase. For a moment, neither man recognized the other.

Sean Connaught raised his pistol but Jeremy fired first. The
bullet passed through Sean's shoulder; the impact knocked him
through the front doors.

Jeremy dropped to the floor to escape the intense heat and
crawled through the doorway. Once outside, he felt the blessed
relief of the night air. The man he'd shot lay nearby, stunned.
Clutching at the sandstone, Jeremy inched himself to his feet
until he stood at full height. In the driveway of the President's
Mansion he saw a man in the uniform of a high naval officer
mount a white stallion. With the roaring of the fire all about
them, the British officers had been unaware of the shooting.

Jeremy drew his other pistol and shouted, "Admiral!"

Cockburn wheeled his horse and looked at the dark figure
limned against the roaring inferno of the White House.

"Draw your pistol, sir," Jeremy cried. "You shan't go un-
punished for this crime!"

Cockburn reached for his gun.

Jeremy steadied his arm and fired just as Sean Connaught
threw himself at him, deflecting his aim. The bullet passed
harmlessly through Cockburn's hat. Then Jeremy collapsed.

A half-dozen soldiers rushed him with fixed bayonets, but they didn't shoot, fearing to hit Sean Connaught, who was still tangled with him.

"Is the man dead?" Cockburn demanded.

"Close enough," Sean said, stemming the blood from his own wound. He rolled the man over with his foot and then recognized him. "Jeremy Brand!" he exclaimed.

He wished it was Zebulon. That would have made his revenge complete.

"Admiral, I think we'd better bring the American with us," Sean said. "Obviously, he was hiding in the White House while we were there, and he may have overheard our plans."

"That's highly unlikely," Cockburn said.

Sean compressed his lips. "I know this man. He may be useful in my effort to gather intelligence."

Cockburn shrugged his agreement. Sean felt the same exultant thrill as when he ran a fox down to earth. Jeremy was slung over a horse and carried to the temporary British headquarters at Rhode's Tavern nearby. There Sean turned him over to the ship's doctor who'd set up an aid station in the tavern's back room. After the British wounded, including Sean, had been tended to, the doctor examined Jeremy. Sean Connaught hovered nearby.

"Broken arm, lost a great deal of blood, shrapnel wound to the head. He's still unconscious, but with the proper care, he may live."

Sean's thin wet lips twitched. He thought of that long-ago day when he'd seen his uncle murdered before his eyes, and by this man's brother. He thought of his Aunt Elizabeth, consigned forever to a life of the living dead. Surely the crimes of this Brand family cried out to heaven for vengeance, and a just God had given him the opportunity to avenge the Connaught name. Zebulon Brand's turn would come soon.

Sean gripped the doctor's arm. "I charge you, make sure you tend to him. I want this man alive. He's a spy, and I have every intention of hanging him as soon as we get back to the fleet."

Chapter 4

THE BRITISH had converted the outbuildings of Rhode's Tavern on F and Fifteenth Streets, into prisons holding captured American militiamen, suspected snipers, and others who'd fought them. Among the hostages were Circumstance and Tanzy.

Admiral Cockburn sat at a table in the tavern's main room, meting out justice. A decanter of wine stood on the table. "Burning makes one deucedly thirsty, wouldn't you say?" he asked Sean. "Who's next?"

Sean, his arm bound in a sling, shoved Tanzy and Circumstance forward. "My aide tells me this colored slave and the child tried to murder one of our soldiers."

"I'm not a slave," Tanzy cried. "And your soldier tried to rape me."

Circumstance nodded her head vigorously. "I saw him."

"Be quiet, child," Sean ordered.

"But it's true," she insisted.

Tanzy gripped Circumstance's shoulders. "Don't say anything. It won't do us any good."

Suddenly the shutters flew open and a great gust of wind swept into the room, blowing papers about and extinguishing the candles. "Bolt the doors and windows," Cockburn ordered. When the candles were relit he regarded Tanzy impatiently. "Do you always have such infernal weather in this city?"

Tanzy kept her tongue, but Circumstance stepped forward. "This storm has been sent by the Lord to drive out the invaders who would destroy our land."

Taken aback, Cockburn let out a short, harsh laugh, but Sean reached out and slapped her. "Children shouldn't be impertinent."

Tanzy sprang at him but another soldier grabbed her arms.

Circumstance stared at the man without flinching; she memorized every detail of his face. She would never forget him. "We'll win," she whispered. "The rain will put out all the fires

20

you've set. It's a sure sign that the Lord wills it. We'll win."

Sean shuddered in spite of himself, and Cockburn said, "Get them out of my sight. They can't do us any harm."

Circumstance and Tanzy were locked up with the other prisoners, unaware that just a few yards away lay Jeremy.

About an hour later, Marianne Connaught, Sean's cousin, swept into Rhode's Tavern on a gust of wind-driven rain. Her face was hidden beneath the hood of a dark cloak, and when she pushed it back, her eyes looked terrified.

Though in her midtwenties, Marianne Connaught looked considerably younger. There was a fragile tentativeness about her. Her pale oval face was framed by her black hair, which had come undone in the storm. Dark eyebrows arched gently over her violet eyes.

Sean came to her instantly. "Marianne, you shouldn't have come here! It's far too dangerous."

"I know, but I had to warn you," she said. Marianne Connaught had been Sean's contact in America, feeding him information about the defenses of Washington. But she had done this almost against her will—she'd been forced into the spying activities by her Aunt Victoria, a confirmed Tory.

Marianne leaned toward Admiral Cockburn. "News of your presence in Washington has reached the surrounding states, and a large force of the regular American army is heading here."

"When are they expected to arrive?" Cockburn demanded, instantly alert.

"In two days—three at the latest."

Cockburn drummed his fingers on the table. "Without the stores from their Navy Yard, I'm afraid we daren't engage their army. We must retreat to our ships. But this weather..."

"My aunt said to tell you that there's a hurricane heading this way," Marianne said. "She's lived through one of these things before."

Sean nodded, and then took her arm tenderly. "Marianne, I've some good news for you. We captured somebody earlier whom I know will interest you." He led her to the rear room, where Jeremy lay. His arm had been set and put in a splint, but he was still unconscious.

Marianne would have fainted if Sean hadn't caught her. "Brandy!" he shouted to a soldier, who quickly brought it. The drink revived her, and color gradually returned to her parchment-white face.

"You know this man, then?" Admiral Cockburn asked.

She nodded. "He's an acquaintance of mine."

"She's entirely too modest." Sean completely misinterpreted her mood. "Jeremy Brand means a great deal more to the Connaughts than that."

"Well, my dear," Cockburn said, "you should know that this night, your... acquaintance not only wounded your cousin, but almost cost me my life."

Marianne fought to keep her voice from trembling. She knelt beside Jeremy; his breathing sounded labored. "He's seriously wounded, isn't he?" she said, looking up at Admiral Cockburn. "Oh, please, let me take him to my doctor."

"Marianne!" Sean exclaimed.

She turned her brimming eyes to her cousin. "You don't understand. Jeremy had nothing to do with my father's death. Am I to hate him just because he bears the same name as his brother?"

Sean straightened and placed his good hand behind his back. "I would hope that you'd detest him because of everything he stands for, a loutish rebel."

"In the years I've known him he's shown me nothing but kindness, and recently—" Her voice caught in her throat but she managed to finish. "—well, he's done me a personal service. I owe this to him. Please, I beg you—"

"It's out of the question!" Sean's face hardened into a mask of hauteur. By the degree of her concern, she'd given herself away. His Aunt Victoria had warned him that something was going on between her and Jeremy, but he hadn't believed her. Before Marianne could say more, Sean said to Cockburn, "Surely you can see that what my cousin asks is impossible. This man was spying on us in the White House. He can't be set free, or even allowed to remain in Washington. He could easily give our plans away."

"Quite right," Cockburn said. He patted Marianne's arm. "My dear, rest assured that whatever you believe you owe this man, it will be faithfully discharged by us. Our own shipboard doctors will see to him. And now you'd best go. I've been on the high seas long enough to know that this storm will hit us before too long. You mustn't be trapped here. We need you in Washington to continue your good work for us."

He helped her on with her cloak. "One last thing. Please alert our supporters that we plan to bypass Annapolis and will strike at Baltimore shortly. Once we've leveled that city, then part of the fleet will sail on to New Orleans, where, God willing, we shall also be victorious. If these fortuitous conditions remain with us, then I'll wager this war will be over in short order, and settled to our advantage."

Marianne stared at Jeremy, his long blond hair matted with blood, his craggy face twitching as if in a nightmare. How many nights had she spent in his arms, how many nights where he'd gradually ripped away the caul of code and usage that had made her less than a woman, how many nights where she'd known such ecstasy that she couldn't imagine life without him. And now Cockburn was going to send him to one of the navy's infernal prison ships, where if he didn't die of his wounds, he would surely perish of maltreatment or disease. And there was nothing she could do about it. Suddenly, the victory she'd worked for all these years seemed hollow, overshadowed by her love for this simple, generous man. With a final heart-wrenching look at him, she left.

As her horse's hooves beat out a steady cadence along the vast empty avenues, Marianne couldn't help thinking of the history of her benighted family. Her father slain in a manner so dreadful she still had screaming nightmares about it . . . her mother plunged into a madness from which she'd never recover . . . and her own life taken over by her vengeful Aunt Victoria, who had two dreams only—to return the American colonies to the rule of the British Empire, and to erase the entire Brand family from the face of the earth. Each day of her childhood, Marianne had been fed that bitter dose of poison. It continued when her Aunt Victoria took her to England for her education, continued when she returned home and became a spy for her cousin Sean, traveling to Philadelphia, Baltimore, and New Orleans on missions for him, continued until the day she met and fell in love with Jeremy Brand. She was eighteen then, and she tried everything to keep him at arm's length, but he, emerging from his own private hell after the death of his Indian wife and being left with a half-breed infant, wore down her resistance until they finally became lovers. She hated the deception, the clandestine meetings, but since she was under-age, her aunt would have taken her away from Washington, and once she'd tasted love, she knew she couldn't live without it. Then when she finally came of age, the war had broken out, and that presented further problems.

For years now, she'd been gathering confidential information and forwarding it to Sean Connaught—the defense plan for Washington, the precise trail of the Lewis and Clark expedition, the political situation in New Orleans. But with the outbreak of war, her feelings took a violent swing. The thought that she might be doing something that could injure Jeremy had almost torn her apart. And now when she saw him lying unconscious and bleeding, she knew where her true loyalties lay. Her existence had been figured with deceit and hatred. Only Jeremy's love had redeemed her, shown her what life could truly be, and now she would do whatever was necessary to save him, even if it meant sacrificing herself.

With those thoughts on her mind, she rode back through the gathering hurricane toward the Connaught plantation in the hills above Washington. A plan was slowly forming—dangerous to be sure, and one that might alienate her entire Connaught clan; nevertheless, for once in her life she would act bravely and do it. "I will," she swore, and the gale snatched the words from her mouth until it seemed a long scream on the wind: "I will!"

Dawn came several hours later, though with Washington now in the grip of the hurricane, the sky remained dark, swirling with lowering clouds. The White House, the Capitol, and other government buildings had burned steadily through the night. Though the walls of the Capitol and the White House hadn't yet collapsed, the intense heat would surely buckle them soon.

The British troops made ready to depart. "It's madness to go out in this weather," Admiral Cockburn said. "However, we've no choice. We just can't sit here and allow the American army to cut us off from our ships."

Since traveling would be difficult in the extreme, only the most important prisoners were taken along. Thus Circumstance, Tanzy, and scores of other people were let go. That was when Circumstance recognized her father being loaded into one of the wagons. "Papa!" she cried. But when she and Tanzy tried to run after him, they were chased off by the soldiers. One wagon held prisoners chained together, and another wagon held the wounded. Cockburn gave the order to march and the files of soldiers and wagons started out.

The storm struck with its full fury, howling along the wide avenues, uprooting trees and lashing everything with torrents of rain. The wind blew off the roof of the Patent Office, and demolished several wood-frame houses along Pennsylvania Avenue.

The beat of rain against his face gradually revived Jeremy. As the wagon bumped along Pennsylvania Avenue, all that had happened slowly came back to him. He raised himself on his elbow and strained for one last look at Washington. "Oh, merciful God, please let Circumstance and Tanzy be safe."

And what of Marianne? he wondered. Dear, complex Marianne, tormented by her Tory family. He'd grown to love her with an unremitting passion. Where was she? Out of this inferno, he hoped. For she had neither the strength nor the sense to cope with the brutality of war.

And then he saw it, the fire-blackened ruin of the White House. His heart contracted and it was all he could do to keep from screaming aloud.

Fire and storm battered at the remains of the building. The roof had fallen in, the interior was gutted. But the walls were still standing. And then he noticed the clouds of smoke—and something else? Was it steam? The torrential downpour was putting out the fire! And to Jeremy, it seemed like an omen.

"It will rise again, I swear it," he whispered. "If I have to rebuild it with my own hands, it will rise again!"

"I would say that was highly unlikely," a voice said quite near to him.

Jeremy twisted and saw a man on a horse riding close to the wagon of the wounded. The man reached down and prodded Jeremy's arm with his riding crop, and the pain almost made him pass out. He blinked and recognized Sean Connaught.

"The only thing you're going to do is swing from the highest yardarm on one of His Majesty's warships," Sean said. "I'll see to that, I promise you."

Chapter 5

ZEBULON REMAINED hidden in the root cellar until the British left Washington. Letitia, the maid who'd been in Rebecca's family since her birth, sneaked some food down to him, along with heavy doses of consoling chatter, but Zebulon, depressed and frightened after his narrow escape, remained inconsolable.

After her first fruitless attempt to talk reason to her husband, Rebecca avoided him. Finally it was Suzannah who went down into the cellar, and taking her father by the hand, led him upstairs. Once out in the daylight, Zebulon's fear vanished as mysteriously as it had manifested itself, and in short order his charming air of bravado reasserted itself.

Later that evening, as he and Rebecca lay abed, he tried to explain what had happened. "You know I'm no coward," he began.

Rebecca thought that was something she didn't know at all. His response to any difficult situation was apt to be unthinking, and she wondered now if he'd really been as much the hero as he'd made himself out to be in the war with Tripoli, ten years before.

Zebulon's voice, low and resonant, rumbled through the darkness. "It was when I fired on those British soldiers and they gave chase, scores of them after me, that I suddenly became aware of the fragility of life. If they'd gunned me down, I would never have gotten a chance to hold Suzannah in my arms, never gotten a chance to teach Gunning how to be a man. All of that would have been snatched from me, but most of all, I would never have gotten a chance to tell you how much I loved you. Loved you from the first day I saw you, and right to this moment."

She'd come to bed determined that he wouldn't have his way with her. For too long now she'd suffered his presence, but the cataclysmic events of the day, her city burned before her eyes, the relief that their house was still standing and that

26

the children were all right, all this conspired against her resolve. And when he moved to her in the darkness she opened her arms and gave herself to him willingly, and with the hope that she might yet manage to salvage something from their marriage.

In the swell and plunge of his massive body she remembered all the things that had happened between them in their lifetime. She'd met him when she was eleven or twelve years old, and he was nearly twenty. Already he had a reputation with all the tavern wenches in the Federal City area, and her father had warned her against him. But that had only piqued her interest, for with the secret knowledge of her sex, she knew that his hunger for her was very different from his other conquests.

To pay off debts when his father had died, Zebulon had sold his half-brother, Jeremy, to Mathias Breech for a seven-year term of indenture. This had rankled Jeremy and created an ill-feeling between the brothers that existed even to this day. Things had eased somewhat when Jeremy's indentureship had been bought by James Hoban, the principal architect of the American Palace, as the White House had been called in those years.

But as the young men grew into maturity, Rebecca gradually became aware of Jeremy, his generosity, his smile that fully demanded a smile in return. But he was poor, with no prospects, whereas Zebulon was already making a mark for himself. In her vacillation between the two brothers, she almost lost them both.

Finally, in a rage against Jeremy, Rebecca had accepted Zebulon's proposal of marriage. That was almost eight years ago; Suzannah was born nine months later, and Gunning the next year. And if in the passage of the time she'd realized the enormity of her error, Rebecca nevertheless consoled herself with her children, whom she loved with an encompassing passion.

Zebulon's breathing became heavy, his endearments sounded hoarsely in her ear, and when he strained for the moment of completion, hoping to bring her to this climactic point with him, she could think only of Jeremy, wonder about his safety. Zebulon cried out, but she was left alone and adrift in some unreachable part of her being.

The following morning Zebulon, a captain in the Washington militia, dressed in his uniform, buckled on his sword, and

jammed his pistols in his belt. He coiled his whip and hooked
it into a special holder on his belt.

Gunning danced around his father's legs, demanding to hold
the pistols, or to play with the whip, while Suzannah gazed at
her towering father in adoration.

"Where are you going?" Rebecca asked.

"The talk is that the British will attack Baltimore next,"
Zebulon said. "We must make a stand there or the country will
fall."

Rebecca bit her lip. "Looters are still roaming these streets
of Washington. The poor of the city have taken it into their
head that this is the moment to get their due."

Zebulon nodded. "I know, and you must stay indoors. With
Eli here, and Letitia, you'll be safe enough."

Rebecca knew he was right about Baltimore. If the militia
didn't make a stand, there would be no country at all. Well,
she'd survived the British, and she'd survive the rabble of
Washington.

With a final wave, Zebulon mounted his horse and galloped
off toward Baltimore, joining a stream of ragged soldiers
headed in that direction.

Throughout that day, Rebecca paced the drawing room of
her house on Eighteenth Street and New York Avenue. From
her windows she could see the smoldering ruins of the White
House. Occasionally she heard the sounds of distant gunfire,
or the cry of a looter being shot. Once she climbed to her roof
and looked at the city. Overturned wagons still lay on Pennsylvania Avenue, witness of the panicked flight of the citizens,
and she felt a wave of revulsion against her fellow Americans
for their cowardice. "If we'd made a stand and fought the
British—from house to house if necessary, and from behind
every tree, as our forefathers did—we would have beaten
them," she said to Letitia.

Letitia nodded; if anybody could have beaten the English,
it was her mistress.

After another hour of fretting, Rebecca dressed in the plain-
est dress she had, a brown cambric, concealed her titian hair
under a dimity cap, and started toward the door.

"Where are you going?" Letitia cried out in alarm.

"There are things I must tend to."

"But Mr. Zebulon, he said not to go out."

"If we listened to everything he said, we'd be in a sorry fix," she said.

"Then you got to take Eli with you," Letitia said.

"No," Rebecca said curtly. "I've got to do this alone. I want you and Eli to stay here and guard the house and the children. If anybody tries to break in, shoot to kill."

Rebecca trusted Letitia implicitly. The heavy-set, dark-skinned woman had been maid to Rebecca's mother, and Rebecca had grown up under her care. As was the custom, Mathias Breech had coupled Letitia with a robust Negro buck, and two of their children had been sold at auction years before. But Rebecca had insisted that Letitia be allowed to keep her youngest child, a son named Tadpole, and because of this she'd gained Letitia's everlasting devotion.

Rebecca hid a small pistol in her reticule, then mounted her stallion and galloped toward the President's House. The closer she got, the more she could see the devastation. The building was simply a shell of its former self. The pristine white walls that Dolley Madison had kept so lovingly painted were now blackened with smoke. Not a windowpane remained. The roof was open to the sky and wood still glowed with embers.

But her mind wasn't on the ruined mansion . . . She continued on her way to Jeremy's house. It had been a cabin when he first moved there, but through the years he'd added rooms to it, a studio where he worked and drew his inventions, a comfortable main room. She couldn't help but remember that he'd done this for her. It was to have been their home. And now that she lived in one of the grandest houses in Washington, she wondered where she would have been happier.

She dismounted and rapped on the door smartly. After some more furious knocks a frightened voice called, "Who is it?"

"Tanzy, let me in, it's Rebecca Breech Brand," she called.

The door opened hesitantly, and Rebecca pushed her way into the room. She found Tanzy clutching a knife in her hand and Circumstance peeking out from behind her skirts.

Rebecca and Tanzy eyed each other warily. A deep antagonism existed between them. For years before Zebulon married Rebecca, he had owned Tanzy, keeping her practically a captive, using her in all the ways that a man could use a woman. When Rebecca agreed to marry Zebulon, the only condition she insisted upon was that he rid himself of the slave, so he put her up for auction. Jeremy, who'd been looking for somebody to take care of Circumstance, bought Tanzy, using his mustering-out pay from the Lewis and Clark expedition. This incensed Zebulon, who assumed his brother would use the slave as he had. But he was very much mistaken, for the moment he owned her, Jeremy set her free, as James Hoban had once done for him. Later, when Rebecca had given birth to Suzannah and couldn't perform her marital obligations, Zebulon once more attempted to force his affections on Tanzy, but when Jeremy discovered this he beat his brother to a pulp, which of course increased the bad blood between them.

Staring at Tanzy now, Rebecca tried to discern what that magical quality was that had so intrigued her husband. Tanzy was tall for a woman, though not quite so tall as Rebecca, and her movements were liquid with grace. Her curly hair was cropped close and her skin, which looked as if it had been polished to a high sheen, was a shade darker than café au lait. Rebecca had to admit that for a mulatto, she was attractive.

"Why are you crying?" Rebecca asked sharply.

As Tanzy struggled to collect herself, Circumstance said, "Papa has been captured by the British."

"Are you sure?" Rebecca knelt beside the child and gripped her shoulders. "How do you know this?"

Wincing under the pressure of Rebecca's fingers, Circumstance said, "You're hurting me."

Rebecca released her grip and stroked the child's hair. "I didn't mean to. Forgive me. Now you must tell me everything."

"I saw him," Circumstance began, her eyes welling with tears. "They put him in the bottom of a wagon. His shirt was all stained with blood. I called to him but he didn't hear me. Like he was asleep." Now the words tumbled from her as relentlessly as her tears. "Oh, please, tell me he's not dead."

Rebecca clutched Circumstance to her breast. Before now she'd never felt especially drawn to Circumstance, since she was the cause of her not marrying Jeremy, but now in the child's distress all those things were forgotten, and Rebecca held her until she cried herself out.

"What can we do?" Tanzy asked.

Rebecca stood up. "We must get him back from the British. Especially if he's as badly wounded as you think. I'll talk to the President. He'll work out some prisoner exchange, and if necessary, ransom him. Now you can't stay here," she said, glancing out the window. "I want you to go straight to my house, while it's still light. Tell Letitia I sent you. You'll be safer there. Oh, and don't worry, Zebulon's gone to Baltimore."

"But Mr. Jeremy, he said to stay here and wait for him," Tanzy said.

"Don't be a fool," Rebecca said irritably. "It's too dangerous here." Rebecca helped Tanzy gather their meager belongings, and then sent them on their way the few blocks to her house.

Then Rebecca rode hard down Pennsylvania Avenue to the offices of the *National Intelligencer* on Seventh Street. When she reached the intersection she saw the editor-in-chief of the newspaper, Joseph Gales, helping his workers to pick up the type that had been scattered in the street by the British soldiers.

"How soon can you be ready to print again?" Rebecca asked as she helped gather the type.

"In two weeks perhaps," Gales said. He looked about him in despair. "There's not a press left unbroken. They've wrecked everything."

"If they have, it's because they realize the power of the press. Now we don't have two weeks, or even one. You must have at least one press ready by tomorrow."

"Impossible," Gales said.

"What if I told you that the fate of the country depended on it?" Rebecca demanded. "What if I told you that without a rallying voice, we could lose the war in the very next week? If Baltimore falls, the nation may never recover. And all we've worked for in the past forty years since our Revolution will have been in vain."

The people stopped gathering type and stared at each other. What Rebecca had said cut through their gloom.

"We must fight or perish," she continued. Then she whispered to Gales, "Tomorrow morning Rebel Thorne will deliver the first of her articles for the *National Intelligencer*. You must distribute them to every home in Washington, and particularly to every legislator and judge. We've lost this battle, but we daren't lose the war."

She mounted her horse and galloped off, leaving Gales and his staff working in a frenzy. This night she would also have her work cut out for her. When Rebecca was in her twenties, a conversation with Abigail Adams about the role of women in society had so fired her with resolve that she began to write articles about the state of the union. Knowing that the opinions of a woman weren't taken as seriously as a man's, she'd written them under a pen name, Rebel Thorne, and sent them anonymously to the paper.

The articles, a blend of political gossip and outraged patriotism, had proven highly successful. Every time a piece by Rebel Thorne appeared in the *National Intelligencer,* the edition sold out. Federalists and Democratic-Republicans alike railed against the pen of Rebel Thorne: Aaron Burr had challenged the unknown writer to a duel for impugning his motives in the election of 1800 when he and Thomas Jefferson had tied for the Presidency, and Thorne had also helped rouse the nation to revenge the barbarities being perpetrated on U.S. seamen by the Tripoli pirates.

Intrigued, the owner of the paper had advertised for the identity of this Rebel Thorne. Finally, realizing that her hidden identity did nothing for her own sense of satisfaction, Rebecca presented herself to the editor. At first he didn't believe her, but when she proved conclusively that she had indeed written the pieces, he swore her to secrecy. "Women in politics simply aren't taken seriously in the United States, and if you want Rebel Thorne's voice to retain its full power, you'll tell no one about this."

And so for a decade, Rebecca had subverted her own wishes. It didn't matter that she had a more comprehensive grasp of the political situation than most of her male contemporaries; their attitudes about women were so ingrained that she had to remain anonymous. It rankled sorely, and it rankled deep.

Rebecca tore her mind away from these dark thoughts. "That's not exactly the issue at the moment," she said under her breath. Her horse seemed to gather strength beneath her as his stride lengthened; the rushing wind tore the cap from her head and her long titian hair fell free, lashing her face. What we must do is rouse the nation, she thought. Imbue them with courage, imbue them with the righteousness of our cause! If we lose this battle it will be a blow against freedom, not only in this country but all over the world. If Tom Paine can do it, then so can I!

So engrossed was she in her thoughts that she paid little heed when her stallion slowed down to avoid an overturned carriage in the middle of Pennsylvania Avenue. The contents were strewn all over the road and the horse picked his way carefully. Rebecca didn't notice the man until he charged out at her from behind one of the poplar trees lining the avenue. His gnarled, calloused hands grabbed at her skirts and he began pulling her from the saddle. Rebecca screamed, but there was nobody to hear her.

Chapter 6

AS THE man yanked and pulled at her, Rebecca caught a glimpse of his besotted face and recognized Blutkopf, one of the overseers of the slave crews that had helped build the White House. An immigrant from Westphalia, he had had grandiose plans for returning to his homeland a rich man. The dreams, though, had degenerated into long bouts with whiskey which cost him his job and left him a sniveling pauper, scavenging through refuse heaps.

"Blutkopf, it's me, Rebecca Breech," she cried as he dragged at her. "You used to work for my father!"

But she might have been talking to the wind. For when the British sacked Washington, all the poor people and derelicts had seized the opportunity to loot for food, clothing, furniture, anything they could get their hands on.

Rebecca brought her riding crop down on Blutkopf's face, opening his cheek. With an animal cry he hauled her out of the saddle. She fell to the muddied earth, and he tore at her clothes, eager to feast himself on the flesh of this beautiful woman.

This can't be happening! Rebecca screamed inwardly, while his hands roamed over her. Then she remembered the small pistol in her reticule. She stopped fighting long enough to draw it out. Thinking that she was acquiescing, he took even greater liberties.

"Stop or I'll shoot," she said, pointing the pistol at his chest. He looked dumbly at her, then lunged for the gun. She didn't want to shoot; she'd never shot anybody in her life, but she saw that it was her life or his. She pulled the trigger and the force of the bullet knocked Blutkopf off of her. He looked with amazement at the growing red stain on his shirt and bellowed, "I am killed, killed!"

Slipping in the muck of the road, Rebecca ran to retrieve her mount, while Blutkopf, his hands flailing the air, came after her, this time to kill her. She reached the stallion and swung herself into the saddle. As he grabbed for her leg she wheeled the horse and kicked him hard. He toppled backwards. Then she galloped off; she looked back once and saw him lying in the mud, but couldn't tell if he was dead or alive.

She managed to get back to her house before she gave way to an attack of near-hysterics. Letitia and Tanzy helped her out of her muddied clothes while she told them what had happened. "Bolt all the doors and windows, don't let the children outside. He knows who I am and may come here!"

The three women fell into a frenzy of activity, and only when the house had finally been barred and shuttered like a fortress did Rebecca allow herself to give way to a fit of crying. It was dark before she managed to control herself. The last gusts of wind from the hurricane swept through the city, rattling the shutters and making Rebecca think there was somebody at every window.

Rebecca went into the children's rooms to say goodnight; she didn't want them to suspect how frightened she really was. Suzannah and Circumstance had taken to each other like long-lost sisters: Suzannah had already given Circumstance one of her favorite rag dolls. In return, Circumstance had drawn her a picture of a pet chipmunk that she said visited her every night. But Gunning, feeling left out, had continually deviled them; once he punched Circumstance until Letitia slapped his hands. When Rebecca looked at the drawing of the chipmunk she realized that the gift of the artist had passed from Jeremy to his daughter. Somehow it made her feel sad, that her own offspring would never carry the seeds of his genius. She tucked them all in, told a special story to Gunning, then retired to her room.

She sat at her pine desk and dipped her quill in the brass-lidded inkstand. She experienced not an instant of hesitation or doubt; the words flowed off her quill as it whispered harshly across the paper.

"Arise, ye sons of freedom! This one battle may be lost, but not the war, never the war! Already the British have been forced to flee from our capital, for our brave men have denied them the use of the naval supplies that they so desperately needed. And so what have the British gained? The burning of a few buildings, a dastardly act worthy of the Hun and the Vandal. And to those misguided cowards among us who would sue for peace, I say: Are we to deliver ourselves and all our hopes for the future into these hands? Never! I call upon every

American, I call upon the sons and daughters of the heroes who fought at Valley Forge, of the heroes who won the day at Yorktown. We can win again, if only we have the will, if only we are imbued with the spirit of our founding fathers, who believed that freedom was man's most precious gift. They fought for that belief, and forged our freedom in flame and fury. Are we to say their deaths have been in vain? Again I say: Never! Arise! Arise!"

She ended the short piece by telling the reader to watch the paper tomorrow for further news. Rebecca had no idea what the British plans might be, except of course, for Baltimore. Logic dictated that they would attack that vital seaport next. But in this volatile situation there would be fresh news almost hourly.

She fell into an exhausted sleep; visions of Jeremy, alone and bloodied, assaulted her. When she woke the next morning she realized that she had to do something. "I can't let him die," she said to Letitia. "I can't."

Letitia said nothing. Since Rebecca's birth she'd been her confidant. Aside from the editor of the *National Intelligencer*, only she knew that Rebecca and Rebel Thorne were one and the same person. And only she knew that despite being married to Zebulon, it was Jeremy whom she loved. These confidences troubled Letitia, for she had a deep superstitious bent. "No good can come of this, no good at all. And that's all I've got to say about that matter."

Rebecca delivered the article to the *National Intelligencer* and was thrilled to learn that they'd gotten one of the presses working. All day long, slave boys and men of good will delivered handbills to anybody who'd take them.

President James Madison and Secretary of State James Monroe returned to the capital on August 27 at about five in the afternoon, surrounded by a guard of about twenty soldiers. Rebecca saw the two men trying to get into the Octagon House, and she hurried across the street from her own house to greet them. The house, which belonged to Colonel Tayloe, had been occupied by the French Minister to the United States, Serurier, but he'd fled the capital for the safety of Philadelphia.

Rebecca's heart dropped when she saw Madison. He looked older than his age of sixty-three by at least a dozen years. His face was haggard; his wizened little body seemed to have shriveled even further under the defeat.

James Monroe, stalwart and tall, also looked ashen. His uniform was begrimed. The men had traveled many miles to get away from the advancing British army, and had just this hour slipped back into the capital.

"Is there no way for us to get in?" Madison asked. "With the White House burned to the ground, we'll need some headquarters for the government."

Rebecca led them across the street to her own house. The twenty soldiers, who were needed more to protect the President from the pillaging citizenry than from the British, bivouacked outside on the front lawn. The children rushed out to gape at them, Gunning expressing a keen interest in their rifles.

"You must have food and drink to refresh yourselves," Rebecca said, and called for Letitia. "I'll send Eli to fetch Colonel Tayloe. I'm sure he'll be honored to let you use Octagon House. But you're more than welcome to remain here. Whatever Zebulon and I have is at your disposal."

"You've been a good friend to me and Dolley all these years, and once again I'm in your debt." President Madison bowed, trying to be gracious, but the spark was clearly gone from him.

Rebecca thought, it can't be easy to see your own capital destroyed, your army flee in the face of an enemy, and to see your own house burned to the ground. If the country did fall and returned to the fold of the British Empire, history would lay the blame squarely on James Madison—a man of political brilliance, and of the highest intent, but a poor leader.

Rebecca sliced a smoked ham and poured some glasses of a heady burgundy. The spirits refreshed Madison and Monroe, and when they seemed a bit rested, Rebecca pressed them for news.

"What of Dolley?" she asked.

"She's safe at Salona. We kept missing each other at various meeting points, but I've left word that I've returned to Washington. I expect she'll join me soon," Madison said.

"Thank God she's safe," Rebecca said, feeling a flood of relief. Rebecca had first met Dolley when she came to Washington in 1801, after Thomas Jefferson had appointed Madison as his Secretary of State. Since Jefferson was a widower, Dolley had acted as his hostess in what he preferred to call the President's House—a more democratic name than "American Palace."

Dolley Madison had taken an instant liking to Rebecca. When she'd become First Lady in her own right at the White House, Dolley had drawn Rebecca into her social orbit, and Rebecca had responded with élan. The Madisons were godparents to both her children, and Rebecca thought of them not only as political figures but as close friends. Indeed, Dolley had almost become a substitute mother for Rebecca, who had been motherless since the age of ten. Rebecca's mother had been a quiet, artistic creature who hadn't the strength or fortitude to cope with the excesses of her garrulous, demanding husband, Mathias. Seeing her mother so abused had left Rebecca with a smoldering resentment against men in general, and was in part the reason she'd vacillated between Zebulon and Jeremy.

"Have you any news of the British?" Rebecca asked.

"I've heard that Alexandria has sued the British for peace and has surrendered," the President said glumly. "The British are now stripping it."

"With that arm of their fleet so close, they could cross the Potomac at any moment and strike again at the capital," Monroe said. "But this time we'll be ready for them. The states are responding and sending us as many men as possible. But tell us of what's happening here."

"The mob has taken over the streets," she said grimly, paling at the thought of what had happened to her. "Unless we restore some order, no one will be able to govern from here."

"The poor of the city have always been a problem. They're like fishes, they live by eating one another," Monroe said. "But we have to put a stop to that immediately. We must declare martial law. Anybody caught looting will be hung."

"Do whatever you think best." Madison was so overwhelmed by it all that he was content to have his friend and protégé take control.

"One other thing, Mr. President," Rebecca said. "I've heard talk that the men in the army and the militia will refuse to serve under General Winder if he's put in charge of them."

"But they must!" Madison said. "Winder is in command."

"Do we dare take another chance with him?" Rebecca asked. "Do so and we risk the morale not only of the army but of the nation. And in that same vein, it's well known that Secretary of War Armstrong consistently refused to make adequate preparations for Washington's defense. People believe that he wanted to see the capital—'this sheep walk,' as he called it— destroyed, so the government could move to some city that was 'civilized,' like Philadelphia, or better still his hometown of New York."

"That will never happen if I have anything to do with it," Madison said, a spark of fight in his voice. "This site was chosen as a compromise between the North and the South, and the capital shall remain here, or the Union could easily be ripped asunder. But you're right about Armstrong; he's a divisive force. It would be better if he were . . . to take a leave of absence."

Monroe nodded and Madison said to him, "Would you be willing to take over the job of secretary of war—while continuing as secretary of state?"

"I will undertake to serve in whatever way I can to protect my country," Monroe replied.

"Mr. President, we have some sad news of a personal nature," Rebecca said, and when Madison looked at her quizzically, she continued, "Jeremy Brand has been captured by the British."

Madison half rose to his feet in shock. "But this is terrible! We must do whatever we can to effect his release." He turned to one of his aides. "Have Jeremy Brand's name put on our list of exchange prisoners. Mr. Skinner, our negotiator, will be on his way to the British fleet shortly. I've also asked Francis Scott Key to go along. He's well versed in international law, and could be of great use."

"Thank you, Mr. President," Rebecca said, then added quickly, "I'm sure my husband will be gratified to know that you're doing everything in your power to free his brother."

The following day, Dolley Madison arrived in Washington, and she and her husband had a tearful reunion. Her meeting with Rebecca was no less tearful.

"Mr. Madison and I plan to live for a few days at my sister's house on F Street, the very place we lived when we first came to Washington. And then as soon as some order is restored, we'll move into the Octagon House. The government has already begun to operate from there."

Dolley looked so crestfallen that Rebecca put her arm around her shoulder. "This isn't the time for sadness. We must do what is needed to win, and with God's help we will, for our cause is righteous."

Dolley made an attempt at a smile. "I've just been reading the very same sentiments from this pamphleteer, Rebel Thorne. I must say my spirits were buoyed."

Madison and Monroe acted decisively to get the government moving again. As soon as the looters realized that they'd be dealt with harshly, they stopped, and a semblance of order was restored in the burnt-out capital.

That night, Rebecca wrote by the light of her flickering candle: "The latest news is that the British have boarded their ships at the Upper Marlboro and are sailing toward Baltimore. Their plan is obviously to capture our principal port, and they have already sworn to level the entire city. Now the battle is joined. Now is the time come for our mettle to be tested. Wellington's Invincibles *shall* be beaten by the sons of those who fought at Saratoga and Bunker Hill! Now is the time for dissension and divisiveness to be over. We fight not for any political party, but for our honor and our nation!"

Rebecca put the pen down. Her head ached with her efforts and yet she realized that she'd left something undone. Then it came to her, growing with each heartbeat, until the pounding filled her ears with its surety. "I must go to Baltimore myself!" she said aloud. "Only that way can Rebel Thorne really report all that's happening."

She grew agitated with the idea, trying to think of all the possible reasons that might prevent her going. The children? Washington was safe for the moment; Letitia and Tanzy would care for them. "And what if I should meet Zebulon in Baltimore?"

She pondered that and decided she could say that she'd come to protect the family's business interests in the city. That was true enough. But to be at the scene of the battle, to report firsthand all that was happening, was an idea that so excited her she could barely contain herself. Yet she knew her real reason for going to Baltimore.

Unless I go and do whatever I can to get Jeremy released, she thought, I'll always live with that regret.

It didn't matter that Jeremy had been having a long affair with Marianne Connaught. It didn't matter that she knew she would never have him. What mattered was that she loved him, and he was in danger, and she must help.

At peace for the first time since she'd heard of his capture, Rebecca fell into a deep sleep. Tomorrow, Baltimore.

Chapter 7

THE THIRD BRIGADE of the British Army led the retreat from Washington. During the night of August 28, they halted and camped at the tiny stone village of Bladensburg.

"It was in this very spot that we broke through the American lines and routed the blackguards," Sean Connaught exulted to the junior officers with whom he was quartered. "And for all time, that battle will be known as the Bladensburg Races!" A round of laughter greeted this and Sean ordered another ration of rum for the men.

On the outskirts of the camp, Jeremy Brand lay in the wagon carrying the wounded. His throat felt parched, his wounded arm ached, and occasionally he'd slip into a slough of delirium. In one such state he relived the battle . . . behind his closed lids he saw the glare of the British rockets as they streaked across the sky toward the American lines. When the first shells of this new weapon exploded among the inexperienced American militia, they bolted and ran.

And then Jeremy thought he heard the voice of Joshua Barney, who'd been in command of his unit. He opened his eyes and blinked when he saw the garrulous old salt standing over him.

"Commodore?" Jeremy said weakly.

Barney put his hand on Jeremy's shoulder. "Ah, my boy, how are you? Are you all right?"

Jeremy managed a nod. "And you?"

"That shell that landed near us broke my leg, but the British doctors put a splint on it. With this crutch, I can get about reasonably well."

Barney held a canteen to Jeremy's lips and he drank slowly. "I've been trying to arrange an exchange of prisoners," Barney said. "Though officially I'm still a prisoner myself, the British haven't been unsympathetic. We'll have you free in no time at all. I'm off to see one of their officers now."

Barney hobbled away toward the officers' quarters. Jeremy looked up at the dark, cloud-swept sky. A surge of hope swept over him. Free...he'd be able to go home...find Circumstance. "Oh, God, don't let anything happen to her," he prayed. "That child is my very life."

The pale moon emerged from behind its cloud cover, only to disappear again. Jeremy had little sense of the passage of time. But once when the moon reappeared, he thought he saw the pale piquant face of Marianne Connaught. Only when he felt her hand clamp down on his mouth did he realize that she wasn't a specter.

"Don't make a sound," she whispered urgently. "There are guards all about."

"What are you doing here?" he blurted, aware how ridiculous the question was even as he asked it.

"I've come to get you out of here," she said, struggling to untie the ropes that bound his hands. "I've two horses hidden in the woods nearby. Can you ride?"

He tried to sit up, but sank back with the effort.

"You must try," she said desperately. She put her arms around his shoulders and tried to lift him up, but the dead weight proved too much for her.

"I'm sorry," he said. "I'm so weak..."

"Rest a minute, then we'll try again."

"Don't worry, Marianne. Commodore Barney told me that he was going to arrange an exchange of prisoners."

"Sean will never let you go."

He blinked, trying to assimilate that. "How do you know?"

"He—never mind. I just know."

Jeremy managed to prop himself up on an elbow. He stared at this gentle creature whose love had given him back his manhood after the death of his wife, White Doe. But now he saw confusion on her face, and more...guilt. He shook his head slowly, "You—?" And then the anger shot through his body, giving him strength. The cords of his neck stood out as he grated, "You've been working with Sean Connaught all along. You and your damnable Aunt Victoria!"

"Darling, please," she whispered urgently. "We haven't much time. The British may be breaking camp shortly. We can talk about all this when you're free."

"Answer me! You've been a spy for them, haven't you? Oh, my God! How many Americans have died because of you?"

She clutched at her throat and struggled to find words.

"Whatever I've done, believe me, I've paid for those sins a thousand times over."

"How easily you say that," he spat. "What a fool I was! How I loved you . . . And all the time we were making love, you were using me, gathering information for the British."

Her face turned deathly white and tears sprang to her enormous violet eyes. She swallowed hard and finally managed to say, "Whatever I've done, whatever misery I've caused, I accept full blame for that, and I'll bear whatever punishment necessary. But there's been only one worthwhile thing in my life, one thing that's given it meaning. And that's been my love for you. I've always loved you. I always will. You *must* believe me."

He snorted.

She gripped his arm. "Oh, my darling, please, please, don't forfeit your life now, just because you're angry with me."

He pulled away from her. "And why should I trust you? What new betrayal would you have in store?"

A low moan escaped her. Her misery was so patent that for a moment he wanted to believe her. But the defeat at Bladensburg, the burning of Washington, and her complicity in all this proved too much for him. He turned away from her. "Get out of here," he muttered. "I don't want anything from you. I don't want to see you again."

Marianne started to protest, but then she became alert. "I hear somebody coming," she whispered. From her vantage point behind the prisoner wagon, she saw Sean Connaught approaching, with Commodore Barney limping along behind him.

Marianne put her hand on Jeremy's chest. "I must go—I can't be found here. Don't listen to anything that Sean promises you. He wants you dead. I know it! And no matter what you believe about me, no matter what you think, I'll never stop trying to free you. Never. Even if I must die in the attempt."

And then, crouching low, she slipped away from the wagon and disappeared into the darkness.

Listening to the crunch of approaching footsteps, Jeremy's heart began to thump harder. Marianne is lying, he thought. I don't need her. Barney will arrange to free me.

But that possibility seemed to evaporate when Jeremy heard the slightly sibilant, clipped accent of Sean Connaught, who was standing close by him now. "Commodore Barney, I've told you before and I'll tell you again. We've reviewed your prisoner-exchange list, and we've no objection to it—with the exception of Jeremy Brand. We caught him spying on us at the White House. Naturally, he'll be dealt with accordingly."

Barney began to protest, but Sean would pay no heed, and shouted, "Fall in and march!" Once more Jeremy felt the wagon begin to bump over the rutted roads, sending stabbing pains throughout his body, and then merciful darkness swept over him.

On the journey from Washington back to the British fleet anchored in the Upper Marlboro, more than a hundred and ten British soldiers vanished into the darkness. Even though these redcoats had defeated the Americans, had captured and burned the capital, they were so impressed with this fertile land and the possibilities of a new beginning that they deserted. When Sean learned this at a roll call, he became outraged. At one crossroads, he fired a bullet into the back of a soldier who'd broken ranks and was heading into the forest. The man's comrades insisted that he was suffering from dysentery and was only going to relieve himself, but Sean was taking no chances.

As the column came within sight of the anchored fleet, Sean heaved a sigh of relief. "We've done it," he said to his junior officers. "In twelve days we've marched fifty miles into the enemy's territory. We've captured the capital, burned Congress to the ground, and the palace of the president, and are now returning safely to our own fleet! You men who've participated in this extraordinary victory will go down in history!"

Sean tried to lead a rousing cheer, but the foot soldiers were so exhausted that they didn't respond, except for two stragglers at the rear who slipped away into the predawn murk.

Jeremy woke to a gentle rocking motion and realized he was aboard a ship. An officer wearing the uniform and insignia of a British naval doctor swabbed at his shoulder wound.

"The bullet's passed clean through," the doctor said to a youth kneeling beside him. But pay particular attention to him; the man's lost a lot of blood, and Captain Connaught wants him alive. Feed him some broth."

"Aye sir," the lad said. When the doctor left to tend to other patients, the boy finished dressing Jeremy's wound. "Lie still," he said. "I'll try not to hurt you."

Jeremy nodded, giving himself over to the lad's gentle fingers. He looked at the boy. "How old are you?"

"Fourteen," he said. Then he leaned forward and whispered, "My name is Wingate Grange, and I'm from Maine."

Jeremy started and tried to sit, but fell back weakly. He studied the boy intently, trying to determine if he was lying. He had long light brown hair that curled slightly at his shoulders, light brown eyes, the beginnings of peach fuzz on his upper lip, and though he still had an innocent air, the hunted look in his eyes indicated that he'd seen enough hard times to be counted a man. "How is it that you're here?" Jeremy asked.

Wingate kept his voice low. "I was born way up north in Maine. Ever been there?"

Jeremy shook his head.

"It's harsh, and sometimes it looks barren with the sea constantly pounding the rocky coast, but I think it's beautiful. As you know, the territory is claimed by both the Americans and the British. Every year, they draw up some new boundary line, but right away one side or the other is sure to violate it. In truth, we people who live there wouldn't care if we were called Canadians or Americans, if we were just left to live out our lives in peace."

"I know what you mean," Jeremy said, nodding.

"When war broke out more than two years ago, a British troop convoy anchored in our harbor. They didn't care what nationality I claimed, Canadian or American. They just argued from the end of their long rifles, and practically every lad in our town was impressed into their navy."

Jeremy swore softly. "That's exactly why we're fighting this damned war. For ten years the British have treated us as if we were little more than their servants. They've captured our ships on the high seas, confiscated our cargoes, impressed our seamen. On the frontier, they've incited their Indian allies like Tecumseh to massacre our settlers. They insist that we return the Louisiana Territory to Spain, yet we all know that they covet it themselves. At every turn they've harassed us, ground us under their heels, until at last President Madison had no recourse but to ask Congress to declare war."

"Best not to excite yourself so," Wingate said. He finished cleaning Jeremy's wound, then put on new bandages.

"Incidentally, where am I?" Jeremy asked.

"Aboard the *Tonnant*, the British flagship," Wingate said.

"They must think me pretty important to put me aboard the flagship," Jeremy said with a wry smile. "I can't think why."

"I know that Captain Connaught insisted on it," Wingate said. "Something about your being a spy. Did you really try to kill Rear Admiral Cockburn? Did you really hide in the White House?" Wingate asked, his eyes wide. He glanced at the cell door to make sure the jailer hadn't overheard.

"I was in the White House," Jeremy said, "though with no intent to spy. And I gave Cockburn fair warning before I fired. No man could ask for more."

Wingate's face lit with anticipation, and his eyes fairly danced. "I've always had a hankering to see the President's Palace," he said. "The American Palace, they call it in my part of the country. Is it as grand as they say?"

"It's a great house, yes," Jeremy said softly, "but greater by far in its meaning." A puzzled look came over Wingate's face, and Jeremy continued, "You see lad, it's your house, and mine, the second home of Americans everywhere. Because the one man elected by the will of all the people lives there. The British know that, know that in that home reside the hopes and aspirations of all men who yearn to be free. And that's why they burned it, as if to destroy that desire for freedom. But that can never be, for the house is not only a dwelling, but an idea as well, and that idea lives in the heart and soul of every American."

"Amen to that," Wingate murmured.

"I swear, I'll see it rise again," Jeremy said through gritted teeth. "Even if I have to rebuild it with my bare hands!"

His exertions had made the blood leave his face, and Wingate quieted him, bathing his forehead with compresses. After a bit, the boy said, "If ever we get out of this mess, I'm going to visit Washington. And I'll set foot in that house, you can bet I will."

Jeremy smiled at him. "And I'll take you on the grand tour, for like as not I'll have it built by then."

Wingate suppressed his laughter lest the jailer hear. The cabin that served as a cell was no more than six feet by nine, with a pallet on the floor, and leg and hand irons securely bolted into the timbers. But since Jeremy was so ill, he hadn't been chained.

"Is there no way to escape from here?" Jeremy asked.

"I've tried twice," Wingate said. "The last time was when

the British fleet anchored here. I thought I could slip away
then, but Sean Connaught had me tied to the mast and whipped.
He's as mean as a ferret, that one."

"Aye, that much I know," Jeremy said. "How did you learn
your skills? You have healing hands."

"My father is a doctor, and though I never thought I liked
the profession, I must have picked up many of the rudiments
from him. When the ship doctors found out I could tie a splint
and apply leeches, and knew how to bleed a man, they pressed
me into service. I do like it better than being a toadying cab-
inboy for the likes of Sean Connaught and the rest of the junior
officers."

Wingate held a bowl of soup to Jeremy's lips and he ate
hungrily. "I guess the fates don't mean me to die yet," Jeremy
said, "not if I'm this famished."

"That's a good sign," Wingate said. "Anyway, the doctor
says you're as strong as a stallion. He says your wounds would
have killed a lesser man."

After the last of the soup Wingate said, "I'd best go, otherwise they'll be wondering why I've taken so long. A word
of warning, though. Watch out for Sean Connaught." Then he
grasped Jeremy's hand. "It's good to shake the hand of a coun-
tryman again. Be of good cheer. I'll come back as soon as I
can."

In the next few days, as the fleet gathered its forces in the
Chesapeake, whenever Wingate could sneak away, he visited
Jeremy. He brought food he'd managed to cadge from the
galley. Jeremy and Wingate would huddle together making
elaborate plans to escape; though they knew that such a thing
was near impossible, it kept their hopes alive.

In the officers' quarters aboard the *Tonnant*, Vice Admiral
Cochrane, Rear Admiral Cockburn, General Ross, and Sean
Connaught held a council of war. A wide-bottomed whiskey
decanter stood in its carved circular niche on the oaken table.
Through the curved leaded windows of the stern, a galleon
moon had just embarked on its journey across the skies, its
passage reflected by its watery twin. Timbers creaked in the
swell of water and wind, as the man-of-war sailed toward its
destination.

Sean Connaught was giving the officers his assessment of
the situation in Baltimore. "We've known for a long time that

the port is little more than a nest of pirates. Their shipyards have supplied one hundred and twenty-six of the privateers that have ravaged our merchant ships. Gentlemen, more than five hundred of our vessels have been captured or sent to the bottom by Baltimore-based privateers."

General Ross shifted uneasily in his seat. He admired Sean Connaught's professionalism, but didn't much like him personally. There was a streak of cruelty in the man that fell outside the bounds of what a proper English gentleman should be.

Sean continued, "In population, Baltimore is the third largest city in the United States, with some forty-five thousand people. But it's by far the richest city in the colonies, with enough booty to make us all very rich men."

General Ross interrupted. "Captain Connaught, we're well aware of the prizes that Baltimore has to offer. What's more to the point is that we are here first and foremost in the service of his majesty's government. The question of prize money must be secondary to the safety of our army and navy."

Sean stiffened at the rebuke and licked his lips. "You all know that I've gone on record for having wanted all of Washington burned to the ground. Both government buildings *and* private property. To my mind, Americans, like dogs, must be treated with great severity before we can make them tractable. In the case of Baltimore, I can think of no reason whatsoever why the entire city shouldn't be razed. In fact, justice demands it."

"Hear, hear," Admiral Cockburn cut in. "I second those sentiments." The foppish rear admiral a strong supporter of Sean's. "Unlike Washington, Baltimore has strategic importance," Cockburn insisted. "I venture to say that if Baltimore falls, the entire American war effort will collapse and they will have to sue for peace on our terms."

General Ross said, "That still doesn't answer the important question. How well is Baltimore defended? How many men can we expect to lose? Gentlemen, I don't need to remind you that what with fighting Napoleon on the Continent, and now battling these colonials, our country has been at war for more than twenty years. Taxes are impossibly high, there's not a home in England that hasn't lost a son or father. Is Baltimore worth risking our army?"

"Let me assure you, General," Sean said, "I've spent many

hours reconnoitering that city." He unrolled a map of the Chesapeake Bay area and pointed to various locations as he spoke. "The approach to the inner harbor of Baltimore is guarded only by a smallish fort, Fort McHenry. It was built in 1798; it's a conventional five-pointed star-shaped structure, but with very weak defenses, perhaps a dozen eighteen-pound cannon."

"Can the Americans man it with more guns?" Ross asked.

"They can, and undoubtedly will, if they can spare them. But that's why I suggest a two-pronged attack. Admirals Cockburn and Cochrane attack with their fleets by sea, while you, General, land at North Point on the Patapsco River, and strike overland up the peninsula to the city. There are no breastworks in Baltimore, no redoubts or trenches. With their defenses spread thin between Fort McHenry and the Patapsco peninsula—not to mention that their army is composed of incompetent cowards—Baltimore must fall to us."

Admiral Cochrane, who'd remained neutral in all these discussions, now stood up, his head nearly grazing the low-beamed cabin ceiling. At sea, he was the supreme commander of the British expeditionary forces; once the army was put ashore, General Ross was in command. Now Cochrane saw fit to exert his rank.

"If burning Baltimore will shorten this war by just one day, or save the life of just one Englishman, then I say it must be burned!"

"Here, here!" Cockburn exclaimed.

Then Cochrane filled the whiskey glasses and handed one to each of his comrades. "To Baltimore, and the end of the war."

"To Baltimore—may it be wiped off the face of the earth!" Sean Connaught said. And then the men drained their drinks and threw their glasses to shatter against the wall.

Chapter 8

REBECCA ARRIVED in Baltimore on the third of September, having ridden the forty miles from Washington on horseback. It would have been easier by coach, but all means of transportation had been commandeered by the militia. As she galloped along the route, she kept a wary eye out for highwaymen, particularly since she carried a great deal of money on her. If a ransom was required for Jeremy's release, she would be prepared.

She breathed a sigh of relief when she saw the outskirts of the city, then she went directly to the Indian Queen Hotel. She and Zebulon always stayed there on shopping and business expeditions; the hotel offered the most civilized accommodations in the area. But now the place was swarming with military men. Smartly dressed Baltimore militiamen in their blue-and-white uniforms strode through the halls, army regulars jostled each other in the tavern, and from Kentucky had come the tall, taciturn frontiersmen with their buckskin clothes, coonskin caps, and long-barreled rifles.

"The hotel is closed to the public, Mrs. Brand," the distressed hotelkeeper told her. "We're now the headquarters for the defense of the city and men are sleeping six to a bed!"

Rebecca tapped her foot impatiently; not even a bribe could get her a room. And then she saw Major General Samuel Smith coming in through the front door, surrounded by subordinates, all talking at once. Taking courage, Rebecca swept over to him. "Sam, how good to see you!" she cried, extending her hand.

His eyes lit with recognition and delight and he bent to kiss her hand. "Madam, you grace Baltimore with your presence. I've just seen your husband at North Point on the Patapsco peninsula. He's in command of a unit there. Shall I send word that you're here?"

She shook her head vehemently. "I wouldn't dream of pulling him away from his duties. In these times, one's country must take priority above all else."

He nodded in agreement, and took her hand as he went to the desk. General Winder, looking harassed and slightly lost, followed in their wake. He had been in charge of the defense of Washington, and was now trying to redeem his reputation by taking command of Baltimore's defense. But nobody was paying any attention to him, and all important issues were being brought to Samuel Smith.

Sam Smith was a gruff, thick-necked bull of a man. He'd served in Congress first as a representative and now as senator. Quick-tempered, impatient with incompetence, and somewhat dictatorial, he'd distinguished himself fighting in the Revolutionary War. Now a major general in the Baltimore militia, he'd been the natural choice of the town fathers to defend the city.

"Sam, I need a room," Rebecca said.

"Impossible. I'm sharing my own with three of my aides."

"Nothing's impossible for Sam Smith," she said, squeezing his arm. "Anything will do—a cot in the cellar or a pallet up under the eaves. Sam, I'm here as a direct emissary from Dolley Madison," she lied. "And on business vital to the nation. More than that I can't tell you. But would I have risked my life to come to a beleaguered city unless it was an issue of life and death?"

The quiet conviction with which she spoke made him regard her with keen interest. He knew that she was a confidant of Dolley's, knew also that in public gatherings she'd raised her voice against the Tories who wanted to surrender to Great Britain. And she was a deucedly handsome woman.

"Madam, you shall have what you ask. Further, you are ordered to have a light supper with me this evening in my room. I need firsthand news of Washington."

"You shall have it," Rebecca said, "along with some other observations that may stand you in good stead in the defense of your city—our city."

Smith started to order some of his officers to vacate their room for Rebecca, but she said, "I won't hear of it. Let me have one of the maids' rooms on the top floor. That will suit my needs."

At six that evening, Rebecca knocked at the door of Sam Smith's room. She'd dressed in the best costume she had brought along, a russet-colored gown a shade darker than her titian hair. Around her neck she wore a river of Brazilian topaz that Zebulon had purchased on one of his South American shipping ventures, and her hazel eyes took on the color and warmth of the gemstones.

Curious, she thought, that in times of war, instead of being demure, women become more extravagant in their dress. Perhaps it's our way of countering the death that men perpetrate everywhere. The look in Samuel Smith's eyes told her that her care with her toilet had not been in vain.

They dined on cold mallard. She'd never cared for the slightly gamey taste, but she didn't let on, praising it and the wine. A dessert of frothy syllabub finished the simple meal. "Would that I could have ordered up six full courses for you, Rebecca, but we're at war," Sam Smith said. "Now tell me what happened at Washington."

"We suffered a debacle, nothing less," Rebecca said. "Our militia was no match for Wellington's Invincibles. More to the point, we had no leadership at all. As much as I love and revere James Madison, he's better suited to the abstractions of political theory than to the leadership of his nation in time of war." She looked Sam Smith squarely in the eye. "The information I give you is meant only for your ears. The President isn't well. He must be protected at the same time that we embrace the truth."

"You have my word, Rebecca," he said, reaching across the table and patting her hand.

"Whatever the faults of Madison, his intentions were pure," she said. "But the same cannot be said of Secretary of War Armstrong. I know for a fact that he resisted defending Washington—refused to have trenches dug, refused to requisition money for the army, refused to admit, even after the British were on the road to Washington, that they would invade the capital."

"Yes, I've heard rumors about that," Smith said. "Some even claim that he *wanted* the capital destroyed."

"The man is a traitor," she said.

"Those are harsh words."

"If not by commission, then by omission," she insisted. "He mustn't be allowed a hand in the defense of Baltimore."

"What of General Winder?" Smith asked.

Rebecca's exclamation was tinged with contempt. "I know that it's unseemly for a woman to express her opinion so," she said, "but how can I not speak out when the very safety of the nation is at stake? General Winder is a fool, plain and simple.

Given a choice between a right and wrong military move, he will choose both, fearing to make a mistake. We might have won the day at Bladensburg, or at least held the British in check; all he had to do was blow up a small bridge across the Eastern Branch of the Potomac, and that would have blocked their access to Washington. But he claimed that he needed the explosives for his men. Can you imagine? And why didn't he think to set fire to the bridge? I'll tell you why—because in times of crisis he becomes so rattled that he can't think straight. The British have no better weapons on their side than *our* Secretary Armstrong and General Winder."

"It presents a problem," Smith said. "Apparently, Madison and Monroe feel as you do, but they're loath to remove Winder from the field. Now Winder is in command of the Tenth Military District, and Baltimore is part of that. So by rights, he should be in full command of all the forces."

"Then we're lost," Rebecca said. She tapped her fingernail against the lead-crystal goblet. "Is there no way to get around this? Couldn't he be put in command of a post that wasn't vital?"

"You've anticipated me, Rebecca," Smith said, alternately amazed and excited by this woman's keen mind and beauty. "I plan to have him command a small detail guarding the western approaches to Baltimore. It's highly unlikely that the British will attack by that route—the water is too shallow for the draft of their warships."

"Splendid! Of course, he'll protest to Washington."

Smith nodded. "But by the time the communiqués go back and forth, the battle of Baltimore will already have been fought."

"What of our other defenses?" Rebecca asked.

"They're no secret," Smith said. "By land, our main defenses will be erected on Hampstead Hill; it offers a commanding view of the eastern road along which the British must come. I want breastworks built there, redoubts, and cannon put in place. Then we have Fort McHenry guarding the harbor."

"How much time do we have before the British attack?" Rebecca asked.

"Five days, six at the most. Perhaps less."

"Can you have the defenses ready?"

"I don't know. But I do know that our worst enemy is public apathy and demoralization. There's a whole segment of the population clamoring for us to sue for peace, so fearful are they of having their property ruined. As though property were the be-all and end-all of a nation's greatness. Ah, where are the old days of the Revolution, when men fought for ideals?"

After dinner, Rebecca was passing through the lobby when she saw a tall, storklike Frenchman hopping from one leg to another as he berated the hotelkeeper.

"But I tell you, I *must* have a coach! I have ordered one for days now. Do you not know who I am? I am Audubert Villefranche. And I must fly from here!"

Rebecca tried to slip away before Villefranche saw her, but she was too late.

"*Alors,* do my eyes deceive me? *Non,* it *is* Rebecca Breech! The one true love of my life." He rushed to embrace her, but Rebecca kept him at arm's length. The smell of his ambergris perfume was overwhelming.

"Hello, Monsieur Villefranche. How are you?"

"How can one be in this hellish city? Oh my dear, the merciful Lord has put you in my path so that I might rescue you. We must fly at once to Philadelphia, and from there book passage back to Paris."

"But Monsieur Villefranche, I'm a married woman."

"I had heard that you married that Zebulon Brand. A great mistake. You should never have refused me. But it is never too late. I too remarried, and am the proud father of *une jeune fille,* Véronique Villefranche, whom I fear I shall never see again."

"And your wife?" Rebecca asked, amused.

"Ah, we've long since decided to go our separate ways."

"But what in heaven's name are you doing here?"

"I invested my fortune and founded an acting company—without question, the finest in all France. My Racine brought tears to Napoleon's eyes, and my Molière—three people had to be forcibly removed from the theater, they were laughing so much. But when Paris fell to the British, I thought it was time to bring the troupe to the United States. And then as soon as we got here—" Audubert tragically pounded his forehead with his fist. "—the ingrates abandoned me. And now this war threatens to kill us all."

Rebecca patted his arm reassuringly.

"Did I not tell you years ago that your capital city should

have been built *above* the falls of the Potomac?" Audubert said.
"That way, the British fleet could never have sailed upriver
and captured it."

My Lord, he's absolutely right! thought Rebecca with a
start. Years ago, when Federal City, as the capital was called
then, was first being built, Audubert Villefranche, Zebulon
Brand, and her father, Mathias Breech, had been involved in
a real estate venture. A self-proclaimed aristocrat, Villefranche
had cut a fine figure, worn the best clothes; he'd come to
America to escape the terror of the French Revolution. Just
about the time that the real estate venture went bankrupt, Napoleon seized power in France, and Villefranche made ready
to return.

"Do you remember how I *implored* you to come to Paris
with me?" Audubert asked.

She had toyed with the notion of becoming engaged to him;
for he'd promised to show her the cosmopolitan life of the
Continent, instruct her in the genteel art of living. Looking at
him now, reduced to near destitution, she thanked God for
giving her the sense not to take him seriously.

"Say, Frenchie, there's a farmer leaving with an empty
wagon for Philadelphia. Says he'll take you," the hotelkeeper
said.

"A *wagon*? Audubert Villefranche in a *wagon*?"

"Says he won't charge you anything."

The Frenchman grasped Rebecca's hands. "I must return
to the arms of *ma jeune fille*. You will not come with me? Ah,
but we will meet again. My love for you is too strong not to
be consummated." And with that, Audubert Villefranche ex-
ited, leaving behind the pungent odor of ambergris.

Later that evening, Rebecca threw on a cloak with a hood
that hid her face, left the hotel by a rear exit, and walked the
streets. If I intend to write about the battle, I need to see what's
going on first hand, she told herself.

But she saw nothing. The houses were dark, there were no
patrols, no breastworks were being erected. After a frustrating
hour of wandering that took her to the darkened waterfront and
as far as the outskirts of town, she returned to her hotel room
and began to write furiously.

She was done in less than an hour, and before dawn the
following day, delivered it to the offices of the *Baltimore Sun*,

with the name Rebel Thorne clearly marked on the envelope. She fretted impatiently throughout the morning, and sent out a half-dozen times for the paper, but was always told that it hadn't yet arrived.

At about noon she was sitting in the tiny lobby, sunk in gloom and convinced that the paper had dismissed the article out of hand, when Samuel Smith burst into the hotel.

"By God, have you seen this?" he shouted to anybody who'd listen. "It's the damndest thing I've ever read!"

Rebecca took the paper from his hand. In bold type on the front page was a banner head: REBEL THORNE SPEAKS. The article said:

"Why do men concern themselves with the defense of Baltimore? Any fool can see that the city is already lost. Why do we waste our time arguing about who shall lead us—Armstrong, Winder, or Smith—when there are no men to lead? Throw open the gates to the city then, I say, and dismantle our forts, embrace the British when they march through our streets, and cheer them on when they burn our buildings, plunder our riches, and rape our wives and daughters. For that is all a Baltimorean is good for; we have that from no less an authority than the redcoats who boast that they shall be in our city, in our storehouses, and in the beds of our loved ones before the week is out. I've seen what they did in Washington and their threats aren't idle. I've seen our Capitol Building, one of the wonders of the modern world, go up in smoke, and I've witnessed their vicious destruction of the White House. Think not that they will spare anyone, but resign yourselves to rapine and plunder. Lick the hand that strikes you, kiss the foot that kicks you, pay fawning homage to the body that invades you.

"For that is all that Baltimoreans are good for. Were it not so they would be out in the streets this very minute, building breastworks, redoubts, strengthening their fortresses, preparing to fight from house to house for their honor as men and citizens of the United States. Were it not so they'd be ready to repel the invader with such a rousing shout that it would be heard across the Atlantic in the chambers of the English Parliament. But the citizens of Baltimore can't do this, say the British— and they should know, for the apathy that exists here is exactly what allowed them to put the torch to Washington. So cease all the internecine quarrels between the branches of the services, cease the worrying, and simply bid adieu to Baltimore. And

those few of you who live through the coming Armageddon—
remember, never tell your children or grandchildren of the
opportunity lost, but carry your secret shame to the grave."

A howl of outrage greeted the article. People met on street
corners, demanding that Rebel Thorne be found and hung as
a traitor. Here and there the passion spilled over into action;
old men took their ancient rifles down from over the fireplaces,
cleaned and oiled them, and then went out to join the militia.

Then Commodore Rodgers arrived in Baltimore with three
hundred seamen from Philadelphia; he combined them with
five hundred flotillamen already in the town, then added David
Porter's force, which arrived from New York. Then the Fifty-
Sixth Virginia arrived, followed by the Thirty-Eighth U.S.
Infantry.

Urged on by General Smith, the local citizens dragged out
their wheelbarrows, hoes, farming equipment, anything that
could help dig ditches, or breastworks, and a line of fortifications began to appear on Hampstead Hill, the most accessible
approach to the city.

Then suddenly another problem developed: Sam Smith ran
out of money and couldn't get the War Department in Washington to give him any more. The situation seemed grim.

"We ran into the same problem in Washington," Rebel
Thorne wrote in another article. "When our General Van Ness
asked Secretary of War Armstrong for funds for the militia,
he refused. Van Ness immediately went to the private banks
and raised money. After all, citizens of Baltimore, if the city
falls, who has the most to lose? Let the banks invest in themselves, and their own safety!"

Contrite, the Baltimore bankers immediately floated a
hundred-thousand-dollar loan for General Smith, and the defense effort moved forward again.

The streets became a nightmare of wagons, carts, cais-
sons—anything that could move was pressed into use. The
hurricane of the preceding week had deposited inches of rain
on the city and the roads were a muddy trap. Rebecca saw
white men and black working side by side—master or slave,
it didn't matter; they'd all closed ranks against the common
enemy.

Youngsters who'd been playing in the streets suddenly found
more gainful work collecting stones and bricks for barricades.
Everybody worked from sunrise to well after dark, with no

thought of pay. Something had happened in Baltimore, an indefinable change in spirit: the arrival of fresh troops, the strong, sure hand of General Sam Smith, and the hell-raising articles of Rebel Thorne had galvanized a frightened populace into a determined fighting force.

But Rebecca had little time for satisfaction. The primary reason for her being in Baltimore had borne no fruit. She'd heard no news about any prisoner exchange. All her efforts to discover anything about Jeremy had come to naught, and each hour she grew more desperate.

Chapter 9

REBECCA HAD expected a great many things to happen in Baltimore. It was, after all, a city preparing for siege. But she hadn't expected to see Zebulon, nor had she expected to suffer so at his hands. And suffer she did.

Zebulon, in command of a militia unit at North Point on the Patapsco peninsula, learned that Rebecca was in Baltimore from General Sam Smith when he inspected his positions. "General, there isn't a British ship in sight," Zebulon said. "I could be in Baltimore in a matter of hours, and be back at dawn tomorrow."

Smith, believing he was doing the couple a service, agreed, and Zebulon galloped off to the Indian Queen Hotel. He arrived at nightfall and charged up to Rebecca's attic room, where he found her seated at a makeshift desk, writing.

She cried out in alarm when he entered, and hurriedly swept the papers into a drawer. Without a word, without a kiss in greeting or preparation, he swept her into his arms and carried her to the bed. Before her horrified eyes he began to rip the clothes off her, tearing the hooks and buttons in his haste.

At first she was so paralyzed with disbelief that she couldn't do anything, but then she tried to fight him off.

"Zebulon, stop! Have you gone mad?"

But his consuming need was far too urgent to be put off by fragile fists, and he kept repeating, "We could both be dead tomorrow!"

She sensed that fear was his spur; the war, the ever-present danger of death—all this moved him to couple with her in a life-giving surge. But it isn't me, she realized with a stab of pain; he could be doing this with anybody. She tried a different tack, lying perfectly still, thinking that would make him lose interest, but to no avail. In his brutish act of passion he didn't notice her tears.

In the middle of the night Zebulon awoke, got up and relieved himself in the chamber pot. Then he had a thought and padded across the bare wooden floor to her desk. Cautiously, he opened the drawer. But whatever she'd been writing, she'd removed it.

She must have hidden it while I was asleep, he thought. Who could she be writing to? He cast his mind back to past events, trying to think if she had a secret lover. There had always been that specter with his brother, Jeremy, but he was either a prisoner of war or dead. Was there somebody else? Was that why she'd been so unresponsive? And the worst punishment of all was that he truly loved her, loved her to distraction. From the moment he'd met her when she was twelve years old, he'd known that she was to be the woman in his life. And though there may have been others between, she'd always remained his ideal. He stared at her fine-chiseled profile outlined by the moonlight and realized again that he'd never seen a woman more beautiful.

If he could have painted a portrait, sung a song, written an ode to celebrate her beauty, he would have. Not having those talents, he could only shower her with gifts. At thirty-five, she was still at the height of her power and passion, and he didn't know of one woman in Washington who could hold a candle to her.

"Yet to what end is it all, if my love is unrequited?" he whispered to the sleeping form. With these thoughts tormenting him, Zebulon fell into a fitful sleep.

He rose with dayspring, and with a hurried, embarrassed kiss, rode back to his post at North Point.

As soon as Zebulon left, Rebecca nervously repeated the precautions she'd taken last night so as not to conceive. What a dreadful indictment of our marriage, she thought, that after sharing his bed for seven years, even thrilling at times to his brutish maleness, now she could no longer tolerate the idea of his touching her, let alone bearing another child of his. If she had had any doubt as to whether or not she still loved him, here was her final proof.

Besides the horror of conjugal rape, another thing Rebecca never expected was to come face to face with Marianne Connaught. She could not have said which experience shattered her more. The meeting occurred when Rebecca entered the Bank of Maryland. Marianne stood in the doorway of the president's office, arguing with the man.

Rebecca started at the sight of her. At once she fell victim
to an inexplicable anger and a host of other grim feelings. The
total effect was to make her feel diminished. But then she'd
always felt that way in the presence of the Connaught heiress.
Nor could she understand why so many men found this pale
cipher attractive. True, she had breeding; she always dressed
tastefully—now she wore a dark purple cotton dress, and a bib
of lavender lace at her throat. But her body was too thin, she
had no breasts to speak of, and the expression in her eyes was
more that of a frightened titmouse than of a woman.

Rebecca waited until Marianne finished her transactions,
then approached her, all the while taking a hard, cool look at
the girl. How old was she now—twenty-five, twenty-six? But
years had been added on to her face by the tension of the
moment. She looked as if she was on the verge of screaming.
For an instant, Rebecca thought that the strain of madness that
wove through the Connaught line had found its way into Marianne.

"I need to talk to you," Rebecca said.

When Marianne recognized Rebecca she visibly shrank; her
fingers tightened around the small purple velvet case in her
hand.

"Where are you staying?" Rebecca asked.

Marianne shook her head, confused. "I don't know. I just
got here. I came immediately to the bank."

"You'll never find a room," Rebecca told her. "The city's
swollen with soldiers." Impulsively she said, "Come with me."

Marianne hesitated a moment, but she was so unnerved that
she would have followed anybody anywhere, and she allowed
Rebecca to take her back to her tiny room at the Indian Queen.

As they climbed the steep flights into the attic, Marianne's
breathing became labored, and once in Rebecca's room she fell
against the table and sank to her knees.

Rebecca half-dragged her to the bed. "What's wrong?" she
demanded, searching her nipped waist for any telltale signs.
"Are you pregnant?"

"Oh, no," Marianne exclaimed, as though no man might
have ever touched her. "I'm sure of it."

"Then what?"

She shrugged helplessly. "Fatigue . . . I haven't slept in a
week. And worry." She started to cry.

Rebecca's impatience evaporated slightly in the face of

Marianne's distress. She reached for the pitcher, poured some water on her scented handkerchief, and pressed it to Marianne's fevered brow. "It's about Jeremy, isn't it?" she said softly.

Marianne gazed up at her with her dark, wounded violet eyes. "Yes, it's about Jeremy," she whispered.

"Tell me," Rebecca ordered.

Marianne told her the full story. Her voice cracked when she told her that Sean planned to take Jeremy back to the British fleet. "He's probably aboard one of their prison ships right now," Marianne murmured.

As her story unfolded, Rebecca listened with growing alarm, understanding for the first time the extent of Marianne's complicity in the British spying operation. Everybody in Washington knew that the Connaughts were Tories, nor were they in such a small minority. But Rebecca had never dreamed that they would be so traitorous as to aid and abet the enemy.

She felt the blood rushing to her head. "While Jeremy was fighting for his country, you were busily stabbing him in the back? I should have you shot!"

For the first time a spark of defiance lit Marianne's face. "Go ahead and shoot me if you dare. Believe me, it would be a relief from the torment I've put myself through. But I'm the only one who can reach Sean Connaught. I'm the only one who can plead Jeremy's case. And if I die, you'll never see him again."

The two women stared at each other, and then Marianne said, "I know you love him." Rebecca gritted her teeth while Marianne continued, "Rebecca, when this is over, you can do anything you want to me. I've been a blind fool, swayed by my family and by a mistaken code of honor—I see that all now. But first let me set him free. Look."

She opened her velvet case, and Rebecca's eyes flinched from the glare of the king's ransom in gems that lay in the jewel box. There lay the emerald lavaliere she'd seen Elizabeth Connaught wear before she went mad. Her fingers reached out and touched the pearl choker that had graced Marianne's fabulously long neck.

"Does your aunt know you've done this?" Rebecca asked.

"No one knows. I brought the jewels to the bank hoping to sell them, or to get a loan on them. But there isn't enough specie in the city for them to make a reasonable offer. So what I must do is give these to Sean as Jeremy's ransom."

Rebecca's eyes widened; clearly she'd underestimated the girl's strength. That she was willing to give up the family heirlooms for her lover . . . "Will your cousin accept a ransom?" she asked.

"The Connaught estates in England are always in need of money, and they've been dependent on our branch of the family for a long time. This will give him the security he's always wanted."

"Suppose he refuses?" Rebecca asked.

"I haven't thought that far," Marianne said wearily. "But he's got to accept. He must!"

"You know as well as I that Sean Connaught has no love for the Brands," Rebecca said.

Marianne nodded dully and then gave voice to her inner fears. "Sean . . . has asked me to marry him."

"Oh, God, no! Does he know that you and Jeremy . . . ?"

"I don't know. When Sean's wife died, he pressed his suit. I never gave him any encouragement, I swear! But his children needed a mother, he said, and of course, if we married, then he would inherit my share of the estate. Aunt Victoria lent her voice to his suit. I've resisted him up to now . . . but if it will free Jeremy . . ."

"You would do that?" Rebecca asked.

"How else can I make amends for all the horror I've caused? My life for his."

And then a wave of unreasoned anger swept over Rebecca. How repentant and noble it all sounded! But what of the men who'd been killed because of the Connaught treachery? Justice demanded that she be punished. And yet Rebecca also knew that her hopes for Jeremy's safety lay with this girl.

If she could pride herself on one quality, Rebecca had always told the truth. A strong sense of morality had been her staff and rod during her life, and even now, with Jeremy's life in the balance, she could act no other way. "Marianne, I must be fair with you," she began. "However this turns out, don't come back to Washington. If you do, I will do everything in my power to see that you're brought to justice."

Marianne shivered, and then she drew herself to full height. "Neither of us knows how fate will unwind this skein," she said. "Time enough to talk of justice and retribution when Jeremy's safe. If he sails off with the British war fleet, then we both know he's lost."

That realization made tears well in Rebecca's eyes and she turned away. "What's to be done?" she whispered.

"I'll need a boat," she said. "A rowboat, preferably. Something that doesn't look suspicious. And a lantern so that I can signal the British ships."

"Where are they?" Rebecca asked, instantly alert.

"They should appear off North Point in a matter of days," Marianne said.

"Are you sure? I know that our lookouts have reported nothing."

"Unless there's been a drastic change in plans, the fleet will anchor at North Point on the eleventh or twelfth."

Two days away, Rebecca thought, figuring madly. Could they get their defenses ready in time? She'd have to get this information to General Smith as quickly as possible.

"Admiral Cochrane's plan is to creep in at darkness and then land before the Americans know what happened."

"You shall have your boat and a lantern," Rebecca said. And then the thought suddenly occurred to her that Marianne might once more betray them, as she had all along. "We'll go together," she said.

Marianne shook her head vehemently. "If they see two people they'll like as not shoot us out of the water. Oh, Rebecca, I know how difficult this must be for you, but you must trust me. There's no other way."

Rebecca nodded abruptly. "But you can't go alone for a boat. You're so nervous you'd arouse suspicion."

"Couldn't we buy or rent one from a fisherman in the harbor?"

"We could, but how long would it be before you were stopped? No, we must get past Fort McHenry before you set out to sea. Let me think." While checking out every phase of the defenses, Rebecca had had occasion to ride the length and breadth of the Patapsco peninsula. "I remember a small fishing point near Bear Creek. I saw some boats there, unattended."

They waited until dark, then taking a lantern from the room, they rode doubled up on Rebecca's horse along a side road to Bear Creek. The road passed through a marshy area, but finally they saw a rowboat tied up at a fisherman's cabin. When they started for it, the howl of a dog frightened them, and they remounted and galloped off. A quarter of a mile deeper into the marsh they had better luck. They found an abandoned rowboat that was still seaworthy, and they pushed it into the currents.

"But there are no oars," Marianne whispered.

Rebecca took up a heavy stone and knocked out a slat from the back seat. "This will have to do. It's about a mile and a half from here to North Point, but you shouldn't have any trouble. The river's currents are with you. Do you have everything?"

Marianne checked her lantern, the slat of wood, and the jewel case. "Everything," she said.

"Go with God, then," Rebecca whispered.

Impulsively, Marianne reached for Rebecca and the two women embraced. Though at heart they were mortal enemies, fate had somehow brought them together to save the man they both loved.

Chapter 10

MARIANNE'S BOAT was borne out into the swift currents of the Patapsco River. On her left, she saw the dim shoreline of Sparrows Point; just around that bend would be Old Roads Bay, which Sean had planned as the main rendezvous point of the British invasion fleet. She tried to paddle toward the bay, but within minutes her delicate hands became blistered.

Dawn's first light saw her boat being swept into the vast expanse of Chesapeake Bay. Gulls hovered overhead, piping their plaintive investigating cries. About two miles away on the left she made out the spit of North Point, but try as she might, she could get nowhere near it. The sun rose from the sea, a molten golden orb turning the towering cumulus clouds into fantasies of pinks and lavenders and pale blues. Marianne scanned the horizon hoping to see a sail, but there was nothing.

Adrift and despairing, she thought, This has been the quality of my entire life. My best intentions have only paved the way to my private hell.

The sun swung to midheaven, a searing white disk that burned a hole in the sky. She hadn't thought to bring any protective clothing, and soon her face flushed with sunburn and her body became parched. She lost all sight of land. One thought and one thought only kept her going. "I must save Jeremy," she whispered. It was the only way she could redeem herself.

She'd slipped into a delirium when a pugnacious little British schooner, the *Cockchafer,* picked her up. By the time she'd regained her senses, identified herself, and implored the captain to take her to Sean Connaught's ship, sea and sky were becalmed in a twilight stillness. Moving slowly in the darkness, the *Cockchafer* sailed to the *Tonnant,* and Marianne was transferred to Admiral Cochrane's flagship.

Sean's face registered surprise, then delight, which he quickly tempered with caution.

"This is most irregular, Connaught," Admiral Cochrane said as he watched Marianne being brought aboard.

"She's our most trustworthy agent," Sean explained. "I expect she'll be bringing us a report on the latest developments in Baltimore's defenses."

Sean started to question Marianne when she stepped on board, but Admiral Cochrane saw her bleeding hands. "Take her to your cabin, sir. We're still civilized gentlemen, I presume. Have the doctor tend to her wounds. I'll be on the bridge."

Sean took Marianne to his cabin and hovered about solicitously while she told him how she'd gotten there. Minutes later, Wingate Grange bounded into the cabin. "The doctor is in surgery with one of our wounded, and sent me instead."

"See to her," Sean said curtly. He stepped outside and went to report to the admiral.

Admiral Cochrane stroked his chin as he listened. When Sean finished he said, "That's an extraordinarily brave young woman you have there."

"One of our best informants," Sean agreed.

Then Cochrane said, "Oh, I've had certain thoughts about your prisoner. What's the man's name?"

"Jeremy Brand. The worst kind of traitorous colonial. He should be hung immediately."

"That may be, but we're not the barbarians these Americans are. I want him given a fair trial. Set an example with him. Time enough to hang him once we've conquered Baltimore. Remember, Connaught, I hold you personally responsible for him. I don't want a repetition of that last incident."

Sean stiffened and bit back a retort. Two prisoners had died while being interrogated by him, and the admiralty had raised certain questions about Sean's methods. Totally unfairly, of course, Sean thought. How did they expect him to get the information that they required? Nevertheless, he saluted Cochrane smartly. "Jeremy Brand will be delivered to you in the best condition possible, I guarantee it."

"Good," Cochrane said. Then he and Sean fell into a spirited discussion of the upcoming battle.

In Sean's cabin, Wingate continued to treat Marianne. He cleaned her hands, gently punctured the blisters with a needle, then laved the wounds with an ointment. "They'll be fine in a few days," he said, smiling at her. But the distress in her face was so patent that he touched her arm. "Is something wrong?"

Marianne leaned toward Wingate. "I must ask you something, but swear you won't say anything. Promise?"

"What?" he asked, completely mystified.

"Is there an American prisoner aboard?"

"There are at least three."

"This man is named Jeremy Brand."

"Why, yes. I tended to him not an hour ago."

"Oh! Thank God he's still alive!" she whispered.

"Alive and on the mend, I guarantee," Wingate said.

"Tell him I'm here," she said. "Marianne."

"Ah, then! He called out your name a number of times when he was feverish."

Tears started to her eyes and she said hurriedly, "Tell him I've come to set him free. Tell him—" She broke off as Sean came back into the cabin.

"Haven't you finished yet?" he demanded of Wingate and dismissed him with a sharp kick. He closed the cabin door, then embraced Marianne. He felt her body stiffen and he recoiled . . . But then, he thought, that could have been because of her injuries. "Well, my dear," he said with a forced smile, "what noteworthy information have you brought us about Baltimore?"

She lowered her gaze and said nothing.

This time he couldn't misinterpret her attitude, and his mind flew back to her reaction when she'd seen Jeremy lying wounded and unconscious at Rhode's Tavern. He hoped against hope that his suspicions were unfounded, and set about putting her to the test.

"Marianne, you know that what I'm about to say has been on my mind for these many years, ever since you reached your majority."

Her pulse began to race.

"I know this is hardly the time or place to declare my intentions once again, but sometimes on the eve of a great battle, truths are given voice that might otherwise not be spoken. Marianne, nothing would please me more than if you consented to become my wife." A long pause followed while they stared at each other.

"All right," she whispered. "I ask only one thing. Jeremy Brand's freedom."

Though he felt as if she'd just thrust a red-hot poker through his heart, Sean's face remained impassive. Before he could say anything, she placed her jewel case into his hands.

"Call this what you will—my dowry, a ransom, whatever you like. But you and your sons will never lack for money."

Sean sprang to his feet, grabbing the jewel case. "I cannot believe that you'd be willing to barter our family's heirlooms for this worthless man's life. Have you no sense of honor? They're not even yours to barter. Jeremy Brand is going to hang! As soon as we've conquered Baltimore, I shall hang him in the public square, as an object lesson to all traitorous Americans!"

Sean's eyes blazed with a mad, unfocused look that Marianne had never seen before, and suddenly she was terrified. "What has he ever done to make you feel this way? How can you hate him so?"

"What has he done?" he fairly shouted. "How much you choose to forget, just to save some cocksman who's warmed your bed. Don't deny it; it's all over your face. A Connaught, with a commoner—you're no better than your mother." His eyes glazed, traveling inward to a distant memory. "Your mother, poor misguided woman, had seen fit to leave her husband's bed and was having an affair with Zebulon Brand, though at nineteen he was five years her junior."

Marianne flinched and pressed her bandaged hands to her ears, but Sean pulled them away. "Unless you hear this, Marianne, you'll never know the truth!"

I do know! she wanted to scream, but kept silent. Since the age of four, Marianne had carried her own recollections of that terrible day, and that memory had forever twisted her life. She had no need to hear it from Sean.

But he plunged on. "When your father discovered he'd been cuckolded, he demanded satisfaction from Zebulon Brand. But showing his cowardly colors, Zebulon refused. One afternoon we were all out riding—your mother, father, me, and you. I was just ending my visit to this country, and though I was only seventeen, I could already see that this bastard nation, harboring the rejects of Europe, was little more than a nest of thieves and malcontents. Then we saw Zebulon galloping along the road that led to Washington. A work crew had just started building the American Palace, and the grounds were a miasmic quag-mire, fit only for mosquitoes and wild animals.

"We followed Zebulon in our carriage, and though Devroe wasn't quite prepared for a duel, I reminded him of his obli-gations as a gentleman and an Englishman. Naturally, he con-curred. We trapped Zebulon in a bog near the edge of the Potomac. Your father leapt from the carriage, his pistols at the ready. Zebulon begged for his life, but all the while the cow-ardly bastard was maneuvering Devroe closer to a nest of water moccasins."

Marianne remembered seeing the coiling and uncoiling vi-pers, remembered how she and her mother had screamed warn-ings to her father. But he was so intent on taking Zebulon's life that he became careless with his own.

"Then Zebulon Brand pushed your father into the nest, where the snakes struck at him until he was dead."

Flecks of spittle had formed in the corners of Sean's mouth. He passed his hand in front of his eyes, trying to regain his composure. "Your mother, seeing the consequences of what she'd done, went quite mad, and so she's remained to this day, the mind of a child wandering in a woman's body. And you have the temerity to ask why I hate the Brands?"

"But Jeremy had nothing to do with that!" Marianne ex-claimed. "He couldn't have been more than ten years old at the time. He had no knowledge of it."

"Blood, my dear," Sean Connaught muttered. "The same blood that flows through the veins of Zebulon Brand flows through his brother's, and I shan't rest until all the Brands and all their issue are wiped from the face of the earth. Only that way can the Connaught name be avenged."

"You're mad," she whispered. "I never knew it until this moment, but you're absolutely insane."

"Not I," Sean said, straightening. "But I think it a piece of insanity that you should be pleading for this man's life when your concern should be with winning this war."

Faint from Sean's retelling of the tale, and from her debil-itating day, Marianne blurted, "Your own honor as an English-man demands that Jeremy be freed. He's no spy and you know it." Then her emotions got the better of her. "I tell you this: Unless you do free him, I consider myself released from my vow to aid you. Further, I'll tell—"

Sean grasped her hands and she almost fainted from the

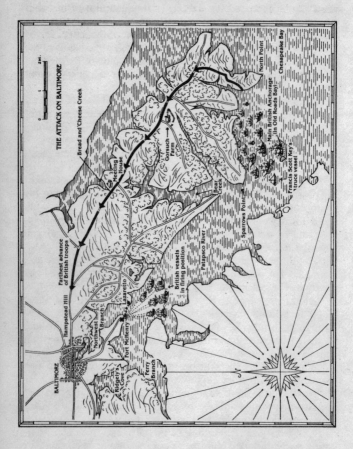

THE ATTACK ON BALTIMORE

Bread and Cheese Creek

Farthest advance
of British troops

Hampstead Hill

BALTIMORE

Northwest
Branch

Ridgely's
Cove

Fort McHenry

La Lazaretto

Perry
Branch

British vessels
in firing position

Patapsco River

Sparrows Point

Bear
Creek

Meeting
House

Gorsuch
Farm

Main British Anchorage
(in Old Roads Bay)

Francis Scott Key's
truce vessel

North Point

Chesapeake Bay

pain. "How dare you dictate to an officer in his majesty's service?" he demanded. "Obviously, you've taken leave of your senses. The sun, perhaps, and the tension of these trying times. Let's hope that it won't be of long duration. But under the circumstances, I've no recourse but to confine you to a cabin until the battle is over. We'll decide the best course of action afterwards."

Chapter 11

AT TWO o'clock in the morning of September 12, the last of the British men-of-war and troop transports were anchored at Old Roads Bay. Two brigs hove toward shore, their bristling guns ready to rake the beach. But there was no sign of any American opposition.

"Not only are the Americans cowards, but they're stupid as well," Sean Connaught said. "If there was any chance of stopping us at all it would have been right here at the beach-head."

"We can be grateful that they have little experience in war," Admiral Cochrane said. "And that both Thomas Jefferson and little James Madison refused to countenance a standing army. The more fools they."

From the porthole of Sean's cabin, Marianne watched with sinking heart as hundreds of redcoats swarmed down cargo nets to waiting small craft. She saw the ship's doctor leave, and with him the young lad who'd been so kind to her, Wingate Grange. Had he given Jeremy her message? she wondered, and then thought ruefully, Not that it makes any difference. Once again, all that she'd tried to do ended in failure.

By the time the sky had lightened, much of the invasion force had landed on the beaches of North Point. They had with them eight cannon drawn by teams of horses.

General Ross rode a black charger at the head of the army; beside him on a white mount rode the rapacious Admiral Cockburn. At 7:00 A.M. the drummer boys beat out a stirring cacophony, the buglers sounded the march, and the invasion force numbering almost five thousand of his majesty's best troops began their march on Baltimore. General Ross, Admiral Cockburn, and an advance scouting party of sixty rode ahead, and quickly outdistanced the main force.

"Where in blazes can the British be?" Zebulon asked, wiping the sweat from his eyes.

Nearby stood General Stricker, in command of the force

guarding Long Log Lane leading to Baltimore, several miles inland from North Point. "Our lookouts reported that the British landed at seven this morning," Stricker said. "At eight o'clock our cavalry units saw them at Robert Gorsuch's farm, only three miles from here. It's now eleven o'clock and there's still not a redcoat in sight."

Zebulon lifted his spyglass and scanned the road. Nothing moved. Then he swept the terrain that General Stricker had chosen as his first line of defense—the point where the two roads leading to Baltimore converged, and where a Meeting House stood. It was a marshy and wooded area; on the right was Bear Creek, and on the left, Bread and Cheese Creek; the Meeting House line extended between these two bodies of water. Stricker had positioned the Fifth Regiment on the right to guard the line at Bear Creek, and on the left he'd placed the inexperienced Twenty-Seventh Regiment. His six guns stood in the center of the line, trained on the road along which the British would have to come.

"General, we should have some reserves in the rear," Zebulon said to Stricker. "General Winder neglected to do that at Bladensburg, and when our front line broke, everybody fled. But it would make a man think twice if he found himself facing his own guns; it just might shame him into fighting."

"Good thought," Stricker said. Quickly he ordered two companies of reserves to the rear of the Meeting House line.

By noon the British still hadn't arrived. Zebulon, increasingly irritated by the heat and the mosquitoes, said, "I think they're gathering their forces, probably to plan a bayonet attack after dark. I say we should go and search them out, make them fight."

General Stricker pondered that. The thing the inexperienced militia feared most was a bayonet attack. The British were masters at hand-to-hand fighting, and Stricker had no doubt that if such a thing came to pass his entire militia would turn tail and run.

Stricker agreed to send out a probing force, but much to Zebulon's chagrin, he didn't appoint him commander. Not that Stricker questioned Zebulon's bravery, but he was impulsive, often rash, and he might sacrifice the men in some harebrained scheme. The general didn't trust a man who carried a whip as a weapon. Instead, Stricker appointed Major Heath to lead units of Captain Benjamin Howard's Mechanical Volunteers and

Captain Levering's Blues, two of the best companies in the regiment. Along with them were eighty riflemen commanded by Captain Edward Asquith, a dozen cavalrymen for added mobility, and one cannon. All told, the force numbered two hundred and fifty men, including a very disgruntled Zebulon. At one in the afternoon, just as a light rain began to fall, the men cautiously crept out of their fortified positions at Meeting House point and started down the road to find the British army.

Admiral Cockburn and General Ross and their advance guard of sixty men were reconnoitering the area, testing the Americans' strength. So far, they'd had an easy time of it, capturing everything along the road. Earlier that morning, the two British commanders had stopped for breakfast at the farm of Robert Gorsuch, where they'd questioned two captured American dragoons.

"How many men are defending Baltimore?" Ross asked.

"Fifteen thousand," said one dragoon.

Ross and Cockburn raised their eyebrows. "Are they militia?" Ross asked between a mouthful of ham and eggs.

"They are," the other dragoon said proudly.

"That's a great relief," Ross said. "As far as I'm concerned, I don't care if it rains militia!"

As they prepared to leave the farm Robert Gorsuch asked, "Will you gentlemen be back for dinner?"

Ross picked his teeth, amused. "No, tonight I'll be eating in Baltimore—or in hell!"

Now several hours later, as the sixty-man British force reached a turn in the road, rifle shots rang out, and the men scattered. Ross steadied his rearing horse. "Obviously the Americans," he said to Cockburn.

"We've advanced too far in front of our army," Cockburn said. "We have no choice but to stand them off."

Ross shouted to his men, "Fire at will!"

The British marksmen opened fire at the Americans hiding behind trees and in ditches and drove them back.

But as the fusillade continued, Zebulon and a handful of men had circled wide in an attempt to outflank the British. "If we manage it," he whispered to a private, "then they'll be caught in our crossfire."

Then he saw the gold-braided hat of an admiral, and what looked like the uniform of a general. He couldn't believe his

luck. In spite of Stricker's passing him over, it seemed as if
fate had intervened to give him a chance to cover himself with
glory.

"That must be General Ross," he whispered to two men
from the Mechanical Volunteers. Off to Zebulon's left, Levering's Blues were creeping through the bog that lay on either
side of the road. "Aim for the general—the one on the black
horse," Zebulon whispered.

"Fix bayonets!" General Ross called to his men. With a
clank of steel, the redcoats clamped their gleaming bayonets
onto the barrels of their guns. "Let the Americans try to rush
us!" Ross said. "We're ready."

"I believe we've engaged a superior force," Admiral Cockburn said. "We face the distinct possibility of being cut off."

"On the other hand, we don't want to give up any ground,
or order a retreat. Think of the adverse effect it might have on
these men," Ross said. "Or on the main army directly behind
us."

The sporadic shooting died down somewhat. The Americans
appeared to have vanished into the tall underbrush. General
Ross said, "I'd best ride back and urge our light infantry on."

"It might be dangerous," Cockburn said. "Perhaps you
should send a detail."

"That would only deplete our force here." Then Ross added
with a smile, "Besides, if I go, our infantry will march a little
faster, you may be sure."

Spurring his horse, Ross galloped off. He'd gotten around
the bend in the road when he came within rifle range of Zebulon
and his platoon hiding in the tall grasses.

"Hold your fire until I say," Zebulon whispered. They all
took aim. And then with his command, a half-dozen rifles
flashed. A bullet tore through General Ross's right arm and
smashed into the side of his chest. The impact was so great
that he was thrown from his horse.

"Got him!" Zebulon cried exultantly.

Before Zebulon and his unit could finish off the general,
they heard the British infantry running up. "Scatter!" Zebulon
ordered his men.

Within moments the first British units appeared. A redcoat
rushed up to General Ross and the general managed to gasp,
"Quickly, send for Colonel Brooke!"

Colonel Arthur Brooke, leading the Forty-Fourth Foot, was

second in command of the entire British army force. Word was
brought to him and to the other staff officers, including Admiral
Cockburn. A medical officer was hurriedly found and he galloped up; Wingate Grange was with him.

"Tourniquet," the doctor said tersely to Wingate, who
wrapped the bandage around Ross's lacerated arm. But the
general's chest wound continued to gout blood with every heartbeat.

"It's useless," General Ross whispered. "I feel the end
creeping up on me." He took a locket from his uniform and
handed it to Admiral Cockburn. "See that my wife gets this,
and commend her to my king and country."

"We must get him back to the ship," the doctor said. "Perhaps there with all my equipment..."

The redcoats scoured the countryside and found a wagon.
Gently, they placed Ross in it; Wingate Grange went along in
the wagon to tend to him. The doctor and Ross's aide, Lieutenant Haymes, went along also, but to save the horse from
pulling too heavy a load, they marched alongside the wagon.

As they bumped along the road, with the rain starting to fall
more heavily, General Ross began to suffer terribly. The pain
became so unbearable that he lost consciousness. Wingate loosened the tourniquet lest the wound become gangrenous. But
he knew that his efforts were useless; General Ross had already
begun to take on the pallor and mask of death.

During this foray Wingate had kept his eyes open, waiting
for the first possible chance to escape. Now he furtively scanned
the landscape. If he jumped from the wagon and made a dash
for it right now, he might just reach the cover of the forest
before Lieutenant Haymes could draw a bead on him. But two
things stopped him.

General Ross was in his last moments, and he couldn't bring
himself to desert him, not if there was the slightest chance that
he could bring him some small comfort. Any dying man deserved at least that. The other and far more important reason
was Jeremy Brand. From the moment he'd met Jeremy, Wingate had felt that somehow his future was inextricably tied up
with this man's. How, he didn't know, nor did he know why.
But he did know that unless he returned to the prison ship and
took special care of Jeremy, he too might easily die.

And so he stayed in the wagon, tending General Ross as
his last breaths rasped hoarsely in his throat. Wingate found

the entire experience unnerving. It didn't matter that Ross was an Englishman; he was a human being first. "How strange," Wingate murmured, "that only death has the power to give us compassion for our fellow man."

General Ross died before they reached the beach. Lieutenant Haymes wrapped his body in the Union Jack, and they took it back aboard the *Tonnant,* where it was immersed in a keg of rum for preservation.

General Stricker's defense line at the Meeting House was tense. Zebulon and his unit had made it back with the news that the British were coming up Long Log Lane in full force. At about two-thirty in the afternoon, the first British rockets began tearing across the sky.

"No cause for panic, men," Stricker shouted. "They're more noise than anything else." The American artillery began to pound the British positions. The British artillery answered, and the infantry on both sides watched the duel.

Zebulon studied the action with a keen eye. "The British are concentrating their fire on our left flank," he said to Stricker. Already anticipating an attack there, Stricker tried to strengthen his lines. But his men, green for the most part, were confused by the sudden command to change positions, particularly while all the shooting was going on.

In contrast, the redcoats took their position like an army of red ants, each unit moving with perfect precision. Colonel Brooke, confounded by the death of Ross, still hadn't assumed full command, so Admiral Cockburn gave the orders to the division commanders. "Spread the Eighty-Fifth Foot out along the entire front line. Back them up with the Forty-Fourth Foot. Have the Twenty-First stand ready on the road to fill in any weak points. Remember this," Cockburn told his troops, "you're fighting for God and country. The men you're facing aren't soldiers at all, but rabble, and traitors to boot. Last but not least, remember the prize money!"

A hearty cheer greeted this. At three o'clock, a distraught Colonel Brooke finally gave the signal to advance. The buglers sounded the charge, and the notes floated across the meadows and swamps.

As the redcoats charged, General Stricker shouted to his artillery men, "Fire!" The cannons spewed forth death in the form of grapeshot. Any available piece of loose metal had been crammed into the muzzles—bits of broken scythes, horse-shoes, chains, hinges, nails.

The front ranks of the redcoats took the grape and it deci-mated their lines, but others automatically filled in, and they kept coming.

"But you see, they can be killed!" Zebulon shouted to his men, and a rifle volley cut down more of the advancing British. Zebulon had the scent of blood in his nose and it smelled good. These invaders had burned his city, and he wanted them dead. "All of you!" he shouted.

When the charging redcoats were a scant hundred yards away, Zebulon leapt from behind his redoubt and fired his rifle, and then his pistols. Now the firing came indiscriminately from both sides, men firing and reloading as fast as they could, men screaming as metal tore through flesh and bone, men breathing their last prayers.

In the midst of the action, for some inexplicable reason, part of the American line, the Fifty-First Regiment on the far left, suddenly broke and ran. They were not under direct fire yet, but all the noise and confusion panicked them. As they bolted they stampeded the Thirty-Ninth Regiment along with them.

"The cowards are running!" Admiral Cockburn shouted gleefully. "Avenge Ross! Don't let them get away!"

Redcoats raced toward the remainder of the American lines. The center and right held their position for more than twenty minutes, fighting the British in fierce hand-to-hand combat. When the Americans ran out of ammunition they used their rifles as clubs, but they were no match for the razor-sharp steel of British bayonets as they ripped into stomachs and cut a swath through the line.

"Retreat!" General Stricker called. He could have saved his breath—his troops were already disappearing into the woods.

Zebulon ran as he'd never run in his life. But decades of profligate drinking and smoking had taken their toll, and he heard the heavy tread of a redcoat gaining on him. Zebulon stumbled and fell over an exposed root. He turned to see a bayonet lunging for his stomach. With a cry he rolled to the side, scrambled to his feet, and tore his whip free. As the redcoat came at him again, Zebulon lashed out and saw the soldier's surprised look as the whip caught him across the eyes. The second whiplash coiled around the redcoat's neck. Zebulon jerked sharply and the vertebrae snapped. Zebulon grabbed the redcoat's rifle and continued running.

As he emerged from the far side of a stand of trees, Zebulon almost ran into General Stricker, who was also running.

"Re-form, re-form, damn it," Stricker shouted, fighting to keep some semblance of order. The retreat threatened to degenerate into a rout. "The last thing we can afford is another Bladensburg!"

They came upon their reserve line, the Sixth Regiment, and Stricker managed to re-form his lines somewhat. But fearing that the British might still rout them, and that this in turn would affect the major defenses at Hampstead Hill, Stricker ordered his men to fall back to that well-fortified position.

"Look smart there," Zebulon said to the men tramping beside him. "Hold your head up. We've nothing to be ashamed of. They're supposed to be Wellington's Invincibles. They've spent a lifetime learning war, but we showed them how free men can fight. And by God we'll fight them again, and this time we'll win!"

When a hasty roll call was taken, General Stricker discovered he'd lost one hundred sixty-three killed or wounded. An additional fifty were unaccounted for, presumably taken prisoner.

But the British had also suffered losses, far more than they'd bargained for. "The count of dead and wounded now stands at three hundred," an aide told Admiral Cockburn.

The admiral paced the Meeting House grounds, where the remainder of his five-thousand-man army had just bivouacked. From under his lowering brow, Cockburn studied the youthful Colonel Brooke. He appeared to be a competent officer, but without Ross's vitality and experience. Cockburn wondered how well the army would serve under him.

"Signal Admiral Cochrane," Cockburn said to his aide. "He should be aboard the *Surprise* by now, preparing to sail on Fort McHenry. Tell him we'll attack the American position at Hampstead Hill just as soon as he'd captured the fort. With our navy on one side bombarding Hampstead Hill, we on the other, once we have them in our pincers, the Americans will crumble, just as they did at Washington. This night will tell the tale," Cockburn said. "The war could be won by dawn."

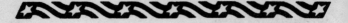

Chapter 12

ADMIRAL COCHRANE, unaware of the death of General Ross, was making slow progress up the shallow Patapsco River. After landing the army and the necessary supplies, he'd transferred his flag to the frigate *Surprise;* it had a shallower draft than the *Tonnant.* At one-thirty that afternoon, Cochrane gave the order to proceed upstream to within firing range of the fort guarding Baltimore's harbor.

"Fort McHenry is the key, Captain Connaught," Admiral Cochrane said. "If we can slip past it, we'll sail into the harbor and be able to give naval support to our army. The fleet will be *behind* the American lines at Hampstead Hill. Once we commence raking them with our broadsides, they won't stand a chance."

Sean smiled broadly. "It will do my soul good to see Baltimore consumed in flames."

But the progress upriver proved slow. They encountered unexpected shoals, and their pilots were inexperienced in these waters. "Damn, look over there," Sean said. "The *Seahorse* has just gone aground."

Cochrane ordered small boats lowered away to take soundings, and the fleet inched upriver. At three-thirty, the *Surprise* managed to sail within five miles of Fort McHenry and was joined by a score of other frigates and brigs. Five bomb vessels and the rocket carrier *Erebus,* which constituted the heart of the attack force, sailed even closer until they were two and a half miles from the fort.

"Do you think that the Americans have any surprises in store for us?" Sean asked. "My guess is that they're too inept."

"I'm not taking any chances." Admiral Cochrane passed the order on: "Every ship is to have her grapnels ready in case the Americans send out fire vessels. Our position is tight here. They might set fire to a number of their ships and sail them among us; it could create havoc."

"My intelligence reports tell of an American inventor named

Robert Fulton. He's devised a sort of long mechanical bomb that moves underwater. Fulton calls this thing a Columbiad."

"Such barbarous weapons are outlawed by the rules of warfare," Cochrane said stiffly. "Incidentally, have you made arrangements for the prisoner exchange?"

Sean nodded. "The American negotiators, a man named John Skinner and a lawyer named Francis Scott Key, have been piped aboard our prison ship. But I've taken the precaution of having the negotiators held on the ship also, at least until this battle is over."

Cochrane nodded his agreement. Yet he mistrusted Sean Connaught; his role in British intelligence gave him a great deal more influence than his rank would indicate. He had many friends in the military establishment, including Lord Bathurst, and it was said that the prince regent himself took an almost ungentlemanly interest in this cloak-and-dagger business.

Sean swept his spyglass along the shoreline . . . Lazaretto on the right bank, to Fort McHenry on the left. His body tensed. "Admiral, something's happening that we didn't anticipate. The Americans are sinking block ships across the mouth of the channel!"

"Damn!" Cochrane swore. "I'd hoped to outflank the fort, but now we've no alternative. We must capture it. All right then, once that's done we'll blast the sunken ships out of the channel and support our ground forces as planned."

In the late afternoon, Cochrane sent a communiqué to General Ross outlining his new plan of attack. But at seven-thirty that evening, the letter was returned with the terrible news that Ross had been killed in action.

"It's a blow to our cause, indeed; it means we must redouble our efforts," Sean Connaught said. "My only fear now is that Colonel Brooke will be too lenient with Baltimore."

Cochrane immediately wrote to Brooke, giving him the plans intended for Ross and adding, "The atrocities committed by the Americans in Canada clearly justify the harshest measures possible against this den of pirates. It must be totally destroyed."

Rebecca fretted, beside herself with worry. She'd seen Francis Scott Key and John Skinner just before they embarked for the British prison ship.

"I don't have Jeremy listed on my exchange sheet," Key

said. "But if he's on the ship, you may be sure that I'll do everything in my power to have him released."

Unable to bear the tension of sitting in her room alone, Rebecca had scoured the streets and suburbs of Baltimore, gathering details for what would be an article about a glorious victory, or a devastating defeat—a defeat that might mean the end of the United States. If she had to give an opinion at this moment, she would have been hard pressed to predict the outcome.

The news that General Stricker had been forced to fall back to the main defense line at Hampstead Hill had caused panic throughout the city. She knew that Zebulon had been in those front lines and she said a silent prayer for his safety. Though she no longer loved him, he was nonetheless the father of her children and she wished him well.

Rebecca guided her horse along the road that led to Fort McHenry and saw cannonballs being transported to the fort. When she reached the narrow part of the harbor she saw sailors working furiously to sink ships across the channel to deny the British fleet access to the harbor. With the English vessels now in full view, it would be a close race.

When General Sam Smith had implored the Baltimore shipping merchants to scuttle their ships, they hadn't taken kindly to the idea. But a scathing diatribe by Rebel Thorne convinced the townspeople that they would have to sacrifice a little, or lose all. Now Rebecca watched as John Donnel's ship *Chesapeake* slowly filled with water and went down, followed by Claggett's schooner *Scudder,* and Craig's brig *Father and Son.* With the line of ships now blocking the channel, Rebecca and everybody else in Baltimore breathed a bit easier. That evening Rebecca found lodgings in a farmhouse close to the fort. She slept fitfully that night and rose before daybreak. The terrain was fairly flat, so she climbed into the hayloft of the farm's barn, where she found an excellent view of the bay and of Fort McHenry. She scanned the area with her spyglass, but it was still too dark to make out anything.

At dawn on September 13, the British bomb vessel *Volcano* began creeping closer to Fort McHenry. Behind her trailed another bomb ship, the *Meteor,* followed close by the rocket-launcher *Erebus.* The *Cockchafer,* the schooner that had picked up Marianne Connaught, sailed in the thick of the ships, and was almost swamped by the arrival of three more bomb ships, the *Terror*, the *Devastation*, and the *Aetna*. Accompanying frigates and sloops also trained their guns on the fort.

At about six that morning, Rebecca recoiled as a huge blast shook the barn. The *Volcano* had fired a salvo for range. A flume of water sprayed into the air as the shot fell short. The bomb vessels and the rocket ship sailed closer until they were less than two miles away. At seven the *Meteor* opened fire, and one by one the other ships commenced firing in earnest.

The roar was deafening and Rebecca held her hands over her ears. The British had refined their siege ships into formidable weapons. They were stubby, only one hundred feet long, and armed principally with two guns, a ten-inch and a thirteen-inch mortar. The mortars hurled shells weighing two hundred pounds a distance of over two and a half miles. Enormous force was required to fire such a heavy shell, and this transferred horrendous strain onto the ship. A complex system of beams and springs crisscrossed the hold to cushion the recoil impact, lest the ship's own firepower blast it out of the water. Each of the five bomb vessels could hurl about forty-five shells an hour. Rebecca watched in awe as the ships bucked and plunged after each blast.

Since the British ships were well out of range of Fort McHenry's smaller cannon, the gunners there were falling far short of their targets. Rebecca's heart contracted as the shells continued to pour into the fortress. General Sam Smith had told her a piece of confidential information: the fort's powder magazine wasn't bombproof. If one shell were to land there . . . As she watched the pounding, it didn't seem possible that the fort could last more than a few hours.

Inside the fort, Major George Armistead tried to boost the morale of his gunners. "Raise the elevation of those guns just a bit more," he said.

"They're raised as far as they'll go," a gunner told him.

"Then add an extra charge of powder."

"Major, that's dangerous," the gunner said. "The barrels can only stand so much."

"We've got to do something," Armistead said. "They're firing at us at will, and we can't even reach them."

The best efforts the gunners could manage was 1,800 yards with the twenty-four-pound cannon, and 2,800 yards with the French thirty-six-pounders. But since the British were bombarding them from a distance of 4,200 yards, Armistead finally gave the order to cease fire. "We might just as well save our shells," he said.

"Now I know what a sitting duck feels like," an infantryman said to his comrades as they huddled in a dry moat that ran partway around the fort.

Rebecca kept an hourly report in her diary. "Ten o'clock and the British seem more determined than ever to reduce the fort to rubble . . . Eleven o'clock, this hour alone I've counted almost two hundred shells, or some three every minute. The noise is deafening and I can't imagine how the men inside the fort are enduring it . . . The sun stands at high noon now and the attack continues unabated. The shock waves literally rock one back on one's heels. The fort's only act of defiance seems to be the huge American flag that flies over its battlements. It measures thirty feet by forty-two feet, so Sam Smith told me, and has fifteen red and white stripes, and fifteen stars on a field of blue. It cost $405.90, and was sewn up by Mrs. Pickersgill and her daughter Caroline." It struck Rebecca that the flag was in its way a spirited defense against the British Empire. She jotted down some ideas—"a lone flag against the great armada . . . symbol of the nation that dared to stand up to the mightiest oppressor in the world. Long may it wave."

At two o'clock, Rebecca saw an explosion and a plume of black smoke rise from the battlements as a shell landed squarely on a gun emplacement, knocking out a heavy cannon and killing its entire gun crew. And then what she feared finally happened—a shell crashed through the roof of the munitions shed. She waited for the explosion, but nothing happened. (Later she learned that the two-hundred-pound bomb still had its fuse sputtering in the munitions shed and was about to explode, when a quick-witted soldier threw a pail of water on the fuse, extinguishing it just in time. For Major Armistead this was too close a call; he had the powder barrels removed and stretched out along the walls of the star-shaped fortress. "Better to risk one or two of them exploding than having the entire magazine go up," he told his men.)

Toward three in the afternoon, Rebecca saw three of the bomb ships moving in closer. "Apparently they believe they've softened up the fort sufficiently and are closing in for the kill," she wrote. "Pray heaven that Major Armistead has enough courage left to return their fire the moment they come within range."

Some erratic shells landed close to the barn and Rebecca decided it was better to be on the ground. She climbed down from the loft and took up a new lookout post. She was unaware of the soldier until he came up behind her and wrestled her to the ground. "Got you!" he shouted.

She cried out as she fell, landing with a bone-jarring thud. She tried to collect herself, see what was happening.

The soldier who'd thrown her was no more than a youth, sixteen or seventeen at most. He was wearing the uniform of a corporal in the Tennessee Volunteers, which meant nothing more formal than buckskin pants and tunic, and a coonskin cap. He carried a powder horn slung over his shoulder, a pistol in his leather belt, and a long, deadly Kentucky rifle.

"You idiot, what's the meaning of this?"

"Idiot, is it? Well, I've been watching you for a spell. Saw you up in that barn yonder. Spying on the fort through your spyglass. You're most likely one of those Tory spies I've been hearing about."

Rebecca was so angry she could only sputter.

"Taking you over to the fort, I am. Deliver you up myself to the commander. See what's so almighty important in those notes you've been writing."

"Now see here, you illiterate fool. I'm Mrs. Rebecca Breech Brand of Washington, and General Sam Smith, who's in command of all the Baltimore forces, is a personal friend of mine."

"Yeah, sure, didn't expect you to say nothing less. My name's Corporal Jonathan Albright, and I'd be obliged if you'd just come along peacefully."

"I swear, I'll have you court-martialed!"

"Couldn't if you wanted to," he said with a grin. "'Count of I'm attached to General Andrew Jackson. Now I'll take those notes, ma'am, if it's all the same to you."

Rebecca's mind worked furiously. This boy's overzealousness was creating a serious problem for her. If he took her to the fort, sooner or later she'd be vindicated. But the information in her notes would certainly reveal her identity as Rebel Thorne, and all she'd worked for these many years would be ruined— not only would her disguise be penetrated, but her influence as Rebel Thorne would immediately be diminished. Think! she commanded herself. He's only a lad, hayseed still in his hair; he shouldn't be too difficult to persuade.

"If you're assigned to General Jackson, aren't you a little far from home?"

He nodded. "I'm a courier for him. Rode all the way from Horseshoe Bend, Alabama way, to bring his dispatches to President Madison."

"Oh? And what's the news?" she asked.

"Defeated the Creek Indians, the General did," Jonathan Albright said proudly. "They won't trouble us anymore."

"Splendid. And how is the General? He's an old friend of mine."

"Guess anybody who ever met Old Hickory calls him friend," he said, his tone clearly indicating that he took what she was saying with a grain of salt.

Rebecca appraised him, trying to find the key. Tall and gangly, with shoulders so bony that they stuck out of his shirt. His eyes were light brown, with thick brown eyebrows and long hair that had turned copper-colored under the summer sun. A bribe, perhaps? she wondered. No, more than likely he responded to authority.

"If you're a courier, shouldn't you be about your business? General Jackson's probably waiting anxiously for your answer from Madison."

"Wasn't that important, to my mind. And this is where the fighting is right now. I thought that they could use an extra gun at the fort. I know the General will understand."

A cannonball hit about two hundred yards away, and Jonathan Albright grabbed Rebecca's hand and started to pull her toward the fort. "Best not stand out in the open this way."

Her shoe caught on a root and she cried out in pain as she wrenched her ankle. Her knees buckled and she sat down hard. "Oh, see what you've done now!" she cried in exasperation and began to massage her foot.

"If you'd come along peaceably, this wouldn't have happened," he said.

Suddenly she lost every vestige of control and screamed at him, "You blasted nincompoop! I'm not a spy!"

Another cannonade pocked the land all about. Jonathan said, "We can't stay here. They're getting the range." He bent down, scooped her up in his arms, and started to carry her.

She beat against his chest with her clenched fists, but in response he crushed her so close that it took her breath away. Though he was thin, he was very strong, and she could feel his hard, flat muscular chest and arms.

He didn't look like Jeremy at all, yet there was something similar about them. His independence, perhaps. With a woman's intuition, she recognized that in any confrontation between them, neither of them would ever give way.

She felt terribly uneasy in his arms. And her feelings were further compounded by the fact that he was about to expose her.

Some corner of her brain registered a high-pitched whistling sound, and then the two of them were thrown into the air by the concussion of a bomb bursting nearby. She landed on a patch of loamy turf and had the wind knocked out of her. Gasping for breath, she crawled toward the lad. He was unconscious.

She put her hand on his chest and felt his rhythmic heartbeat. She doubted that he was seriously hurt. He would come to shortly, and she would be in the same predicament. She stood up and tried to hobble away, but with her ankle injured, she knew that she wouldn't get very far before he overtook her. And he'd interpret her running away as a sure sign of her guilt.

"There's only one thing to do," she whispered.

She reached for his belt and yanked out his pistol. Then she took his powder horn, poured out some of the black powder on the ground, and lit it with his flint. In the puff of smoke and sizzling fire, she fed her notes to the flames.

She knew that some of what she'd written in these pages was the best of her life. She might not be able to capture the immediacy of how she'd reported the battle. But she had no choice except to destroy the pages, and she cursed the fact that she'd ever laid eyes on this young man.

Several minutes later, Jonathan Albright regained his senses. He sat up and shook his head. Then he spotted the charred remains of the pages and guessed what she'd done. His long hand moved reflexively to his belt.

"No, I have it," she said, and pointed the pistol at him. She'd expected some kind of pleading from him—he had to pay a little for what he'd made her do—but there wasn't the slightest vestige of fear in his eyes. "Before you get any more silly ideas, I *am* Mrs. Rebecca Breech Brand, I *do* live in Washington, General Jackson *is* an acquaintance of mine, and I'm *not* a spy."

"Then why'd you burn those pages?"

"That has nothing to do with you, nor is there any reason that you should know. But if I was a spy, I could have shot you while you were unconscious." Then she handed the pistol back to him. "And now, you've caused me enough grief for the day. Would you please leave me alone? If I never see you again, it will be too soon."

Jonathan Albright searched her face, not knowing what to believe. But then he looked out to the gleaming waters of the bay and the white sails of the advancing British ships.

"They're coming in in force now," he said, and scrambled to his feet. He shook his head to clear it. "Don't know who you are, or why you're here, ma'am, or if you're telling the truth. Seems to me you're acting like you got something to hide. But I can't waste any more time with you."

Then, scooping up his rifle, Jonathan Albright started running toward the fort, his lanky body tensed for battle.

Chapter 13

THE LOOKOUTS in Fort McHenry shouted, "The British are coming within range!"

"Now's our chance, lads," Major Armistead called to the gun crews huddled near the embrasures. "We've taken their blasted shelling for hours without a chance to fire back. Keep steady now, let them get closer—a mile should do it. Don't fire until I give the word."

Rebecca watched as the ships hove closer. "Why don't they fire?" she asked, clenching her fists. She wrote furiously, "The fort seems to have been stunned into submission after the dreadful pounding. Now the British ships are less than a mile away, and still there is no response from our men."

And then suddenly every gun inside Fort McHenry opened up. Shock waves rolled over Rebecca as she scrambled to her feet, unmindful of her ankle. Her heart beat with elation as she saw the shells land amid the british ships.

The *Devastation* took a shell in her port bow, and sprang a leak. The *Volcano* took five straight hits, and a shell struck a gunboat and killed several Royal Colonial Marines.

A great cheer went up from the fort nd they redoubled their efforts, firing furiously.

Aboard the *Surprise*, Admiral Cochrane scanned the battle action. "Recall the bomb hips immediately," he orered, and the signal flags went up on the line ordering all vessels out of range.

"If I may make a suggestion . . ." Sean Connaught said.

Cochrane looked at him with impatience. "Yes, what is it?"

"It might be wiser to attack after dark. The fortis a stationary target, while our ships would be moving about, making them more difficult to hit."

"Excellent point," Cochrane said. "Send a message to Colonel Brooke' headquarters. We will attack at one in the morning. When he sees the American flag hauled down from the battlements of Fort McHenry, that will be his signal to assault Hampstead Hill. By then we'll be in position to give him all the support he needs to crash through their defenses and roll on to Baltimore." He turned to Sean and said grimly, "This night we'll administer the *coup de grâce*."

Colonel Brooke and his army were bogged down in the mud. The British had advanced from the Meeting Hous area, skirting the trees that had been felled across the road to slow them down. Another torrential rainfll hd turned the road into a muddy sump, and teams of men and horses strained in their leather harnesses, draggingthe cannon and supplies through the mire.

Earlier that day, they'd reached the crest of a knoll and gazed at Baltimore, which lay less than three miles away. "There's the prize, men," Brooke said. "By tomorrow, you'll all share the booty. Whatever we can't cart or sail away will be burned to the ground."

Only one final obstacle blocked the way to Baltimore, Hampstead Hill. Colonel Brooke and Admiral Cockburn climbed onto the roof of an abandoned farmhouse to get a better vantage point. They studied the fortifications through their spyglass.

"They've done quite a job," Admiral Cockburn said. "I make out trenches and palisades all along its length. There must be ten thousand men there, at least."

"And every tree and house that might have afforded us some protection has been razed," Brooke said. "While the Americans have a clear line of fire."

"None of that will do them any good once Admiral Cochrane and the fleet sail into the harbor. Then our warships can rake all of Hampstead Hill from the rear. They'll be caught in our pincers. After one concerted bayonet charge on their line, the Americans will break and run like they did at Bladensburg. Baltimore will soon be ours."

Rebecca huddled in the empty farmhouse, her spyglass trained on the fort. Erratic bombs occasionally exploded nearby. She'd never been so frightened in her life. What she wanted most was to get away from here, but her ankle had swollen so badly that she couldn't walk. Gradually, as the British shelling increased, she forgot her own pain and fear and thought, If the British fleet was trapped in the Chesapeake, then perhaps Jeremy . . . Everything hinged on Fort McHenry now, and she sent prayer after prayer to the valiant men manning the ramparts.

At one o'clock the dark sky erupted in a dazzling display of bombs and rockets and streaking missiles as the British fleet commenced their final assault. Many poorly fused british bombs never reached the fort, but exploded in midair, turning night into day for brief flashes. Rebecca had never seen anything like it—starbursts of light sporadically illuminated the fort and the huge flag that still flew in the center of the compound.

In a cove near Old Roads Bay, Francis Scott Key and John Skinner watched the bombardment all through the night. Key's efforts to locate and free Jeremy had come to naught, but he had managed to arrange for the release of a number of other American prisoners. But since the British wouldn't allow them to leave the prison ship until the battle was over, all he could do was watch the duel that grew more violent with each hour.

Key was a lawyer with a literary bent. As he watched the streak of red rockets and the bursting bombs, the lines of a poe began to form in his head. He jotted them down hurriedly on the back of an envelope he happened to have in his pocket. Every time a bomb exploded, he prayed fervently that he still might see the American flag flying over Fort McHenry.

Aboard the British flagship *Tonnant,* Jeremy pressed his aching body against the door of the brig. Most of the skeleton crew of British tars were at the rail watching the battle, and Wingate Grange had been able to slip away and see Jeremy.

"I'm sorry I haven't been able to see you before this," Wingate said hurriedly. "A woman's come aboard. She said to tell you. Her name is Marianne."

Jeremy grabbed the boy's shoulders. "You're sure?"

Wingate nodded. "I tended her wounds myself. She rowed all the way out to the ship and her hands were blistered."

"I suppose she's with Sean Connaught?" Jeremy said, his face clouding. "Spying for him again."

"I don't know anything about that," Wingate said. "But I did hear them arguing. At any rate, she said that she had come to set you free."

Jeremy stiffened. "To free me," he repeated derisively. He

looked sideways at the boy. Was Wingate part of a plot that
Marianne and Sean were hatching? No, the lad was too simple
for that, but they could be duping him. Then the unbidden
memory of what Marianne had sworn at Bladensburg came
back to haunt him. Could he have been wrong about her?

The muffled roar of exploding bombs reverberated through
the brig. "What about the battle?" Jeremy asked Wingate.
"What's happening?"

Wingate told him as quickly as possible.

"Will the British be able to take the fort?" he asked weakly.

Wingate shrugged. "I don't know. I only know that the flag
is still flying. That's what the lookout reports from the crow's
nest."

"Pray God," Jeremy whispered, "pray God."

"We're almost four hours behind schedule," Colonel Brooke
said to Admiral Cockburn. "What can be keeping the fleet?
Has the flag been hauled down yet?"

They had to wait for another bomb burst before they could
see that the flag was still flying. "Damn!" Admiral Cockburn
swore. "I say we attack anyway, flag or no flag."

"Admiral, when General Ross died I automatically became
commander of his majesty's ground forces. In my judgment
it would be sheer suicide to attack Hampstead Hill without the
support of the fleet. I don't need to remind you that we have
other objectives, including a rendezvous with General Pakenham at New Orleans—a target just as vital as Baltimore, if
not more so."

"Would you have us be known as cowards?" Admiral Cockburn demanded.

Colonel Brooke paled. Though he was many years Cockburn's junior in age and experience, he drew himself to his full
height. "This is my decision, and I will pass it along to my
officers. We will wait until dawn. If the fleet has been successful, we attack. But if Fort McHenry has not been captured,
we withdraw, and live to fight another day."

With an oath, Admiral Cockburn strode off.

Rebecca's eyes burned, her head pounded, and there was
such a ringing in her ears that she thought she'd be forever
deaf. Am I mistaken, or is the bombardment slowing down?

she thought. She stood up, limped to the door, and stepped outside. In the east, dawn was rising, and in the early light she caught a panoramic view of the battle scene. There were the British ships, still firing away, but intermittently now. And there was the solid presence of Fort McHenry, bomb-pocked, with the walls shattered in many places. Then she lifted her eyes up to see the red, white, and blue flag still flying defiantly in the stiff breeze. She blinked at what she saw next. The British bomb ships were turning and sailing away!

She raised her hands to the sky. "Thank God! We've turned back the British! Oh, thank God!" And then her body seemed to dissolve from the tension and lack of sleep and she sank to her knees and wept uncontrollably.

All of Baltimore erupted into a gigantic celebration. Soldiers and citizens roamed the streets, arm in arm, drinks in hand. Bonfires burned at street crossings, and everywhere the citizens talked of the wonderful victory. They had turned back the invincible British! The burning of Washington, though not avenged, was now a little easier to bear.

When Francis Scott Key was finally released by the British, he went to the Indian Queen Hotel, where he prepared to leave for Washington. Rebecca heard he was there and sought him out. "What of Jeremy?"

"I'm so sorry," he said to her, "but they wouldn't even acknowledge that he was a prisoner, let alone release him."

Rebecca kneaded her hands. "Did you see a young woman there, Marianne Connaught?"

Key shook his head. "I know Marianne, but she wasn't on the prison ship."

Rebecca slumped to a chair and rested her head in her hands. Key came to stand at her sie and pressed her shoulder. "All we can do is keep trying," he said gently.

She nodded, and at last she managed to calm herself. Then the two of them talked quietly, sharing their experiences of the battle. He showed her the poem he'd written.

Rebecca read it with growing interest. It seemed to have just the right combination of fear and defiance about the outcome of the battle. "It's wonderful," she breathed. "I wish I could have written something like it. You must have it printed."

"Do you really think so?" he asked, obviously pleased. "Do

you remember the poem I wrote honoring the heroes of the
Tripoli Wars? I used the song, 'To Anacreon in Heaven.' I was
thinking of setting this poem to it."

Rebecca hummed it to herself as she read the verses. "That
might work. You'll have to change the meter in a few places,
but that shouldn't be too hard to do."

Key set to work right there. When he was done he took it
down to the *Baltimore American and Commercial Daily Advertiser* and had it struck off as a handbill. Hundreds of copies
were soon circulating throughout the city. The song caught on
immediately and was sung everywhere.

Then there came another piece of dazzling news. On September 11, almost at the same time as the Battle of Baltimore
was being fought, a British army of eleven thousand men,
under the command of Sir George Prevost, invaded the United
States from Canada. They struck at Plattsburg, New York, but
were thrown back. And a fleet of English ships was annihilated
on Lake Champlain by the consummate seamanship of Captain
Thomas Macdonough.

But though the nation was cautiously celebrating the double
triumphs at Baltimore and Lake Champlain, Rebecca experienced them both as Pyrrhic victories. As she headed back to
Washington in a coach with Zebulon at her side, she listened
half-heartedly to his tales about the fighting at Meeting House
Road and Hampstead Hill. But her eyes were scanning the
waters of the Chesapeake, as though she might conjure up the
British ships which were out there somewhere.

Tears rolled from her eyes.

"I know," he said softly. "It's just relief that this is over
and that we've both come out of it safely." And then he began
to hum the bars of Francis Scott Key's song:

> ". . . And the rocket's red glare,
> The bombs bursting in air,
> Gave proof through the night
> That our flag was still there . . ."

The tears continued to roll down Rebecca's cheeks, for a
battle won . . . and a love lost.

PART TWO

Chapter 14

"I'VE NEVER heard of such a piece of idiocy!" Rebecca exclaimed to Dolley Madison. "They can't be serious. They *mustn't* move the capital out of Washington."

The two women were sitting in the upstairs drawing room of the Octagon House, the Madisons' temporary residence. Colonel John Tayloe's house, built to fit the wedge-shaped lot at the corner of New York Avenue and Eighteenth Street, was directly across the street from Rebecca's own dwelling, and consequently she and Dolley had become even closer.

Dolley rose and moved to the window; usually she dressed in gay pastel colors—beiges and yellows were her favorites—but of late she'd taken to wearing dark grays and muddied browns, which did little for her pallor. "My dear, come and look at this," she called to Rebecca.

Rebecca went to her side. She stared at the burned-out shell of the White House, visible down the avenue. Not a piece of glass was left in the empty windowframes, and the stone on the northwest corner of the building had totally crumbled, giving the building the appearance of an ancient ruin.

"Everything that Mr. Madison and I owned, reduced to ash," Dolley murmured. "But that's the least of it. With the White House burned to the ground, New England ready to secede from the Union, and the entire nation in a turmoil, there are times when I feel that a malevolent star is casting its light on this nation."

Rebecca slipped her arm around Dolley's waist. "Come now, you mustn't give in to your despair. All my life I've looked to you for comfort. And so has the rest of the nation. When things looked darkest, your optimism buoyed us, assuring us that things would ultimately right themselves. Now the country needs you more than ever—for you, like the White House, have become a symbol. You daren't desert us."

Silent tears streaked Dolley's rouged cheeks. "I search everywhere for some sign of light, but I find only gloom."

Rebecca gave her a reassuring hug. "You're tired, that's all. It's been a terrible summer. But take heart. We did best the British at Baltimore, and the news from the Great Lakes continues to be splendid."

"But New Orleans," Dolley said in a near whisper. "Mr. Madison believes the British will strike there next, and we're so woefully unprepared."

"We've put our fate in the hands of one of our best generals," Rebecca said. "Andrew Jackson will know how to deal with the British."

The women moved away from the window. Dolley stirred the fire that blazed in the hearth. "This house is always so chilly! My maid Sukie tells me that her rheumatism is acting up because of the dampness in the cellar."

"You'll be back in the White House soon. I know such a thing doesn't seem likely right now, but if we have the will, then anything is possible."

"Do you really think so?" Dolley asked. She took the scented handkerchief that Rebecca handed her, dried her eyes, and smoothed the streaked rouge.

"The way things are going, we don't know where we'll be a month from now. Philadelphia sent a commission with an invitation to move the government back to its old quarters on Chestnut Street," Dolley said. "And with the promise that the President and I could have a house there, rent-free."

"Very enterprising of them," Rebecca said. "And why wouldn't they want that? They know what benefits would accrue to them if the government moved back there."

"And New York City has given Mr. Madison the choice of several buildings, all of which I hear are quite splendid."

"Nothing in this nation has ever been as splendid as the Capitol and the White House," Rebecca retorted.

"Oh, I quite agree," Dolley said hastily. "But do you know how much they say it will cost to rebuild the White House? Nearly three hundred thousand dollars! You know that Congress will never appropriate such a sum."

"Then we must make them," Rebecca said. "And we must begin rebuilding the entire capital."

"Well, I suppose we must do what we can and then trust in the Lord," Dolley said, trying for a smile.

"I say that we must do more," Rebecca said. "It's not an ill star that hovers over our destiny, but malevolent people who won't carry their share of the burden, who think only of themselves and their own safety, and who run in the face of the enemy. That's not the way we won our War for Independence, and it's not the way to win this war."

"My dear, you're beginning to sound just like that reporter—what's his name?" Dolley asked.

"Nor can our present woes be blamed on any political party, be it Federalist or Democratic-Republican. But each man, *himself*, must be held accountable for his actions!"

Even as she spoke, Rebecca was formulating an idea for an article. She believed implicitly in what she'd just said. Of course leadership was vital, but far more important was how each individual felt about himself and about the destiny of his country. Without that pride, without that courage, any nation was doomed. "The country must be made to see that!" she exclaimed with such vehemence that Dolley started.

They returned to the settee and continued working on the bandages they had been rolling. "I'm so worried about Jeremy Brand," Dolley said, and Rebecca's heart thudded.

"Have you heard anything further?" she asked, trying to keep her voice level.

Dolley shook her head. "We've tried everything. No news at all."

The roll of bandages slipped from Rebecca's hands and ribboned out across the parquet floor. Dolley reacted to her distress, but said nothing. She'd always believed that Rebecca should have married Jeremy, and in fact had advised her to do just that. But in these family matters it was best to remain discreet.

Rebecca's mind worked furiously. The only people who might conceivably have more information were the Connaughts. But both Marianne and Victoria were reported to be away, and no one knew when they were expected back.

"Have you heard the latest news from England?" Dolley asked. "The President just received a communiqué sent by packet boat from our negotiators in Ghent. They say that Lord Wellington has refused to take command of the British army fighting over here, and has advised Parliament to end the war with a peaceful settlement."

"Pray God that it happens," Rebecca said. "But we mustn't give up too much, either in territory or in our demands. It mustn't appear that we lost the conflict, or we'll become prey for every rapacious country on the Continent, all of them with their greedy eyes on the New World."

"The President quite agrees," Dolley said. "And he's sent messages to that effect to our negotiators at Ghent."

"Our cause is in good hands with John Quincy Adams," Rebecca said. "He's even shrewder than his father. He'll squeeze the last possible concession from the British, and make them think that they're enjoying it into the bargain. And what news of your son?"

Dolley's face brightened. "Oh, Payne Todd is doing wonderfully well. I do hope that this experience suits him. Though it's still too early to tell, I think he's perfectly cut out for a diplomatic career, don't you?"

Rebecca nodded, but only for the sake of the deep affection she felt for Dolley. The least suitable position for Payne Todd was a diplomatic post. He was only in his twenties, but he had a firm reputation as a wastrel and a slacker, a ne'er-do-well with grandiose dreams that he could never quite bring off. Yet everybody in Washington looked the other way for Dolley's sake. She'd lost her first husband and a son in the plague of fever that had decimated Philadelphia in 1791, and only Payne Todd and she survived. After a brief, tempestuous affair with Aaron Burr, Dolley had married James Madison—Martha Washington herself had given the blessings to this union. James Madison was seventeen years older than Dolley, and no bigger than half a piece of soap, as Burr had said. Since they had no children, Dolley poured all of her maternal instincts into her only son.

"Whatever happens, we've got to stop this attempt to move the capital from Washington," Rebecca said. "If we were forced to move, the world would view it as a British victory. So we must rebuild the Capitol and the White House, and the sooner the better."

At twilight, Rebecca walked across the street to her house. There, she and Zebulon discussed the latest in the household crisis. Because of the difficulty between Circumstance and Gunning—the two always seemed to be fighting about one thing or another—Tanzy had taken the child back to Jeremy's cabin.

"I probably ought to feel more of a family tie to the child, but I must say I'm not sorry to see the little hellion gone," Zebulon said. "There's something queer about that girl."

"Well, she is a half-breed," Rebecca said. "But I've more important things to discuss." She repeated what Dolley had told her about moving the capital.

"I don't understand why you're so upset," Zebulon said. "I couldn't care less where they move. I've always viewed it as a place chosen out of a compromise, rather than for its own natural qualifications. It was little more than a wilderness when we first knew it."

"True," Rebecca said, "but we've come far beyond that. Hamilton and Jefferson chose this spot more than twenty years ago. The North got what it wanted—the Federal assumption of the Revolutionary War debt—and in return, the South got the capital located here. Since then we've seen the beginnings of a city rise here. Industry and wealth have poured into the community. Does that count for nothing? You must use whatever influence you have with the legislators to prevent them from moving."

"But why?" he demanded. "Why *not* move to a civilized city? That way we'd have all the conveniences we'll never have here, not in our lifetime."

"Is that the extent of your horizon, to settle for *conveniences?*" She made the word sound like a petty crime. "In a larger city, in a society already entrenched, we'd be lost, nobodies. Perhaps that suits you, but I'll never settle for that. Here in Washington, the Breech-Brand name still exerts some influence."

Her fiery approach to all matters had always piqued his appetite and he took her in his arms. "Tell me something, would you love me any more if I became President?"

"I'd love you if you were more sensible," she said, extricating herself from his embrace.

At that moment, Letitia brought in Gunning and Suzannah. "They come to say goodnight," Letitia said. Both children were wearing nightshirts made of thin flannel, and their faces and hands were scrubbed. Zebulon scooped them up and the children squealed with delight when he nuzzled them.

God, how they love him, Rebecca thought. Even more than they love me, she had to admit. For he made no demands on them, showered them only with affection, while she had been unfairly forced into the role of the disciplinarian. Suzannah was no problem; the child was an angel. But Gunning, knowing that his father would give him anything, had already turned into something of a problem.

She looked at Zebulon. At forty-two, he hadn't lost his formidable appeal; he was still considered one of the most attractive men in all Washington. I wish I could love him, she thought with a sinking feeling. But the good Lord had seen fit to make her feel otherwise, and try as she might to resurrect her old passion for him, she couldn't.

When she and Zebulon retired for the night, what she'd begun to dread, again came to pass. He insisted on his conjugal rights. She pleaded fatigue, but that didn't move him. Whereas tension made her feel withdrawn, it only made him more sexually excited.

She couldn't have said why, but this particular night she found the entire experience devastating. Long after he'd fallen asleep, revulsion tore at her with grisly claws. "Used," she whispered into her pillow, "that's the way I feel, used."

She wanted to scream her rage into the darkened room, wanted to beat at him with her fists, overwhelm him, render him helpless . . . as he did to her each time they made love.

There's only one solution, she thought. I must divorce him. That thought gave her some courage, and she began to total up all that they owned . . . the stone works, the shipping interests. But the nation was staggering under the burden of the war, and she doubted whether she could realize very much from the sale of any of these properties. I could start writing full time, she thought with sudden hope, perhaps earn a living that way. With those thoughts pursuing her, she finally fell into a deep, troubled sleep.

The next morning, after the children had been sent to their tutor, and Zebulon had gone to the Breech-Brand Stone Works, Rebecca wandered around the house, distracted, her head pounding.

A half-dozen times she interrupted Letitia at her chores until finally the maid put aside her broom and asked, "All right now, Miss Rebecca, what's wrong?"

The moment the question was out of the slave's mouth,

Rebecca burst into tears. Letitia held her, rocking her back and forth the way she had ever since she'd been a little girl.

"I don't know what to do," she whispered. "If he touches me again, I think I'll take a knife to him! I've got to divorce him!"

"Now you hush!" Letitia exclaimed. "Hush and listen to me. It happens sometimes with a woman, that she doesn't want to when her man does. But that's the way it is and it's no good crying about it. And no good thinking about divorce, neither. This feeling will pass, you'll see. You made two beautiful children, and if you had any sense, you'd make more. It's not too late. Keep your mind occupied. And that's all I have to say about that matter."

"I *am* going to divorce him," Rebecca said resolutely. "He can have everything except the stone works, which belonged to my father. And this house. My father built that for us. The rest is his to keep."

Letitia gripped her shoulders and shook her. "Now I've listened to a lot of your foolish talk through the years, but I'm not listening to any of this. What about the children? They loves their father to pieces. You've got to stay married, if only for them. You hear me?"

This only brought forth more tears from Rebecca, tears that seemed to come from the core of her being. "Something else is bothering you," Letitia said. "I ain't known you for all these years without knowing that."

"It's Jeremy," she whispered. "The British refused to release him. Oh, he's dead, dead, I just know it."

"You don't know no such thing!" Letitia exclaimed. "Instead of just worrying, it's best that you set your mind to thinking how you can find out about him."

"Damn, damn! Where can the Connaughts be?" Rebecca exclaimed. "If something doesn't happen soon, I'll go mad!"

Chapter 15

ON SEPTEMBER 19, President Madison summoned Congress to a special session. Dolley and Rebecca made their way arm-in-arm toward Blodgett's Hotel. It had served as the Patent Office and now was practically the only government building left standing in the city. The session would be held there.

"Though Congress is officially recessed," Dolley said to Rebecca, "the President declared this an emergency."

"I hear that Thomas Jefferson has offered to give the government his library," Rebecca said.

Dolley nodded. "It's the best library in all America; he wants it to replace the books that the British burned. It will become the nucleus for a Library of Congress."

"Perhaps that will have some influence with the legislators," Rebecca said. "These men are frightened of their own shadows. But the people want the capital to remain here. Just look there."

She pointed to a gang of men who were working spiritedly to clean up the mess caused by the British. Even the aging Major Pierre L'Enfant had returned to Washington. "I've come back to help rebuild the city that I conceived," he said.

Dolley and Rebecca took seats in the corner of the grand ballroom of the hotel, and listened to the debate. Rebecca saw Thomas Jefferson in the room. "Obviously he thinks this is important enough for him to come to Washington," she said. "You know he almost never leaves Monticello."

Dolley nodded. "He doesn't like to leave Sally and the children alone. It's been nearly a decade since the scandal broke, but it still pains him sorely."

As well it might, Rebecca thought as she looked at Jefferson. At seventy-one, he appeared more like a man in his fifties. He'd bedded his mulatto slave Sally Hemings when she was fifteen years old, and had sired five children by her. It caused a great scandal during his presidency, and even now the gossipmongers still whispered about it.

The debate about the location of the capital quickly developed into one of the most heated in the history of the nation. Representatives Richard Stockton of New Jersey and Jonathan Fisk of New York were two of the most vocal advocates of change. Every day, Dolley and Rebecca went to the sessions loaded down with hampers of food and drink, which they gave to the legislators defending Washington. It wasn't until October 15 that the move to abandon Washington was beaten back in the House of Representatives by a vote of eighty-three to seventy-four, a narrow margin of nine votes.

"The Senate must still confirm it," Rebecca said on a rising note, "but I believe we have the votes there." She approached President Madison. "Mr. President, someday the nation will understand your wisdom about this and thank you on bended knee."

He looked up at her and a smile creased his wizened face. "Not those who happen to be in the capital on any sticky day in the summer."

Now accommodations had to be found for the various federal agencies. The State Department was quartered in a house recently occupied by Judge Duval; Treasury occupied the former home of the British minister; the War Department moved into a building standing next to the Bank of the Metropolis; the Navy Department used a house belonging to Mr. Mechlin, near West Market; and the General Post Office set up business in a new house that belonged to Mr. Way.

Though renovations were currently underway to provide meeting chambers for the legislators in Blodgett's Hotel, the building was clearly inadequate, and plans were quickly made to build a long brick building on Capitol Hill; it was soon dubbed the Little Capitol.

Rebecca Breech Brand managed to get the contract to supply the brick and stone for some of the new government buildings being constructed. The profits would be small but steady, and that gave her some peace. October moved to the height of autumn, and November, passing through, withered leaves. Rebecca reflected that that was the way she felt. So many weeks, and still no news of Jeremy.

And then one day, the itinerant barber who plied his trade between Washington, Georgetown, Alexandria, and Bladensburg, told Tanzy a piece of gossip, who told it to Mrs. Madison's maid Sukie, who ran across the street to tell Letitia, who immediately came bursting into Rebecca's bedroom sitting room.

"The Connaughts is just come back!" she exclaimed.

An hour later, Rebecca was galloping along the road to the Connaught estate in the hills above Washington. There was a sharp edge to the late November air, and Rebecca drew her miniver-lined cloak more tightly about her. The land had taken on the subtle colors of approaching winter, the earth was brown and bare, dead trees poked dead fingers at the sullen sky. The six-columned Connaught mansion faced out across the rolling hills. The silver-gray Potomac threaded its way through the valley, and in the distance, Rebecca could make out the burned buildings of the capital.

"I'll bet this view pleases the Connaughts," she muttered. Then she gave the reins of her horse to the waiting stablehand and swept into the gracious hexagonal entryway with its curved stairway.

When Rebecca was announced, Victoria Connaught peered at her through her lorgnette—it was not an affectation; cataracts had blurred her eyes with a milk-white glaze. "I had not expected to see you here, ever," she said, "particularly after what you last said to me."

Rebecca took a deep breath, trying to control her anger. Remember, she warned herself, you're here for a different purpose than arguing with this virago. The two women had an instinctive loathing for each other. Even when in her teens, Rebecca had disliked this Tory aristocrat who was always trying to lord it over her neighbors. Victoria Connaught was close to eighty now, but she still ruled certain segments of Washington society with an iron hand. The antagonism had reached the flash point at a town meeting at the start of the Second War for Independence; Victoria Connaught had proposed an immediate surrender to the British. Merely recollecting that confrontation ripped away any vestige of control from Rebecca's temper.

"I'm not here to make apologies," she said through gritted teeth. "I believe now, as I did then, that traitors to one's country should be shot. And I state again, that if I caught anybody giving aid to my enemies, I would pull the trigger myself!"

Victoria Connaught looked like she might be about to have a fit of apoplexy. Her gnarled, beringed fingers gripped the head of her walking stick as though it were a weapon.

"It's your stupidity and the stupidity of people like you that has caused the havoc we see in Washington," she whispered.

"Madam, I've not come all this way to argue with you. I've come to see your niece, Marianne."

"In that case, you could have saved yourself a trip," Victoria said. "She's not at home, nor is she expected."

"This is urgent, a matter of life and death."

"I'm afraid I can't help you. And now, if you'd be good enough to leave . . . You've caused me enough pain this afternoon."

A door at the far end of the drawing room slid open and a fine-boned woman in her forties entered. "Wait," she said softly, and came forward. She wore a deep plum-colored gown that made her dark hair seem even darker and accentuated the smoky gray color of her eyes. Her skin was as pale as a corpse's; the resemblance to Marianne was startling.

"Elizabeth, go to your room immediately," Victoria Connaught exclaimed.

But Elizabeth Connaught paid no attention to her. She turned to Rebecca and said in a far-away voice, "I'm looking for Marianne also."

Rebecca stared at her with fascination, as one might look at a delicate hybrid rose. She must have been at least ten years older than Rebecca, but there wasn't a line on her face . . . as though time had stopped for her that dreadful day when Zebulon—

Elizabeth Connaught interrupted Rebecca's thoughts. "Have you seen Marianne? We've so much left to do. Look." She held out a strip of needlepoint, tracing the buildings neatly stitched into the canvas, of the Capitol in flames, and the White House erupting in gold and orange fire that lit up the black night. "You see?" she said eagerly, "the fire has eaten tomorrow."

Then she stared at Rebecca, and seemed to shrink back. "Who are you?"

"I'm Rebecca Breech," she said softly.

Elizabeth's eyes looked vaguely into the past. Then her face opened in a smile when she recognized Rebecca's titian hair. "Yes, oh yes, Rebecca. You had the most beautiful hair in Washington. I always wanted hair that color. I thought that if

I did, then Zebulon . . ." Her voice broke off. "Zebulon," she repeated, and her eyes widened in horror. "And Devroe and— Oh, merciful Lord, no!" She screamed, a piercing cry that brought the servants running. They led the sobbing woman out of the room.

Rebecca clutched at her bosom, almost undone.

"See what you've done?" Victoria Connaught whispered, and she suddenly sounded like an old, defeated woman. "Can you and the Brands never leave us in peace? Must we always suffer from your excesses? At long last, madam, is there no spark of common decency in you?"

Rebecca shrugged that off. "Where is Marianne?" she insisted. Her heart was torn because of what had happened to Elizabeth, but it wasn't her fault that she'd gone mad, or her fault that Devroe Connaught had brought about his own death. No, I can't accept blame for that, Rebecca thought resolutely. Let others live in the past; I've more urgent things on my mind. The future . . . and Jeremy.

Victoria stood up. She had been besieged by the ailments of the old. The flesh on her neck and bosom had long ago turned crepy, her step faltered, and her voice sounded aspirate.

Yet she's still formidable, Rebecca thought. Formidable and dangerous. Because she believes, and all her life she's acted on those beliefs.

Victoria took a certain pleasure in saying, "Marianne has left with her cousin Sean. He sent me a communication shortly before the fleet sailed. By now they should be in Jamaica."

"Jamaica?" Rebecca repeated, startled. "And what of Jeremy Brand?"

"I'm quite sure that Sean will see to it that traitors and spies get what they deserve. And now, unless you leave of your own volition, I'll forget that I'm a Connaught and a lady, and I'll have the servants throw you out."

Rebecca swept from the room. Outside, she mounted her stallion and rode hard down the winding paths to the city. Jamaica . . . probably a staging point for the rest of the British fleet and troop transports that had been dispatched from England in a last effort to finish off the war. Then Dolley was probably right; New Orleans would be their target. But what of Jeremy? Was he alive?

When she reached her house she didn't stop when Gunning

called to her but raced to her sitting room and locked the door. She lit a candle, and as the aureole of light filled her eyes, she dropped to her knees at her bed and prayed, "Dear Lord, please . . . I'll suffer anything, even Zebulon—only keep Jeremy safe."

Chapter 16

SEAN CONNAUGHT stood at the bridge, legs spread to accommodate the gentle rocking of the ship. He felt as expansive as the great white sails of his sloop, puffed out with the fair wind. He watched as the plunging prow cut through the aquamarine waters of the Gulf of Mexico. Stretching as far as his eye could see were the sails of the British fleet, some fifty vessels in all. One of the mightiest invasion fleets that the British had ever assembled in the New World, it included ten thousand crack troops, commanded by Wellington's brother-in-law, General Sir Edward Pakenham. Their destination: New Orleans, queen city of the Mississippi, and gateway to the American continent.

"And we shall have it," Sean muttered, hitting the palm of his left hand with his long leather-covered truncheon. "We shall have it all."

He turned to an aide standing at attention near him. "I'm ready to see the prisoner now."

"Aye, sir," the aide said, wondering if the American languishing in the brig was still alive. Sean and the aide started down to the brig.

Of late, Sean Connaught hadn't had much time for Jeremy Brand; after the British had decided to abandon Baltimore for the greater prize of New Orleans, his days had been taken up with the considerable planning for the conquest of that city. Plans to incite the native Creole population to turn against the Americans, plans to incite the colored people to revolt, plans to entice Jean Lafitte and his pirates to join the British.

But what Sean didn't know was how the American general, Andrew Jackson, intended to defend the city. New Orleans was enclosed within a palisaded wall with a fortress at each corner. Would Andrew Jackson defend the city from within its walls? Or would he choose to fight at some strategic battleground outside? Because of his association with the White House, perhaps Jeremy Brand might have some useful information.

The aide unlocked the cell, and Sean reeled from the smell of bilge gas. He heard the sounds of rats scurrying about, and jerked back his foot when one of them ran over his boot.

Crouched in a corner, Jeremy roused himself from his torpor and blinked at the shaft of light lancing through the door. Then he recognized Sean Connaught. Dressed in his immaculate white uniform trimmed with gold, and silhouetted in the light, he looked like some avenging angel.

Sean started to question Jeremy, but gagged. "Bring him to my cabin," he said. "The stench in here is unbearable."

They dragged him to Sean's cabin and propped him up in a chair. Sean dug his fingers into Jeremy's thick blond hair and snapped his head back. Jeremy had difficulty understanding any of Sean's questions. He stared at him with eyes glazed and hurting from the light. "Where is Marianne?" he whispered. "I know she's aboard. What have you done with her?"

Not even the punishing blows that Sean gave him with his truncheon could make him say anything save "Where is Marianne?"

Sean's arm ached from his exertions, but it was a deeply satisfying ache. "Take him back to his cell. We'll try again tomorrow."

Every day thereafter, Sean questioned Jeremy in his own quarters. Oddly enough, Jeremy experienced these interrogations as a mixed blessing. They were painful, sometimes even torturous, depending on Sean's mood, but at least they got him out of the hellhole of the brig.

During one particularly brutal session, Jeremy fainted and couldn't be revived, and Sean sent for the doctor's apprentice, Wingate Grange. Wingate managed to bring Jeremy around with a heavy dose of smelling salts, but he was sickened by his condition.

"Stay here in case he should fake another seizure," Sean ordered Wingate. Then he resumed his questioning. "As I was saying, Mr. Brand, I know you took part in the Lewis and Clark Expedition to explore the Louisiana Territory. It will go easier with you if you tell me everything you know."

"I'll tell you nothing," Jeremy muttered. He gritted his teeth as Sean's fingers dug into his wounded arm, and then passed out.

"Perhaps he truly doesn't know anything," Wingate ventured.

"Shut your mouth, boy! You speak only when an officer addresses you. And then you ask for permission."

Wingate's cheeks flushed and his eyes glinted with anger. "Sir, if this man continues to be treated this way, he'll die."

Sean lashed out at Wingate with a backhand blow, and his heavy signet ring opened the boy's cheek. "I'll have you lashed for insubordination!"

"That won't stop this man from dying!" Wingate insisted, his hand pressed to his cheek. Then he tried a desperate gamble. "If he did die after I'd just treated him, naturally I'd have to report the circumstances to my superior."

Wingate held his breath, waiting for Sean's reaction. Other prisoners had died during Sean's interrogations, and Wingate knew it had created something of a scandal in the admiralty.

Sean prodded Jeremy's body with the toe of his glossy boot.

"Sir, if I may have your permission to speak?" Wingate asked.

Sean glared at him and then nodded curtly.

Wingate pushed forward his next question very carefully. "Perhaps it would be easier to extract the information you want if the prisoner was stronger. A bracing walk around the deck every day might bring him around."

He narrowed his eyes and looked at Wingate suspiciously. Then he snorted, "Well, we are in the middle of the sea, aren't we? He can't get very far. All right, get him strong enough so that he can talk. Even if he doesn't, at least he'll be able to make it to the gallows on his own two feet. I planned to hang him in Baltimore, but now it will have to wait until New Orleans."

Every day, Wingate took Jeremy out of his cell, helped him up the narrow companionway, then walked him around the deck. The days arched toward winter, and the sea looked like beaten silver in the sun. The waves were tipped with whitecaps from the driving wind.

Chained in leg and wrist irons, Jeremy remembered how the youthful slave Eli had been so manacled when he and the rest of the slave construction gang laid the foundation of the American Palace more than twenty years before.

The first few days, Wingate practically had to hold Jeremy up, but the bracing sea air and the extra food that Wingate managed to slip him gradually brought him around.

"Why doesn't Connaught kill me and be done with it?" Jeremy wondered aloud.

"Part of it is because he takes pleasure in all this," Wingate said. "And another part is because he's hoping to get information from you."

"But truly, I don't know anything," Jeremy said. Then he gripped Wingate's arm. "Where is Marianne?"

"She's in one of the cabins below," Wingate said, keeping his voice low. "She knows you're still aboard and alive," Wingate finished. "Sean taunts her about you every night when he goes to her cabin to dine."

"They're not—?" The question hung unfinished on Jeremy's lips, but Wingate couldn't escape its meaning.

"No, no," he said hastily. "He's tried to bed her. I know that much, but she won't. He's far too proud to force her. He thinks to wear her down. But don't worry, he never will."

"He's a beast," Jeremy muttered. "God forgive me, but that man deserves to die."

They continued walking around the deck. "Where are we now, do you think?" Jeremy asked.

"Three, maybe four days away from New Orleans," Wingate said. "Sean believes you know the defense plan for New Orleans. I've heard him say as much to Admiral Cochrane. It's how he justified taking you along with the fleet."

Jeremy shook his head wearily. "I don't know any such thing. It's clear the man's gone totally mad, and he'll say and do anything in order to exact his revenge." Jeremy stared at the endless armada all about them. "We've nothing to match this navy. Our only hope is to beat the British off in a land battle."

He stumbled and Wingate grabbed him. "Maybe we've done too much for today. It'll be a long time before you get your full strength back."

"We don't have a long time," Jeremy said. "Somehow we've got to escape, get to General Jackson."

"They keep very close watch," Wingate said. "A few impressed seamen have tried it. Connaught almost plans on it. And then he kills them in the act. He says it's like shooting rats. That way, he doesn't have to make any excuses for his penchant for killing. I beg you, don't try anything foolish. He's just waiting for something like that to happen."

"Somewhere in his plan there's a flaw," Jeremy murmured.

"There always is with a savage like that. We've got to find that flaw and use it to our own advantage."

They walked a few feet further and Jeremy whispered, "Could you lay your hands on a length of rope? Long enough to go from this deck to the sea? When it's dark, we might climb down and..." He went on, weaving what seemed like an impossible plan of escape.

"And we've got to take Marianne with us," Jeremy said. "We can't leave her."

Wingate thought that the whole idea was too farfetched to even consider; yet when he lay in his hammock that night, having just fought off a petty officer with amorous intent, he found himself figuring, planning, hoping for a chance for freedom.

Sean Connaught's interrogations of Jeremy took a peculiar twist. Because of Admiral Cochrane's orders, Sean couldn't risk having Jeremy die. Feeling thwarted, he turned the sessions into a battle of wills, with Sean determined to grind his enemy, and the enemy of his country, under his heel.

"You stupid man, don't you know when to concede defeat?" he demanded as he hit Jeremy across the face with his truncheon.

Jeremy spat blood. As weak and debilitated as he was, Sean's attacks somehow made his blood quicken, goaded him into responding. Jeremy muttered through clenched teeth, "We'll never give up."

"Fool, we've burned your capital. Don't you remember seeing your precious Washington going up in flames? And we've burned your American Palace."

Jeremy's breath came in short, hard gasps. "Maybe you can destroy a building, even a city, but you'll never be able to destroy the idea of liberty. No matter what you do, that idea will always rise again."

Sean hit him in the groin, a stunning blow that made Jeremy double over. "That's for Marianne." He began to pace the room, growing angrier with each step. "You Americans, you talk of liberty, but you still have secret royalist desires. Why else would you have named the mansion of your president the American Palace?"

Jeremy struggled for breath, then managed to say, "It means...something very different...in our minds. It's a palace, true, but a palace of the spirit. A palace where aspirations can be nurtured. For it isn't the fortress of a despot, but the home of the one man we've chosen to lead us." His voice took strength from his conviction. "This home embodies all those things man has craved since he first understood the meaning of the word freedom. And our palace, the American Palace, is the symbol of that freedom!"

His eyes shone with the fervor of belief, his face became incandescent with the knowledge that he was right—even Sean Connaught knew he was right—so Jeremy hardly felt the blow from the truncheon that knocked him unconscious.

Early one morning Wingate came into Jeremy's cell and shook him awake. "Sean Connaught is about to leave the ship. I just heard it from one of the crew!"

Jeremy gripped the boy's shoulder. "How long will he be gone?"

"I don't know. I only know that he and two of his aides are taking a longboat and heading for the Louisiana shore."

"One of his spying missions," Jeremy said grimly. "Well, then, this is our chance. We must do it now or never. Have you made the arrangements we planned? Does Marianne know? Can you get her safely past her guard?"

Wingate nodded. "I've hidden a length of rope. As for Marianne, she's already bribed her guard, and has promised him more."

"What about my jailer? Have you thought of how to deal with him?"

"Leave him to me," Wingate said, smiling. "I don't think he'll trouble us at all."

That night, with his heart beating loud enough to be heard in the captain's quarters, Wingate began to carry out his plan. He stowed hardtack, dried beef, and a canteen of water into his haversack. As prearranged, the tar usually stationed outside Marianne's door was nowhere in sight. Wingate slipped into her cabin and handed her some clothes. "I've stolen these from one of the cabin boys. Put them on; your skirts would only be a hindrance."

She changed hurriedly. Then, taking care to avoid the deck-hand on watch, Wingate and Marianne stole to Jeremy's cell. Earlier that evening, Wingate had put a sleeping draft into the jailer's winecup, and now he was snoring peacefully. Wingate

carefully extracted the keys from the man's belt and opened
the door.

Jeremy rushed out and swept Marianne into his arms. They
clung to each other desperately. "Darling, darling," he whispered.

"Be quick, I beg you," Wingate whispered, tugging at Jeremy's shirt. "They could sound the alarm any moment."

Marianne hardly heard the boy; she was conscious only of
Jeremy's embrace. Though he'd gotten frightfully thin, his
strength was the same, the same strength that had cherished
and loved her these many years, the strength that had allowed
her to cast aside the insanities of her family and become a
woman.

The words tumbled from her, repentant, begging forgiveness
for what she'd done.

He put his hand over her mouth. "Hush now. The only thing
that matters is that we're together."

Wingate half-dragged them apart. "Please!"

Jeremy nodded, then said to Marianne, "Are you game?"

"Anything, as long as you're with me."

They crept back up the creaking ship's ladder, expecting
at any moment to be discovered, but they reached the top deck
without incident.

"I've hidden the ropes at the stern," Wingate whispered.

Crouching, they made their way stealthily to the rear of the
sloop. The evening mists had rolled in from the sea; the swirling
clouds of fog obliterated any light that might have come from
the crescent moon, and turned the lanterns on the sloop into
blurred aureoles.

"I'll go first," Wingate said, and hoisted himself onto the
rail. He threw the rope over the side, then, hooking his leg
around the rope, clambered down the twenty-five feet until he
slipped into the water.

"I've never done anything like this before," Marianne said
faintly.

"It's the only way we can save ourselves," Jeremy whispered. He boosted her onto the rail, then swung himself over.
"Hang on to my neck," he said as he started down. She clung
to him fiercely. Midway, his strength failed and they fell the
last ten feet into the sea.

Moments after they hit the water they heard a sentry call,
"Who's there?"

The three of them treaded water noiselessly. But the night was so dark and the fog so thick that they weren't seen. The current gradually took them away from the ship and then they struck out for shore. "The water is colder than I'd imagined it would be," Jeremy said. "Keep moving."

Wingate cried out when a jellyfish stung him across his arm. He tore away the tentacles that had seared his skin like hot wires. At last, after swimming for what seemed like an eternity, their feet touched the sandy bottom of the shore.

They dragged their way up onto the marshy plain of the Mississippi delta. "Careful," Jeremy said. "There may be snakes or alligators around."

He allowed them to rest until they'd gotten their breath back and then pushed them on. "They've probably discovered we're gone by now, and they're sure to send a boat out searching for us. We must be gone from here."

They slogged their way deep into the swampy terrain. Jeremy helped Marianne through the sucking mud. "Tell me," he said urgently. "Tell me everything you know about Sean's plan for New Orleans."

"He bragged about it every day," she said. "The British are taking a force across Lake Borgne."

"Lake Borgne?" Jeremy repeated. "But if I remember correctly, that's impassable to large ships."

She nodded. "But Sean's thought of a way around that. They've outfitted some forty flat barges and manned them with a thousand marines. Sean says the Americans have only five gunboats on the lake, and he expects that he'll win a swift victory. Once that's done, and a beachhead's established, then the main British army under General Pakenham will join them. Together they'll strike for New Orleans."

Jeremy's breath came faster as he increased his pace. "Hurry! General Jackson may not expect an attack from that quarter. We've got to warn him!"

Half a mile behind them, they were being tracked by Sean Connaught, two of his aides, and a Creek Indian guide.

"Well, it worked as we planned," Sean said. "Though I didn't expect the idiots to involve Marianne in this. But what's done is done."

One of the aides lost his boot in the mire and Sean swore softly, "Hurry, you fool! We mustn't lose them."

As they slogged through the swamp, Sean congratulated himself on his plan, visualizing the report that he would make to Admiral Cochrane. "Jeremy Brand escaped and was heading for New Orleans..I had no choice except to put a bullet through his brain." And he would have these witnesses to prove it.

But about a mile later, just as Sean was closing the gap with Jeremy, another of the seamen stepped into a quagmire. For half an hour they struggled to pull him free, but finally the bog claimed him. And in that time, they lost Jeremy's trail. Sean cursed the dead seaman, cursed the Creek tracker, but finally managed to control himself.

"No matter," he told himself. "I know where they're going. Time enough to kill him in New Orleans." And then another thought came to him, one so daring, so absolutely in keeping with his sense of justice, that he knew he must do it. Once in New Orleans, he would ferret out the headquarters of General Andrew Jackson. Lie in wait for him . . . "Just let me get close enough for one shot and this war will be over!"

Chapter 17

THREE DAYS later, Jeremy, Wingate, and Marianne stumbled out of the sucking swamps, more dead than alive. Ticks clung to their flesh and the mosquitoes had almost driven them mad.

"But we made it," Jeremy said hoarsely, as he pointed to the timbered walls that surrounded the city of New Orleans.

"General Jackson—where is he?" Jeremy shouted to a sentry atop the ramparts of the crumbling Fort Charles.

The soldier kept his rifle aimed at them while he yelled for his commanding officer. Then they went through an interminable interrogation—the officer, a dandified Creole, questioned Marianne in French. At last he was persuaded that they weren't British spies.

"He doesn't know where General Jackson is," Marianne told Jeremy.

"Ask him about Governor Claiborne," Jeremy replied. "Perhaps he can help."

Marianne questioned the officer, then reported, "He says that the governor is probably at the Cabildo, and Jackson may be there also."

They started for the Cabildo, the seat of the government in Louisiana, and finally reached the Place d'Armes, where it stood. It had been built by the Spaniards in 1791 when they owned the territory. Next to it stood the Cathedral of St. Louis, and its Refectory, a structure built in the same style as the Cabildo to give the grouping harmony. The square opened onto the broad, gunmetal-gray expanse of the Mississippi River.

As they hurried toward the Cabildo, Jeremy gazed at the beautiful structure. It stood two stories tall, and was built in the typical style of Spanish architecture, massive-walled, with a broad arcade on the street level, and the arcaded design repeated in the nine huge fan windows that stretched across the entire facade.

"It's a handsome building," Jeremy said. "But it lacks the

grace that the White House has...had." He added bitterly,
"If the British ever do manage to conquer New Orleans, you
can be sure they'll put the torch to the Cabildo also."

Inside, the three of them were shunted from one harassed
clerk to another. The air was heavy with the babble of French,
Spanish, and English from people seeking solutions to all sorts
of problems arising from the war. Finally, they wound up in
the anteroom of the governor's office, and were told to wait.

"I met Claiborne in Washington a few times," Jeremy said
to Wingate. "That was when I was working as a journeyman
architect on the American Palace."

"Will he remember you?" Wingate asked.

"I don't know."

"What's he like?"

"Well, he comes from a prominent Virginia family. While
he was a congressman, he caught the attention of Thomas
Jefferson. When Aaron Burr and Jefferson were tied for the
presidency back in 1800, and the election was thrown into the
House of Representatives, Burr's faction tried to influence
Claiborne—along with anybody else they could. But Claiborne
steadfastly supported Jefferson, and as a reward, Jefferson appointed him governor of the Louisiana Territory."

When they were finally admitted into the governor's presence, Jeremy quickly found that Claiborne had no recollection
of him, and so he got directly to the point and asked about
Jackson. He thought it best not to go into too much detail about
his mission to the general, for Jeremy had a deep mistrust of most
politicians. Hadn't Secretary of War Armstrong and Secretary of State Monroe been in part responsible for the American debacle at Bladensburg? Jeremy wanted no repetition of
that. What he had to say was for Jackson's ears only, with no
dissident, misinformed voices between.

Claiborne shuffled the papers on his desk. "General Jackson
has just moved into his new headquarters on Royal Street. If
you hurry, you may find him there."

Buoyed by hope, Jeremy, Marianne and Wingate left the
Cabildo. As they stepped outside into the raw day, Jeremy's
knees buckled and Wingate grabbed him to keep him from
collapsing.

"We must get you someplace where you can rest," Marianne
said.

Jeremy shook his head vehemently. "Time enough for that

after we warn Jackson." Leaning on Wingate for support, Jeremy started out again.

Marianne had been to New Orleans a number of times with her Aunt Victoria, often as a courier for British intelligence, and she knew the city fairly well. She led them through streets of thick-walled brick houses, most faced with stucco to protect the houses against the dampness.

Despite his weariness, it registered in Jeremy's mind that most of the buildings were two stories tall with tile roofs. They were painted in pastel yellows, greens, and blues. Fanlights over the windows and doors were a repeated architectural detail, but the most distinctive ornamentation was the wrought-iron fronts that appeared on most every building. New Orleans artisans created their own forgerons, and Jeremy saw ornate filigrees of leaves, flowers, arrows, initials, and acorns, all done with exquisite artistry. They cast delicate shadows on the pastel buildings, giving the city a quaint fairy-tale quality.

"But it's so different from Washington," Jeremy said. "We have magnificent vistas, and the houses are far between. Here there are no front lawns and the buildings crowd directly onto the street."

The narrow sidewalks and gutters were jammed with men who'd come to defend the city: Tennessee volunteers, Kentuckians, the gruff, brawling riverboatmen, the dandified officers of the New Orleans militia, their uniforms and faces polished to a gloss, free men of color from Santo Domingo, and Choctaw Indians who'd fought alongside Jackson and acted as his scouts. The Choctaws wore war paint and breechcloths and little else. Threading through the crowd were the painted women of New Orleans, plying their timeless trade. The normal population of the city was about eighteen thousand, but the war had swelled that to almost twenty-five thousand.

Jeremy, Wingate, and Marianne had to pause at one corner blocked by two gargantuan riverboatmen who fought with reckless, joyful abandon to see which of them would win the right to use the wooden sidewalk.

"Those sidewalks were once flatboats," Marianne said, and at Wingate's doubtful look, explained. "The flatboats are floated down the Mississippi with their cargoes, and once they reach here and the cargo unloaded, the boats are broken up and used for these sidewalks and sometimes for buildings. It's cheaper to build new flatboats than to haul them back up river."

Both of the riverboatmen fell into the mud, there to continue
their battle while the rest of the pedestrians walked on. At last
they reached Jackson's headquarters on Royal Street. Once
inside, they were amazed to find everything being run with
strict, military efficiency.

Jeremy was also surprised by the gracious proportions of
the house. Through the rear windows of the drawing room, he
could see a shaded courtyard still in bloom in the weak winter
sun. An aide led them to Jackson's private office.

Major General Andrew Jackson, recently promoted to that
rank by President Madison, was a towering, forty-seven-year-
old frontiersman. His iron-gray hair matched the flinty quality
of his eyes. In his recent and bitterly fought campaign against
the Creek Indians, and against the Spanish and British in West
Florida, he'd taken ill, and his face still had an unhealthy pallor.
But his toughness was reflected in his superb posture; the force
emanating from the man clearly commanded respect.

When he'd rushed to New Orleans less than two weeks ago,
after determining that the British indeed planned to conquer the
city, Jackson had found a divided populace. New Orleans had
first been a French settlement, had then passed into the hands
of Spain, and then Napoleon had acquired it. Most of the
citizens didn't know where their loyalties lay. Surly Creoles
eyed Jackson with suspicion, the Spanish were outright antag-
onistic, and the free men of color had always looked with doubt
on white Americans. Was this uncouth-looking, dictatorial
frontiersman any better than the British?

But Jackson had addressed them in the Place d'Armes, and
in a short, heartfelt speech had said, "I will save this city or
die in the attempt. There is no middle ground."

The force of his personality was so undeniable that the
citizens, having first viewed him as a conqueror, now embraced
him as their savior. Jackson had also been shrewd enough to
send for his wife, Rachel Donelson Jackson, and their nephew,
Andrew Junior, and they'd arrived as quickly as possible.
Rachel's presence in the city lent force to Jackson's claim that
he would defend New Orleans with his life.

Jackson looked at Jeremy; his manner was direct and abrupt.
Clearly he had no time to waste. Then he caught sight of
Marianne standing directly behind Jeremy. Though dressed in
male clothing she was obviously a woman, and Jackson's mood
changed immediately. He couldn't have been more solicitous;

he offered her a chair, and ordered that a decanter of wine be brought.

A buxom woman with a squarish face came into the room. Jackson rose and greeted her. "This is my wife, Rachel."

She had a kind face, with nothing in the way of airs or pretensions about her. She was smoking a corncob pipe, and she offered it to everybody in the room: "Smoke, honey?"

Marianne delicately refused. Wingate took a puff and gagged. "Well, I can see that you're all busy," Rachel said, "so I'll just be about my marketing." With a little wave goodbye she was gone.

Jackson's face became almost beatific. "There goes a walking saint on this earth."

Jeremy, agitated by the delay, blurted, "The British plan to sail into Lake Borgne, then press on from there to New Orleans."

Jackson didn't seem at all surprised. "We already know that. We received word of their penetration yesterday." Then Jackson stared at Jeremy, searching his memory. "Brand, you say your name was? I knew a Zebulon Brand once."

"My brother," Jeremy said.

Jackson's long lean face took on the semblance of a smile. "Then you must be the man that went with Meriwether Lewis! Damned important expedition that—gave us claim to all the territory in the Pacific Northwest. We'll have it one day. Now tell me everything. From the beginning—and don't leave out a detail."

Jackson listened with increasing agitation as Jeremy recounted his tale. "You were captured in Washington?" Jackson demanded, and insisted on knowing everything about that battle. When he heard of Secretary of War Armstrong's incompetence, he snorted. "We no longer need worry about him. That reporter Rebel Thorne exposed him in a series of articles that almost brought about his impeachment. He was forced to resign. At any rate, President Madison replaced him with James Monroe."

Jeremy grimaced, remembering Monroe's ineptitude also.

Jackson laughed. "I like you, by God. You have the courage of your opinions and aren't afraid to speak out. Now as for Lake Borgne, in a surprise move, the British hauled their flatboats to the lake and there engaged a force of five American gunboats under the command of Lieutenant Thomas Ap Catesby Jones. The British had forty-two barges, each with one cannon in the prow, and the barges were manned by a thousand of their best marines and sailors. Jones was hopelessly out-gunned, and outmanned, having in all twenty-five cannon and about two hundred men.

"Still, Jones might have fought them off, but as luck would have it not a breeze riffled the waters of the lake, and the barges, rowed by the sailors, surrounded our gunboats and overran them one by one."

"Oh, if only we could have gotten here sooner!" Marianne exclaimed.

"Have no fear," General Jackson said. "The British can't get far. I've given orders to have every bayou and tributary leading to the Mississippi blocked."

Marianne shook her head. "You don't understand. Sean Connaught knows every route leading to the city. He's had agents infiltrating for years, bribing the local Spanish and Portuguese fishermen to show him these routes. He—" She broke off, unable to go on.

But Jackson hadn't taken her outburst seriously. "I hear that Admiral Cochrane boasts he'll have his Christmas dinner in New Orleans. Well, if so, *I* shall be presiding over that dinner! Now don't you worry, Miss Connaught. We're taking every possible precaution. I've asked the legislature to declare martial law. So far, they've done nothing but argue about it. If necessary, I'll declare martial law myself!"

"Sir, I'm a captain in the Washington militia," Jeremy said. "I'd be honored to fight under your command."

"Include me in that too, General, sir," Wingate said eagerly. "I know a little something of medicine."

A smile creased Jackson's craggy face. He put his long calloused hands on Jeremy's and Wingate's shoulders. "That's the kind of spirit we'll need to win," he said. "But the two of you look as if you're ready to fall down. You need sleep, plenty of it. I'd invite you to stay with us, but every bed in the house is full. I'll have one of my aides see that you're quartered. When you're rested and your wounds are healed, we'll talk about posts for both of you."

Ordering an aide to find them accommodations, Jackson walked them to the front door and stood framed in the doorway. Perhaps it was the flash of sunlight reflecting off metal, perhaps it was an instinctive reaction to danger, but Jeremy shoved

Jackson aside just as the shots rang out. Two bullets plowed into the doorframe, a scant two inches from Jackson's head.

Marianne screamed as soldiers rushed to the front door, shielding the general.

"There, on the roof!" Wingate shouted, pointing.

They looked up and saw three crouching figures fleeing along the rooftops. A Kentuckian raised his long rifle, aimed, and fired, almost in the same motion. One of the fleeing men clutched his chest, staggered, and then pitched forward, falling into the street. Some soldiers raced around the corner, trying to head the other assassins off, but a few moments later they returned, breathless. "They got away."

"Of course they did," Jackson grunted. "This city is an armed camp. All they had to do was disappear into the crowd. By the Eternal, New Orleans is crawling with spies. That does it! I'm imposing martial law. Post signs everywhere," he ordered an aide. "Curfew at nine tonight. Anybody caught out after that will automatically be considered a spy and will be dealt with accordingly."

They turned over the dead man and Marianne gasped when she saw his face. "It's one of Sean's aides!"

Jeremy studied the man. No doubt about it—Marianne was right. And then it came to him. "What fools we've been! We thought we were so clever in our escape. Well, I'll wager that the entire thing was arranged by Sean Connaught. He probably followed us here." He turned to Jackson. "General, my humblest apologies. It's only by a stroke of the sheerest luck that we avoided calamity."

"For a moment the thought crossed my mind that you all might be accomplices in this," Jackson said. "But only for a moment. After all, it was you who pushed me out of harm's way. And I thank you for that."

He extended his hand and Jeremy gripped it, feeling the energy strong and vigorous pulsing from him.

Marianne began to shiver. She leaned against Wingate for support and whispered, "But it means that Sean is here in New Orleans! We'll never escape him, never!"

Jeremy put his arm around her shoulder, trying to reassure her, saying that everything would be all right now that they were with the Americans. Yet somewhere deep within him, he knew that Sean would never give up the hunt until either he or Jeremy was dead.

Chapter 18

GENERAL JACKSON'S aide set them up in two tiny rooms under the eaves of a half-brick, half-timber house on St. Charles Street. They slumped onto their pallets and within minutes were fast asleep. Their exhaustion was so profound that twenty-four hours elapsed before any of them wakened. They ate some soup called gumbo, that the proprietress of the house brought them, and then went to sleep again.

The next morning, Wingate knocked on the door of Jeremy and Marianne's room. "I've got some clothes for us, bandages and medical supplies I managed to cadge from a supply sergeant," he said. He dressed Jeremy's wounds, and then tended to Marianne's cuts and bruises. "I also managed to lay my hands on these—compliments of General Jackson." He placed two pistols in Jeremy's hands.

"All these things cost money," Jeremy said. How did you come by them?"

"One of General Jackson's aides knew we were penniless and gave me some dixies," Wingate said.

"Dixies? What's that?"

Wingate handed him some paper currency and Jeremy inspected it. "Why, it's printed in English on one side and in French on the other."

Marianne nodded and explained, "When the United States took over the Louisiana Territory, the French didn't know which currency to use—American or French. Being eminently practical, they printed up a new ten-dollar bill. On one side it read 'ten' in English, but on the reverse side it read 'dix'— French for ten. The paper money became known to the riverboat men as 'dixies,' and soon the word became so popular that the city of New Orleans itself is now called Dixie."

"In truth, I'd heard of it being called Dixie before," Jeremy said, "but I never knew where the word came from."

Wingate headed toward the door.

"Where are you off to?" Jeremy asked.

"I've had more than enough sleep, so I'm going from house

to house collecting more medicines and bandages. When the battle comes, we mustn't be caught short." He saw the concerned look on Jeremy's face and said, "Don't worry, I've already cleared it with General Jackson's command, and they've given me leave."

Marianne and Jeremy listened to Wingate's footsteps as he descended the oaken stairs. "I can't imagine a finer lad than that one," Jeremy said.

"We'd probably both be dead if it wasn't for him," Marianne said. Then she moved to the tiny French windows that opened out onto a courtyard still fragrant with hibiscus, oleander, and frangipani. The sun cast a warm glow on the amber-colored walls.

Jeremy stood beside her, gently easing his arm around her small waist. "One might never know there were filthy streets outside. Or a filthy war."

They glanced at each other shyly. Marianne said, "We've been so close to each other for the past months, and yet so far away, we might just as well have been in different worlds." She cast her glance down, suddenly embarrassed. He'd been her lover for more than four years, he'd known every part of her, as she'd known every part of him. She'd thrilled to his touch and to his embrace, and yet now . . . "I feel the way I did the very first night that we . . ."

He smiled at her and kissed the top of her head. "I know what you mean. But don't worry. I'm still so weak that you've nothing to fear."

She clutched his arm. "Listen to the bells." The sound of mellow, joyous church bells were coming from the Ursuline Convent, ringing out a French Christmas carol. "It must be very close to Christmas," she said, excited as a child.

"About a week before, I would guess," he said. "We've been locked up in that damned ship so long that we've forgotten."

Hand in hand, they watched the twilight steal over the courtyard, turning the golden walls to a dark amber as the light faded. And then with a heart-catching cry they could deny each other no longer. They embraced, so determined to capture all that they'd hungered for in this lifetime, all that had been denied them through no fault of their own.

"A new season, new hope," he whispered, as he loosened her clothes. He drew her to the pallet and made love to her,

gently, and then·with growing desire, until finally their impassioned kisses led him to become as one with her. She
clutched him fiercely, thrilling to the union, and whispered that
he was the only man she'd ever loved, the only man she'd ever
known, and that she would know no other . . . ever.

In her heart she knew this was true. But she couldn't bring
herself to tell him of her dreadful premonition, something so
awful that every time she tried to fathom it she turned away
from the truth. This was to be the end of their love, for he was
going to face death . . . she knew it in the very fiber of her
being, knew it as only a woman in love can know it, and so
it spurred her on to fantastic flights of lovemaking. And he,
rejuvenated by this display of her love, grew whole in body
and spirit, knowing that he'd found the one thing that could
make him complete, a woman to love, a life to share.

They spent that entire evening in their room. The woman
of the house, a jolly octoroon, brought them their meals. The
days drifted one into the other. They never ventured outside—
hiding from enemies, real and imagined, but really discovering
themselves again. A few days before Christmas, he woke to
find that she'd cracked a walnut shell and filled the empty half
with sprigs of tiny baby's breath. Smiling, she presented it to
him.

"But it isn't Christmas yet," he said.

"In this world, who can be sure of anything?" she laughed
gaily. "Take it, along with my heart."

"I've no present for you but this," he said huskily, and
devoured her body with kisses.

The more they made love, the more that they wanted, and
they spent hours, holding, touching, kissing.

"I'm an old man," he said in wonder. "Almost thirty-three,
and yet you make me feel full of the sap of youth again."

Her heart stopped when he said 'thirty-three' and he noticed
her pale. "What's the matter?" he asked, raising himself on an
elbow.

"Nothing," she whispered. "Only—thirty-three, that's how
old Jesus was when . . . Oh, darling, I'm so frightened," she
murmured, and clung to him.

"But of what? We're safe here."

"You don't know Sean Connaught. You don't know how
vicious he can be when he's thwarted. He'll find us, I know
he will."

"Hush, nobody's going to find us. We gave General Jackson his description. He wouldn't dare stay in New Orleans."

When she didn't answer he looked at her inquisitively. "Do you know something you're not telling me?"

She shook her head in alarm. "Oh, no! I've told you everything. It's just that he's been in this city so many times, and he has another identity here. They think he's a French trader, for he speaks French fluently. He frequents the gaming houses, he knows Jean Lafitte, and for several years he's been trying to get him to join the British forces. Also, he's agitating the colored people in the city to rebel against the Americans."

"They tried that in Washington and Baltimore, but it didn't work," Jeremy said.

"Yes, but New Orleans is different. Remember, it was a Spanish and then a French city long before it became American. If Sean succeeds and the British win, then he'll have us in his clutches again."

"Don't worry, the British will never win."

"How can you be so sure?" she asked.

"Because this isn't their land. Because they haven't earned it by the sweat of their brow and the spilling of their blood. Because they come as conquerors, and not as men who love the land. And so they shall never win."

Another night of love, and then a morning of tenderness coupled with plans that somewhat assuaged her fears. She whiled away the time telling him what she knew of the city. "There were so many tragedies in New Orleans all the time—plagues of fever that wiped out the populace, floods that came every year no matter how high the levees were built, and the fires that twice obliterated the city—that the New Orleanders began to live as if each day was their last. And so now they call it the City That Care Forgot."

"That's not what I've heard it called," Jeremy said, grinning.

"Oh, I know it's called Sin City, and worse," Marianne said. "I know there are more fancy houses here than in any city on the whole continent. And what's more, they're proud of it! And I know that a Creole would rather go to balls and enjoy the afternoon siesta than do business, business, business, all the time like the puritanical Yankee traders who have nothing on their minds but the making of money." She said the last with a slight pout, and he was amused with the change that had come over her.

"Remember, we're all not Connaughts, with vast fortunes to fall back on. But all right. We'll forget business today and do nothing but have fun!"

"Be careful, your wounds," she exclaimed with a cry as he grabbed for her.

"They're nothing compared to the wounds I'd have if you didn't love me," he murmured.

"Oh yes, yes," she said, throwing her head back while his mouth roved against her neck, and then to her breasts.

"Nothing can hurt us, no one can find us, no war, no Sean, nothing," she whispered. Her heart ached with such contentment that she knew that even if she died at this very moment, in the Lord's Book of Life she would be counted as one who'd found complete happiness. Gone were all her guilty feelings about having betrayed him and the country, gone her fears about her Aunt Victoria, gone everything except the sure knowledge that she loved him and that he loved her.

"Have you seen Wingate?" Jeremy asked Marianne one night.

"He left earlier," she said. "I think he feels he's in the way. Oh, Jeremy, have we been cutting him out? After all he's done for us I couldn't stand that."

Much later that night Jeremy heard Wingate's tread on the steps and padded down the hallway to his room. He knocked and Wingate opened the door. He looked like he was close to tears.

"Something's troubling you, lad, isn't there?" Jeremy said. "Tell me, it can't be that bad."

Wingate kept his gaze down and shrugged his shoulders.

Feeling it was best not to press the matter, Jeremy waited patiently. Finally Wingate said in a voice that still had the timbre of youth, "Oh, well, I guess I'm just not like other men." With the floodgates opened, he said in a rush, "When I was up in Maine just before the British impressed me, a bunch of the older farmhands were going to town at the end of the month. They took me along because they said it was time for me to be a man. They got liquored up and took me to one of those fancy houses. Well, I got so scared that I couldn't do it, and all the ladies and the farmhands—they laughed at me. I never did go back to that town again."

"How old were you?" Jeremy asked.

"Old enough—twelve, going on thirteen. Most of my other friends that age had already...Anyway, when we got here, and you and Marianne...well, anyway, I saw all those painted women on the streets and I figured that now was the time. After all, I'm almost fifteen! I gave one of them all the money I had...but it was just like the first time. I just can't, I just can't do it!"

He hung his head in his hands and Jeremy put his arm around the boy's shoulder. "Maybe in a way, God's been watching over you," he said softly.

Wingate jerked his head up and looked at him through glistening eyes. "What do you mean?"

"I've got it in my head that you're one of those chosen people who'll only be able to give himself if he's in love."

"You mean that?" Wingate said. "You're not just saying it? All those sailors on the British ships, the things they kept telling me..."

"I can make you this promise," Jeremy said. "There'll come a time in your life, and not so far off, when you'll look back at this moment and you'll laugh. When you fall in love, all your fears will disappear—just the way mine did when I was young."

The slightest ray of hope lit Wingate's face.

"Now you'd best get some sleep," Jeremy said, and rose to leave. At the door he turned and said, "One last thing. If ever I have the good fortune to have a son, I couldn't wish him to be a finer lad than you are."

Sean Connaught sat in a rundown tavern in a derelict section of New Orleans called the Swamp. He felt safe in this part of town because no officers of the law ever dared venture into this quarter. Located some ten blocks in from the Mississippi River, the Swamp consisted of a jumble of houses, bars, whorehouses, gambling dens, and flophouses, where a Kaintuck riverboatman might indulge himself in all the pleasures of the flesh, and probably get killed for his pains. This bar was a favorite haunt of Jean Lafitte; though there was a price on his head, here he could be safe among his own kind. Sean waited for Lafitte anxiously; on this meeting could well depend the outcome of the battle for New Orleans.

Two of Sean's New Orleans confederates had stationed themselves in strategic positions in the bar. Near the front door

stood Hercule Bordeaux, a giant of a riverboatman, with a red
turkey feather in the hatband, signifying that he was a champion
and would take on all comers. Guarding the rear of the bar was
a Spaniard who went by the name of Sariano. His face was
sharp with a long pointed nose and lips that tended to disappear
into his mouth. He carried a long stiletto in a sheath strapped
to his chest. To the casual onlooker, he appeared unarmed;
many men had died because of that misimpression.

Sean watched with growing irritation as the raucousness in
the tavern increased. In a dark corner, one of the Kaintucks
argued with a comrade over the attentions of a prostitute, and
finally crowned his companion with a bottle of rum. Then he
picked up the squealing girl and carried her to a booth where
they hammered out their bargain on one of the hard benches.

Sean looked away in disgust. Marianne and Jeremy—did
they also couple like animals? he wondered, and felt his gorge
rise in anger. He couldn't imagine why anybody would want
this territory of criminals and misfits; except for its enormous
wealth, it would be better off left to the savages. But in the
decade since the United States had purchased the Louisiana
Territory from France, the tonnage through New Orleans had
increased tenfold, with no end in sight. Goods from the frontier
couldn't be hauled over the Allegheny Mountains, nor could
the manufactured items from the eastern states or from Europe
be transported that way. The river, the mighty Mississippi,
afforded the easiest access to and from the interior of the country, an area that would one day be a vital market for all goods.

Sean stiffened when he saw Jean Lafitte enter the tavern.
He rose from his seat and motioned, and Lafitte sauntered to
him. Lafitte was an odd-looking man; some might think him
handsome. He wore a wide-brimmed hat, and his dark hair
curled and bunched on the nape of his neck. He had long, dark
moustaches that stuck straight out to the sides of his face. His
expression was fierce, and yet as the crowd parted to make
way for him, he appeared somewhat amused that he could
command so much attention.

Lafitte sat down and a barmaid immediately brought him
a mug of rum. The men exchanged pleasantries. "My sym-
pathies, Jean. I understand that the Americans raided your
hideout at Barataria and have sworn to hang you," Sean said.

Lafitte shrugged. "They call me a pirate, but in fact I operate
under letters of marque from Cartagena. Besides, there are so

many people in New Orleans who want what I sell—contraband whiskey, black ivory . . . Ah yes, you British know about the slave trade, don't you?"

"I know that last year, Governor Claiborne offered a reward of five hundred dollars for your capture."

Lafitte threw back his head and laughed, a deep rich laugh that reverberated through the room. "Then you probably know that in turn, I offered a reward of five *thousand* dollars for the capture of Governor Claiborne!"

Sean shrugged with annoyance. "Let's get down to cases. This past September, I arranged for Captain Nicholas Lockeyer of the British Navy to visit you. He was authorized by me to offer you a commission in the British Navy, and the promise of thirty thousand dollars if you would join forces with us."

"Ah, then it was you who made such a generous offer," Lafitte said.

"I also know that you forwarded my offer to the members of the New Orleans legislature. I assume it was an effort on your part to extract a better offer from them."

"Ah, but you're a real trader!" Lafitte exclaimed, and then took a long gulp of his rum. He wiped his mouth with the back of his hand.

"I'm here to reiterate my offer, and to make the sum of money more attractive. Fifty thousand dollars."

Lafitte said nothing.

"All right then," Sean said, "I will ask only one thing of you. I happen to know that General Jackson has asked you for several thousand flints from your store of ammunition."

Lafitte raised his eyebrows. "Your intelligence network is better than I thought. But I will save you some work. Jackson asked for all I had—some seven thousand flints, to be exact."

"And your answer?"

Lafitte shrugged noncommittally.

"I ask you to consider this carefully," Sean said. "You know that our navy now commands Lake Borgne; we'll be in New Orleans shortly."

Lafitte leaned forward, looking at Sean intently. "It's a long way from Lake Borgne to New Orleans. Twenty miles of impenetrable swamp."

Sean's lips thinned into a bitter smile. "No one knows better than you that the area is crisscrossed with bayous and canals. Jackson can't possibly guard them all. Sufficient to say that

I can assure you as an officer and as an English gentleman that the British army will soon be in this city. I urge you to throw in your lot with the winning side."

Lafitte shifted his body in his seat. "If the British win, their navy is the strongest in the world, and no doubt they will soon move to crush me. But if the Americans win, they will be grateful for the help that I give them, and leave Jean Lafitte to his peaceful work."

"I give you my word that—"

Lafitte cut him off with an abrupt motion of his hand. "Enough. There is an even greater reason why I cannot entertain your offer. Most of the men that follow me are Americans, and they will not raise their arms against their own countrymen."

With an oath, Sean scrambled to his feet. As he did he heard the click of a pistol cocking, and realized that Lafitte had had his pistol pointing at his stomach under the table all the time they'd been talking.

Consumed with anger, Sean started toward the door and accidentally bumped into a loutish Kaintuck wearing a stocking cap and a loop earring.

He roared at Sean, "Watch where you're going, you sniveling little runt," and raised his fist.

With a nimble move Sean ducked the blow and in the same motion pressed his pistol against the lout's stomach. In the din of the bar the muffled report was barely heard. Sean continued walking at an even pace while the man gradually slumped against the wall and fell to the floor, dead. In short order, he was carried outside without anybody paying too much mind.

Sean's two accomplices followed him out into the street. Hercule Bordeaux adjusted the patch over his right eye. He'd lost it in a fight with another riverman, but Hercule had gone on to gouge out both of the other man's eyes.

"I'm ready for you to take me to them now," Sean told Hercule and Sariano. "Are you sure that they're the right people?"

Sariano nodded. "The girl answers your description to the letter, and she's with a wounded man. They went to this house with a young boy, but the last time I checked, he wasn't there."

"I want them all dead," Sean said, still feeling the effects of his disappointment with Lafitte. "No questions, no mercy, just dead. I've wasted enough time on them already."

"Don't worry, we'll make short work of them," Hercule said. "But a wounded man and a girl, and you need two of us? Ha! How do you expect to win a war if you can't do such a little job yourself?"

"I have my reasons," Sean said. "Now do as I say and you'll be paid handsomely. Just remember, dead."

Chapter 19

MAKING SURE to avoid the army units patrolling the streets, Sean Connaught and his two accomplices made their way to St. Charles Street. Sariano scouted the house. The boy was still not there, and they entered stealthily and made short work of the landlady, bludgeoning her into unconsciousness.

The three of them began to climb the stairs. Sean paused at a door where he heard voices. He tried the doorknob gingerly but the door wouldn't budge. "It's locked," he whispered.

"What is that to Hercule?" The giant grunted and heaved his shoulder against the wood. But the heavy oaken door held. With a bellow of rage Hercule charged at it again, and this time the hinges gave with a splintering crash.

But inside, the delay had been long enough for Jeremy to scramble out of bed and grab his pistols. Sariano came through the door, his drawn stiletto flashing in his hand. He ran straight for the bed where Marianne crouched against the headboard, the covers drawn up around her naked body.

Jeremy fired, and Sariano's hands clutched at his heart. The knife fell out of his hands with a clatter as he crumpled to the floor. Before Jeremy could take aim again, Hercule sent his fist crashing against the side of Jeremy's head. Jeremy felt the pain radiate out from the blow as he hit the floor, felt a boot smash into his face and the warm sticky fluid that was blood streaming from his nose.

"Finish him," Sean said.

But Hercule's attention was elsewhere. Sean aimed at Jeremy, but crumpled as he was in the corner, and blocked by Hercule's massive form, he couldn't get a clear shot.

Hercule yanked the coverlet from Marianne. Her skin was so translucent that in some places the finest tracery of veins showed through. "It would be a pity not to have some pleasure from that one before she is dead, eh?" Hercule grunted as he grabbed for her.

Marianne's scream pried Jeremy to full consciousness. He groaned, and Hercule looked down, surprised. "I thought I had finished that one, no? He has a hard head." He raised his cleated boot high above Jeremy's head, ready to bring it down and crush his skull like an eggshell.

Jeremy rolled as Hercule's foot came down, and he fired his pistol at the same time. The bullet caught Hercule in the other eye and he clawed at his face, the blood gushing through his fingers. He collapsed across the bed and lay still.

Sean leaned against the wall, white-faced. "I'd forgotten you were such an excellent shot," he said to Jeremy, who was trying to raise himself from the floor. "But that doesn't matter now, does it?" Sean said. "Both your pistols are empty."

Jeremy and Marianne stared at him; his eyes were wide and oddly unfocused, and flecks of spittle flew from the corners of his mouth. "Before I kill you both, I want you to experience a little of purgatory right here and now. May you burn for all eternity with the knowledge of what is about to happen." He turned to Marianne. "We've been planning this for a very long time, haven't we, cousin?"

She shrank at this. Jeremy reached across the bed and gripped her hand.

"Very touching," Sean said. "But she knows full well the extent of her complicity."

Jeremy's glance darted from Sean to Marianne. For a moment he felt the old pang of doubt about her. But even as he looked at her, he saw somebody very different from the frightened girl he'd always tried to protect. She *had* helped him escape from Sean's ship. She *had* led them safely to New Orleans. And in the past blissful days, her lips, her body, and her heart had all proven to him that she was true to him.

"I love you," he murmured, and tightened his grip on her hand.

"Shut your mouth!" Sean ordered. Then he said, "Our plan has been in operation in British intelligence for the past decade, ever since we allowed our banks to loan you the money to buy the Louisiana Territory from that monster Napoleon. Within days, General Pakenham will arrive here to take command of our army. Aside from Wellington, England boasts no greater general than Pakenham. When we've conquered New Orleans, our army will march up the Mississippi while our armies in Canada will descend. Once joined, they'll sweep east and push your damned country into the sea!"

As Jeremy listened to Sean's ravings, he recalled that he'd

warned President Madison about this very possibility just before
the war had broken out. If New Orleans was lost . . . it could
very well mean the end of the United States of America.

Sean's eyes had darkened to a lowering gray and his words
came in short, hissing bursts. "Your fool Jackson believes that
our army is mired at Lake Borgne. What he doesn't know is
that within the day—the day, I say!—our armies will have
crossed through the swamps and will emerge at the Mississippi
no more than eight miles below New Orleans!"

Jeremy could see that Sean was telling the truth, could see
the pleasure he was exacting by tormenting them with this
information. He knew that his own life meant very little in the
context of his country's greater good—nobody's life could
mean that much—and in a desperate move he lunged for Sean.

But Sean had been prepared for this and fired. Jeremy felt
the searing pain as the bullet passed through his shoulder,
knocking him back against the wall. Sean raised his other pistol
and took careful aim. But with a cry, Marianne flung herself
at her cousin. They struggled briefly, and then there was a loud
report. Marianne's back arched as she took in her breast the
bullet intended for Jeremy.

"No!" Jeremy shouted, and stumbled for Sean, picking up
the stiletto that Sariano had dropped. Seeing that he didn't have
enough time to reload, Sean turned and fled down the steps.
Jeremy tried to pursue him, but wounded as he was, Sean
eluded him, and disappeared into the warren of streets. Jeremy
dragged his way back upstairs and found Marianne lying across
the bed.

Her face had taken on an unearthly pallor, and her lips were
bloodless. He cradled her head in his arms. "We must get you
to a doctor," he murmured. He tried to lift her, but she cried
out in pain.

"Don't," she breathed. "I have only a few moments left."

"Oh God, don't say such a thing," he moaned.

"Listen to me," she whispered. "My life has been a waste.
Riddled through with hate and error. I was never strong enough
to fight my family, even though I suspected they were wrong.
And then I met you."

The pool of blood in the hollow of her breasts widened with
each of her heartbeats. "Don't talk," Jeremy said. "I'll get a
doctor. Oh, where's Wingate?" he cried out in anguish.

She clutched at him with the last of her remaining strength.

"Don't leave me, please. I don't want to die alone. Hold my hand."

He twined his fingers through hers as if trying to impart strength and life through his touch.

"My love," she whispered, "what happened is just retribution for the greivous sins I've committed. I couldn't let you die because of that. Don't weep, for you have given me enough love to last for eternity, and so you've given me eternal life."

With that, a spasm shook her body; her dark, luminous eyes opened wide and then turned blank and unseeing.

A cry of a wounded animal tore from his throat and he wept for her . . . wept for himself, wept from a grief so unbearable that he knew he would never recover from it.

The only thing more compelling than his grief was what Sean had told him. Weak from this new gunshot wound he threw on his buckskins and stumbled down the stairs. Unmindful of his bleeding, he ran through the dark night to General Jackson's headquarters.

Chapter 20

THE DOLOROUS bells of the Cathedral of St. Louis were announcing dawn when Jeremy reached Jackson's headquarters. Inside the Royal Street house, Jackson's aides moved with quick precision, carrying the latest communiqués from their outposts to their commander. Jeremy was ushered into a room whose walls were hung with maps. A fire crackling in the hearth fought vainly to dispel the wet chill of the morning.

Jackson jumped to his feet when he saw Jeremy. "By God, man, what's happened? Send for a doctor!"

Voice shaking with emotion, Jeremy told him what had happened as briefly as he could. Then Jeremy finished, "Sean Connaught told me that within the day the British army will have crossed the Lake Borgne peninsula and be at the Mississippi. That would put them within striking distance of New Orleans."

Jackson strode to the map and studied the area. "It's a trick," he said at last. "Every canal, every bayou, every access road in that area has been blocked. I've given explicit orders to that effect. If the British had been sighted, my scouts would have warned me. You see, from Lake Borgne, the British can just as easily strike at Mobile and catch us off guard there."

When Jeremy protested this, Jackson's impatience vented itself. Where military matters were concerned, Jackson had an arrogance that would accommodate no other viewpoint than his own. But after his first outburst he calmed down somewhat. "I sympathize with your loss, Jeremy. If such a thing were to happen to me . . ." He shook his head.

He gave orders that Jeremy was to be quartered in the house, and a doctor found to treat him. Numbed, Jeremy slipped into a state of deep lassitude, dozing fitfully, only to waken with a cry when he remembered what happened. Wingate came running into headquarters about a half hour later. When Jeremy told him what happened, he wept unashamedly. Jeremy reached out and comforted the boy, and in so doing, managed to regain some of his own senses.

He gripped Wingate's shoulders. "If Jackson doesn't listen to us, then Marianne's death will have been in vain, and that would be the worst thing of all."

Wingate nodded and saw to Jeremy's wound. "It's clean. The bullet's gone right through your shoulder without hitting anything vital." He bandaged the shoulder and put his arm in a sling.

Shortly before one o'clock that afternoon, Jackson's headquarters erupted into a frenzy of activity. One of Jackson's aides barged into Jeremy's room and dragged him out. "The general wants to see you!"

In the map room, Jackson strode back and forth across the hardwood floors, his hands knotted behind his back. He jerked his head in the direction of a Creole in his late twenties. "Gabriel Villeré has just arrived with the damnable news that a British force two thousand strong has broken through along Bayou Bienvenu. They've captured the Villeré plantation!"

"The British are just eight miles below New Orleans," Villeré whispered. Villeré had been captured by the British but had jumped from the window of his plantation house and, under a hail of bullets, had escaped into the surrounding swamps. From there he'd made his way to New Orleans to warn Jackson.

"By the Eternal, I'll smash them!" Jackson swore. "They shall not sleep on our soil tonight!" Jackson's face was contorted with fury, but as Jeremy watched, the general regained control and took command of the situation. Once more Jackson had Jeremy repeat his story and this time he listened intently. Then he put his hand on Jeremy's shoulder, and though he said nothing, Jeremy knew it was his way of apologizing.

At least the man's got enough guts to admit his error, Jeremy thought. Then once more he felt the confidence of the man surge through him. It also charged every other officer in the room. Jeremy couldn't help comparing him to President Madison and to Monroe. This man is a natural leader, he thought, and I'd follow him into hell.

"There's no way we can defend New Orleans from within its walls," Jackson said. "The forts are in a terrible state of disrepair and the British would overrun them in short order. No, we must defend the city from without its walls. And unless we march this very night, the British will have conquered us by morning. Gentlemen, prepare."

• • •

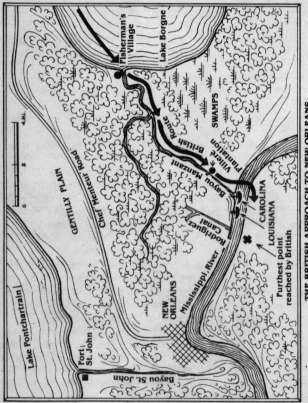

THE BRITISH APPROACH TO NEW ORLEANS

Panic spread throughout the city when the citizens learned of the British breakthrough. But under Jackson's iron grip, New Orleans collected itself, and then found its spirit. Optimism became infectious, merchants reopened their shops. The Kaintuck riverboatmen, always eager for a scrap, viewed the coming battle with delight. From all quarters of the city, Jackson rounded up whatever forces he could. His army regulars in their tight blue uniforms, the Creole militia got up in their finery and looking like they were going to a ball, Brigadier General John Coffee's tough Tennessee volunteers, Colonel Hind's Mississippi dragoons, Choctaw Indians in their fierce war paint, and about two hundred free men of color. In all, Jackson managed to muster a force of some two thousand men. Jackson also welcomed Jean Lafitte and his pirates into his army. He'd once called them "hellish banditti," but that judgment was put aside in the face of the greater enemy.

The flat disk of the winter sun was sinking into the west when Jackson and his men marched out of New Orleans. Jeremy and Wingate were in the vanguard, Wingate with a haversack full of medicinal supplies on his back. Wingate had pleaded with Jeremy to remain in New Orleans, but he would have it no other way but that he must join the fight this night.

Citizens lined the streets and the Creoles, putting aside their detestation of the Kaintucks, sang "Yankee Doodle." The Americans, in a rare burst of camaraderie, answered in their pidgin-French version of the "Marseillaise."

With night falling, the army moved swiftly and silently through the bayou countryside. Jackson had ordered two American warships, the *Carolina* and the *Louisiana*, to creep as close as possible to the British encampment.

"At seven-thirty tonight, our ships will open fire. That will be our signal to attack," Jeremy told Wingate. "Surprise is the key. It's exactly what George Washington did at Valley Forge about forty years ago. He attacked on Christmas Eve, when the British and Hessians least expected it. And that's what Jackson plans to do tonight."

In the darkness, the *Carolina* and the *Louisiana* crept to within three hundred yards of the British camp bivouacked at the Villeré Plantation. Promptly at seven-thirty, the two warships opened fire. Shortly thereafter Jackson's forces charged and engaged the redcoats who'd been relaxing around their campfires. The audacity of the attack threw the British completely off guard.

After their initial shock, the superbly trained British forces regrouped, and the battle raged for five hours. A dense fog rolled in from the river, effectively negating the firepower of the *Carolina* and the *Louisiana,* since they could no longer distinguish the battle line. Jeremy fought like a madman, searching through the darkness for the flash of red that would signal a redcoat. Several times he took chances that risked his life, but with Marianne dead he cared about nothing.

About midnight, General Jackson ordered a withdrawal from the Villeré battlefield to a position a half mile upriver at the Macarté plantation. The Rodriguez Canal, an irrigation ditch about fifteen feet wide and four feet deep, separated the two plantations, and Jackson ordered his men to take up defensive positions on the far side of the ditch.

Reluctantly, Jeremy withdrew from the battlefield. He approached Jackson and saluted smartly. "Sir, if we press them this night, we can beat them back."

Jackson shook his head. "The British are accustomed to precision military fighting, and our men aren't. In the fog and in this darkness we'd surely be beaten. And I've word that the British reinforcements—another two thousand strong—will soon be here."

Guards were posted, and all through the night the men kept vigil, sleeping when they could. The following morning, Jackson set up his headquarters in the Macarté plantation house. The two-storied house had galleried porches on all four sides and stood about two hundred yards from the canal.

The weather had turned raw, and stiff winds and rain lashed the area. The tramp of army boots in the entrance hall, the cries of the wounded whom Jackson had housed in the elegant building, was in harsh contrast to the graciousness of the mansion facing on the Mississippi River.

Jackson called a council of war with his staff of officers and engineers. Major Howell Tatum, Jackson's chief topographical engineer, was present, as were Hyacinthe Laclotte, an assistant engineer, and Major A. Lacarrière Latour, Jackson's chief engineer. Jeremy, because of his building expertise—besides spending twenty years helping to construct the White House, he had also helped design and build Forts Mandan and Clatsop while on the Lewis and Clark expedition—had been asked to contribute his thoughts.

"We have a natural defensive position in the Rodriguez Canal," Jackson said. "How can we best utilize it?"

"What about cutting through the levee and flooding the grounds immediately in front of the line?" Jeremy asked.

"We've already investigated that possibility," Major Latour said. "Unfortunately, the river is too low to be of any help."

"Then we must do with the moat," Jeremy said. "We should widen it wherever we can. Also, throw up a breastwork on our side of the canal."

"But there are no building materials anywhere," Hyacinthe Laclotte said, pointing to the treeless cane fields.

"Use whatever is available," Jeremy said. "Have our men uproot the stunted cypress in the swamps, use wagons, furniture, everything. Build the ridge as high as a man's shoulders, so that he can rest his rifle on it, and at the same time be shielded from the enemy's fire."

"How long a breastwork?" Jackson asked.

"Running from the Mississippi to the cypress swamp."

"How long a distance is that would you estimate?" Major Coffee asked.

"I paced it off this morning," Jeremy said. "About nine hundred yards."

General Jackson ran his fingers through his thick shock of hair. "It means our men will be spread thin, and it will be a tremendous amount of work. But if we can hold both ends of the line, then I have every confidence we'll be secure."

Jackson strode to the wide french doors and flung them open. A gust of brisk air swept in from the river, and Jackson pointed to the mighty body of water that meandered through the savannah. "Our work is cut out for us. If we win this battle, the Mississippi becomes an American river for all time, and the way is opened for the westward expansion of our nation. Within a generation we shall people this land from sea to shining sea. If we lose—but we won't lose! By the Eternal, we won't!"

In turn Jackson spoke to each officer in the room. He had the ability to make each man feel that he and he alone held the key to the future, and it made a man want to fight all the harder.

As the energized officers were about to depart Jeremy said

suddenly, "General, the British rockets!" He quickly explained about the new British weapon, the Congreve rocket.

"Pass the word along to the men," Jackson ordered. "Tell them that these damnable rockets are more noise than anything else, and not to be feared."

On the twenty-fifth of December, a salvo of British guns made the Americans believe that the redcoats were attacking. But the British were simply celebrating the arrival of General Sir Edward Pakenham, the new commander of the army. Sean Connaught, who'd joined the British forces, was overjoyed at the general's arrival.

Sir Edward, the brother of Wellington's wife, was thirty-seven years old and at the peak of his military career. He'd brought with him an additional three thousand soldiers. Along with the four regiments who'd fought at Washington and Baltimore were fresh troops including the Ninety-Third Foot, the Ninety-Fifth Foot in their distinctive green rifleman's jackets, and the Fifth West Indian Regiment, reputed to be the best of the black colonial fighters. Altogether, the British army now numbered fifty-seven hundred soldiers.

"We could beat them with half these men," Sean Connaught said to Pakenham.

"We're in a damned awkward position," Pakenham said, surveying the field through his spyglass. "The Mississippi is on one side, a swamp on the other, and confronted by that damned ditch."

"Believe me, sir, at our first bayonet charge they'll tuck their tails between their legs and run," Sean said. "Look at them! They're nothing but rabble. Our men refer to them as 'dirty shirts.'"

A broadside from the *Carolina* and *Louisiana* whistled overhead and exploded nearby. Pakenham said, "Those gun boats are a nuisance. Something must be done about them."

Under orders from Jackson, the *Carolina* and the *Louisiana* had continued to pour fire and lead into the British camp, making life miserable for the British soldiers who were trying to prepare for battle. "Do you have any suggestions, captain?" Pakenham asked Sean.

"Leave it to me, sir," Sean said with a crisp salute.

He ordered nine fieldpieces set up on the levee, including

two nine-pounders capable of firing hot shot, four six-pounders that could fire shrapnel, two howitzers, and a mortar.

Anxious to prove himself to Pakenham, Sean took sightings of the closer boat, adjusted the incline of the guns, and then personally lit the first fuse. With a roar, the hot shot flamed across the sky, and with devastating accuracy set the sails of the *Carolina* afire. Salvo after salvo tore into the ship. Sean watched with glee as the American seamen scrambled into the river to escape the burning vessel. "Like rats," he said, clenching and unclenching his fists. Then a tremendous explosion erupted as the *Carolina*'s munitions magazine blew up.

With a mighty cheer from the redcoats, Sean then trained his guns on the *Louisiana*. Too late he realized that he should have tackled the larger ship first, for the *Louisiana*'s sailors had scrambled into their rowboats and were towing her out of the range of his guns. I've lost her through stupidity, Sean thought, but he kept his mouth shut. The *Louisiana* took up a position across the river, and with her heavier cannon, continued to bombard the British camp.

"The British won't sit still for this long," Jackson said. "They'll attack soon. Keep building that breastwork, boys. We've got to be ready for them!"

Chapter 21

ON DECEMBER 28 General Pakenham decided that he was sufficiently prepared. "Send out a reconnaissance force to test the American strength," he ordered.

Jackson studied the superbly trained soldiers as they marched forward. "They sure look pretty," he said. But when the redcoats came within range, his artillery and the cannon on the *Louisiana* opened up and caught the British troops in their crossfire. The British were beaten back and retreated to a position about two miles from the Rodriguez Canal.

All during this time, Jeremy and a crew of men worked furiously to strengthen the embankment. They piled up the mud and soil until it was shoulder height, and then continued the line deep into the cypress swamp to a point where it would be impossible for the British to breach it. The future of New Orleans depended on whether or not this line would hold, and Jeremy poured every drop of his energy into the task. Further, it helped him forget.

The number of gun emplacements along the ditch was increased from five to twelve. But the ground was unstable. Then Jeremy hit on a solution. He sank bales of cotton into the muddy ground, then built wooden platforms atop them to support the twenty-four- and thirty-two-pound cannon. This prevented the artillery from sinking into the muck.

On New Year's Day, the British, under cover of a heavy morning fog, brought up their fieldpieces and prepared to assault the American line. When the fog lifted, they were greeted with an extraordinary scene in the American camp. Andrew Jackson had chosen this day to hold a grand review of the army in order to bolster their morale. Citizens from New Orleans in all their Sunday splendor had come to watch the parade.

"We'll make short work of this," Sean Connaught said, and gave the order to fire. Sean, assuming that Jackson would be quartered in the Macarté house, gave orders to direct the fire there. He also knew that was where the wounded were being treated, but it made little difference to him. In the first few minutes, more than a hundred shells and rockets tore through the wooden building.

Wingate, who'd spent the last few days tending to the wounded, tore around the house, slapping out the small fires that had started from the shelling. Outside, the ranks of the American army and the visiting citizenry fled before the bombardment. Within minutes, though, Jackson had taken command and the American artillery returned the fire.

Jeremy watched anxiously as round after round was fired; but the guns on their platforms didn't sink into the mud the way the British fieldpieces were doing. Within two hours, the American gunners had knocked out all the British positions.

At the day's end, General Pakenham was in a rage. "I curse the piece of imbecility that's confined me to this narrow plain. Since I cannot maneuver, the only thing I can do is smash straight through Jackson's line."

"Exactly, sir," Sean said. "The Americans will never be able to withstand a direct frontal assault."

"But we need more men for that kind of operation. We must wait for the Seventh Fusiliers and the Forty-Third Regiment," Pakenham said.

"When will that be, sir?" Sean asked.

"Within the week, certainly," Pakenham said.

"We run the risk that during that time the Americans will be building their own defenses," Sean said.

Pakenham nodded. "But because of the original miscalculation that's boxed us into this position, we have no other choice."

The Americans did more than just build their own defenses, and every night for the next week the backwoodsmen, many of them expert Indian fighters, would sneak through the sugarcane fields or through the cypress swamps to the British lines and slit the throats of the sentries. Or a marksman might find a redcoat outlined by a campfire and send a bullet through him. The raids became so brazen that the redcoats were always kept off balance, frightened of going to sleep too near a fire, and then freezing in their wet clothes if they slept too far away. But at last their morale was given a great boost when the British reinforcements arrived.

"I've never seen anything to compare to the savagery of

these Americans," Sean complained to General Pakenham.
"They've turned this conflict into something uncivilized. Truly,
they are barbarians."

"It will be over shortly," Pakenham said. "Now that our
reinforcements have joined us, we'll attack at dawn. Day's end
will see us in New Orleans."

"I have no doubt that this will go down in history as one
of England's greatest victories, and as your own glorious hour,"
Sean said.

General Pakenham nodded his thanks. "Let us pray to God
that it comes to pass."

At the Macarté plantation house, General Jackson sat in a
cane chair. He'd been taken ill suddenly with a severe pain in
his chest, and sweat beaded his forehead. All the other doctors
being out in the field or in New Orleans, Wingate had been
pressed into service. His fingers trembled as he gently kneaded
the general's chest and back, trying to alleviate the pain.

"It's this damned bullet," Jackson said to Jeremy, who stood
nearby. "I took it in one of the duels I fought, and the doctors
were never able to dig it out. They tell me it's still lodged near
my heart and they can't get at it."

Wingate blotted the general's forehead with a towel and
handed him a cup of hot comfrey tea. He continued to knead
Jackson's back, which had knotted up from the pain.

"How old are you, lad?" Jackson asked.

"Fourteen," Wingate said.

"And will you follow this profession?"

"I don't know, sir. My father is a physician, but barely
earns enough to maintain our family."

"Aye, I know the lot of a doctor isn't easy. But you have
healing hands. I'm feeling better already. You know, lad, in
this country you can become anything you want. Anything, I
say. Why, I had no formal education at all. Where I was born
in Waxhaw, just a tiny frontier settlement in the Carolinas,
there were no schools. But by the time I was nine years old,
I'd taught myself to read, and recited the entire Declaration of
Independence to a bunch of illiterate frontiersmen! From there
I struck out to Tennessee, bought land, and lived in a log cabin
I call the Hermitage. But one day I'll build a finer—"

An aide rushed into the room. "General, the scouts report

fresh activity in the British camp. They're bringing up their guns again and battalions are forming."

"Pass the word along to the men," Jackson said. "With their reinforcements here, they're likely to attack at any time. What's the hour now?"

"A little after midnight," Jeremy said.

"Between now and dawn then," Jackson mused. "Closer to dayspring, I'd wager."

"General, the commanders want to know if there's been any change in the contingency plan," Major Coffee asked.

"None!" Jackson thundered, half-rising from his chair. "I'll retreat to the city if necessary, and fire it, and in the surrounding flames we'll fight them. Everything will be put to the torch— supplies, dwellings, everything. Then we'll occupy a position above the city and cut off all supplies coming downriver. That will force them to leave our land. I have no love for the British," he spat.

Jeremy blinked, in awe of the elemental force that the man generated. To defeat the enemy, he was prepared to destroy an entire city! Yet Jeremy realized that this very determination was the margin between victory and defeat.

"Leave off now, lad," Jackson said to Wingate. "And thank you. You've eased the misery in my bones. Now it's time to smash the British." Wingate helped him on with his navy blue coat with golden epaulettes and a stiff collar embroidered in golden thread. "When I was thirteen years old I served as a messenger for the American troops in our War for Independence," Jackson said. "I'm proud to say I took part in several skirmishes, but then I was captured. One of the British officers, a haughty fellow, demanded that I polish his boots. When I refused, he became so angry that he hit me on the side of the head with his saber. And that's the scar you see right here."

He pointed to a slash mark that ran down the side of his face. "No, I have no love for the British."

Then Jackson strode from the room. Wingate gathered his supplies. "I don't think I've ever met a man like that," he said to Jeremy.

"Nor I," Jeremy said as he checked his powder and flints. "Everything he's done in this life he's done for himself. That's why the frontiersmen all understand and trust him. He was the first man elected from Tennessee to serve in the House of

Representatives, and he also served in the Senate. But he's not a man used to sharing power that way, so he resigned and went back to Nashville, where he could be top man. Unless I miss my guess, Jackson's aspirations stop only at the White House. That is, if there's a country left after this battle, and if we ever rebuild the President's House."

Wingate slung his haversack over his shoulders. "But he'd make a wonderful President, wouldn't he?"

"Probably. Pity he'll never achieve it."

"Why not?" Wingate asked, surprised.

They went outside. The predawn chill made them draw their coats tighter around them. Jeremy said, "Well, there's a grave scandal surrounding Jackson and his wife. The gossip has been around for years and it just won't die."

"What?" Wingate asked, wide-eyed.

"It's very complicated, but you see, Rachel was married before, to a man named Robards. He had a reputation as a drunkard and a wife-beater. Rachel left him. She thought he'd gotten a divorce, and so she married Jackson, whom she'd known for a while before. Then Robards came back and he hadn't gotten the divorce after all!"

Wingate whistled.

"Robards accused Rachel of adultery and bigamy and accused Jackson of licentiousness and of stealing his wife."

"Was there really any truth to the charges?" Wingate asked, feeling somehow that he had to defend Jackson.

"I honestly believe that it was an innocent error," Jeremy said, "though Jackson's enemies claim that he and Rachel had known each other, in the biblical sense, even during the time she was Mrs. Robards. Finally, Robards was granted a divorce and Jackson and Rachel remarried, but the scandal's followed them. Jackson's fought a dozen duels over Rachel's honor, and killed a number of men, too."

"No!" Wingate exclaimed.

Jeremy nodded. "The bullet near Jackson's heart was gotten in just such a duel. From a man named Dickinson, I think."

"What happened to Dickinson?" Wingate asked.

"Jackson killed him. So you see, that's why Jackson will probably never be President. Because in this diehard Puritanical nation, the electorate won't tolerate that kind of scandal."

Wingate wanted to know more of the details, but suddenly Jeremy had to break off the conversation. He discovered that in the heavy rain that had fallen, a section of the embankment had caved in. "Bring some light this way!" he shouted.

Some soldiers came running with lanterns. "It's a bad breach," Jeremy said, inspecting it. "And likely to get worse until we repair it. Get your shovels, men! Hurry!" He turned to Wingate. "Let's hope that the British don't attack before we repair it. Otherwise they could pour through our line right here. And there's not much time before first light."

Chapter 22

IN THE British camp, General Sir Edward Pakenham stood in his lamplit tent and reviewed his plan of attack with his officers. In the tent were General Samuel Gibbs, Colonel William Thornton, and Lieutenant Colonel Thomas Mullens of the Forty-Fourth Infantry. Sean Connaught, called in for intelligence, had donned his best white uniform and polished his saber and pistols.

"At three o'clock this morning, Colonel Thornton will cross the Mississippi with fourteen hundred men, and shortly before dawn will launch an attack on Andrew Jackson's west bank line. Once Thornton captures the American batteries across the river, he'll shift the gun positions so that they can rake Jackson's main defenses *behind* the Rodriguez Canal. Though Jackson may believe he's safe behind his cowardly ramparts, this will teach him differently. He'll find himself outflanked, and by his own guns. We on this side of the river will launch a frontal attack."

Pakenham turned to Colonel Mullens. "If you'd be good enough to repeat your orders."

Mullens cleared his throat and stammered, "During the night, my unit will creep as close as possible to the American lines, and with the rocket signal, attack." He paused, then added hurriedly, "We'll be carrying fascines of sugar cane, and scaling ladders. No matter how heavy the fire from the American lines, we're not to stop until we've thrown the bundles of cane into the canal until it's filled, then cross over and set up the scaling ladders on the embankment."

"Exactly," Pakenham said. "The second wave of troops will be directly behind, and they'll scale the ladders while our riflemen pick off any Americans foolish enough to show their heads above the ramparts."

Pakenham finished the rest of the details and then dismissed his men. As Sean was leaving, he called him aside. "I say, Connaught, it might be wise for you to check on Mullens. He's

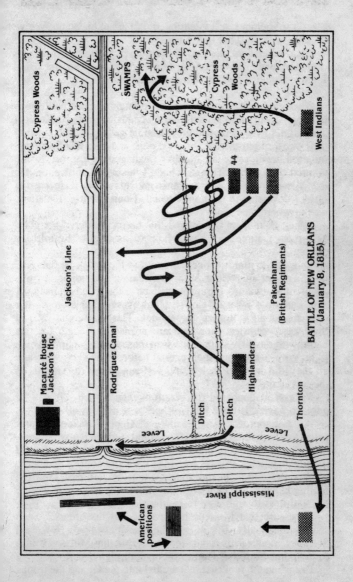

BATTLE OF NEW ORLEANS
(January 8, 1815)

Cypress Woods

Macarté House
Jackson's Hq.

Jackson's Line

Rodriguez Canal

Levee

Mississippi River

American positions

SWAMPS

Cypress Woods

West Indians

44

Pakenham
(British Regiments)

Highlanders

Ditch

Ditch

Levee

Thornton

a good soldier and well intentioned, but apt to be vague. We've no idea how he'll act under fire."

Sean nodded and left. All during the preparations, Sean was obsessed with one idea—to breach the American line, find Jeremy Brand if he was there, and kill him.

Though General Pakenham had thought out the battle plan in great detail, unforeseen snags began to develop. Colonel Thornton's expedition had great trouble getting their boats into the river through the canal they'd dug, and instead of fourteen hundred men, only six hundred managed to get off in the allotted time. Also, Thornton hadn't made any allowances for the Mississippi's strong currents and his boats were carried farther downstream than anticipated. Consequently, his attack was nowhere near ready.

When Pakenham discovered this he reconsidered his plan. "Thornton's force will be no help to us at all," he told his officers.

One of the junior officers urged that the attack be delayed, but Sean cut in, "General, if we remain any longer in this pestilential swamp, our men will be totally demoralized. A man can fight what he can see, but every night more of our men are found with their throats cut. This very night we lost three more sentries. Our men are primed and eager for this battle with the dirty shirts. I've seen these American militiamen fight; why, we burned their capital before their very eyes, and all they did was lift their skirts and run. They're cowards to the last man."

Pakenham pondered his position, then sighed. "It will be good to have this dirty job finished once and for all."

As day approached on January 8, General Pakenham prepared to fire the rocket signal that would start the British charge. "I trust you made sure that Mullens has gotten his fascines and scaling ladders," he said to Sean. "It's imperative that there be no interruption in the attack. First the fascines, then the scaling ladders, and then the troops following hard upon them." He said it as though it were in litany.

"I'm sure that Mullens has carried out his orders," Sean said automatically. But in truth he hadn't checked. However, Sean put it out of his mind. Inconceivable that Mullens would forget something that vital to the overall plan.

But when the rocket signal arched into the air and the troops moved forward in perfect cadence, Sean discovered that Mullens had indeed forgotten to bring along the fascines and the ladders!

Sean began to curse at him and Mullens dissolved into a mass of nerves. "Is it any wonder that I forgot? My men have been fighting off guerrilla attacks all night long!"

"I'll see you're hung from the highest yardarm for this!" Sean swore and slapped Mullens across the face. Then he sent the troops back to get the equipment.

But by the time the ladders and fascines were finally brought to the front ranks, dawn had broken and the British had lost the advantage of surprise.

General Samuel Gibbs and his Scottish Highlanders attacked the American left and center with a force of about three thousand men. The eerie sound of the bagpipes floated across the savannah to be answered by the American fife and drum corps playing a spirited rendition of "Yankee Doodle." As the British advanced across the open fields they came within range of the American artillery.

"Fire!" General Jackson shouted, and the cannons spewed forth their molten death, tearing gaping holes in the concentration of redcoats. With superb discipline, the British soldiers filled in where their comrades had fallen.

"They'll be within rifle range soon," General Jackson shouted as he rode up and down the line, offering encouragement. "Take aim, my boys, and make sure that every shot counts! And keep up that 'Yankee Doodle Dandy'!"

Then the charging British soldiers carrying their fascines and scaling ladders came within rifle range, and the Kentucky and Tennessee marksmen opened up. The red line of soldiers wavered under the fierce volley, re-formed, then wavered again as the second line of marksmen stepped forward behind the American ramparts, fired, then stepped back to allow the third line to fire. By that time, the first line of marksmen had reloaded and were ready, and so the fiery, unrelenting death poured into the British ranks. Unnerved, the redcoats dropped their ladders and fascines and returned the fire, causing hopeless confusion to the soldiers coming up right behind them.

Near the river on Jackson's extreme right, some British troops managed to penetrate the American lines, but most of them were trapped and the remainder were cut down by the heavy fire.

Jeremy and Wingate were in the thick of the battle, Wingate loading Jeremy's guns and handing them to him. As Jeremy fired again and again, he felt at last that the rape of Washington had been avenged. Yet he was sickened at the sight of the terrible carnage. Some men literally had their heads torn off, others lost limbs, and the bodies of the British began to fill the ditch.

To Jeremy's left, a thirty-two-pound cannon loaded with musket balls hit a division of charging men squarely in the center, killing two hundred of them outright. The fields ran red with the blood of the dead and dying. Then, unable to withstand the fierce firepower, the British line broke and ran!

"Stop, you cowards!" General Gibbs shouted, waving his sword overhead, but a fusillade of bullets smashed through his body. He too fell dead.

Seeing that the attack on the right was failing, General Pakenham tried to rally his men for a final assault. Early in the battle his knee had been shattered by a bullet and his horse shot out from under him. Now he mounted another horse. "Strike at the American line," he shouted, and galloped forward. "We must do it now or lose!" he called to Sean Connaught, who had also mounted a horse and galloped beside him.

The fields were marked with dead soldiers, but finally the decimated ranks of redcoats reached the canal. But with no fascines to fill the moat, and no scaling ladders anywhere, all they could do was stand there helplessly and take the bullets fired by the marksmen. Then those soldiers too broke and ran.

"Run damn you, run!" Jeremy shouted as he aimed at a redcoat and saw him stumble into the ditch.

"Regroup, regroup!" Pakenham shouted at his retreating men, and then another bullet struck him, this one in the spine. With a gasp, he fell from his horse. The blood gurgled from his mouth as he whispered, "Lost through want of courage!" and then he rolled over, dead.

Sean Connaught didn't take time to help his commander. His only thought now was to reach the American line. If but one British soldier could breach it, then the others would take courage and follow and the day would still be theirs.

"Over there, look!" Wingate exclaimed, grasping Jeremy's arm. About two hundred yards away they saw a rider, dressed in the immaculate white uniform of a captain in his majesty's navy, charging forward on his stallion. As he dodged and weaved through the field, he miraculously avoided being hit.

"By God, it's Sean Connaught!" Jeremy cried. Without another word he tore himself from Wingate's grasp and climbed over the rampart. He was impeded by his wounded arm, but finally he reached the top. He stood up and shouted, "Sean, Sean Connaught!"

All about Jeremy, the marksmen stopped firing to see what madness infected this man. Sean didn't hear Jeremy, but kept charging straight for the moat. But then he saw the figure on the ramparts, and wheeled his horse in that direction, irresistibly drawn to the man who stood like a sentinel stone.

It wasn't until the man clambered down the far side of the rampart and waded through the four-foot-deep canal that Sean realized who it was. Digging his spurs into his horse's flank, Sean made straight for him. "The good Lord has answered my prayers!"

"Oh God, somebody," Wingate yelled. "Jeremy can't fight him off! Not a man on a horse!"

Though he'd never raised a gun against anybody in his life, Wingate cocked the rifle and aimed for Sean Connaught, just as other shots rang out. But the gunshots succeeded only in killing Sean's horse. Sean rolled to the ground, and recovered in time to see Jeremy coming at him from the near side of the canal.

Sean drew his saber and charged at Jeremy, a man possessed. Jeremy took quick aim and fired, but the flint of his rifle had gotten wet in the moat, and the gun clicked harmlessly. Then Sean was upon him and Jeremy fell back before his attack.

Sean lunged and Jeremy barely had time to dodge, the saber slicing through his buckskin jacket. Jeremy grabbed the barrel of his rifle and swung wildly, seeing Marianne's face as she'd taken the bullet meant for him. And all because of the cruelty of this man, this man who'd hounded them to death, this man who'd said he wouldn't be content until he'd seen the United States destroyed.

With a cry of elemental rage, Jeremy swung again. His blow caught Sean on the collarbone and broke it. Sean looked with surprise at his limp arm, and then the saber fell from his hand. He sank to his knees, not believing that this could be happening to him . . . the most intelligent man in his class, the best swordsman . . . being bested by this lout who'd turned his beloved against him? No, he *couldn't* let that happen!

With his free hand he took his pistol from his belt, cocked it, and aimed at Jeremy. The men's eyes met, and then a smile creased the corners of Sean's mouth. "Prepare to meet your hell!"

Before Sean could pull the trigger, a British rocket exploded near them, kicking up sprays of turf and momentarily blinding him. Sean rubbed his eyes, blinked, trying to get Jeremy in his wavering sights.

Jeremy snatched up Sean's saber and lunged.

Sean never felt the cold steel of the sword as it plunged into his throat. But his mouth opened in a circle of horror as he saw his own death. He fell forward, and as he hit the ground, the blade was pushed through to the hilt.

Jeremy's knees were buckling and his guts were heaving, and then somehow Wingate was at his side, supporting him. Dimly, Jeremy became aware that the firing all around them had stopped. He raised his eyes and looked around. The field was strewn with the British dead; those still left alive were running away. And then a great shout rose from the American ranks. The battle had been won! And with that roar ringing in his ears, Jeremy collapsed.

Chapter 23

"THE BRITISH sustained losses of more than two thousand men in the battle for New Orleans!" Rebecca read aloud from the headline story in the *National Intelligencer*. "The American forces, under the command of General Andrew Jackson, lost only seven dead and forty wounded. Surely Jackson is the savior of our nation!"

Rebecca jumped to her feet and whirled around the room, her green cambric skirt flaring. "Never has there been a greater victory," she exclaimed. "Now we're assured that the Louisiana Territory is ours for all time. And England must give up all hope of ever forcing us back into the Empire."

"*And* we shall never be able to annex Canada," Zebulon said sourly.

"True, but I find that a small price to pay for what we've gained," she said. "With this victory, peace must come soon, and with terms more favorable to us. Don't you realize that for the first time the United States will be considered a bona fide power by the world's nations? Our experiment in democracy is an experiment no more, but a living reality."

With a quick twist of his hands Zebulon cracked his knuckles. His face looked moody, and his thick, broad shoulders were slightly hunched, as if he were expecting to be hit. "I find it difficult to get excited about your abstractions," he said. "I haven't wanted to worry you before, but the truth is, we stand the very distinct possibility of being ruined."

Rebecca felt her spirits droop. What had he done this time?

"We've lost two ships running the blockade near the Canadian border," he said.

"Oh, Zebulon! I *begged* you not to get involved with the smuggling trade." She wanted to scream but knew that wouldn't do any good. "What are we going to do?"

He shrugged. "Well, we'll inherit Jeremy's property, and whatever possessions he owns, but that won't amount to much."

Rebecca stiffened. "Is he dead, then? Are you keeping something from me?"

He shook his head. "There's been no further news of him, so clearly he's lost to us."

"But if he is dead, won't everything go to Circumstance?"

Zebulon snorted. "Since when are illegitimate children entitled to share in an inheritance along with good Christians? Thank God the country hasn't yet come to that sorry pass."

Rebecca passed her hand over her forehead. "Jeremy told me he married the child's mother."

"What nonsense!" Zebulon barked. "Marrying an Indian in the wilderness? And with Meriwether Lewis performing the ceremony? What court would believe that?" Then his shoulders slumped. "At any rate, it's all moot, because there isn't enough money to make a difference to us. However, we do have one ship left. I propose to go to New Orleans and pick up a cargo of slaves on consignment. Washington needs to be rebuilt, and there'll be a crying need for slave labor. Just one such cargo and we'll be back in business again."

Rebecca's face drained of color. "Zebulon please, don't do this. What if you're caught? Trafficking in slaves is illegal; you could be imprisoned. And then what about the children?"

"What about the children if we don't recoup our losses?" he demanded. "I won't have my son trapped in the same poverty I was. It's a slow death."

She moved to him and put her hand on his arm, a gentle sign of affection that she hadn't been capable of in months. "Zebulon, whatever our financial difficulties, we can work them out if we do it together. In these past months, the stone works have begun to make money. And it will get better, I know it."

He wavered, caught somewhere between desire for her and the suspicion that she might be using her charms to get her own way. Gently, he loosened her hand and pressed it to his lips. "We'll do both. You've always wanted a free hand with the stone works, and this is your chance. And I'll take the ship to the Indies."

Smarting under his rebuff, she withdrew her hand. But more was at stake now than a mere question of wills. This journey would be a disaster...she felt it echoing in the windswept chambers of her heart. "Don't go, I beg you. I have a dreadful feeling that something awful will happen."

He threw back his head and laughed, a deep rich throaty laugh that seemed to vibrate through the room. "Rebecca, you're getting as superstitious as Letitia and the rest of the slaves." With that, he strode from the room to take Gunning horseback riding.

That night, when Zebulon and Rebecca went to bed, he tried to rekindle the spark of warmth he'd felt earlier in the afternoon. But the moment had passed for her and the best she could do was suffer his advances. With a groan of frustration he turned and rolled to his side of the bed.

She lay there, wondering how many more nights she could endure this. Tomorrow, she resolved, I'll have Letitia turn the sewing room into another bedroom. Put a lock on the door . . . and with those thoughts tormenting her, she finally fell asleep, feeling very much like a prisoner in her own bed.

On the evening of February 15, 1815, President and Dolley Madison entertained a handful of close friends in the main drawing room of the Octagon House. The President sat in a tall wing chair in the high-ceilinged room, looking much like a little lost boy. Dolley fussed about, adding another log to the fire, serving wine and cakes to Dr. and Mrs. William Thornton, and Zebulon and Rebecca Brand. An air of anticipation pervaded the conversation, for momentous news was at hand.

Everybody there knew that Henry Carroll, carrying news from the peace conference in Ghent, had arrived in New York on Saturday, February 11, aboard the *Favorite*. The ship had taken thirty-eight days to cross the Atlantic. The journey by coach from New York would take another five days, but his arrival was imminent.

About nine that evening, at an hour when respectable people were already in bed, the butler, French John Souissat, came into the drawing room. "James Monroe and Henry Carroll are here to see the President."

Dolley clutched her bosom. "Oh, pray that it's good news."

The President rose slowly and approached the tall, dignified Monroe. "Is it peace?" Madison asked in his soft voice.

Monroe straightened to his full height, dwarfing the President. "Yes, we think so. Mr. Carroll has the treaty with him. It awaits your approval."

Henry Carroll handed a copy of the treaty to Madison. Madison clutched the packet, then went to a table and began to read. But Dolley couldn't wait for her husband's assessment. She embraced Mrs. Thornton, kissed Rebecca soundly on both cheeks, and then rushed out of the drawing room into the circular entrance hall. "Peace!" she shouted. "Oh, it's peace at last!"

Her maid Sukie ran down from the upper floors, and the President's freed manservant Jim Smith hurried up from the basement.

"Open the wine cellar," Dolley said. "Serve our best to everybody in the house. And to anybody who comes in from the street! Rejoice!"

The news swept through the city, and people rushed out into the avenues. The night was clear and cold, but nobody cared. A crowd gathered around the Octagon House and serenaded President Madison with a rousing rendition of "Yankee Doodle." One enterprising young lad found some fireworks, which arched into the air, their multicolored sprays blazing joyously in the night sky.

Then somebody began to sing the song that Francis Scott Key had written during the siege of Fort McHenry, and soon all the voices were joined in "The Star-Spangled Banner."

Remembering all that had happened, Rebecca's eyes filled with tears. It had been a long and terrible war, but one that the nation had had to fight for its own preservation. And the Union had survived.

But no matter how profound her joy, it could never be complete, for in some corner of her heart she mourned for Jeremy. Zebulon was right: he must be dead, for every effort she'd made to locate him through the War Department or through Dolley's good offices had come to naught.

And then she could think on that no more, for the crowd was swirling around her, pushing the melancholy thoughts from her mind. She stood on the steps of the Octagon House and called out, "This night, who would *not* be an American?"

Washington stayed drunk for two days. When Rebecca recovered sufficiently, she wrote an article for Joseph Gales of the *National Intelligencer,* on the significance of the war.

"In these glorious days, who would not be an American?" Rebel Thorne began. "To those who complain that we gained no territory, I submit that we gained something even greater, a compelling sense that we are one people. Can a nation ask for anything more? Everything will follow if we but believe in ourselves and in our destiny. Our vast West with all its riches beckons to us, and I see a shining future with the United States leading the entire world to a new appreciation of the dignity of man. Oh, quickly, let us rebuild our American Palace, this palace of our spirit. I celebrate this victory, I celebrate our people, I celebrate our nation!"

Several days later, over the tears and protests of Gunning and Suzannah, Zebulon prepared to sail from Georgetown in his merchant ship. He clambered into the rigging and called down to the children, who waved to him from the dock: "I'll only be gone a few months, and when I come back, this ship will be loaded with treasures for all of you!"

Rebecca watched as the sails caught the wind and the ship moved out of the tiny harbor. She'd heard Zebulon say the same thing so many times, and so many times she'd seen it all ruined. Was there some flaw in her husband that would always insure that he failed? All the schemes he'd been involved in since his youth . . . Selling government lots from a pirated copy of a secret map of the Federal City layout. That venture had never worked because his prices had been so exorbitant. Then his involvement with Aaron Burr's mad scheme to split the United States in two. Then his smuggling ventures which had cost the Breech-Brand enterprises their two best ships. And now he was risking their final vessel in illegal slave trade. Always the lure was the chance at an instant fortune. And always the schemes failed.

Gunning, clutching her skirts with one tiny fist, shook his other fist at the dwindling sails. "I want Papa back! I want him!" He started to cry and when Suzannah tried to comfort him he punched her. Rebecca picked him up and kissed him. Then she gave the boy to Letitia, who carried him to the carriage, all the while trying to avoid his pummeling fists.

"Never did see a child as mean as you!" she cried.

Rebecca swung Suzannah into the carriage. Well, with Zebulon gone, she'd have several months of freedom. But she had to make up her mind to do something. She couldn't go on this way, living with somebody she no longer loved, enduring his demands because of a legal document. She'd seen the same thing happen to her own mother, and it had led her to an early grave. "No," Rebecca said suddenly to Letitia. "I won't let that happen to me."

That afternoon she went to see Francis Scott Key on M

Street in Georgetown. "I want to divorce my husband," she said. "I don't know how I'll manage, but I will. And not only will I survive, I'll also flourish! It's time for me to show the world that I don't need anybody but myself!"

Key let her talk until she'd exhausted her foul humors about Zebulon. When she'd quieted he said, "Whatever you decide to do, it will have to wait until Zebulon comes back. There'll be questions of answering your charges, the disposition of the property, the custody of the children."

"He can have whatever he wants," she said. "Except for the stone works, which belonged to my father, and the children— they belong to me."

Francis Scott Key leaned back in his chair. "Well, though divorce is frowned on, you do have certain rights. In all probability, the stone works would go to you. And barring some outrageous behavior on your part, like adultery, the court would probably grant you custody of the children. But as I said before, you must wait until Zebulon returns."

"All right, then, I'll wait. But I want you to institute proceedings the *moment* he comes home."

Feeling righteous, Rebecca left the Key home. "Well, at last I've done it," she said to herself. Whichever way her life turned out, at least it would be by her own design.

A week later, while Rebecca was recaning a chair, Letitia answered a knock on the door and screamed. Rebecca rushed into the hallway and came face to face with the ghost of Jeremy Brand. She stared at him, unable to speak. He looked like a shade, having lost thirty pounds. Every bone in his face showed through the translucent skin. Her impulse was to clasp him to her bosom, comfort him, but all she could do was stare at him.

Jeremy took Rebecca's silence as annoyance and tried to explain why he'd come here. "I've just arrived on the packet boat from New Orleans. I stopped at my house, but Circumstance and Tanzy weren't there and I wondered..."

Suzannah came tripping through the entrance foyer and stopped dead when she saw him. "Uncle Jeremy!" she cried, and flung herself at him. Then the dam was broken and they all crowded around him—Gunning, who'd run in, and Suzannah, and Letitia, and then somehow Rebecca found herself in his arms, feeling his strong embrace, her heart overflowing with an indescribable happiness.

"Letitia, some tea, food, quickly," she ordered.

Drying her eyes on her apron, Letitia bustled out into the kitchen and returned with a tray laden with cold chicken, slices of venison, and a wheat loaf she'd baked that morning. Rebecca sent the children off with Letitia, and while Jeremy ate, he told her briefly what had happened. He faltered when he came to Marianne's death, and Rebecca had an overwhelming sensation that they'd had such a scene before . . . when he told her of the death of White Doe, Circumstance's mother.

"Sean Connaught is dead also," Jeremy said. "Killed in the battle of New Orleans." He thought it best to spare her the gory details.

Rebecca set her tea cup down. "I think he leaves two orphaned children in London. Dreadful. I shudder to think what will happen to Victoria when she hears this. I have no love for that woman, but Marianne and Sean were the two people she loved most in the world."

Jeremy nodded. "I'll have to pay my respects and tell her."

Jeremy finished eating and took his leave. When he reached his home, Circumstance and Tanzy were there, and amid the cries and tears of joy they were reunited.

Tanzy fussed and fretted over him. He looked so thin and so sad that her heart ached.

"I knew you'd come back," Circumstance whispered in her father's ear. "Every night before I went to bed, I'd say a prayer to the wind that it would carry you back. And sometimes I saw you in my dreams, and I knew you were alive."

Jeremy crushed his daughter to him. This strange enchanted child was all he had left. "I'll always be with you from now on," he murmured. "I'll never leave you again."

Chapter 24

SHORTLY AFTER returning to Washington, Jeremy went to call on President and Mrs. Madison. Dolley was euphoric at seeing him; they'd had a long and affectionate relationship since the early days of his work on the White House.

After he'd given Madison every detail of the Battle of New Orleans, the President nodded thoughtfully. "Andrew Jackson is a man to watch; he'll be a contender one day for the presidency."

Jeremy nodded. "Sir, what can I do now to help?"

"Why, you must rebuild the White House. The Senate will soon vote on whether to support the House of Representatives design to have the capital remain in Washington."

"But they *must* vote that way," Jeremy said. "What's the alternative?"

"To build a new Federal City deep in the interior of the country, safe from any invading forces," Madison said.

"That would only expose the new capital to the ever-present danger from hostile Indians," Jeremy said. "And what of communications with the rest of the country, and with Europe? How would we ever know what was going on? We could easily find ourselves in another situation like the Battle of New Orleans, where the war raged on even though the details of peace were being worked out."

"My sentiments exactly," Madison said.

"When will we know?" Jeremy asked.

"Sometime next week," Madison said. "Assuming they vote yea, I'm going to appoint James Hoban as principal architect to restore the White House."

"But that's wonderful!" Jeremy exclaimed. "Why, I worked with him from the time I was ten until Benjamin Latrobe replaced him."

Madison nodded. "I'd thought seriously of asking you to be principal architect, but Hoban has given the country great service and deserves this honor."

"Absolutely," Jeremy said. "I'd have it no other way. Every-

thing I learned about architecture I learned from him. It will
be wonderful working with him again."

"Splendid, splendid," Madison said. "Well then, until next
week—and say a little prayer for the wisdom of the Senate."

Dolley Madison saw him to the door. "I see that you favor
your right arm. Is it serious?"

He smiled and shook his head. "It'll take more than a British
bullet to get rid of me. Though I must confess it hurts like the
devil when it rains."

They both laughed. Then Dolley grew pensive. "I've de-
bated long and hard whether to tell you this, but in all fairness,
I must. I know she's far too modest to tell you herself, but
Rebecca moved heaven and earth to set you free. You have a
good friend in that woman."

Jeremy, somewhat surprised by this piece of information,
put it in the back of his mind, where it could do nobody any
harm. But whatever his daylight resolve, darkness had a way
of resurrecting the past, and in his sleep he'd toss and dream
of her. She'd been his first love; he would have married her
a decade ago, but the fates had conspired against that. Once
Jeremy woke in the middle of the night with the drifting forms
of White Doe, Marianne, and Rebecca plaguing him. As soon
as he opened his eyes, two of the shades dissolved into the
darkness, but the memory of Rebecca remained, alive and vital.

"But she's my brother's wife," Jeremy whispered to himself.
And so he held his desires in an iron grip.

A week later the Senate voted to have the capital remain
in Washington, and amid the general rejoicing of the populace,
the planning commission named Benjamin Latrobe to supervise
the rebuilding of the Capitol, and James Hoban to oversee the
construction of the White House.

The greeting between Jeremy and James Hoban was like
that of a father and son. Hoban crushed him in a bearhug.
"How good to have you back," he said. "I told them I couldn't
rebuild it without you, and that's the truth. In fact, you'll have
to take up a lot of the slack now that my bones are old."

Hoban and Jeremy had worked on the original construction
of the American Palace in 1792, and had known each other for
almost twenty-five years. Hoban, close to sixty, was the father
of ten children; his wife was weary indeed.

The winter was still too harsh to commence building, so the

two men spent long hours going over the original plans. Often
Jeremy would sit alone in his studio and try to determine ways
to make the construction go faster. He was dominated by a
passion to rebuild it as quickly as possible, as if to wipe out
the indignity that it and the nation had suffered in that grim
war.

Circumstance would steal to his side and stare at the plans,
asking questions about this room or that, and Jeremy would
spin tales to her of the old days, when John Adams and his
wife Abigail had first lived there, and then Thomas Jefferson,
probably the most brilliant man that the nation had yet produced, and then the Madisons.

"And you worked for James Hoban when you were a little
boy?" Circumstance asked.

He nodded. "Just about your age. You see, when my father
died, we needed money to pay off his debts, or else he would
have been buried in a pauper's grave. So Zebulon sold me as
an indentured servant to Mathias Breech—he was your Aunt
Rebecca's father."

Circumstance listened attentively, making connections in
her own mind.

Jeremy continued, "Well, Mathias was apt to get drunk and
be a little free with his fists, and James Hoban saw that—I
guess it was on the very day that we were laying the cornerstone
of the American Palace—and he bought my indentureship papers. And the moment he did, he freed me. And we've been
friends ever since."

"But why are you and your brother always fighting?" Circumstance asked.

"Who told you that?" Jeremy asked.

"Gunning. He says that you wanted to marry his mother,
but his father got there first. And that I'm a bastard. What's
a bastard?"

Jeremy's fair complexion turned red with anger. "Gunning
is a silly boy, and I'll have to talk to his mother about him."

Circumstance, sensing how angry she'd made her father,
slipped her hand into his. "Papa, I didn't mean to make you
angry. I heard another story. Shall I tell you?"

He nodded.

"I've heard this tale everywhere in the city—oh, all of
Tanzy's friends repeat it, and even the children in the streets.

That the day that the White House falls down and no longer stands on its original foundations here, that is the day the United States will be no more."

Jeremy smiled. "Well, that's a legend associated with many capitals in the world, but I guess it has more meaning now that our palace has been burned. But I promise you, we'll rebuild it just as good as new and it ever was."

One evening he told her about Wingate Grange, and how wonderful he'd been. "In fact," Jeremy said, "I doubt if I'd be here today if he hadn't taken care of me."

"Then I shall love him," Circumstance said. "Where is he?"

"He had to go back to Maine to tell his parents he's all right. Well, perhaps one day he'll come and visit us."

In March of 1815, President and Dolley Madison moved from the Octagon House. Rebecca loaned the Madisons her slaves, Letitia and Eli, to help them pack.

"We must remove to the Seven Buildings," Dolley said to Rebecca. "There we'll be better accommodated, and in a more healthy region. The President hasn't been well since we came to this house, and the servants are constantly sick from the dampness in their basement quarters. We're all coming down with rheumatism."

The Madisons rented the corner house of the complex located at Pennsylvania Avenue and Nineteenth Streets, N.W. The annual rent was five hundred dollars, and they rented another building for office space for three hundred. The new location was still within walking distance of Rebecca's, so she still saw them almost every day.

"Have you had any news of Zebulon?" Dolley asked her.

Rebecca shook her head. "Nor do I expect any for several more months. These sea voyages can be interminable."

Rebecca had confided her dilemma to Dolley, who patted her hand. "I pray all will go exactly as you want it," she murmured.

And then spring came with its fire-green grasses, the ground thawed, and Jeremy and Hoban began a detailed inspection of the White House. The peculiar smell of fire still hung over the wreckage.

"What we must be concerned with first is the removal of

all the damaged walls, and the preservation of any good structure," Hoban said. "With Congress as parsimonious as ever, we've got to economize."

The quarries at Aquia, which had supplied the original stone, had been exhausted, and Hoban sent Jeremy out to look for new sources. He found some suitable quarries near Baltimore, and discovered that Rebecca had already entered into an arrangement with these quarries to transport and dress any stone that they sold. The work drew them together. One day Jeremy said to her, "What an extraordinary coincidence that you'd already contracted for the quarry stone."

"No coincidence at all," Rebecca said. "Remember, I grew up in my father's stone works and have some passing knowledge of building materials. I simply visited all the quarries in the area and chose the two that had similar stone."

Jeremy nodded his head in admiration. Then he said, "The damage is worse than we thought. The walls of the north and south fronts have to be taken down almost to the level of the first floor. The fire cracked the sandstone in a way that's made it unusable. And on the east and west fronts, the center sections that contain the Venetian windows have to be removed clear down to the basement and rebuilt. You can see for yourself the gaping hole on the west side."

"How long do you think it will take to rebuild?" Rebecca asked.

"Well, the first building took ten years before it was ready for occupancy, but we don't have that kind of time. I'd say two years, three at the most."

"Well, then we've our work cut out for us, don't we?" she said. "You'll have the first load of stone delivered within the week."

While stone was being cut for the exterior, Jeremy also had to cope with new wood for the interior. All the wood had to be cut to size, then put in seasoning bins before it could be used. Fortunately, he had all the previous board-foot estimates, and ordered thousands of feet of new mahogany for the interior trim, and also the best grade of yellow pine.

The raw spring winds turned into the gentle breezes of June and then to the stultifying heat of summer. The grounds of the President's House were once again filled with workmen; plaster dust and sawdust filled the air.

Rebecca came daily to observe the building; she ran the

Breech-Brand stone works with a sure hand, economizing wherever she could, instituting new practices; though she ran into a fair amount of antagonism from the local workmen, unused as they were to taking orders from a woman, she not only survived, but prospered.

Only one thing preyed on her mind: the lack of news from Zebulon. She should have had some word from him by now. The children asked daily about their father, and she could only tell them to be patient—but she herself was far from feeling patient. Each day her fantasies about Jeremy grew, and he, immersed in work, seemed to have buried his despair about Marianne. Sometimes she would catch him looking at her . . . she'd seen that look often enough not to mistake it. He still cared for her—she knew that in the very fiber of her being. If only Zebulon would come home! She could resolve everything and get on with the business of her life.

Chapter 25

AS JEREMY watched the building rising again, his own spirits began to take wing. The White House grounds were a hive of activity, and he was now overseeing the work of almost a hundred and fifty men. Thirty stonecutters dressed and fitted the sandstone blocks supplied by the Breech works. Forty carpenters labored with saws, hammers, and nails. Four stone setters fitted the blocks into place on the scaffolding that Jeremy had constructed. Six brickmakers stoked the kilns and baked their bricks. Fifty laborers, some from the old crew of Germans and Irish who'd originally worked on the palace, had been employed. But for the most part the common day laborers were slaves, the strongest chosen to do the heavy work. Jeremy prevailed on Rebecca to rent out Eli to him, and the two men worked alongside each other, more friends than master and slave. Stone carriers whipped their oxen, dragging the blocks of stone. Then they were loaded into sturdy leather cradles and hoisted up to the scaffolding where Jeremy and Eli, along with the four masons, eased them into place.

President Madison, in concert with Hoban and Jeremy, decided this was the appropriate time to begin the construction of the South Portico. "From start to finish, Mr. President, it will cost us twenty-one thousand dollars," Hoban said.

Madison approved the figure and the work progressed. In short order Jeremy was able to report that the foundation was laid and the arcade of the basement was ready to be set.

The South Portico had originally been designed by Benjamin Latrobe during his tenure as chief architect of the mansion under President Jefferson. But the elliptical portico Hoban chose to build was substantially different in design. The two architects had totally different attitudes about the philosophy of building. Whereas Latrobe preferred grand designs that would call attention to the architect, Hoban preferred to construct any new additions in the style of the building. And so in his version of the South Portico, he had two small flying staircases descending in a graceful sweep from the main floor to the ground level, leaving the center open for a direct approach to the basement. Madison thought this might allow for a dignified approach to a reception room located there, perhaps for diplomats. The portico was graced by six columns, two stories tall, with capitals of the Ionic order, but with American roses in full bloom decorating the four sides of each column.

The North Portico was also begun, and Jeremy estimated it would cost twenty-seven thousand dollars.

The summer gave way to the melancholy rush of fall, and with the fresh autumn winds the danger of Potomac fever was swept away. The pace of rebuilding the capital increased, for as much construction as possible had to be finished before the onslaught of winter.

One evening, Rebecca sat before the fire in her study, reading the Bible to the children. Suzannah sat at the foot of her mother's chair, one arm flung over Rebecca's knees. Gunning poked and jabbed at the fire, sending sparks flying onto the hearth. Rebecca read, "And Cain talked with Abel his brother: and it came to pass, when they were in the field, that Cain rose up against Abel his brother, and slew him. And the Lord said unto Cain, Where is Abel, thy brother? And He said, I know not: Am I my brother's keeper? And He said, What hast thou done? the voice of thy brother's blood crieth unto me from the ground."

Rebecca stopped when she heard a knock on the door. "Who can it be at this hour?" Letitia was in the kitchen, preparing the dough for tomorrow's bread and so Rebecca answered the door.

A sailor with his hat in his hand and a muffler around his neck shifted from leg to leg, obviously distressed. "Ma'am, I—my name is Ezekiel Bight, and I was the ship's mate on your husband's vessel, the *Rebecca.*"

Even before he said anything, Rebecca knew that something dreadful had happened. "Come in, please," she said, and led the way to the study.

Ezekiel Bight moved to the fireplace and warmed his back. "Ma'am, this isn't a pretty tale, and maybe the children..."

"I want to stay," Gunning shouted. "Where's my pa?"

"It's all right," she said to Ezekiel. "They have a right to know." She thought it best that they hear it directly from the source; otherwise, they might never believe her.

"Well, ma'am, the cruise started out ordinary enough. The winds were fair, the currents good, and we made good time to New Orleans. There we picked up a cargo of slaves—a good lot of black ivory, Mr. Brand said—and we started back. Halfway home, fever broke out belowdecks—maybe it was the overcrowding, or the heat, who can say?—but every morning we'd consign more of the black devils to the sea. To add to it we were becalmed. Not a breeze stirred for four days; the sun just blazed down and killed more and more of the slaves."

"Oh God, I told him not to go, I told him!" Rebecca said fiercely. "What happened then, man? Please get on with it."

"Mr. Brand and some sailors got into the longboats and began to tow the ship, hoping to bring her to a place more favorable to the winds. For another three days we rowed until we thought our arms would fall off. But then the good Lord sent a saving breeze, and we were on our way again. Or so we thought. But the wind grew stronger, then turned into a gale, until we realized that we were in the grip of a hurricane. It drove us far off course, to sea lanes that few of us knew, somewhere near Pensacola. There we ran aground. The ship broke up within minutes, a terrible grinding against the sandbars that ripped out its hull. We took to the boats, but they were swamped with all hands. For some reason, Providence elected to save me, though the sea gave me up more dead than alive. I lived on that sandspit for months, eating fish and crabs, and searching for my comrades, hoping against hope that somebody else was alive. But all I found were dead bodies. And this."

He reached into his jacket and took out a watch.

"That's Papa's!" Gunning yelled and grabbed for it.

Ezekiel Bight let the boy have it. He looked at Rebecca. "I know it was your husband's, ma'am. Many's the time I saw him look at it. I thought you'd want to have it."

She nodded, then asked softly, "And his body?"

"I gave all of them a decent Christian burial, and marked their graves with a wooden cross. It was the least I could do."

"But Zebulon Brand," Rebecca insisted. "Did you positively identify his body?"

Ezekiel scratched his head. "Well, ma'am, the sea does funny things, and then there's the fish. So I doubt that even a man's own mother would know him for positive. But of course, there's the watch."

Rebecca nodded, her eyes filling with tears. Whatever their difficulties, she'd never wished such a fate on Zebulon. Suzannah saw her mother crying, and began to sob also. And then Gunning joined in, howling lustily for his papa, until Rebecca called Letitia to take them to their rooms. When she'd regained her composure, she asked, "And how is it that you managed to get here?"

"I kept a signal fire going night and day from our ship's wreckage, and one day, after months of hopeless waiting, a British merchant ship spotted it and took me aboard. They dropped me off at Charleston, and I made my way here."

Rebecca listened while Ezekiel repeated the details. Then rose to leave. She took him to the door and pressed some money into his hands. "Thank you for coming. I know you must be needy after such an ordeal. When you're rested, come to the Breech-Brand stone works and I'll see that you're paid your wages for the journey."

"Thank you, ma'am."

"Oh, and one other thing. I'd appreciate it if you told my lawyer the same tale you told me."

Rebecca went upstairs and took the children into her room and allowed them to sleep with her. Long after their tears had dried and they'd fallen asleep, she lay awake and watched the moon shadows on the ceiling. She felt burdened with an indefinable sadness, and more, an indefinable guilt. Did I wish this to happen? she wondered as the silent tears spilled from her eyes. Then, with her children pressed close on either side of her, she managed to fall asleep.

Rebecca went into a period of deep mourning. As soon as he heard the news Jeremy called to pay his respects. "If there's anything I can do, anything you need . . . money?"

She shook her head. "No, nothing. Except . . . a boy needs a father. If you could look in on Gunning occasionally, perhaps take him riding, or hunting . . ."

"Of course," he said. "As soon as his pain's eased."

Rebecca's house was filled with callers. Zebulon and she had been very popular in Washington, and most everybody in the government paid condolence calls. Chief Justice Marshall, who'd married them, came, as did President Madison and James Monroe. Dolley brought hampers of food, and even

Elizabeth Kortright Monroe, wife of James Monroe, who rarely paid any social calls because of ill health, came to pay her respects.

People everywhere, crowding the parlor and the library, speaking softly about the tragedy, kept Rebecca from plumbing her own grief—or worse, from discovering that she had little. After the first wave, the flood of callers diminished, and only Dolley kept up her daily visits, always full of cheer and optimism.

With Zebulon gone, and their last ship lost, Rebecca found herself strapped for available cash. Jeremy tried to give her what little he had, but she refused.

Then one day he said to her, "Why don't you sell Eli to me?"

"Perhaps. Let me think about it," Rebecca said. Rebecca had always felt uncomfortable around Eli; she knew that he hated Zebulon, knew that Zebulon kept him around out of some perverse need to lord it over the slave. Now here was the perfect chance to get rid of Eli, and in a way that would benefit her and the children.

About a week later, when Jeremy came to the stone works for some supplies, she said to him, "All right, I will sell Eli."

Rebecca had Francis Scott Key draw up the papers. Jeremy didn't tell Eli anything about his plans until he'd paid Rebecca. Then he brought Eli back to his house. Tanzy and Circumstance were smoking some meat and stopped when the men came into the kitchen. Jeremy poured them all glasses of hard apple cider.

"I don't believe in slavery," Jeremy began. "I think a man will work twice, three times, as hard for something he really believes in, especially if he's free. And so . . ."

He reached into his pocket and handed Eli the papers. "From now on, you're a free man. Says so right there."

Eli stared at him, stunned. "I can't read!" he blurted.

"Take my word for it," Jeremy said, grinning. "You're free. And I've already registered the papers with the government."

Silent tears rolled down Eli's ebony cheeks.

"All I ask is that you work for me long enough to pay back some of the cost of buying you," Jeremy said.

"Oh, yes, yes!" Eli exclaimed. He gripped Jeremy's hand. "You'll never regret this. I swear it on the blood of my father."

Then Eli turned to Tanzy and crushed her in his arms. "Free!" he whispered again and again, "free."

Within a few weeks Eli and Tanzy were married, Jeremy serving as witness for the couple. Eli tried to find lodgings near Jeremy, but Washington was hostile to free Negroes living in the heart of the city. Finally, Eli and Tanzy moved across the Eastern Branch of the Potomac to a settlement of free blacks in Anacostia.

Every morning at dawn they'd row across the river. Tanzy would go to Jeremy's house, to do the household chores and to look after Circumstance; Eli would join Jeremy's work gang at the White House. The couple worked harder than they ever had, but they flourished; they were both free now, and that made all the difference.

"Still, I don't like the feeling in Washington," Eli said one evening to Tanzy. "It's still a southern city, and I think there's a better place for us."

"Where?" she asked.

"I don't know. New York, maybe, or Pennsylvania. And as soon as we work off our debt to Jeremy, then I'm for looking for some land to homestead. What do you say?"

She clasped her hands together. "I don't know. I love that child so."

"They could always come visit us, couldn't they?" Eli asked softly.

Recognizing how she'd upset her husband, Tanzy said quickly, "Of course they could. I'll go wherever you want."

He slipped his arm around her waist. "Only a few more years then, maybe sooner, and we'll really be free, working on our own land."

The new year came in with the ringing of the new bronze bell at the Church of St. John. Designed by Benjamin Latrobe in the form of a Greek cross, the church was being erected on the north side of the President's square. President Madison had already come to worship there—though it was still incomplete—thus establishing it from its inception as the church of the Presidents.

Rebecca stood at the window of her drawing room, watching a gentle snow fall, and wondering what might happen to her next. She remembered an old wives' tale that her mother had once told her, that whatever you do on New Year's Eve, you'll do for the rest of the year. But she couldn't countenance the thought of another year of such loneliness. Across the snow-dusted fields she saw the dim outline of the White House. Each day it looked more complete, at least from the outside. All the cracked and crumbled stone had been replaced, and the outlines of the North and South Porticos were beginning to take shape.

Jeremy had told her, "The American Palace will be grander now than when it was first built." Rebecca saw him almost every day, thrown together as they were through business. His preoccupation with completing the building had helped him forget his own recent tragedy. But if he had any idea at all that she existed—as a woman with deep desires and passions—he gave her no sign. Wearily, Rebecca turned from the window and made her way upstairs to her empty bed.

"Miss Rebecca, you got to stop that pining," Letitia said. "Mister Zebulon wouldn't have wanted it."

A lot you know, Rebecca thought. But her maid was right: she had to lift herself out of this despondency. She plunged into writing again, anything to occupy her mind. But it wasn't her mind that was rebelling, but her body, fraught with a growing groundswell of desire. Daily, she took to going to the Little Capitol, the long low brick structure just completed where Congress was temporarily meeting. There she listened to the three great orators of the land, John C. Calhoun of South Carolina, Henry Clay of Kentucky, and Daniel Webster of Massachusetts. Each in his own right was hypnotic and compelling: Clay, given to carousing of nights, and to hard liquor that just seemed to oil his tongue . . . Calhoun, the picture of the perfect southern gentlemen, urbane and witty, and dedicated to the preservation of states' rights . . . and Daniel Webster— Black Dan as he was called for his jet black hair, piercing eyes, and beetle brow—who lost no opportunity to raise the question of abolishing slavery. At the moment, the debate raged over protective tariffs. Calhoun, arguing for the South, was in favor of the protective tariffs; Webster, championing the North, argued against.

Rebecca recognized the question as dangerous, but she found that her pen had lost its heart; instead of striking sparks with her articles, she could only sow dissension. "I am turned into something poisonous," she whispered, and watched her tears blur the ink on the page. She ripped the sheet into shreds and threw it into the wastebasket, aware that her own mood was dictating her feelings about political matters. She wondered whether congressmen were as vulnerable to their own moods.

A piece of legislation might or might not pass, depending on whether a senator's domestic life was serene. It seemed like such a fragile way to govern, yet she knew no better way.

Here was a lesson to be learned: a certain selflessness had to dominate in the decisions of the truly dedicated lawmaker. But the nation was still caught in the battle of regionalism, each party seeking what was good for the North, South, or the frontier, rather than what was good for the country as a whole.

The months dissolved one into the other and Rebecca moved through them like a sleepwalker. It registered but made little impression that Suzannah was growing into a charming, sensitive child, with a disposition so sweet that she beguiled everybody. Gunning, without his father's constant attention, had grown even wilder. The times when Jeremy had taken the children out, Suzannah and Circumstance had gotten along wonderfully well, but Gunning resented Jeremy, resented Circumstance, and let them both know in no uncertain terms.

In some secret chamber of Rebecca's being, a place known only to women at a certain moment in their existence, Rebecca recognized that her life was contracting.

I'm nearly thirty-seven years old, she thought. Soon, I won't be able to bear children. This loss threatened and frightened her. She knew that if she was ever to have another chance at love, love in its fullest ramifications, the time was now. The need and the sureness of it grew more compelling with each passing day.

But just as people have a way of shaping events, so events have a way of shaping their lives, and in the fall of 1816, an opportunity for Rebecca presented itself in the form of Dolley Madison. She came to Rebecca's house in full sail.

Chapter 26

"I CAN only stay a moment," Dolley said, "my carriage awaits me to take me to the next home. My dear, we must all work for the election of James Monroe as our next President. Mr. Madison believes him to be the best choice for the difficult decisions that lie ahead. We cannot let the Federalists win, not after they talked of seceding from the Union. And Mr. Rufus King, who will carry their banner, is the worst kind of Federalist."

"I couldn't agree with you more," Rebecca said, suddenly galvanized into energy. She pledged some money for Monroe's election campaign, promised to speak to all the legislators she knew personally, but it was with her quill that her real work began.

"Elect a Federalist?" Rebel Thorne demanded. "Why that would be like turning one's back on a highwayman intent on mayhem! Let us never forget that it was the Federalists who called for the Hartford convention and came to Washington with their demands for an immediate surrender to the British, and on the British terms! If we didn't heed their demands, they would secede from the Union. How can anybody believe that such a party deserves the support of any loyal American? Thank God Andrew Jackson's victory at New Orleans sent these traitors back to their homes with their tails between their legs. And now can they ask us to elect Rufus King?"

Rufus King threatened to shoot Rebel Thorne on sight, the Federalists tried to downplay the charges, but the *National Intelligencer* printed and reprinted the articles; papers in Boston, New York, and Philadelphia reprinted them. Monroe was elected with an electoral vote of 183 to 34.

"If it's not one crisis it's another," Dolley Madison said to Rebecca as they rode to Georgetown. "Really, the way the various branches of the government carry on, it's like dealing with children."

"What is it this time?" she asked.

"Well, James Monroe told John Gaillard, the acting President of the Senate, that he planned to take the presidential oath of office this Tuesday, the fourth, at noon in the chamber of the House of Representatives."

"It's a pity that the Capitol Building couldn't be finished in time for the inauguration," Rebecca said. "Every time I see that little brick building, I'm reminded of what the British did."

Dolley nodded. "Anyway, the Senate decided they would put their wonderful red chairs in the upstairs chamber of the House."

"That seems very generous of them," Rebecca said. "They usually won't even give the House the time of day."

"Isn't that the truth," Dolley said. "And so the House turned the tables on them! Not only did they refuse to take the chairs, claiming that they preferred their own plain democratic chairs, but Speaker of the House Clay is throwing his weight around and claiming that he fears for the safety of the building if too large a crowd congregates, the implication being that very few from the Senate will be invited upstairs! What ever shall we do?"

Dolley's carriage bumped along the road to Georgetown. Her gown, gold jewelry, and feathered headdresses had all come from Paris, but there were last-minute things she needed for the inaugural ball.

Dolley's yellow coach with the puce interior and yellow curtains on the windows was a familiar sight to the citizens of Washington and Georgetown, and many people waved as she passed. Dolley waved and called out to those she knew.

"I can't imagine Washington without you," Rebecca said. "You've been friend, confidant, even a mother to me these many years."

She squeezed Rebecca's hand. "And I've seen you grow from a girl into one of the most beautiful women here. Maturity becomes you, my dear; these hard times have softened and mellowed you. And I'll make a prediction: if you keep that softness, you'll grow even more beautiful. For beauty is just a reflection of the spirit, isn't it? And if the spirit is beautiful, then it must ultimately shine through."

Rebecca felt on the verge of tears, and leaned over and kissed Dolley's cheek.

When they got out of the carriage Dolley exclaimed, "What a wonderful day! It's as mild as summer, and here it is only the first of March."

"Then that's the answer, isn't it?" Rebecca asked as they hurried into the crowded dry-goods store. "Why not have the inauguration outdoors?"

"But where?" Dolley asked. "And how will people see? There isn't a building left standing in Washington that's large enough to hold the crowds."

"There must be minds finer than mine that can figure out where to hold an open inauguration. Perhaps even build a structure, like at the racetrack, that can hold a few hundred people and give them a view of the proceedings."

"Quickly, then, buy whatever you need; we must return posthaste to Washington," Dolley exclaimed. "I must tell this to Mr. Madison as soon as possible. All isn't lost yet."

"I'm sure Jeremy Brand would be able to build something that's satisfactory," Rebecca said.

"But of course. The man has golden hands. Hurry, we must fly!"

Dolley told James Madison who told Monroe, and they made a hurried trip to the White House, where they found Jeremy completing the last course of stone on the top floor. Madison and Monroe told him the plan and asked, "Is such a thing possible?"

"It would be better if we had a month," Jeremy said. "But since that's impossible, we'd better start right now." He scrambled down from the scaffolding and called the work crew together, quickly outlining what had to be done. Wagons were rounded up; they took all the available lumber, gathered more when they got to the construction site at the old Capitol, and work began to build a temporary portico and viewing stands at the front of the little brick Capitol building.

"This will be Washington's first presidential inauguration held outdoors," Jeremy said. "To my mind it's the better way. We'll erect a platform, and the President can deliver his inaugural speech to the crowd instead of everybody being crammed into a chamber."

For two days hammers and saws never stopped. At last, on midnight of March 3, with torches held aloft so that the men could see to hammer the final nails, the platform and viewing stands were completed.

"The gods seemed to have smiled on our efforts," Rebecca said to Dolley and James Madison, as they rode along in the Madison carriage. They were part of the throng of citizens on horseback, in carriages, and on foot who were escorting James Monroe from his residence at 2017 I Street to the little brick Capitol.

"Don't you think James Monroe looks splendid?" Dolley asked.

"Yes, though a bit old-fashioned," Rebecca said.

Monroe was tall, slender, and at fifty-eight was in the prime of his life. He was considered somewhat of a vain man. Though styles had changed considerably, and most men in the nation had long ago adopted the wearing of long pants, Monroe still affected tight knee breeches, white socks, and shoes with silver buckles. His cutaway coat showed his fine physique and taut waist, and the lace stock at his neck framed his handsome face.

"Whenever I look into those clear blue eyes, I think of what Thomas Jefferson said of him," Dolley exclaimed. "That if you turned James Monroe's soul inside out, there would not be a spot on it."

Members of the Marine Corps marched nearby, followed by the Georgetown Riflemen, and corps of infantry from Alexandria. The military considered Monroe one of their own; he'd left William and Mary College at the age of eighteen to join the Continental Army, and that experience had left a lasting impression on him.

The entire party arrived at the little brick Capitol. Monroe, President Madison, the Supreme Court justices, and other members of the illustrious company went inside to the Senate chamber on the main floor, where Vice-President-elect Daniel Tompkins was sworn into office. Then they repaired to the elevated platform outdoors, and were cheered by the crowd in the stands.

"Have you ever seen so many people?" Dolley whispered to Rebecca as she looked out at the sea of faces. "There are at least seven or eight thousand people here. Did you ever think you'd see such a thing when Washington first became our capital?"

Rebecca only half-heard her, for she'd spotted Jeremy in the crowd. He was standing at the foot of the stands with a worried expression on his face, as though expecting the structure to collapse because of the throngs who'd clambered onto it, trying to get closer to the President-elect.

Chief Justice Marshall, who had been a classmate of Monroe's at William and Mary, rose and administered the oath of office. The moment Monroe finished, artillery salutes sounded from the Navy Yard, the Battery, and Fort Warburton.

The President and his wife were escorted home, where he received the visits of foreign dignitaries, members of Congress, and the Supreme Court. Then those same visitors went to call on former President Madison and Dolley.

"What will the capital be like without you?" Rebecca said to the Madisons. "It seems like you've always been here."

"It has been long, hasn't it?" Dolley said.

"Interminable," Madison said in a near-whisper.

"Seventeen years of my life," Dolley said. "And I must say the happiest of them."

Rebecca felt a pang of apprehension. With Dolley in the White House, she'd always been assured of a warm welcome; there hadn't been an important political or social event in which she hadn't participated. But Elizabeth Kortright Monroe was bound to be another story. She lacked Dolley's pervading warmth, and had firm ideas of her own as to how the President's House should be run. Already she'd announced that she wouldn't continue Dolley's habit of returning social calls. The rumored reason was her ill health, which made traveling over the rutted roads so difficult. But there were other reasons; Elizabeth Kortright had been born into an extremely wealthy Tory family in New York, and though her father lost his fortune in the Revolutionary War, she'd never lost sight of her aristocratic background. Her travels on the Continent with her husband while he was minister to France had further made her into a highly sophisticated and cosmopolitan woman. In comparison to the grand capitals of the world, Washington represented a step down to her.

"Well, my girl," Rebecca muttered to herself, "we shall see how well you manage without a friend at court."

She felt a presence at her back, and then became aware of the smell she knew so well, of wood shavings and tobacco and clean scrubbed skin, and a certain maleness that made her body alert. She turned and faced Jeremy.

His smile was broad, creasing the dimples in his cheek,

dimples not quite so deep as Zebulon's. His intense blue eyes
had their old sparkle, as if a veil had been lifted from them.
Time was slowly healing him.

"Remember the days when only a few hundred people managed to come to an inauguration?" he asked.

She nodded. "I think Washington is beginning to grow up."
She tried to sound nonchalant but her heart was beating loud
enough to drown out her words. "Will I see you at the inaugural
ball tonight?"

He shrugged. "I hadn't thought to go. But if you're planning
to ... Are you going with anybody?"

"I was planning to go with the Madisons," Rebecca said.

"Nonsense," Dolley cried. "You're to pick her up, Jeremy.
What woman in her right mind would prefer an old couple to
the attentions of a handsome young man? I'll hear no more of
it! Escort her and we'll save a place for you at our table."

Rebecca was swept away by Vice-President Tompkins, and
both Dolley and Jeremy stared after her. "It's a pity for such
a rare creature to be unmarried," Dolley said. She looked point-
edly at Jeremy and he blushed.

"She is my brother's wife," he murmured.

"All the more reason," Dolley said, poking his arm. "The
Old Testament is just full of instances where a man would
marry the wife of his deceased brother. Why, you'd just be
following the advice of the Scriptures!"

Chapter 27

"I CAN'T GO —I look terrible!" Rebecca said to Letitia. "Take a note to him; tell him I've taken sick." Rebecca turned this way and that in front of the full-length mirror and despised what she saw. An aging woman in a somber black gown, oppressed by her widowhood.

Letitia went to the closet and came back holding a flame-yellow satin damask dress that had always been Rebecca's favorite. "I can't wear that!" she exclaimed, "Zebulon hasn't been gone a year."

Letitia said nothing, but went about the business of collecting the accessories—a strand of pearls that had belonged to her mother, a silk stole that matched the gown, high-heeled shoes that laced above the ankle, designed to show a lady's instep during the dance.

She protested weakly when Letitia unhooked the black dress and practically pushed her into the other garment. But when she saw it against her skin, giving it richness and life, her protest diminished and an excitement gripped her. "Oh, let them talk!" she said. "They'll talk anyway."

An hour later she was ready. She knew that this was one of her golden nights, when the gods conspired to make everything come out right. Her eyes, tincted with the tiniest drop of belladonna, appeared huge and luminous, changing from topaz to emerald depending on the light and on her mood. She had noticed a few gray hairs in her fall of titian hair, but tonight they weren't visible, and her skin, pampered with rosewater and massaged with an essence of cinnamon and cloves, fairly glowed.

"There!" Letitia said proudly. "Ain't nobody more beautiful than you. Now don't you start crying and ruining all the work we did!"

Rebecca embraced her. "Oh, God—I don't know why, but I feel terrified."

"I know why. And you know why. Long time ago I told

you not to listen to nothing but your heart, and Miss Rebecca, it's your heart talking tonight!"

The children came in to wish her goodnight. "Oh, Mama, you look so beautiful," Suzannah said. "I hated that black dress you wore all the time."

Gunning just glowered. When she bent to kiss him goodnight, he punched her. Reflexively, she slapped him. He stared at her, not crying, not saying a word, but condemnation flared from his eyes.

Jeremy arrived shortly afterwards in a carriage that he'd borrowed from James Hoban. His mouth fell open when he saw her. "You look so—different!" he exclaimed.

He helped her into the carriage. Gunning started for them, mayhem on his mind, but Letitia grabbed him and hurriedly shut the door.

Liveried slaves holding torches aloft lined the street approaching Davis's Hotel. The night was wonderfully balmy, and stars were flung across the sky. Anybody who could afford tickets had come to the inaugural ball, and the hotel was mobbed. The women had outdone themselves; jewels blazed on bodies dressed by the finest couturiers in Europe.

The men also had dressed in their finest clothes. Don Luis de Onís, the Minister from Spain, wore a burgundy velvet outfit with gold buttons and a chestful of medals. The French Minister dazzled the assembly in gold skin-fitting pants, and lace at the throat and cuffs in a metallic gold fabric. But Rebecca thought that none of them cut as handsome a figure as Jeremy in his dark-blue homespun suit. His only concession to style was a ruffled white shirt.

It was the first inauguration since the war, and the mood in the grand ballroom was euphoric. John Quincy Adams was there with his wife, the very English and very cultured Louisa. She looked a little peaked, but then she always was apt to look a little peaked.

"Isn't John Quincy's resemblance to his father uncanny?" Rebecca asked. "The same receding hairline, the same sharp nose, the same scholarly, aristocratic deportment."

Jeremy nodded. "Though he doesn't have nearly the paunch nor the temper of his father. Remember how Abigail Adams ranted and raved about slaves being used to build the White House?"

"And how she hung her laundry in the East Room to dry

because there wasn't any other place for a clothesline?" Rebecca asked, laughing. She drew the Adamses aside and told them the tale, much to their amusement.

"And how is your dear mother?" Rebecca asked. "I cannot tell you what a profound influence she's had on my life."

"On practically everybody's life she touches," John Quincy said. "I suppose one normally says this about one's own mother, but she is a remarkable woman."

"I agree," Rebecca said. She wished that she could tell them that it was because of Abigail Adams's influence that she had begun to write her Rebel Thorne articles. "Martha Washington thought her the smartest woman in America. And so do I," she said. "Oh, they were giants in those days!"

"I confess I agree with you," John Quincy said. "I'm fond of telling this story—my dear Louisa has heard it innumerable times, but it bears repeating now."

Louisa murmured her agreement, and for the first time Rebecca realized how alike Louisa and Abigail looked! She wondered if it was true that men tended to marry women who resembled their mothers. Here was a case for it.

"To begin with, she's a woman of profound moral conviction, much of which she tried to instill in her children, though I fear we'll never come up to her mark. When the fighting broke out around Boston, we were standing on a rise outside of our farm at Braintree, watching the Battle of Bunker Hill. And she said, 'These are the times in which a genius would wish to live. It is not in the still calm of life or the repose of a pacific station that great characters are formed. The habits of a vigorous mind are formed in contending with difficulties. Great necessities call out great virtues."

"And it's true," Jeremy said. "All the men of that time—Washington, your father, Jefferson, Madison, and even Burr and Hamilton—were formed in the crucible of our nation."

"And Monroe is the last of that generation," Rebecca said. "We shan't see the likes of them soon again."

The Adamses moved off to greet other people. Rebecca said, "You know that Monroe has named Adams his secretary of state, don't you?"

"I'd heard the rumor," Jeremy said.

"Dolley said that Monroe had consulted Madison and Jefferson about it, and the Virginians decided that it was best to have the entire country represented in the cabinet. Adams, from the North, for State; Calhoun, from the South, as secretary of war; William Crawford, from the West, as secretary of the treasury. It's time for the country to be healed, fractured as it was between Federalists and Democratic-Republicans."

"Adams as secretary of state?" Jeremy repeated. "Then there's a good chance that he'll succeed Monroe."

"If I know these politicians, they're all jockeying to succeed Monroe. Calhoun is a strong contender—he has the grace of a southerner, and all our Presidents except Adams have come from the South—from Virginia to be exact. But the secretary of state has an excellent chance to succeed to the presidency. After all, Jefferson was secretary of state; so were Madison and Monroe. So Adams is a good possibility, even though he's a northerner."

"Then there's Andrew Jackson—I hold him in very high esteem," Jeremy said. "He strikes me as being presidential timber."

"Yes, I met him at the trial of Aaron Burr," she said. "No question about it, the man has stature. But he's so raw. Do you think the nation's ready for a frontiersman?"

"Well, assuming that Monroe serves two terms, it will be eight years from now."

"That's practically a lifetime away," she said softly.

"Indeed it is, and we'll talk this night away if we don't dance." So saying, Jeremy swept her into his arms.

She moved with him as he glided into a waltz, moving faster in the grand ballroom. Never for a moment did she falter or mistrust him. The great chandelier with its glimmering candles and sparkling crystal drops seemed to send out revolving rays of light. As they spun faster, the couples began to clear the way, and the orchestra, seeing this, played with more verve until the other couples cleared a large space for them on the floor, entranced to see this beautiful-looking couple, she with her skirts and hair flaring, he guiding her with sureness. Rebecca was aware that they were dancing alone, and suddenly she felt very naked under the stares of all Washington. But Jeremy knew nothing save the dance, wedded as he was to holding her in his arms. I'm happy! she thought suddenly, trying to catch the elusive moment. Happy!

The music ended with a resounding finale and the crowd applauded. The young gallants mobbed Rebecca for the next dance. The younger generation of women pouted, piqued that this woman, at *her* age, should still be the belle of this inaugural ball.

But Jeremy, clutching Rebecca's hand, hurried her out of the ballroom. At the door they came face to face with Victoria Connaught. Dressed all in black, with a black veil over her head and long black gloves, she looked like some ancient apparition of death.

Victoria's head snapped alert when she heard Rebecca's voice, and she turned her cataract-veiled eyes in their direction.

Jeremy stopped before her. "Madame Connaught, it's Jeremy Brand."

"I know who you are," Victoria said, hatred contorting her features.

"I've called at your plantation a number of times, but you were always away. I wanted you to know how sorry I was about Marianne's death."

Victoria's lips trembled. Then she whispered, "You killed her." Her trembling finger moved out, pointing directly at Rebecca's heart. "Watch out, he'll kill you too."

Jeremy reacted as if a rapier had gone through his heart. It was Rebecca's turn to hurry him outside. "She's an evil woman, consumed by hatred because she and her Tory cohorts lost the war. Jeremy, she'll say anything to hurt you."

They got into the carriage and drove around the forested lanes of Washington. She saw the tears rolling down his cheeks and she leaned over and kissed them away.

"Don't—you mustn't, or you'll break my heart," she whispered.

He stopped beneath an ancient oak tree just on the outskirts of town. In the darkness, he took her in his arms and kissed her. The kiss had been stored inside of him ever since that night long ago just before he went on the Lewis and Clark expedition. "I love you."

He said it only once, but she captured those words in her heart where they would last her for a lifetime. He spread his cloak on the ground and drew her down to him. They lay there, entwined in each other's embrace, not knowing, not caring where they were except that the completion that had been denied them these many years was suddenly about to happen. In the fear that it would happen too quickly, that they wouldn't be able to savor the wonder of it, they'd stop, gaze at each other, touch, kiss again, until they were inflamed to a point where they had to slip out of their clothes. Her skin prickled with the coolness of the night air, but had she been in the Arctic she would have been warmed by the feelings in her breast. She loved him, she loved him more than life itself, for all these years she'd been living a sort of death, not knowing what love could really be like.

He gazed at her in wonder; the vision that he'd glimpsed so long ago was again a reality before him. He ran his hands over her smooth skin, so white it looked almost ghostly in the moonlight. He kissed her breasts, and felt her clutch his head tighter to her. Then his mouth was all over her, preparing her, building her to a moment when she thought she must faint from desire; and when he became one with her she was ready, welcoming. Whorls of stars, worlds apart witnessed their ageless motion, and the rhythm of love was the rhythm of being, and they moved as one, reaching, building, and then bursting forth in an ecstasy that carried their souls to the stars. Quiet, return, to a place of words whispered for the ages, of promises made never to be broken. Only this time Rebecca knew that they would never be broken. They were both older, wiser, both scarred from the lives that they'd led until this moment. He loves me, she thought. A woman knows such a thing, and she knew it in the depths of her being.

And suddenly she felt so strong, so released from a lifetime of tension, that she knew she could conquer anything. All she need ever do was remember this moment, and know that the gods had allowed her to have it. She felt so exhausted she could barely move. Yet somehow he was aroused again, demanding, insistent. The Brand blood flowed in these two brothers, and there was no denying them when their blood surged; one might just as well try to stop the sap in a tree.

She hadn't been prepared to lose all control, every vestige, until she might have been some wanton, dancing naked around a fire, or a bacchante in a religious rite, drunk on love and the worship of his body. If she could have devoured him she would have, but she found instead that he led her to places never dreamed of before, opened the door to her life.

Chapter 28

AND SO their love began in earnest. Whatever their youthful passions had been, they had been tempered and forged by maturity. Rebecca was like a changed woman, and everybody in Washington remarked about it. Tongues wagged, but tongues wag in any small town, Rebecca thought.

Rebecca's father, Mathias, had left her the old Breech house in Georgetown, and though she'd rarely used it before, now it became their meeting place. They agreed not to tell their children.

"Not just yet," Rebecca said. "It's too soon after the loss of their father. Suzannah's no problem, but Gunning—well, he's apt to be difficult."

They made love at every possible moment—as if, having denied themselves all those years, they had to make up for time lost. The days were liquid, melting into each other. Whatever hard edges Rebecca had were mellowed by these months of love; she piled presents on Letitia, smothered the children with affection, and on the rare days she couldn't see Jeremy, she wrote glowingly of the new Monroe administration.

About the new Rush-Bagot Treaty between Canada and the United States, in which each nation agreed to have only eight warships on the lakes, she waxed enthusiastic. "Surely this is a sign that we intend to live in peace with each other. And if we don't have to waste our monies on weapons of defense or war, then we can direct our energies toward capturing the dream that is America.

"As such an example we have the construction of the Erie Canal, which is slated to begin this July fourth. Running 363 miles, with a depth of four feet, the canal will connect Buffalo, via the Hudson River, with New York. This is the kind of ingenuity that America is capable of, for it will open the northern territories to the principal cities on the east coast. Baltimore beware: unless you construct a similar canal, New York will soon outstrip you as the principal seaport in the nation."

•   •   •

"I never believed I could be this happy," Rebecca told Jeremy one evening. They'd just made love, and their bodies glistened with light sweat. The windows were open to the cool evening breezes. Jeremy lay stretched out alongside her, the line of his thigh against hers and the curve of his powerful haunches rekindling a thrill in her. Though he was thirty-five, he still had the physique and the ardor of a younger man. She bent and kissed the ugly scar on his shoulder, and the one on his upper left arm. With a lazy motion she tumbled on top of him, and he rose to the occasion, eliciting a tiny cry from her.

"Oh, don't, I've never—"

He cut her off with a kiss. "And why not? Love is like the sea—you must plunge in, gambol in the waves, and come up laughing." So saying, he began to rise and plunge beneath her. She rode the waves then, exulting in the strange new sensation, until with a quick motion he turned them so that their positions were reversed, and like two twined sea creatures, they rode the crest of their wave to safe harbor.

"We must think of getting married," he said, a while later.

"The children."

"We can't allow them to rule our lives. With some tenderness and a great deal of love, they'll come around, you'll see."

"I'm so worried about Gunning."

"We'll go on a picnic, all of us," he said. "And tell them then."

Though beset with trepidations, Rebecca finally agreed. When she got home that evening, she told Letitia to pack a picnic hamper for the following day, Sunday.

Jeremy arrived with Circumstance. She looked scrubbed, and just a trifle unsure. Gunning stuck out his tongue at her.

"I thought I'd take you all to the President's House," Jeremy said. "You can see the progress we've made. After that, we'll go down to the Potomac and have our picnic."

That really seemed to interest Gunning, and Rebecca breathed a little easier. The grounds were covered with stacks of lumber, piles of plaster of paris, blocks of the Baltimore sandstone. Gunning clambered on top of everything, balancing himself on a plank between two piles of sand.

"He's absolutely fearless, isn't he?" Jeremy said. "He reminds me of the way Zebulon used to be."

"He may look like me, but he's got Zebulon's devilment, I'm afraid," she said.

They entered the White House. Some rooms were already finished; in others the studs and lath were still visible. "The plaster of paris will be mixed with sand and water and horsehair, and then be applied over that," Jeremy told the children. They climbed up to the main floor, and their voices echoed in the huge space of the entrance hall. "Thomas Jefferson said that this entrance was all stomach," Jeremy said, "and large enough for an emperor, the Pope, and the Grand Lama."

Gunning raced into the East Room. The windows had all been restored, and the parquet floors were about to be laid. Circumstance and Suzannah bowed to each other and then began to practice dancing lessons they were learning, looking so adorable in the huge space that Rebecca wanted to dance with them. I can learn to love that child, and I will, she told herself, as she stared at Circumstance's exotic beauty. Then Gunning broke in on the girls and the three of them whirled round and round until their laughter honeyed the air.

Gunning broke free and spun toward Jeremy, "Take me to the next floor."

Jeremy shook his head. "Only the joists are in, none of the floorboards yet. It's just a skeleton."

"When do you expect it to be ready?" Rebecca asked.

"President Monroe wants to hold a New Year's levee in the White House this January. He feels that since John Adams held the first levee on that date when the American Palace opened, that it would be fitting. Everybody in the government will be invited. So we're working as hard and as fast as we can. Of course, we won't be finished—Congress is as stingy as ever with its appropriations—but these rooms on the main floor will be done, and they're the most important."

Jeremy scooped Gunning up and put him on his shoulders. "Reach," he said. "Reach and you can touch the ceiling!"

Then they all went outside and strolled across the grounds, past the elm trees that Jefferson had planted and the mulberry bushes that Dolley Madison had put in, and they chose a spot with a clear view of the Potomac.

"Look! What's that?" Gunning cried, pointing at a strange boat with huge paddlewheels on its sides.

"That's a new steamboat," Jeremy said. "They've got them plying up and down the Hudson River and the Mississippi now, and I bet this one won't be the last you'll see here."

Letitia had packed a huge basket—thick slices of smoke-house ham, southern-fried chicken, a corn loaf and a wheat bread, slabs of freshly churned butter, vegetables and fruit plucked that morning from her garden, and milk still warm from the cow. She'd also included a bottle of Madeira for Rebecca and Jeremy.

After they'd eaten, the children ran off to play along the river's shoreline. "Mind you, watch out for snakes and varmints," Rebecca called after them.

She and Jeremy lay on the blanket, slightly drowsy from the wine and the warm sun, staring up at the fantasy of clouds that swept by overhead.

"I wonder what it is in our youth that makes us all so . . . unseeing," she said. "I keep thinking of the years we've wasted."

"If we had married early on, would our own demons have prevented us from seeing the things we see now?" he mused. "Perhaps the fates were wise in making it turn out so, bringing us together at a moment in our lives when we can truly appreciate our blessings."

"Of course, you're right." And she wondered anew at the sureness of his instinct. Unquestionably she was smarter than he was, sharper, more socially adept. But in the ways of the heart he was like a sage, and that, of course, was ultimately what mattered.

Suddenly their reverie was interrupted by the cries and shrieks of the children. Rebecca collected herself, but Jeremy had already bounded up from the ground and was running toward the commotion.

Jeremy arrived on the scene in time to see Gunning grab Circumstance by the hair. She, being three years older than the boy and as agile as a cat, turned and smashed him in the nose. Caught off balance, he fell and she was atop him in an instant, pummeling him. Jeremy caught her under the arms and yanked her away.

"What's happening, what's going on?" Rebecca cried as she ran up. She took a handkerchief from her bodice and stemmed the blood flowing from Gunning's nose.

"She hit me!" Gunning cried, fighting to get at her. "She hit me!"

Circumstance's face was bloodless and her eyes had turned

as hard as aquamarines. "Look what he did." She pointed to
a freshet where a baby raccoon lay drowned. "He held it under
the water. I saw him, but before I could stop him—" She broke
off, and tears started to the corners of her eyes.

"She's a liar," Gunning cried.

Rebecca turned to Suzannah, who was standing nearby.
"Did you see it?" she demanded.

Suzannah shifted from leg to leg, looking first at Gunning
and then at Circumstance, not knowing where her loyalties lay.
Then she dropped her eyes and whispered, "Gunning did do
it, I saw him."

"She's lying too!" Gunning yelled, squirming to break free
from Rebecca. "Anyway, you said we could, you read it to us
in the Bible."

"What are you talking about?" Rebecca demanded.

"You said God gave us dominion over the fish in the sea
and the animals on the land. You read it to us yourself."

"Gunning, it doesn't mean that!" she exclaimed. "Not tor-
turing some helpless creature. Gunning, you must never—"
She broke off when his flailing fists hit her in the breast. With
a reflexive motion she smacked him across the face.

He burst into tears, wailing more from the shock of being
struck in front of everybody than the hurt. "You wouldn't dare
hit me if Papa was here!" He kicked at Jeremy. "You're doing
this on account of him."

Rebecca hauled him back to the picnic clearing. Gunning
swore under his breath, "It's her fault, that half-breed bastard.
I'll get her for this, I swear."

With the afternoon ending in discord, Rebecca thought better of telling her children about Jeremy. Obviously, it made
more sense to wait a little longer, until they'd grown more
accustomed to the possibility of having a new father.

"Whatever it is you're selling, we don't need any," Tanzy
called to the young man standing at the open door of Jeremy's
house.

"I'm not selling anything," the young man said. "Is this
where Jeremy Brand lives?"

Circumstance came running to the door. "I'm Circumstance
Brand."

"Are you, then?" he said. "Well, your father's told me all
about you. He didn't lie when he said you were pretty."

Circumstance regarded the thin young man. He had a wonderful open smile, warm brown eyes, and curly hair not quite blond, not quite brown. His trousers were too short, and his shirtsleeves also, for he was still growing. His Adam's apple bobbed prominently in his neck. "I know who you are," Circumstance said.

"Who, then? if you're so smart," he said, laughing.

"You're Wingate Grange," she said.

His eyes opened in surprise. "How did you know?"

"My father described you to mè, and I knew that one day you'd come, so I could thank you." She stood on tiptoe and kissed him on his cheek.

She moved out of the sun and he looked at her, really seeing her for the first time. "You're staring," she said.

He caught himself and shook his head. "I'm sorry. I don't think I've ever seen eyes like yours before. They're as pale as the sky."

For what must have been the first time in her young life, Circumstance blushed. They stood there, stumbling over their words, each sensing that something desperately important had just happened in their lives, but too young and inexperienced to know how to handle it. Jeremy found them that way when he came to the door.

He caught Wingate in a bearhug and half-lifted him off the ground. "How wonderful that you're here! How long can you stay? Tanzy, fix something for Wingate to eat; he must be starved."

While they ate, Wingate told Jeremy all that had befallen him since New Orleans. "When I reached our farm in Maine I found everything in ruins. The year before, the British had raided the coast. My mother had died of overwork and grief, and my father—well, he hadn't much cause for living after she'd gone. My brothers and sisters were all scattered; most of them had headed west. I had my choice: to head west also, or to do what I'd always wanted, study and become a doctor. With my family gone, it didn't much matter where I studied, and I heard that the university in Georgetown had a fine course in medicine, and so here I am! I'll have to get a job to earn enough for tuition, but I've a strong back and I'm willing."

"You'll stay here," Jeremy said. When Wingate started to protest, he said, "We've a spare room we can make livable in short order—put in a Franklin stove and build some furniture for you. And I can always use an extra hand on the White House."

"That's wonderful," Wingate said, but then his voice turned solemn. "I can stay only if you'll let me pay my room and board. I couldn't let you or anybody else think that I'd come here to live off you."

Jeremy clapped him on the shoulder. "Whatever makes you comfortable, lad. And why shouldn't you be here? You saved my life twice over; if it weren't for you, I wouldn't be here!"

And so Wingate moved into the Brand household. The first day, exhausted from his trip, he slept around the clock. On the second day he began work at the White House. Jeremy hired him on as a common laborer, and promised to arrange his hours so that he'd be able to start courses at Georgetown when he'd saved enough money.

"I'm going to become the best doctor in the whole United States!" Wingate exclaimed, and something in the boy's ingenuous optimism made Jeremy believe him.

Wingate proved invaluable to Jeremy; not the least of his qualities was his general good humor. He'd haul bags of plaster up to wherever they were needed when the laborers or slaves proved too slow. One day, he scrambled up on the outside scaffolding and started painting the fire-blackened stone with white paint. The scaffolding didn't reach far enough, and in leaning out, Wingate almost fell.

"It's a problem," Jeremy said. "One I've been working on for a long time. Whenever we need to paint a building, a huge structure has to be built."

"What's the answer?" Wingate asked.

"A movable scaffold," Jeremy said. "And I've constructed a model of it; I've got it in my workroom." When they stopped work at dusk, Jeremy showed Wingate the model.

"You see, there are places where lumber isn't readily available, and sometimes it's awfully expensive. But this could be used over and over. A construction or paint crew could carry it around."

"How does it work?" Wingate asked, intrigued.

"Simple. The painter—or stonecutter, or bricklayer—will stand on this basic platform. It has a guard rail in the back so that the worker won't fall off. Huge grappling hooks attach it to the top of the building. By this system of ropes and pulleys, the platform is raised or lowered to whatever height necessary."

Wingate inspected the model. "But once it's in the position, what keeps it there? Won't it fall down, just from the weight of the workers?"

"Ah, that's been the thorniest problem," Jeremy admitted. "You see, other people have been working on a similar device, but it's the problem of how to hold the scaffold in place that's the real stickler. So I've invented this safety lock on the ropes. The moment the upward or downward motion stops, this small gear slips into place and locks the rope in position."

"Wonderful!" Wingate exclaimed. "Will it work?"

"Without a doubt," Jeremy said. "In fact, I've taken it to the Patent Office to get a patent on it. If anybody wants to use it, they can, and then I'd get a small royalty."

"What do you call it?"

"Oh, just movable scaffolding. I figure that one day, if enough royalty pennies come in, Circumstance may have a decent dowry."

"Is she . . . spoken for already?" Wingate asked.

"At eleven? Why, she'll change her mind twenty times over before she marries, I'll wager."

"No I won't," Circumstance said, coming into the work room. "When I've made up my mind, there'll be no changing."

"And how will you know?" Jeremy asked, amused and somewhat delighted to see how intensely Wingate was reacting.

"I'll just know," Circumstance said.

Chapter 29

TOWARD THE end of September, President Monroe began to move piecemeal into the White House. The workmen couldn't help overhearing Mrs. Monroe's vociferous complaints; she preferred the accommodations of their gracious house on I Street to this gaunt shell that seemed like it could never be made into a home.

Jeremy and Rebecca had gone riding into the hills above Washington, and from their vantage point looked across the rolling plain to the city that had slowly begun to take shape again. "The total cost to rebuild the White House, including the porticos, will be half a million dollars," Jeremy said.

"A small price to pay for so potent a symbol," Rebecca said. "And darling, you've made it rise again from the ashes."

He nodded absently. "Well, it has been part of my life since I was a boy. Though I must say I'm not totally satisfied with this final result."

"But it looks wonderful," she protested.

"The facade does, yes. But we could have dealt with the interior in sounder structural ways."

"How so?" she asked. Since her livelihood depended in part on her knowledge of building techniques, she made sure that she always kept up with current methods.

"For one, we used some timbers that were badly fire-scarred. I would have preferred to use new, seasoned beams, but Congress was sparing with its appropriations."

"As usual," she said.

"But my main concern is about the interior walls. When we built the first mansion, they never were on especially solid footings, and the land at Foggy Bottom has become even more unstable."

"But the interior walls don't support the load, do they?"

"No, not at the moment. But if we're building this house for the ages, then we should have a little foresight. Rebecca, wonderful things are happening in the land. We're entering a time when we may see all sorts of vast improvements. For example, there's talk of one day being able to have running water brought into the house through pipes in the walls!"

"Really? How extraordinary!"

"There are other refinements in men's minds that are too dazzling for me to comprehend. But all of those improvements might well have to be concealed within the inner walls, and unless those walls are supported by sound footings..." He paused significantly.

"Then they could sag and pull the roof in," she finished.

"Exactly. But it's almost impossible to persuade Congress to visualize anything as subtle as that. And then, of course, the whole nation wants the mansion rebuilt and occupied as soon as possible."

"That's understandable," she said. "It's a way of quickly forgetting what happened."

"That's the most compelling reason," he agreed. "So we'll just have to make do."

"How close are you to having the whole place ready?"

"I spent all day yesterday unloading the new furniture that the Monroes ordered from France. It's as beautiful as anything I've ever seen. They spent the twenty thousand dollars Congress allotted wisely."

"Monroe had better be careful," she said. "He'd do well to remember that this is an *American* Palace, and deserves to be furnished with the best that *this* country has to offer. Unless we start taking pride in our own artisans, instead of mimicking the French and English, we'll never develop a style of our own."

Jeremy swung her into his arms and kissed her. "The Monroes must have read your thoughts. They've just ordered a batch of other furniture from William King in Georgetown. He charged them sixteen hundred dollars for twenty-four chairs and four sofas."

"Will everything be ready for the New Year's levee?" she asked. They sat against the base of a tree; she picked a buttercup and held it under his chin, seeing the dot of reflected light.

"Ready or not, the public will be there. It's been more than three years in the rebuilding, and the people are anxious to see what they've paid for."

"Well, in a manner of speaking, it is their house, and the Monroes are only its temporary residents. Though from the

way Eliza Monroe Hay is carrying on, you'd think she expected
a lifetime tenancy."

Eliza, the eldest daughter of the Monroes, had been reared
in France when her father had served as minister. She counted
among her friends the great and near-great of European royalty,
and in the rough-and-tumble of Washington society was de-
cidedly ill at ease.

"I know what you mean," Jeremy said. "She's stamped her
foot once or twice with Hoban, demanding changes, but he's
rebuilding it exactly as Congress ordered—a replica of the first
house. But everybody in the city is saying that Eliza has a
serious case of 'queen fever.'" Then he reached for her.
"Enough of them," he said huskily.

They made love then, on the moss-covered earth, rolling
among the bright autumn leaves in their abandon. She exulted
in their love, felt her body become one with the earth while
her spirit soared upward on the shafts of sunlight, and she knew
a oneness so absolute it was akin to an ecstasy. When at last
they were done, she lay sobbing in his arms. He stroked her
hair and soothed her until quiet and reason returned.

"Rebecca, we've waited long enough. And we've hidden
our love long enough. We must get married."

"All right," she whispered.

He propped himself on an elbow. "Next month?"

"The first of the year," she said. "I'll need that much time
to get things arranged. And then it will have been almost two
years since Zebulon died."

"All right, then, the first of the year, right after the President's levee on New Year's."

Crates and boxes continued to arrive from the Continent,
loaded with more furnishings for the White House. From the
I Street house, Mrs. Monroe moved several of their valuable
pieces of Louis XVI furniture. But the White House still looked
bare, and so Monroe sold his entire collection of furniture to
the government to be used in the Palace, with the stipulation
that he could buy it back when he left.

The winter was the mildest in memory. At Christmas time,
people drove around in open carriages and walked the avenues
without their greatcoats. New Year's Day finally arrived, and
the citizens began to arrive at the mansion at around noon. The
reception was planned to last until three; soon the place was

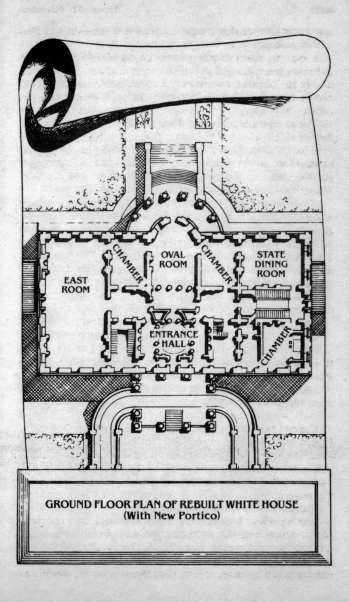

GROUND FLOOR PLAN OF REBUILT WHITE HOUSE
(With New Portico)

thronged with senators, judges, representatives, heads of government departments, foreign ministers, distinguished citizens, and some strangers who happened to be in Washington and had just wandered in.

"It all looks so wonderful," Rebecca said, squeezing Jeremy's arm. She wore a dark-green velvet dress, though she almost hadn't worn it because it was so tight. Her breasts and hips seemed fuller, but Letitia had finally managed to squeeze her into it.

Mrs. Monroe had decorated the Oval Room using light crimson satin for the upholstery and a matching crimson satin for the curtains. The gilded Empire furniture was from the finest Parisian cabinetmaker, Pierre-Antoine Bellangé. The hearth blazed merrily, and light sparkled from the fifty-candle crystal chandelier. The President and Mrs. Monroe were receiving in this room, but the crush was so great that Rebecca and Jeremy could only inch forward. "They say that she spends a hundred dollars a week just on candles alone," Rebecca said, eyeing the ornaments of silver and bronze on the tables and mantelpieces. Then she caught sight of Monroe, standing ramrod tall.

"I feel like I've stepped back in time," she said to Jeremy. "It's like the days when Washington and Adams were President. They say Monroe's so vain about his legs that he still wears breeches in order to show them," Rebecca said.

And then she gasped when she saw Elizabeth Kortright Monroe. At forty-nine, she was still a splendid-looking woman, though in fragile health. She wore a black velvet gown trimmed in ermine, her hair piled high in puffs, and her cheeks were artfully rouged. "But she's sitting on a platform!" Rebecca exclaimed, loud enough to be heard throughout the room.

Several other ladies heard and expressed their surprise. "We didn't fight our Second War for Independence so that our leaders could take on airs and graces," Rebecca said. "And if they persist in that kind of behavior, they may easily find themselves shunned."

In the milling crowd Rebecca saw Stephen Decatur and his wife; they'd just built a house on the corner of the President's Park, which was fast becoming the most fashionable neighborhood in Washington. The John Van Nesses greeted Rebecca and Jeremy, and then they were introduced to Maria Monroe, the President's youngest daughter. She was barely sixteen but

was already affianced to her first cousin, Laurence Gouverneur.
All of Washington seemed excited about the prospect of the
first wedding of a President's child in the White House.

As they moved closer on the receiving line, Rebecca saw
Eliza Monroe Hay in animated conversation with Victoria Connaught. The two women were babbling on in French, laughing
gaily at each other's *bon mots*—and, by the use of a foreign
language, cutting everybody else out of their conversation.
"How quickly we forget," Rebecca said to Jeremy. "Victoria
Connaught was a spy for the British, yet because of her wealth,
she now has access everywhere."

Waiters served refreshments, but Monroe, not being as
wealthy as either Madison or Jefferson, served more coffee,
tea, and fruit punch than wine. But Mrs. Monroe's fruit-juice
julep and lemon cake were delicious.

At last Rebecca and Jeremy reached the platform and were
presented to the Monroes. Rebecca nodded to both the President
and Mrs. Monroe, but refused to curtsey. Mrs. Monroe flushed
slightly, but made no comment. But Rebecca's defiance wasn't
lost on Eliza Hay; pinched and bound by her slavish belief in
court protocol, she approached Rebecca, her fan fluttering in
agitation. "It's Mrs. Brand, isn't it?" she said with hauteur.
"I remember my husband telling me about you and your husband at the trial of Aaron Burr."

Her husband, George Hay, had been the prosecuting attorney for the government in its treason case against Aaron Burr,
in which Zebulon had also been implicated.

Rebecca turned crimson with Eliza's insult. Seeing her embarrassment, Eliza plunged her stiletto deeper. "Most of the
nation is convinced that verdict was a miscarriage of justice.
Over a legal technicality, traitors were set free, that's what my
husband says."

Jeremy tried to lead Rebecca away, but she pulled her arm
free and faced Eliza Hay. "Madam, your husband errs, as he
erred so often at the trial. A poor lawyer will always blame
technical difficulties for his own inefficiency. Remember also,
madam, if that trial proved anything it is that no government
agency—or lawyer or even the President of the United States—
is above the law. For somebody so concerned with an ancient
case, you do seem overly friendly with Madam Connaught,
who supplied a great deal of money for Burr's enterprise. And
in addition, was a known traitor during the late war. Before

you besmirch another person's good name, make sure that your own is above suspicion."

Then Rebecca turned her gaze to the dais on which Elizabeth Monroe sat. "I had thought that these royalist pretensions disappeared after we'd won our War for Independence, or why else did we fight?" Rebecca turned to leave and said in an aside to Elizabeth, "Beware, madam, lest you come down with a dire case of 'queen fever.'"

"Well, you've certainly thrown down the gauntlet," Jeremy said as they walked away.

"And why not?" Rebecca said, her ears still burning with anger. "Monroe is an elected official, and as such he deserves our support and our prayers—but *not* our slavish obedience. And who elected Eliza Hay? Not I, nor anybody else I know. Would George Hay be attorney general if he wasn't married to the President's daughter? I think not. This country is supposed to be a democracy, not one based on family sinecures."

"You're so beautiful when you're angry. When you're angry and right," he added hastily.

One crisp January afternoon, about two weeks after the formal opening of the White House, Rebecca sat in her room.

"Are you going riding again?" Gunning asked, cutting the air with her plaited crop. "Why can't I go with you?"

She took the crop from him. "You know I like to ride alone. It's the only time I have to think."

The corner of his full mouth turned down and he kicked the leg of a chair. "I hate it when you leave us alone."

He's right, Rebecca thought as she threw her cloak over her shoulders and headed toward the door. Time for me to stop stealing moments, time for me to marry Jeremy. He was waiting for her at this moment at her Georgetown house . . . I'll tell him this afternoon, she thought.

As she approached the front door she saw the doorknob turn. For some inexplicable reason she felt her stomach contract. Then the door swung open, and framed in the oblong of light stood Zebulon.

PART THREE

Chapter 30

ZEBULON MUTTERED hoarsely, "My darling," and stumbled toward her. She caught him as he fell, and his weight dragged them both to the floor. She heard herself shouting, "Letitia, come quickly!" while another part of her brain raced, trying desperately to think of a way out of this horrendous situation.

Then Gunning and Suzannah were at her side, screeching and crying and hugging their father. Rebecca and Letitia managed to carry Zebulon into the drawing room and lifted him onto the settee. "Oh, Mr. Zebulon," Letitia moaned, "he's most near played out. Will he die?"

Rebecca gauged her husband. "I think it's only exhaustion."

Zebulon's clothes hung in tatters and his toes stuck through the soles of his shoes. He'd always had a dark complexion, but constant exposure to the sun had turned his skin nut-brown. His hair had grown gray enough to be noticeable, one thatch on his right temple waving back into his blue-black locks. But the major change lay in his eyes, the frightened expression marked him as a haunted man.

"Who is President?" Zebulon whispered.

"James Monroe," Rebecca said.

"I must get to him!" He tried to get off the settee but fell back. "Bring him here."

"Impossible! The President won't come here," she said.

"He will when he knows why. Tell him I have information about the Spanish and British plans in Florida. Rebecca, *please.*"

"Letitia, come with me." Rebecca took her maid outside. "You and Tadpole take the carriage and ride to the house in Georgetown. Jeremy's there. Tell him what happened. But he's not to come here. Under any circumstances."

Letitia rolled her eyes with fear, but Rebecca pushed her toward the stables. "Hurry!" Then Rebecca lifted her skirts and ran to the White House.

The guard stationed at the sentry post outside the front gate

escorted her inside. In the Cabinet Room she found President
Monroe conversing with Secretary of State Adams. As quickly
as she could, she explained what had happened. Both men
thought her news significant enough to accompany her back
to her house.

When President Monroe saw Zebulon he exclaimed, "My
God, man, you're ill! Couldn't this wait until tomorrow?"

Zebulon shook his head weakly. "You must hear me out."

The men and Rebecca pulled up chairs and sat in a semicircle
around him. Zebulon began his tale. "I was heading for New
Orleans on . . . a cargo run, and we neared the port of Pensacola.
I warned my navigator about the treacherous sandbars that lay
all about. They'd always been marked with buoys, but now the
dastardly Spaniards and their Indian cohorts had purposely
moved the markers and we hit a sandbar. The ship broke up
and sank."

"But why would the Spaniards do such a thing?" Adams
asked, bewildered.

"For the salvage," Zebulon said. "The port grows fat on the
cargoes of the ships they lure onto the reefs, God curse them.
Most of my crew drowned, but I was washed onto the mainland.
A tribe of Seminoles captured me, and held me captive for two
years!" He held his head in his hands. "I was . . . abused, forced
to do menial work. The sun didn't rise or set without their
threat to put me to death."

"A terrible tale," Monroe said, "and one that confirms all
we've heard about the fate of our settlers captured in that area."

"It's far worse than anything you've heard," Zebulon said.
"The Spaniards, in league with the English, foment revolution
among our slaves across the border and offer them sanctuary
in Florida. Why, with my own eyes I saw a fortress manned
with two hundred and fifty escaped slaves! Fort Negro, they
call it. It's sixty miles north of the mouth of the Appalachicola
River, and by its very presence incites our slaves to rebel and
run away."

"It can't continue like this," Monroe said to Adams. "Florida
has been a thorn in our side for many years. Something must
be done."

Zebulon had a swallow of water and continued. "I came
face to face with two Englishmen—a Scot named Alexander
Arbuthnot, about seventy years old, but a dangerous man never-

theless, and Robert Ambrister, a swaggering braggart who daily preaches insurrection to his Indian followers. They raid our settlements in Georgia, then flee back over the border and we're rendered impotent. I saw at least a half-dozen of our captured settlers die of mistreatment, and sometimes they were slaughtered just to provide amusement for the Indians." Tears started to his eyes and he choked back his anger. "Sir, they mean to invade us! They're gathering arms and men right at this very minute!"

President Monroe laid his hand on Zebulon's arm. "You must control yourself. We've been aware of this problem for some time, and have in fact ordered General Jackson to take whatever measures necessary to remedy the situation."

"I still believe we can negotiate a peaceful treaty with Spain for the sale of Florida," Adams said. "I've been involved in delicate negotiations with their ambassador, Don Luis de Onís."

"The only thing they understand is force," Zebulon interrupted. "We'll solve nothing unless we invade first and pound them into submission."

"How did you escape from all this?" Adams interrupted. He was a man versed in the art of negotiating; cries for war had always offended him.

"I became friendly with one of the squaws assigned to guard me," Zebulon said, and then his eyes slid away from Rebecca's. "The squaw took pity on me, that's all. One night, she cut the ropes that bound me to my stake, and I escaped. I traveled only at night, hiding in the swamps by day while the Seminole devils sought to track me. Finally I made it over the border to Georgia. From there, I traveled as fast as I could to get here."

Voice fading, Zebulon told them a few more details.

President Monroe said, "Thank you. We'd be obliged if you'd prepare a full report for us. I want to forward it to General Jackson. But for now, you'd better get some rest."

Then President Monroe and John Quincy Adams took their leave. Outside, Adams said to Monroe, "We could have saved ourselves a trip coming over here. We didn't learn anything new."

Rebecca, her mind and body reeling with conflicting emotions, heated some bean soup for Zebulon. With shaking hands, she fed it to him. What am I going to do now? she thought, on the edge of desperation.

About fifteen minutes later, the situation became even more difficult when Letitia returned. Rebecca's heart plummeted when she saw that Jeremy was with her!

With the two brothers in the same room, the air crackled with tension. Rebecca looked first at one and then the other, her heart thudding dully in her breast. Though Zebulon had sailed from Georgetown before Jeremy's return from New Orleans, and therefore hadn't known if Jeremy was alive or dead, he appeared to take his brother's presence for granted. Perhaps it's Zebulon's exhaustion that's keeping him from asking any questions, Rebecca thought. But that wasn't the case with Jeremy. He wanted to know everything that had happened to Zebulon, and most important, what Zebulon's plans were now. Rebecca grew increasingly frightened with the tight, grim look on Jeremy's face. He'd always been slow to anger, but when he did lose his temper . . .

At last Jeremy turned to Rebecca. "Could you give us five minutes alone?"

A pleading look flashed into her eyes and she remained rooted. But Jeremy took her elbow and gently led her to the door.

"What are you going to do?" she whispered. "Please, don't do anything drastic. The children—"

Jeremy didn't answer, and closed the door after her.

Rebecca tried the doorknob, but he'd locked it. She hurried into the kitchen and tore into Letitia. "I warned you not to bring Jeremy here. Oh, am I going to whip you!"

"He wouldn't listen," Letitia whimpered. "I begged and begged. I swear, he wouldn't listen. You know how he is." Letitia clutched her hands, terrified of what had come to pass, terrified for her mistress.

In the drawing room, Jeremy paced back and forth before the settee where Zebulon lay. He didn't know where to start, how to break the news about himself and Rebecca as gently as possible. And even as he looked at his brother's gaunt form, he felt a stab of pity for him. Should he give Zebulon a day or two to recover?

"This is a happy day for us all," Jeremy began. "We thought sure that the Lord had taken you."

Zebulon nodded, barely able to keep his eyes open. "Thank you. It's wonderful to be home . . . to be able to pick up my life again." His head lolled to one side and his words became slurred and almost incoherent. "I swear, I'll never leave Rebecca again . . . the only thing that kept me alive was the thought that one day I'd be able to hold her again."

Jeremy colored to the roots of his fair hair, but his brother didn't notice his reaction. Then Zebulon's eyelids drooped and he dozed off.

Jeremy gripped Zebulon's shoulders and tried to shake him awake. "Get up! Get up, damn you!" He couldn't allow this situation to remain unresolved. They *had* to have this moment of honesty between them; Zebulon had to know that he planned to take Rebecca with him. But nothing that Jeremy did could rouse Zebulon; he'd passed out completely.

Jeremy stared down at his brother, the sad and tormented memory of their youths sweeping over him. Zebulon had always thwarted him, stood in his way, from the time he'd sold him as an indentured servant, to winning the hand of Rebecca, and to this very moment.

Jeremy punched his palm with his fist. "By God! I won't let it happen again, I won't!"

He left the drawing room and strode into the kitchen. Rebecca sat slouched in a chair, numbed. "Pack your things," he ordered her. "You're leaving with me right now."

She looked at him blankly. When he tried to lift her to her feet, she pulled back.

"I can't stand the thought of your being under the same roof with him," he exclaimed.

"Neither can I," she whispered. "But what about the children? How could I do such a thing, abandon them?"

"I mean to take them with us."

She stood up slowly and faced him. "Can you imagine what the courts would think of that? My running off with another man? I'd lose them for certain. No, I must stay here and settle this with Zebulon. I'll come to you as soon as I'm able."

"No, I won't permit that!" he said through clenched teeth.

"Jeremy, please!" she cried, her voice somewhere between a plea and a moan. "You're tearing my heart out. I love you, you know I love you. But I can't do anything to jeopardize my children."

Their argument raged around the kitchen. He cajoled, insisted, warned her that no good had ever come of being dishonest, but always her response was the same.

Then they heard Zebulon moaning and crying out in his sleep. Wild-eyed and trembling now, Rebecca practically dragged him to the kitchen door. "Oh, please trust me. I swear, nothing will happen. Tomorrow I'll have Francis Scott Key start the divorce proceedings. But please, go now."

As much as he hated to, Jeremy left. He stepped out into the night, which had turned damp with the tendrils of fog moving in from the Potomac and shrouding the White House in its mists. He wasn't at all calmed by Rebecca's assurances. Yet what could he do? She was still legally married to Zebulon. She did have the children to protect. . . . He strode along the ruts of New York Avenue, shuddering under a chill not entirely caused by the bitter weather.

Chapter 31

WITH LETITIA'S and Tadpole's help, Rebecca finally managed to get Zebulon into the big four-poster in their bedroom. He reached for her, his hands suddenly demanding, but she was able to put him off. Fortunately, he passed out almost immediately. She went to the small guest bedroom opposite the children's room and undressed. Feeling so weary with all that had happened, she too fell asleep within moments.

Her sleep was tormented with dreams, of Zebulon, of violent hands reaching for her, of a pressing weight that smothered her. Suddenly she was pried awake by a sharp stab and found Zebulon in bed with her.

"Don't be frightened, my darling," Zebulon whispered. "You don't know how long I've hungered for this. Every night of my captivity I thought only of sharing your bed again. Only that thought sustained me. And now..." He reached for her again and she jerked away. When he persisted she bit him hard. She scrambled out of bed, but with a lunge that belied his fatigue, he grabbed her shift and pulled her back.

"Zebulon, don't!" she cried, fighting him off. "Whatever we had, that was gone long before you left."

"I love you," he whispered hoarsely. "I've always loved you."

"Zebulon, *please*..."

His attack became more brutal, and she knew that despite the children, she had to scream, waken the household and prevent this terrible thing from happening. But before the cry could leave her throat, his elbow caught her on the jaw and knocked her out.

She regained her senses to find herself being possessed, his raw jagged rhythm keeping her pinioned to the bed. She tried to writhe free, but he was still stronger than she was. No! she screamed inwardly in her rage, and then with a groan of release his body jerked convulsively. Then he rolled away from her.

She dashed out of bed and hurried downstairs to do whatever she could. "I mustn't conceive, I mustn't!"

By now the entire household had wakened, and Letitia found her mistress outside at the pump, furiously trying to draw water. "Naked in this cold?" Letitia cried. "You'll catch your death. Come inside, come!" she insisted, and led her numbed, shivering mistress back into the house.

Early the next morning Rebecca went to the home of Francis Scott Key in Georgetown and instructed him to file the papers for her divorce.

When Zebulon found out, at first he laughed it off. "Oh, your mother is in one of her moods," he told Gunning. But when Zebulon finally realized that Rebecca was serious, he reacted with hurt, and then anger.

"I'll never give you a divorce!" he shouted. "The two of us swore, for better or for worse, and by God, I'm holding you to that!"

Rebecca realized that the best thing she could do was to get out. Because they'd already been married when they built the house on New York Avenue the property legally belonged to Zebulon. "Even though my father bought and paid for everything," Rebecca stormed to Letitia, who stood nearby, wringing her hands as Rebecca packed.

"Miss Rebecca, you can't do this," she said.

"I can, and I will!" Rebecca herded the children into the carriage and drove to her Georgetown house. Then she went directly to Chief Justice John Marshall, and explained the situation to him. Marshall advised against divorce, but when she broke down in tears, he agreed to help.

"I'll write out a restraining order forbidding Zebulon to visit you," Marshall said. "I'll have a word with the constable myself, tell him to keep his eye out for Zebulon."

Somewhat relieved, Rebecca tried to live with some kind of normalcy. But wherever she went—to the dressmaker's, to the greengrocer's—she felt condemning eyes on her, saying implicitly, a woman's place was with her husband, no matter what. "The devil take them," she muttered under her breath.

When Jeremy tried to visit her, she refused. "For the next few months, or at least until the divorce is settled, it's better that we not see each other."

"But that's madness!" Jeremy said. "I won't have it."

"Zebulon will do everything he can to make our lives miserable. And there's Suzannah and Gunning to consider. I simply can't risk any complications."

In mid-March, Rebecca's worst fears were realized. One afternoon when she could no longer deny the truth, she went to the study and poured herself a snifter of brandy. She sat before the fireplace, feeling the heady warmth of the liquor burning in her throat, feeling the warm tears that coursed down her cheeks.

Letitia found her this way. "Oh my, oh mercy me, what's the matter?" she asked. Then she saw the helpless look in Rebecca's eyes and guessed. "Oh, Lord," she whispered. "Most times it be good news, but now . . ."

"What am I going to do?" she whispered.

"You're going to do what God meant you to do and have the baby. And trust Him to lead you to the right path." She put her arm around Rebecca's shoulder and the two women sat there rocking slowly back and forth.

At the end of April Rebecca saw the first telltale signs of her pregnancy and hid it as best she could. What made everything more confusing was that, after that night with Zebulon, she couldn't be sure whose child it was. No matter, since because of her marital status, Zebulon would have to be listed as the father. God only knew what that would do to Jeremy.

To keep from going totally mad, Rebecca turned her pen to the events of the day. Much to the surprise and delight of the nation, Andrew Jackson, under orders from President Monroe, had invaded Florida, and had, in effect, engaged in a war with the Spaniards. Jackson's enemies—and he had many who feared his political ambitions—demanded that he be censured.

Rebecca went to the House of Representatives and listened as Henry Clay, with his usual flair and deadly brilliance, castigated Jackson. "According to our Constitution, only Congress has the power to make and declare war. Yet Andrew Jackson has taken on this sacred obligation himself. Are we about to enter another era of the Caesars?"

The gallery, ever fickle, responded to Clay's clever manipulations with applause and resounding cheers.

Rebel Thorne counterattacked with a vengeance.

"What really prompts Henry Clay's concern? Is it indeed

the Constitution, or is he afraid of Jackson's political ambitions? It's no secret that Clay himself plans one day to be President. Then let him fight it out man-to-man instead of hiding behind the Constitution. Fellow Americans, suppose you lived on the Georgia frontier and had seen your family massacred by the Seminoles and other Indian tribes. Yet when you pursued them, you had to stop at the border of Florida. Are we to remain forever helpless in the face of this outrage against our people? The history of Spain on this continent has been one of rapine and plunder, with the stolen wealth sent back to the mother country. They have not settled the land, nor tilled it with the sweat of their muscle, nor watered it with their blood. Only Americans have done that. Andrew Jackson knows that, and I for one, along with all our brave settlers on the western frontier, thank God for his courage."

Rebecca kept hearing reports about Zebulon, that he was frequenting the taverns in Washington and Georgetown, that he'd mortgaged the house on New York Avenue to pay off his gambling and drinking debts, that he'd tried to borrow money on the Breech Stone Works. Fortunately, Rebecca was able to speak to Van Ness, the bank president, and since she was the principal stockholder of the stone works, Zebulon was thwarted.

In spite of her distress, each day saw Rebecca become more contented. She took on an almost preternatural beauty, and people turned to stare at her. Somehow, she knew that this was the last child she would ever bear, and her mind and body poured the very best that was in her into this new life. She had her deep suspicions about whose child it was, but not even that mattered anymore, for it had taken on an existence far removed from the pettiness of her daily battle with Zebulon, or even the star-crossed quality of her love for Jeremy. I am a conduit for God's work, she thought, and this idea nourished her for the difficulties which she knew lay ahead.

"You seem in a foul mood," Wingate called to Jeremy. Man and boy were balanced precariously on the movable scaffold hooked to the roof of the White House. Jeremy clambered around the wooden platform as sure as a mountain goat, but Wingate had never gotten the hang of it and held onto the railing for dear life.

"I suppose I am sour," Jeremy said. "And I'm sorry for it,

lad. It's not your fault that I'm having problems. Hand me a load of those bricks."

Wingate brought him a hod of bricks. Though President Monroe had long since moved into the mansion, work still continued. Twelve new fireplaces had been installed, and now Jeremy and Wingate were finishing the brickwork on them. Ordinarily the bricklayers would have done this, but they refused to work on this new-fangled invention of Jeremy's, so he and Wingate had set about to prove that his scaffold was safe.

Chafing under the delay of Rebecca's divorce, and of not being able to make love to her, Jeremy had buried himself in his work. He'd refined his movable scaffold, and the Patent Office had granted him a patent.

Casting a leery look at the ground, Wingate said, "I keep thinking that the scaffold will slip."

"It's not possible," Jeremy said. "I've designed the safety lock, so that the heavier the load we're carrying, the tighter the grip becomes. You see, lad, in the old days, a workman might depend on a half-hitch to secure his ropes. And his knot might be as good as the way he felt that morning. I've seen men plunge to their deaths through their own carelessness. But with the double safeguard of ropes and this locking device, we ought to be able to prevent a fair number of accidents."

"James Hoban told me that your invention will soon be used in every building site in America," Wingate said.

Jeremy shrugged. "Let's hope so. It could mean that Circumstance will have enough money for a suitable education. Perhaps enough left over for a dowry."

Wingate almost dropped his second load of bricks.

Jeremy turned away and smiled. He'd seen Wingate fall more securely under his daughter's spell. Nothing would please him more than if the two of them one day married. But that was something only the fates could decide—certainly not anybody as remote as a parent.

From his vantage point at the top of the White House, Jeremy could see the surrounding hills, see the Potomac River winding close by. Government buildings were beginning to sprout up everywhere, and down the sightline of Pennsylvania Avenue he could see that the Capitol Building was almost ready for occupancy.

About an hour later, Jeremy saw Circumstance skipping

across the White House grounds, coming toward them. At
twelve the first flush of young womanhood was overtaking his
daughter, and it filled him with pride . . . and an oblique sense
of regret. Soon he would lose her to another man. He could
only hope that the man would be worthy of her, this creature
who was so unlike any other girl in Washington. The fact that
her mother was a princess in the Shoshone tribe was reflected
in Circumstance's carriage, in the clear, unwavering expression
in her eyes, and in her innate grace. Yet these fools in Washington talked behind her back, calling her half-breed, and
worse.

"Father?" Circumstance called up, "I'm going to meet Suzannah. We're picking wildflowers for the table. Dinner will
be at four, so don't be late again or Tanzy will be cross."

And with that she was off, seeming to float across the
greensward. Jeremy watched as she headed toward Georgetown, sometimes breaking into a run and throwing her hands
in the air as though she might catch the wind.

Circumstance stalked a rabbit in the bush near the river,
creeping so close to it that when the startled creature finally
saw her it could only cower. Circumstance stroked it and sent
it on its way. Then she saw her cousin coming along the forest
trail and called, "Suzannah!"

The two girls ran to each other and embraced. Hand in hand
they walked through the sighing forest. Circumstance said,
"Today, I learned all about how a young lady should act in the
drawing room. I hated it. I also learned how to sew the silly
embroidery around the edges of a handkerchief. How much
better it is to make clothes you can *wear*. Father showed me
how to make a shirt out of buckskin."

"Really?"

"And now they're teaching us how to dance," Circumstance
said and mimed the stately court dance. "It's so stiff and silly!"
She flung her arms wide, pinwheeled around the clearing. She
fell to the ground and Suzannah joined her, laughing.

"Sometimes I just can't stand all these clothes," Circumstance said, and before Suzannah could stop her, she shucked
them off. Then she raced across the clearing, and plunged into
the Potomac, diving and swimming with the abandon of a river
otter.

Suzannah watched, torn between the fear of what her mother

would say and the attraction of the fun her cousin was obviously having. Then she slipped out of her own clothes and ran into the river. "But I can't swim," she called to Circumstance.

"Don't worry, I'll teach you. Just float for now."

Under Circumstance's gentle instructions, Suzannah overcame her fright. Soon the two girls were floating on their backs, hands barely touching, faces turned to the fantastic forms in the clouds drifting overhead.

On shore, a pair of hazel eyes stared at the girls intently. Then Gunning crept through the stands of reeds and cattails to get a closer look. He'd followed his sister, thinking to ambush and frighten her. But then she'd met Circumstance, and they'd taken off their clothes. Almost ten years of age, Gunning was already his father's son. He squirmed with pleasure when he thought of what he would like to do with Circumstance . . . use her, the way his hound used a bitch in heat. "Well, one day," Gunning swore, keeping his passion in hand.

The river's currents slowly carried the girls downstream. "Will your mother have her baby soon?" Circumstance asked.

"Letitia says it will happen any day now," Suzannah said. "The other day she mumbled something that I didn't understand."

"What?"

"Just pray that the baby has black hair. What did she mean by that?"

"I don't know," Circumstance said.

Chapter 32

ZEBULON SAT in the smoke-filled Tunnecliff's Tavern, swilling down tankards of ale and bellowing the latest popular song along with the rest of the half-drunk patrons. Andrew Jackson had captured the Spanish city of Pensacola, hung the two British agitators, Arbuthnot and Ambrister, and had secured the Florida-Georgia border. Jackson's stock had never been higher, and the roisterers sang:

> Come all ye sons of freedom
> Come all ye brave who lead 'em
> Come all who say God speed 'em
> And sing a song of joy!
> To Jackson ever brave
> Who nobly did behave
> Unto immortal Jackson
> The Spanish turned their backs on
> He's ready still for action,
> O Jackson is the boy . . .

Before Zebulon could begin the second verse, a hand clutched his shoulder and he turned to look into the scrofulous face of Sisley Urquhart, Victoria Connaught's servant.

"My mistress would see you," Sisley said. "She's waiting in a carriage outside."

Zebulon shrugged off Urquhart's hand. "After hating me for more than twenty-five years, what can she want with me now?"

"It concerns your wife."

This put Zebulon immediately on guard. He checked his pistols—loaded—then rose and strode toward the door, trying not to weave. The June night felt balmy, a gibbous moon hung low in the sky, washing the capital in pale silver light. The black Connaught carriage, emblazoned with the gold coat of arms, stood parked in a copse of weeping willows just behind the tavern.

Victoria Connaught, dressed in black, with a towering black poke on her head, leaned out the carriage window as he approached. He cocked his guns. "No need for your pistols, sir," she called to him. "I'm just an old Christian woman waiting for God's call, and can do you no harm."

Zebulon stared into eyes that were milky white, almost ghostly, and felt a shudder course along his spine. "Well?" he demanded. Then he noticed the shadowed figure sitting beside Victoria and raised his pistols. "Who's that?"

"My nephew Devroe Connaught, son of Sean. He's come here to investigate the manner of his father's death. The boy is named after my late brother, Devroe, whom you have cause to remember."

"Old news," Zebulon said irritably.

"Not to me," Devroe muttered in the high-pitched cracking voice of a youth.

"Hush, child," Victoria said. "We've other matters to tend to this evening," She turned her near-blind gaze toward Zebulon. "Strange, isn't it, how the man being deceived is the last to know. So it was with my brother, when you were seducing his wife. And so it is with you."

"You lie, you stupid harridan!" Zebulon cursed.

"Do I? Well, all during the time that you were gone, the pure, virtuous Rebecca Breech Brand was having an affair. And with your own brother!"

Zebulon fell back a step. Even while he heard his own protests, what Victoria had said lacerated his soul. "You'd say anything to wound me," he said weakly.

"I would indeed," Victoria spat. "Though this is the truth. Ask her whose child she's carrying. Place her hand on the Bible and make her swear that the bastard she's carrying in her womb isn't the consequence of sin and the cause of perdition."

Then Victoria waved to her driver and the carriage sped off, leaving behind the echo of her high-pitched laugh.

Zebulon lurched back into the tavern and proceeded to drink himself into insensibility. As he slipped into a stupor he heard Victoria's taunting voice. Had something happened between Jeremy and Rebecca? He struggled to recall the days of their youth. Jeremy had always had a violent attraction for Rebecca. Once he'd even beaten his brother bloody for interfering with his courtship of Rebecca. Well, it wasn't too late to do the same thing again. "Of course the child is mine, it has to be!"

As his head sank to the table puddled with ale, Zebulon croaked, "If it's true, I'll kill him..."

Rebecca went into labor one evening in late October. She knew the birth would be difficult; she was well past the safe age for having a baby, and so instead of using a midwife, she sent Letitia for Doctor Smith. She suffered the pains in silence, willing all of her strength so that the child might have safe passage into the world. The ordeal went on for hours, then a full day passed and still she suffered with an intensity that left her gasping for breath.

With the last of her strength she clutched the doctor's hand. "The child must live. Do whatever you must. Forfeit my own life if necessary, but this child must live!"

Her last plea to the doctor ended in a sharp scream that saw the child born.

"Bravo," Doctor Smith said. "Bravo! It's a fine boy. I've never seen such wide shoulders."

Only when Rebecca saw that her son was whole and healthy and heard his lusty cry did she permit herself to slip into unconsciousness.

Her recovery was slow, complicated by the fact that her situation with Zebulon wasn't yet resolved. He demanded to see the baby, and since he was listed as the father, she couldn't deny him.

Zebulon gazed intently at the boy. He looked like his complexion was fair, but since the baby had been born without hair and his eyes were still closed, Zebulon's suspicions couldn't be further corroborated. "We'll see," he muttered to himself. "We'll see."

Rebecca couldn't bring herself to name the child Zebulon Junior—that would have been a travesty—and calling him Jeremy was out of the question. She said to Letitia, "One of the last things I heard before I fainted was Dr. Smith saying, 'Bravo!' And that's what I'll call my son—Bravo Brand."

Rebecca went to the bookshelf and took out the oversized, leather-bound family Bible. She ran her fingers lovingly over the illuminated frontispiece, and then turned to the family page. There was Suzannah's name... born 1807; and Gunning, born, 1809. In her neat fine hand, Rebecca wrote, "Bravo Brand, 1818."

• • •

October gave way to the quick winds of November, which sharpened into December's cold. Jeremy came to see Rebecca often, gazing long at the child, who with each passing week began to look more and more like a miniature version of himself. "He has hair as fine as a dandelion," Jeremy said.

"And eyes bluer than yours," she murmured. "There's no mistaking whose son he is."

"None. Though I must say that my joy is tempered by my sadness for Zebulon."

"I feel much the same way," she said. "But our marriage was over long before you and I . . ." She shrugged helplessly. "Zebulon is strong. He's always had . . . interests outside the marriage bed. He'll survive." Then she changed the subject. "What's happening in Washington?"

"Oh, they wouldn't dare do anything without you in attendance," he said, laughing, then he grew serious. "Henry Clay has a movement afoot in Congress to censure Andrew Jackson. And Jackson's friends have advised him to come to Washington to look after his interests. I've written him myself and added my voice to the warnings. He wrote back and said he'd be here sometime around the end of January."

"And it's almost Christmas!" she said, squeezing his hand. "I can't believe the year has flown so."

"What news of the divorce?"

She shook her head. "The courts have a surprising lack of consideration when a *woman* files for divorce. There's nothing to be done but to wait. I asked Justice Marshall to look into it, and he promised he would."

"Is Zebulon giving you any trouble?"

"So far he's behaving himself. I think the worst is over."

Andrew Jackson arrived in Washington on January 23, 1819. "He came overland from Nashville," Jeremy told Rebecca. "People in every town along his route came out and feted him."

"From all the talk I hear, the same is true in the capital," she said.

He nodded. "President Monroe wanted to throw an official reception for him at the White House, but Jackson refused, saying that he would do no such thing until Congress cleared his name. Jackson won't be pushed around by anybody, whether it be Congress or the President of the United States."

"Mark my words, Jackson has his eye on the presidency."

"I still say the choice would be a good one," Jeremy said. "At any rate, Jackson's agreed to have John Quincy Adams host a party for him and asked me specifically to attend. I wish you'd reconsider and come with me. You've been cooped up too long."

"Why search out trouble?" she asked. "When the divorce is granted, we can do whatever we want for the rest of our lives."

"I suppose you're right. Though these political functions have little meaning for me unless you're there."

All that week Rebecca listened to the gossip about the Jackson soiree. Anybody of note in Washington planned to attend. Finally she wasn't able to stand the tension any longer and told Jeremy that she'd go with him.

Months of convalescence after Bravo's birth had left her feeling fragile, and she took extra pains to be presentable. "Every hypocrite in Washington will be out for my scalp," she told Letitia. "Well, since they're going to talk anyway, we might as well give them good reason."

She spent the week with a dressmaker and fabrics and designed a gown for herself of emerald-blue velvet.

"It doesn't look like it's the style everybody will be wearing," Letitia said.

"You're right, it isn't. For one, the waist isn't up under the bosom, but in its proper place. Furthermore, most women will be wearing huge muffs and towering pokes with waving ostrich plumes. I can't imagine a style more ridiculous. Really, women can be so silly."

When she had her final fitting, she and Letitia studied the tight waist, and the scooped neckline that bared a good part of her arms and shoulders. "It's too much, isn't it?" she said.

"By a whole lot," Letitia said, nodding vigorously. "Going to get you in a heap of trouble, and that's all I got to say about that matter."

"I suppose you're right." Rebecca spent the evening sewing up an emerald gauze capelet to be worn over her shoulders. But the suggestion of bare skin showed through the gauze and somehow that made her seem even more naked.

When Jeremy and Rebecca entered the Adamses' drawing room, conversation stopped, then resumed, louder and more animated. Everybody in the room knew the details—or at least the rumors—about the Brand brothers and the woman they both loved.

"She's a scarlet woman," Victoria Connaught said, peering at Rebecca through a lorgnette as thick as a magnifying glass. "And she's practically naked."

"That may be, Aunt Victoria," her great-nephew Devroe said. "But she is very beautiful."

"Scarlet women usually are," Victoria said, "else the devil wouldn't choose them to be his handmaidens."

"Jeremy, my boy!" Andrew Jackson's voice boomed out across the room. The men made for each other, Jackson in all his military finery, with the gold epaulettes on his shoulders and the high, stiff embroidered collar that made him appear even more erect, and Jeremy in his plain blue wool homespun suit. They embraced, clapping each other on the back.

"This man helped build my ramparts at the Battle of New Orleans," Jackson said to anybody who'd listen. "With my own eyes I saw him leap over our battlements and engage a British officer who was trying to breach our wall. Bravest thing I ever saw. Killed him dead."

Jeremy blushed under the praise, and then his eyes met Victoria's. From the pained expression on his face, she knew, and she clutched Devroe's arm. "The British officer he killed was your father!"

"But—how do you know that?" Devroe asked.

"Look at him! The guilt is written all over his face."

Jeremy stared at Devroe. He bore an amazing resemblance to his father, Sean Connaught. The same slate-gray eyes, the lank blond-brown hair that had no body to it, the sloping shoulders. But he also had the same sharp, discerning expression.

Rebecca joined Jeremy and Jackson, and the general turned to her. "Ah, Mrs. Brand, isn't it?"

"But how gallant of you to remember," she said. "It's been more than ten years since we met, and then under trying conditions."

"One never forgets a woman as extraordinary-looking as you," Jackson said softly.

Rebecca felt the flush suffuse her body. As commanding

as he could be with men, so was Jackson the gallant with the ladies. It's altogether an irresistible combination, she thought. He will be President.

Jackson, who'd heard all the rumors about the Brands, very quickly appraised the situation, and bestowed his benevolence on Jeremy and Rebecca. He, after all, had found himself in much the same predicament, having married his Rachel before she was divorced from her first husband. Jackson leaned toward Jeremy and whispered, "In love and war a man must make his decision and then stick to it, no matter what the rest of the world thinks or says."

"Thank you, sir. Now what of your own progress with the government? How does that go?"

Jackson fastened his gaze on Henry Clay, who stood across the room talking to his own clique of supporters. "Clay insists that I acted unconstitutionally. But President Monroe knows better, for as Commander in Chief, it was he who gave me my orders. But now Monroe doesn't have the backbone to admit it, and instead runs scared before Congress. Well, by God, they shan't intimidate me!"

The voices grew louder, the argument more heated. Henry Clay's voice rose above the hubbub, "The gist of the matter is, does a President have the power to order an invasion force into land owned by a foreign country, without the full authorization of Congress? Think carefully how you answer, for it may affect not only your situation, but future generations to come."

"It's a complex question," Rebecca said to Jeremy, "with right and wrong on both sides. I understand Clay's point. If a precedent was set, and an unscrupulous President came to power, he could circumvent Congress and the Constitution."

"It depends on the leader then, doesn't it?" Jeremy said.

Rebecca nodded thoughtfully. "And on a watchful and informed electorate."

A quarter of an hour later Jeremy said, "We should go. It's your first evening out, and you mustn't overdo it." They said their goodbyes to John Quincy and Louisa Adams, and to General Jackson. When they reached the vestibule, they found Victoria Connaught blocking the door.

She raised a trembling, bony finger and pointed it at Jeremy. "You killed Sean Connaught, didn't you?" In her other hand Victoria clutched a glass of burgundy and she gulped it to ease her constricted throat. Jeremy said nothing and she screamed, "Answer me!"

"Madam, it was on the field of battle, and we fought our differences like gentlemen."

"And you killed Marianne also," she screeched.

"I had nothing to do with Marianne's death. And if the truth were known...Well, never mind, it would do no good to resurrect that pain. Madam Connaught, whatever's happened between our families, isn't it time to let the past bury the past?"

"Never!" she cried, her face working in an apoplectic fit. "You Brands are all murderers." She turned to Devroe, "I swear on the graves of my brother, and my niece, and of your own sainted father, that these people are worse than murderers. Everything they touch—" In the midst of her tirade, Victoria Connaught started to choke violently.

Devroe Connaught stood by helplessly, not knowing what to do. Jeremy grabbed the old woman and led her to a chair. "Get Doctor Huntt, quickly!" he ordered Devroe. "He's in the drawing room."

By the time the doctor came back, Victoria's eyes were popping from her head. Her gnarled fingers scrabbled at her throat, searching for the relief that wouldn't come. She turned to Jeremy and with the last of her heaving breaths gasped, "May you never know...a moment's peace...May you Brands and your seed be cursed for all generations to come!"

Then Victoria Connaught strangled on her own gall. Dr. Huntt listened to her heart, and shook his head. "I'm sorry. She's dead."

Aside from the handful of people in the foyer, none of the other guests were aware of what had happened, and the reception continued in full swing.

Jeremy touched Devroe's arm. "I'm sorry, I really am."

But Devroe was too distraught to say anything. He walked away, his aunt's curse ringing in his ears. As he rode back to the plantation with Victoria lying on the seat, he patted the dead woman's hand. "Don't worry. I will do whatever is necessary to bring about their downfall. All of them."

When he reached the estate, Devroe went to his Aunt Elizabeth's sitting room; there she sat, doing her infernal needlework. "I'm afraid I've some bad news," he said. "It's Aunt Victoria. She got into an argument with those damned Brand people, and her heart just gave out."

Elizabeth's fingers stopped in midstitch. "Dead?" It looked as if a candle had suddenly been lit behind her eyes. "Dead?" she repeated. She jumped up and rang for the butler. "Bring some wine, the best in our cellar!"

"Madam, how dare you?" Devroe demanded.

She whirled on him, her black eyes flashing with an anger that Victoria had suppressed for decades. "I am the mistress in this house now. And we shall do as I say!"

Elizabeth's spiral back into sanity lasted all of one week, and then she slipped back again. Thereafter, she would move back and forth between her own fanciful inner world to the world of reality. Always, a vision of the same man drew her to the present, the prospect of seeing Zebulon Brand again. The passions of her life had stopped on the day that her husband had tried to kill Zebulon, but instead had himself been killed. In her lucid periods, Elizabeth spent hours before her mirror, fingers dipped in unguents and ointments, preparing for the day when she would meet Zebulon.

Chapter 33

ON A blustery day in March, 1820, Zebulon kept watch outside Rebecca's house in Georgetown. He waited until she left, then entered through the back gate. He saw Letitia laundering clothes in a vat of slow-boiling water. A little ways away, Bravo crawled on the ground, playing with spring's first daffodils. Zebulon strode to Bravo quickly and before Letitia could stop him, picked the boy up.

"Mr. Zebulon, don't!" Letitia cried, trying to snatch Bravo from him. "Miss Rebecca, she'd kill me if she knew you was here."

Zebulon pushed Letitia aside. He undid Bravo's bonnet while the boy smiled at him. Flaxen hair curled around the boy's head, and the eyes . . . so blue that for a moment Zebulon thought he was looking at Jeremy when he'd been a child. He felt a sharp twinge along the base of his spine, as though he'd been emasculated. For a year and a half he'd tried to deny his suspicions, but he could deny them no longer.

Then Zebulon let Letitia take the boy from him. "Don't worry," he muttered, "my argument isn't with the child." Then Zebulon vanished as quickly as he'd come, leaving Letitia trembling.

Zebulon bided his time, planning, waiting for the right moment to present itself.

Several weeks later, Jeremy and Rebecca went calling on James Hoban and his wife and family in Georgetown. It was a delightful evening, with much laughter, and the Hoban children, all ten of them, in constant activity.

"How happy they are," Rebecca said as they walked through the balmy spring evening. "Their lives are so filled with love and caring. If only the good Lord had seen fit to make our family the same."

"It's not too late," Jeremy replied. They passed the town crier and bade him a good night, and he returned their greeting with a tip of his hat.

"Our lives seem so figured with tumult and tragedy," she said. "Is it in our natures to be so? Is that why we were all drawn to each other?"

Jeremy said thoughtfully, "I imagine that every life is shot through with tragedy. Scratch the surface of someone who seems happy, and often you'll find a profound sadness—the loss of a loved one, of a child."

"Thank God we've been spared that," she said fervently. "Our children, all four of them, seem a healthy lot."

"Aye. If there's anything I'm proud of in this world, it's them. And they all bear the Brand name."

"Yet they're as different as the seasons."

"When I look at them, I see our future realized. Mark me, Rebecca, these are no ordinary children. Along with the Brand name, they carry the Brand passions."

She took a playful swipe at him. "Oh? And what about the women who bore them?"

"And the Breech brains and beauty," he added hurriedly. But then he grew serious again. "I'd wager my soul that each one of them will carve out a destiny for himself in this city and in the nation."

She squeezed his arm. "I love it when you talk that way. I don't know why I'm feeling so full of optimism this evening. Perhaps it's because, though Zebulon's still fighting the divorce, he's left us in peace."

Jeremy chuckled. "Zebulon usually isn't one for peaceful measures. But who knows?—perhaps age has mellowed him."

They said goodnight at her door. "I wish we were spending the night together," he said.

She touched his cheek. "You know I wish the same thing. But if I should have to take the witness stand during the divorce proceedings, I want to be able to swear that since learning Zebulon was alive, I haven't committed adultery. I owe at least that much to Suzannah and Gunning."

Jeremy thought that this was an odd way to show one's concern for children, and had told her as much before. But he was so secure in her love that he didn't press the issue. Those insane cravings of youth that could only be satisfied with lusty carnality had with maturity given way to a serene, abiding love. One that could withstand the tests of distance and abstinence.

"I love you," he said. "And that won't change if we don't

sleep together for a month, or a year, or however long. Though I'd prefer it otherwise." He gave her a tiny goose and she gave him a tiny scream. "But if that's what puts your soul at ease, that's what you shall have."

With a promise to see each other on the morrow, they kissed. Then Jeremy mounted his mare and rode slowly back to Washington. Overhead, the vast whorls of the Milky Way swept across the heavens, and he savored the beauty of the brilliant spring night. Ahead in the distance, he could see the twinkling lights of Washington . . . candles lit in windows, oil lamps shining in front of several government buildings.

The city was slowly stretching to fill in the grand design of radiating boulevards and elegant circles that Pierre L'Enfant had conceived almost thirty years before. It might take another century to be realized, perhaps even longer, but this night, under the benevolent heavens, and with peace in his heart, Jeremy knew that one day it would happen. He saw it in his imagination . . . a city of magnificent vistas, one that would make the heart spring up and the spirit soar. And he was filled with a rush of pride that he was part of it.

The scars left by the British invasion were almost gone, mended by the architects William Thornton, Benjamin Latrobe, and James Hoban, and by the efforts of the work force, both free men and slaves. And Jeremy thought that as the city healed itself, so he too had become whole again. He wondered at the resilience of the human spirit that had allowed him to survive first the death of White Doe, and then of Marianne.

Of course, he'd been lucky enough to have Circumstance; she'd been his lifeline. Then God, or fate, or whatever force it was that played a role in man's unfolding destiny had seen fit to bring him and Rebecca together. With her he'd found peace, found an unbounded hope for the future. He began humming a Purcell air:

> When to true love's melting,
> Melting
> Heat exposed—

He broke off as he picked up the sounds of a horse galloping up behind him. Jeremy turned in his saddle in time to see Zebulon riding out of the night, his arm raised. He heard the deadly whirr in the air, recognized it for what it was, but before he could dodge, the rawhide whip cut him across the shoulders, and the force of it knocked him to the ground.

Zebulon galloped straight toward him. Only by rolling into a ditch was Jeremy able to avoid the stallion's flailing hooves. The whip landed again, opening his cheek to the bone, and Jeremy heard Zebulon shout, "That's for seducing my wife!" Again the stinging lash, "And that's for cuckolding a brother, and that's . . ."

The blows continued to rain down on him and Jeremy knew that with one or two more whiplashes, he'd be unconscious and at the mercy of his brother.

Zebulon was besotted with wine, but that only seemed to increase his formidable power with the whip. It had always been his weapon, perfected on countless voyages with slaves.

In a desperate move, as the whip came at him again, Jeremy thrust his forearm in front of him. He felt the rawhide tear through his clothes and skin. The pain was so excruciating that he thought his arm had been broken. But before Zebulon could pull the whip away, Jeremy clamped his right hand on the coils and, with a violent yank, brought Zebulon crashing down off his horse.

They rolled in the dust. Zebulon, always the stronger and bulkier of the two, at first had the better of it. But nights of dissipation in the District's taverns had taken their toll. Jeremy began to land some solid punches of his own.

They scrambled to their feet, standing toe to toe, slugging it out in the dark night. Behind them, the white form of the American Palace stood like a silent sentinel, mute witness to the passion that had flowed between these brothers since their youth . . . a passion of love and hate commingled that called down through the ages to a time when brother had first raised his hand against brother.

With a lightning lunge, Jeremy butted his head into Zebulon's midsection, doubling him over. He followed through with a hard right cross to the jaw, and as Zebulon toppled, hit him with a left to the chin that snapped his head back. Zebulon crumpled to the ground and lay there.

Chest heaving, Jeremy said, "This time I'll let you go. Let you go because of the love I've borne you most of my life. But if you should ever come at me again, or give Rebecca one second's trouble, then I'll kill you."

Zebulon crawled to his feet and stumbled off into the darkness. He pressed his hand to his bloodied face and muttered, "We'll see who kills who."

Zebulon seethed. Night after night in the bars and bordellos of Washington, he was consumed by his betrayal at the hands of his brother and wife. He felt as if a gigantic worm was in his stomach, eating his innards, each day devouring a little more of him. The days blurred along with his senses; some nights he cried in his drunken stupor, sometimes from the loss of Rebecca's love, sometimes because once more his brother had supplanted him.

And then the date for the divorce hearing was announced: several weeks hence. Zebulon grew wild-eyed and gaunt; reason left him. He knew only that he must see his brother, settle this cancer that was eating him alive. One waning Saturday afternoon in late July, he left Tunnecliff's Tavern, where he'd been drinking all day, mounted his stallion, and cantered along Pennsylvania Avenue. The capital looked deserted, most Washingtonians had fled the city's stultifying heat for the cool watering places in the mountains. Both Zebulon and his horse were in a lather when he reined in at Jeremy's cabin.

When he knocked, Tanzy came to the door. He hadn't expected to see her and he started, overcome with a rush of lascivious memories. Years ago, when she'd belonged to him, he'd forced her to serve him in ways that even now made him tremble. Her decade of freedom had only made her softer, more desirable, and his eyes devoured her.

"What do you want?" Tanzy demanded. "Best you get away from here before my man Eli comes back."

Zebulon snorted. "I owned you once, and I'll own you again," Zebulon muttered, and reached for her.

Then Circumstance was at the door. She and Tanzy had been dressing a side of beef and she still had the meat cleaver in her hand.

Zebulon glared at the little half-breed bastard. "Where's your father?"

"Still at work," she said, pointing to the White House.

With a final glance at Tanzy, Zebulon strode away, muttering under his breath, "Bastards! That's the only kind of children he spawns—bastards."

He came to the low brick fence surrounding the eighteen

acres of the President's House, and swung his legs over the wall. He cut across the lawn toward the mansion. As he walked, he took a flask from his pocket and gulped the bourbon mash. It burned his gullet as it went down. The grounds were empty; the workmen had already quit for the day. The White House too was unoccupied; Mrs. Monroe, suffering from her persistent ailments, had gone with the President to their home at Oak Hill, some fifty miles away.

Then Zebulon dimly made out a figure working high up near the roof of the White House. He squinted, and made out a kind of platform. On it stood Jeremy. He was adding a final coat of paint to the chimneys he'd completed. He was alone.

Lines of rope hanging from the scaffolding caught Zebulon's eye. The ropes were anchored so that they kept the scaffold platform on an even keel. Like a sleepwalker, Zebulon drifted toward the ropes.

Perched on the scaffold, Jeremy had seen Zebulon weaving across the lawn. Now Zebulon was standing just beneath him, but in the gathering darkness, Jeremy couldn't make out what he was doing.

Zebulon's fingers moved with a will of their own. He had no idea of what would happen if the ropes were untied; unlike his brother, he'd never had a head for things mechanical.

"Zebulon!" Jeremy shouted from above. His brother didn't answer. Jeremy had no wish for another scene with Zebulon, but it was time that he understood that Rebecca had made her choice. Jeremy unlocked the safety device in order to winch the scaffolding down, knowing that the ropes he'd tied on the bottom would hold him level.

But at that moment, Zebulon loosened the final knot. He pulled violently on the ropes and one end of the scaffold lurched downward, throwing Jeremy to his knees. He grabbed for the sides, but the incline was too steep and he slid farther and farther until his legs hung over the edge of the platform. "Zebulon, for the love of God, the rope, straighten the—"

His words were cut off as he fell, his hands grasping for purchase in the empty air. The falling sensation was akin to a dream...so Adam must have felt when he fell from grace...Oh, heavenly Father, absolve me from any sins I may have committed against my fellow man, and I do humbly beg your forgiveness...

He hit the ground with a fearful crump. Then, he plunged into darkness.

In Jeremy's house, Wingate Grange sat in the kitchen with Tanzy and Circumstance. He'd come to tell Jeremy that he'd just been accepted for matriculation at Georgetown University. He'd saved enough money to be able to afford his education.

"Father will be home soon, and he'll be so excited!" Circumstance cried, unable to contain her pleasure for her friend. Suddenly she stood stock still, the glass of lemonade she was bringing to Wingate slipped from her fingers. She turned deathly pale.

"What's the matter, child?" Tanzy asked, alarmed.

Circumstance passed her hand in front of her eyes. "Something's happened to father!" she cried, and raced out of the kitchen, running for the White House.

By the time the White House servants appeared, Zebulon had already tied the scaffolding ropes again so that nothing looked amiss. "Oh, my God, my brother just fell!" he exclaimed. "I was just coming over to see him when I saw this damnable contraption slip." He pointed to the dangling scaffold. "Hurry, help me get him inside. Somebody go for a doctor."

They carried Jeremy's limp form in and made him as comfortable as they could in the butler's room on the ground floor. Then Circumstance, Wingate, and Tanzy came running.

Circumstance cried out when she saw her father.

Wingate grabbed her shoulders. "It won't help him if you get hysterical." She nodded that she understood and Wingate knelt beside Jeremy, examining him before the doctor came.

"How is he?" Circumstance asked anxiously.

Wingate choked on his words. "He's alive, but barely. He fell almost four stories. Every bone in his body must be broken." Tears started from his eyes, and it was Circumstance's turn to comfort him.

"Don't worry, he won't die," she said resolutely. "He promised that he'd never leave me. He told me that right after he came back from the war. No, he'll never leave me."

Dr. Smith finally arrived and went through the motions of an examination. "It's a miracle that he's alive at all," he said shaking his head. "But I'm afraid that there's little hope."

"No," Circumstance said. "No!"

Wingate took Tanzy aside. "Ride to Georgetown and tell Rebecca. Quickly."

Within the hour, Rebecca swept into the White House. Zebulon made a move toward her but she rushed by him and went directly to Jeremy. "What happened?" she demanded.

But nobody could tell her except that there had been an accident. "Can he be moved?" she asked Doctor Smith.

He shook his head.

"Then we'll have to make do right here," she said.

For two days Rebecca, Wingate, and Circumstance kept vigil over Jeremy. "I won't let you die," Rebecca whispered in his ear. "Not after we've finally found each other. The Lord couldn't treat us so unfairly." He didn't respond, but continued to lie unconscious. The tears fell from her eyes, hot and blinding. "If you die, then I'll die also. You *must* live."

During the third day Rebecca's heart sprang with hope, for Jeremy opened his eyes. "Oh, thank God," she said, smiling at him. But he couldn't answer; all he could do was stare at her with wounded eyes. His body contracted with pain and she thought he might go mad with the agony of it; each spasm cut through her heart. He remained this way until Circumstance came to relieve her.

"Wake me instantly if there's any change," she said to Circumstance, and then lay down in a corner of the room and collapsed into sleep.

Circumstance took up the vigil, bathing her father's forehead with cool cloths. She stared at him; the once wonderful body lay twisted and misshapen. Hands clasped, Circumstance began to rock back and forth, and in a supplicating motion lifted her hands to the Great Spirit.

"I will give you anything," her soul sang out, "I will give you my own life if only you'll let him live." The sound of her rhythmic chant seemed to pour strength and will into Jeremy's broken body, and he moved his head slightly.

She murmured, "Oh, yes, you will live!"

Jeremy's lips parted and she leaned closer to hear him as he tried desperately to speak. Every word burned out what little life was left in him, but he had to tell her, to warn her.

He gasped, and a look of such torment crossed his face that

Circumstance's blood ran cold. "Father!" she whispered, clutching his hand, "Father!"

Jeremy managed to form one phrase, and the blood bubbled from his lips as he said, "Cain...and Abel." And then his eyes, so blue that they had always seemed like the sky reflected, turned blank and unseeing as the last of his life slipped away.

Circumstance cried out then and Rebecca and Wingate came running. Circumstance sat there, clutching Jeremy's hand. Wingate held a mirror under Jeremy's nostrils, but there was no sign of life. Gently, he released Circumstance's hold and then he brushed Jeremy's eyelids shut, and as he did, the light went out of Circumstance's life.

Rebecca sagged against a wall, unable to think, unable to move, rooted to that spot by a sadness so elemental she thought that she too would die. Her eyes felt hot and burning, her throat constricted, from the pent-up tears that wouldn't come, for if they did, it would be proof that he was dead.

And then with a primordial scream the floodgates broke and she became a wild woman, tearing her hair, and crying out in anguish. She cried then for all the days that would never be. She cried for herself, she cried for Jeremy, and she cried that Bravo would never know his father. Great wrenching sobs tore from her body, and then when she thought she had no more tears left, she cried for the cruel cheat that was life itself.

Chapter 34

REBECCA SAT in the pew in St. John's Church. She bowed her head and prayed for God to give her strength to go on. For weeks after Jeremy's death she'd moved through the days like one of the living dead, unable to think, unable to hold herself together. Letitia and the children learned to walk softly in her presence, for at the slightest sign of agitation, she might burst into tears.

Her despair descended into the deepest part of her being. She couldn't pass the theater without thinking, Jeremy and I will never go there again, couldn't see a cantering stallion without wondering what he would have looked like mounted on it, couldn't see a young couple in love without her heart withering.

In the dark hours of the night she conjured up the scene at the White House. With the information she'd been able to piece together, she relived the accident. With the intuition of a woman in love, she sensed that Zebulon had been responsible for Jeremy's death, and there were moments when she wanted to kill him with her bare hands. But what would that accomplish except to jeopardize the future of her children? She had no proof of Zebulon's guilt, and the courts didn't convict on the basis of a woman's intuition.

She still had her head bowed when she felt a presence in the pew beside her. "Mother, please come home," Suzannah whispered. "I promise, Gunning and I will be ever so good, if you'll come home."

Rebecca stroked her daughter's cheek . . . then she rose and slowly followed her out of St. John's. There was no saving grace for her here, anyway. Only the call of her children proved strong enough to carry her back into the mainstream.

In the next weeks events moved so swiftly that Rebecca almost had no time to mourn. Unbeknownst to her, Zebulon had petitioned the courts to have himself appointed as Circumstance's guardian.

"Why on earth would he do something like that?" Rebecca said to Letitia. "He's never paid any attention to her at all. Why the sudden solicitude?"

Her question was answered when the courts not only appointed Zebulon as guardian, but also named him administrator of all her affairs. "Of course!" Rebecca exclaimed. "The royalties from Jeremy's invention will go to her, but as her guardian, he'll be in control of all her money."

With the moral outrage huge in her chest, Rebecca betook herself to the house on New York Avenue and confronted Zebulon.

"You can't do this," she insisted. "You can't cheat her out of her rightful due. Enough has happened to the girl already."

Zebulon glared at her. The house was a slovenly mess. Empty bottles lay about, half-eaten meals cluttered the dining table, and ants had been busily building their colonies.

"I'm doing the girl a favor," he said. "We all know she's illegitimate and not entitled to anything Jeremy left. But I'll take care of her. Fortunately, she doesn't require much," he said with his off-center grin. It had once been so attractive to Rebecca, but now it struck her as devilish. "She has no head for the niceties of civilization as you and I know them."

"Have you no heart?" Rebecca whispered.

"About as much heart as you," he snapped. "Don't think I've forgotten that you wanted Jeremy to send her to an orphanage when she was a baby, so the way would be clear for you to marry him. And now you accuse me of having no heart?"

"That was more than a dozen years ago," she said hotly. "People change—at least I'd like to think that I did. Though it's obvious that you've remained the contemptible swine you've always been!"

He got to his feet, laughing. "Ah, we were once so well matched, and we could be again."

"I'll see you in hell first!" She stormed out of the house and drove her carriage directly to the Capitol Building. She sought out Chief Justice Marshall in his basement offices and told him the predicament.

He considered the problem for a bit, going so far as to search through a few of his law books. "I'm afraid there's little you can do," he said finally. "Zebulon has precedent on his side."

"Is justice to be mocked because of a precedent?" she demanded. "What's going to become of that poor child? I can't let this happen. I owe at least that much to Jeremy."

"Rebecca, think. Even if this was brought to the courts, with the climate so violently anti-Indian, what chance would a child of mixed blood have with an all-white jury? There is a possible solution, though."

"What?"

"If you remained married to Zebulon—"

Rebecca jumped to her feet.

"—then at least you could have some effect on the way Circumstance was raised. But once divorced you'd have no rights at all."

"Do you realize what you're asking me to do?"

"It won't be as bad as it sounds," Marshall began. "You'd remain legally separated, of course. That way, unless it was your choice, Zebulon would have no conjugal rights. You'd continue to reside under separate roofs, and knowing Zebulon, I'll wager he'd much prefer to have Circumstance living with you. All he's concerned with is the guardianship."

Rebecca thought about that long and hard. Beside Circumstance's well-being, there were other, equally serious considerations. If she went through with the divorce proceedings now, unnecessary attention might be focused on Zebulon, particularly in relation to the manner of Jeremy's death. Any such suspicions could only harm Gunning and Suzannah.

Night and day Rebecca worried the problem; at last, and quite uncharacteristically, she opted to do nothing for the moment. As Marshall had predicted, Zebulon quickly grew tired of having Circumstance underfoot, and when Rebecca suggested that the girl come live with her in Georgetown, he agreed. He had what he wanted, control over her affairs; her presence could only cramp his style.

But concerning Tanzy, Zebulon had other, nefarious plans. He waited until Eli left for Pennsylvania to investigate homesteading some land there. Then Zebulon quietly went about implementing his scheme.

Life in Washington went on. Congress prepared to ratify the Adams-Onís Treaty: the ease with which Andrew Jackson marched through Florida convinced Spain to cede the territory to the United States for five million dollars. Adams, with his usual diplomatic brilliance, managed to define Spain's holdings

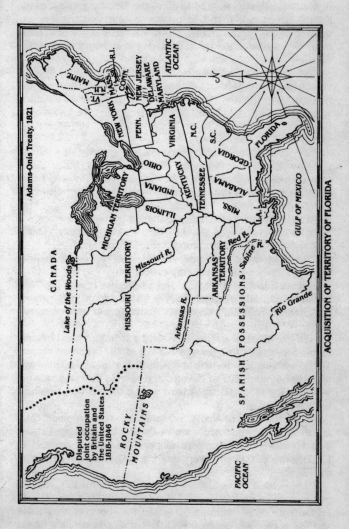

ACQUISITION OF TERRITORY OF FLORIDA

in the Southwest as limited to all of the Texas area west of the
Sabine River. Spain still held sway over a vast territory extending to the Pacific Ocean, but it was an uneasy and volatile
rule, with insurrections already sparking in Mexico and Cali-
fornia.

Rebecca sat at her desk in the Breech-Brand Stone Works,
calculating the debits and credits. She was trying to teach the
procedures to Gunning, but the boy seemed to have the attention
span of a gnat. "According to these books, we've lost money
this year," she said.

"Why?" he asked laconically.

"Because the economic recession that started last year has
gotten worse," she explained. "The Bank of the United States
is insisting on a tight money policy and has foreclosed on many
of the mortgages of settlers on the frontier, and the ripple effect
is reaching us here in Washington. Rightly or wrongly, the
West feels that an Eastern Establishment is running the country
with little or no regard for their own special interests. That's
why they're organizing around Andrew Jackson."

"Oh, who cares?" Gunning blurted, bored beyond the telling
of it. He dashed out of the tiny office.

Rebecca looked after him and shook her head. The only
person who could ever handle him was Zebulon, and without
his father in constant attendance, Gunning was running wild.

The Presidential elections, usually a source of great interest
for Rebecca, this time moved her not at all. On December 6,
1820, without any formal opposition, President Monroe was
reelected, getting 231 of the electoral votes. One electoral vote
was cast for John Quincy Adams so that the election wouldn't
be unanimous.

"Why did they do that?" Suzannah asked her mother. Suzannah and Circumstance were in the kitchen helping Letitia,
Tanzy, and Rebecca prepare dinner. Tanzy, still devoted to
Circumstance, came in every day from Anacostia to help with
the chores.

"This country has always had its eye out for any royalist
pretensions in its Presidents," Rebecca said. "It's why Washington society is shunning Mrs. Monroe, because they think
she has a case of 'queen fever.' But notice how she's begun
to drop her superior airs. Woe to any President, or his First
Lady, who comes to believe that they're anointed, rather than

elected. That's why the one vote was cast, as a symbol that this is a government of the majority of the people. Not that we have much to worry about with James Monroe—he's so placid, so Christian, so right in all things." Rebecca chuckled. "Some call this the Era of Good Feeling. I call it the Era of Boredom."

Circumstance deftly filleted a striped bass and pounded it flat, then seasoned it. "I remember my father once telling me..." Her voice caught in her throat, but she forced herself to go on. "He told me about an old legend, of an Indian chief who put a curse on the White House."

"What ever was it?" Suzannah asked.

"That any President elected in a year ending in zero would die while he was in office."

Suzannah's hand flew to her mouth. "Does that mean President Monroe will die in office?"

Rebecca shook her head. "I remember that legend also. It was at the Battle of Tippecanoe that Tenskwatawa the Prophet, the brother of Chief Tecumseh, laid down the curse. But as I recall, several other things had to be in effect. Some strange configuration of the planets—Saturn and Jupiter, I believe. And the astrologers tell us that for some reason, that configuration doesn't happen in this twenty-year cycle."

"But *will* it ever happen that way?" Suzannah asked.

"I don't know that much about the heavens," Rebecca said, smiling. "Also, the curse was specifically leveled against our General Harrison, who defeated Tenskwatawa." She sighed. "All things being equal, I don't think we have too much to worry about with Mr. Era of Good Feeling in the White House. Monroe is so benign that no curse could ever affect him."

The girls laughed.

"Watch out, now," Tanzy said as she dropped dumplings in the kettle of bubbling soup stock. The savory odor filled the kitchen. They heard a knock at the front door and Letitia went to answer it.

Tanzy dried her hands on her apron. "Maybe it's Eli," she said hopefully. Her husband, still away in Pennsylvania, was expected home any week now.

Letitia came back and said, "There's two men at the door and they're looking for Tanzy."

"Oh my God, something's happened to Eli!" she exclaimed and raced for the front hallway with everybody following her.

But when they reached the foyer, the two men stepped

forward and clapped handcuffs on Tanzy before she could resist.

"What's the meaning of this?" Rebecca demanded. "What are you doing in my house? I'll have the law on you!"

"We *are* the law," one of the men said. "We're bounty hunters, and we're arresting this woman for an escaped slave."

"What? That's ridiculous," Rebecca cried. "By whose order?"

"According to these here papers, she was the property of one Jeremy Brand."

"That's right," Circumstance interrupted. "But my father freed her." She ran to Tanzy's side, but the other bounty hunter shoved her away.

"When this Jeremy Brand died, she automatically became the property of his brother, Zebulon Brand, there being no other legal relatives."

"But that's not so," Circumstance exclaimed, fighting to get at Tanzy. "I'm Jeremy Brand's daughter, so even if she hadn't been freed, Tanzy would belong to me."

"Don't pertain, 'count of you're a bastard, and got no rights in this." With that, he yanked on the chains and dragged Tanzy along.

She started to scream and kick, calling out for Eli, saying she would kill herself rather than return to Zebulon. Rebecca grabbed a vase and came at one of the men, but he drew his pistol.

"Wouldn't want me to shoot anybody now, would you?" Then the men lifted Tanzy bodily and carried her out of the house.

Rebecca clutched the children to her. "Don't worry. It's a horrible mistake. We'll clear it up as soon as the court opens in the morning." But she said it with an optimism she was far from feeling.

Chapter 35

IN THE district courthouse, Rebecca ran into a tangle of red tape. "The whole thing is so complicated," she told Circumstance. "All the papers your father filed to free Tanzy were burned when the British sacked Washington. There isn't a record left of anything."

"But what are we going to do?" Circumstance asked.

"Much of it will depend on your testimony," she said, squeezing the girl's hand. "Do you think you can do it?"

"I must," she murmured. "Tanzy's life depends on it."

Circumstance took the stand at a preliminary hearing before Judge Dothier, a hard-line southerner and a slaveowner himself. She placed her hand on the Bible and swore to tell the truth, though she didn't need a book to do that.

"My father bought Tanzy at a slave auction and then immediately set her free," Circumstance said.

"Immediately?" Judge Dothier asked.

"That's what he told me," she said.

Zebulon interrupted. "May it please the court, such evidence is nothing more than hearsay, particularly since this girl would have been a two-year-old child at the time. Hardly a credible witness."

A burst of laughter broke out in the courtroom, and even the judge smiled. Zebulon continued, "Further, though this young lady claims to carry the name of Brand, there is absolutely no proof as to her own legitimacy."

Circumstance felt the blood drain from her face. The talk she'd heard all the years of her growing up, the whispers of the schoolchildren, the knowing looks of the ladies in society . . . now suddenly it was all out in the open.

"My father told me that Captain Meriwether Lewis married him and my mother, White Doe, while they were on the Voyage of Discovery across the continent."

Zebulon's snicker ignited more laughter in the courtroom. "There is no record of that either, and Meriwether Lewis was an unstable man at best. Remember, he committed suicide in 1809. But even if Lewis did go through such a mock ceremony, surely he did it as a joke. He had no authority to perform any marriage. On that basis, I ask that this witness's testimony be stricken."

"Granted," said Judge Dothier with a bang of his gavel.

Rebecca stiffened. The rest of the evidence went as badly for Tanzy. It's all happening this way because of the times, Rebecca told herself as she tried to figure a way out of the morass. At this very moment, the capital was in a turmoil over the provisions of the Missouri Compromise. The issue of slave versus free states had turned into an ugly confrontation.

In a bitterly fought battle in Congress, a compromise designed to maintain the balance of power in the Senate had finally been hammered out. Under the terms, Maine was to be admitted to the Union as a free state, but Missouri could draw up whatever state constitution it liked. Slavery had existed in that territory since the early days of the French settlers. But the North had rammed through a stipulation that in the rest of the Louisiana Territory, slavery would be prohibited above the latitude of thirty-six degrees, thirty minutes. Missouri was to enter the Union, as a slave state. The thirty-six–thirty line became the slave-free state boundary, and among the more rabid lawmakers, it was considered almost a part of the Constitution.

But most southerners felt that they had given away too much in the compromise, and a number of minor insurrections had further clamped the lid of repression down on the slave issue. It was in this bitter atmosphere that Tanzy's trial was being held.

Then it was Rebecca's turn to take the stand. "Your honor, my brother-in-law, Jeremy Brand, told me that he freed Tanzy in return for five years of her labor."

"Did you see the papers?" Judge Dothier asked.

"I did not," Rebecca said. "But I know who did. Francis Scott Key prepared them and registered them at the Hall of Records."

"Then why isn't he in this courtroom?" Judge Dothier asked.

"My understanding is that Mr. Key is currently in New York on business," she said. "We've sent an urgent letter requesting his return, but as yet there's been no response. You know how slow the mails are."

Zebulon scoffed at that. "Your honor, can't you see that this is but another delaying tactic? By right of inheritance, I claim this woman as my property."

A low muttering of agreement came from the spectators and Judge Dothier banged his gavel. "Order!" The delicate balance trembled and swayed. Tanzy's manacles clanked as she gripped the sides of her chair.

"Until such time as can be proven otherwise, the court finds for Zebulon Brand," Judge Dothier declared. "If Mr. Francis Scott Key returns and presents other evidence, the court may reopen the case."

Tanzy leapt from the chair and stumbled toward the large window that looked out onto the street. But before she could hurl herself through the glass, the bailiff grabbed her. The courtroom erupted in pandemonium; several self-righteous men declared as how the girl's actions proved that niggers were nothing more than savages, and best be kept in their place.

Rebecca took a crushed Circumstance home. "Don't worry, this will right itself," she said. "Justice is often blind, but in the end the scales balance themselves."

"But there are so many people in Washington who *know* that my father freed Tanzy, yet none of them came forward."

"It wouldn't have done any good anyway," Rebecca said. "Their testimony would also have been considered hearsay. In a less hostile atmosphere, the judge would have surely found in Tanzy's favor, or at least placed her in the court's custody until Key's testimony could be heard. But because of this damned Missouri Compromise, and the hatred it's generated, he's afraid that a ruling in favor of a Negro might cause rioting. We mustn't forget that though Washington is our capital, it's also a southern city with a southern mentality."

Circumstance grew pensive. "What will happen when Eli gets back?"

"Pray that he doesn't return until Key gets back and can free Tanzy."

The days slipped by, and still there was no word from Key, nor was there any knowledge of his whereabouts. He had become active in an antislavery movement and traveled to New York and New England to galvanize support to prohibit the smuggling of slaves from Africa. Though their importation had officially been banned by the government in 1808—Jefferson and Madison both felt that Negroes were tipping the balance of the population to a dangerous degree—Eli Whitney's invention of the cotton gin still made slavery an attractive financial policy for the South.

Tanzy was plunged back into the hell which she'd once known. Zebulon kept her imprisoned in a basement room of the house on New York Avenue. For almost a week he fed her a meager diet. He remembered how strong she'd once been and thought it best to break her spirit. Then one evening when he thought she was worn down enough, he went to her cellar chamber.

He'd taken the precaution of having her manacled to the wall, and when he entered she stared at him, wild-eyed. "I wouldn't want you to do anything as wasteful as taking your own life," he said with his off-center grin. When he released her, she tried to fight him off, but though he was in his late forties, he was still strong. He crushed her in his arms. "I've never spared myself, either in work or play, and now with you it will be no different."

"But what do you want with me?" she cried, struggling to get away from his lips. "You can get any woman you want—younger, prettier."

"Ah, but it's because you resist—that makes it all the more desirable. And you always had a way of making me feel like a stud bull."

"Eli will kill you when he comes back."

"You don't understand. I own you. And if Eli gives me any trouble at all, I'll have his freedom taken from him also."

He used her in all the ways a man could use a woman, and then thought he'd even invented some new ones. All the bitterness he felt toward Rebecca and Jeremy he pounded out on Tanzy. He spent hours with her, until he was raw with fatigue and with his excesses.

Eli's never coming back, Tanzy thought. Something must have happened to him. Oh, please, dear God, then let me die.

"I cannot let this go on," Rebecca said to Letitia. "Maybe if I spoke reasonably to Zebulon—*something!*"

"What you aiming to do?" Letitia asked. "Nothing crazy, I hope."

"Nothing like that. I'm too old." Taking her courage in both hands, Rebecca went to see Zebulon. She found him in the study of the New York Avenue house, talking to a portly man with thick spectacles.

"Ah, my dear wife," Zebulon said, and introduced her to Mr. Deering.

Rebecca recognized him as a partner in one of the leading building and contracting firms in Baltimore.

"Madam, a pleasure," Mr. Deering said. "I cannot tell you how pleased I am to be associated with a company like the Breech-Brand Works."

"We're equally delighted," Rebecca said. She hadn't the faintest idea of what he was talking about, but she had every intention of finding out. "How soon will the matter be finalized?" she asked artlessly.

"Oh, I'm sure that Mr. Deering prefers not going into such mundane things again," Zebulon interrupted.

"Not at all," Mr. Deering said, obviously fuddled by Rebecca's presence. "We should go into production on the Brand movable scaffold within six months, I'd say. With your share in the profits, plus the royalty on each scaffold, I can assure you that we'll all do very well. Very well indeed."

In short order, Rebecca extracted the rest of the information from Mr. Deering. "We have reports on the census of 1820," he said, "and they're astonishing beyond belief. Our nation is fairly bursting at the seams. We now have a population of more than nine million, five hundred thousand people!"

"That is extraordinary," she said. "How did the cities fare?" That had always been a primary concern of hers, for cities meant buildings of brick and stone, all of which could help rejuvenate the Breech-Brand Stone Works.

"New York appears to be the largest, with a population of about one hundred and twenty-four thousand."

"Due no doubt to the construction of the Erie Canal," she said.

"Precisely," Mr. Deering said, looking at her in surprise. "Very astute of you. Everybody is flocking to New York; the canal system connecting it and the Hudson River to Buffalo and the Great Lakes will be the shortest route to the West."

"If only the South had that kind of transportation system," she said. "Really, we must do something or we'll stagnate here."

"Philadelphia has one hundred and thirteen thousand people," Mr. Deering said, reading from his notes. "Then there's Baltimore with sixty-three thousand, and Boston with forty-three thousand. One of the biggest surprises is New Orleans. The population doubled, to more than twenty-seven thousand people."

"I recall what President Jefferson once said about New Orleans," Rebecca said. "Remember, Zebulon?"

He glowered at her but she went blithely on, "Its position at the mouth of the Mississippi will one day make it the mightiest port in all America, if not the world."

"As you can very well see, all this exploding population means housing and building. We believe that the movable scaffold with its ingenious safety lock can play an important part in reducing costs. Though there was that unfortunate accident, we've tested it quite thoroughly, and judged it safe. In fact, we cannot understand how the accident happened at all. So I look forward to great prosperity for us all."

After Deering left, Rebecca confronted Zebulon. "I hope you'll deal with this wisely. It could benefit the children enormously."

Zebulon regarded her with a lowering look. "I'm perfectly capable of deciding how and on whom to spend the proceeds."

She had come here to plead with him about Tanzy, but she blurted, "Have you no shame?"

"You speak to me of shame? You who bore my brother's bastard child? Who's shamed me in the eyes of every decent person in Washington? Or did you think your secret was unknown?"

She turned pale but with a supreme effort of will kept control of herself. "You were believed dead. Jeremy and I planned to marry, but then you returned. You wouldn't give me a divorce. I make no apologies for my actions. But now here you are, in full view of Washington, and your children, using a woman whom you know to be free. Yet you keep her in bondage. How do you think Suzannah feels? I ask you in the light of everything decent, in the light of all your hopes for their future, give up this madness—for that's what it is, madness."

Zebulon poured himself a shot of brandy and bolted it down. "I'm not doing anything that every man in this territory hasn't done. Even your precious Thomas Jefferson still keeps his

Sable Sally as a slave, and refuses to free the children she's borne him. And your friend Marshall—he's been known to dip his wick in his mulatto concubines. Perhaps if you'd been a more loving wife I wouldn't have had to stray from the fold."

"That's nonsense!" she exclaimed. "During our marriage I never denied you anything."

"Never anything but your love," he said softly. "How do you think a man feels knowing that his wife barely tolerates him? How long do you think love can last under such conditions? For whatever's happened to our marriage—to us, to Jeremy—you bear some blame."

"Perhaps I do," she said, her very spirit aching with these truths and half-truths. "I don't know anymore. But if that is the case, then there's no reason why we can't handle this like decent human beings. Zebulon, you're not a boy anymore, led around by the tail of youthful passions. Do the decent thing. Let Tanzy go."

"No," he said flatly.

"Zebulon, if you don't, I have a terrible feeling something awful will happen, something that will have horrible consequences not only for you, but for all the Brands."

"I never knew you to be one for omens and superstitions," he snorted. "I thought you left such nonsense to the little Indian bastard."

"Zebulon, please, if you have any feeling at all for Gunning and Suzannah—"

"They'll be amply provided for," he interrupted. "That's why I've entered into this business arrangement. And now if you don't mind, I've some urgent business—in the slave quarters."

His meaning was unmistakable and Rebecca cringed that he could have turned into such a beast. How much of it *is* my fault? she wondered. But that was a hopeless question, one that might never be answered. The important thing now was to protect the children, ensure their future, and she began to see that perhaps Chief Justice Marshall hadn't been so far wrong. If she and Zebulon divorced, she'd have absolutely no say at all in any business transactions. And while she had precious little say anyway, because of the accident of having been born a woman, nevertheless it was still something. As she swept from the house on New York Avenue, Rebecca decided that for the moment, she would quietly drop the divorce proceedings.

Three weeks later, Eli came riding back to Washington on his mule. His heart was bursting with joy, for he'd found a wonderful Quaker community in western Pennsylvania. They'd allowed him to put a deposit down on two acres of land, and they'd welcomed him into their community. At last he and Tanzy would now be among people who considered them human beings.

The moment Circumstance saw Eli she ran to him and clutched him, unable to speak.

He shook her. "What's happened? Where's Tanzy?"

"Zebulon," she whispered.

He dashed into the house and almost knocked Letitia over. "Where's your mistress?" he shouted.

Rebecca hurried downstairs, and explained what had happened. "I beg you, don't do anything rash," she said. "You'll only play into Zebulon's hand."

"All my life, white people been telling me that. They took the best years of my life, bound them in chains, and told me, don't do anything rash. They take my wife away from me and they say, don't do anything rash! And where's this got me? When can I shake Heaven for the wrongs done me and mine? When, I say?"

With that cry, he bolted from the house. He vaulted onto his mule and rode away toward Washington.

"I've got to stop him," Rebecca said. She ran upstairs to her bedroom, Letitia following her.

"Eli's right. He has been treated terribly, but he'll only make it worse for himself. He's doing exactly what Zebulon wants!"

"What you planning to do?" Letitia moaned.

"I don't know." Rebecca opened the dresser drawer and took out the pistol she kept there. She'd rarely used it, and her fingers fumbled as she loaded the gun.

"Oh, Miss Rebecca, don't!"

"Have Tadpole saddle my mare. Hurry." Minutes later Rebecca was galloping toward Washington. If only I don't get there too late, she thought, her heart racing in cadence to the horse's hooves.

Chapter 36

ELI REACHED Washington a little after sunset, but the last rays held the White House in its golden grip. The work gang of slaves chanted in rhythm as they were led away from the grounds where they'd been repairing the outbuildings.

Eli remembered his own years on that gang, slaving to build the American Palace. And in the land of the free . . . The fist of oppression clutched at his throat and he kicked the mule faster toward Zebulon's house.

He dismounted some distance away, then made his way stealthily toward the rear of the house. He entered, quickly determined nobody was upstairs, and crept down into the basement. He heard the murmur of a voice coming from a room . . . it sounded like Zebulon, and then his heart stopped when he heard a whimper—Tanzy! Eli crashed through the door and landed on the floor in the semidark room. The only light came from a flickering candle in a tall brass candlestick near the bedside.

Zebulon stared dumbfounded at Eli from the bed where he'd been toying with Tanzy. She lay spreadeagled, hands and feet tied to the bedposts. Zebulon grabbed for his pistol, but Eli sprang at him and knocked the gun aside.

"Been hungering for this for years," Eli said, and smashed his fist into Zebulon's face. He followed this with a hard left into Zebulon's solar plexus, knocking the wind out of him. Zebulon doubled over and crumpled toward the floor. Eli hit him on the way down, and Zebulon lay motionless.

Eli grabbed Zebulon's throat, but a weak cry from the bed made him turn. "Don't kill him," Tanzy whispered. "If you do, we'll never be free."

He released Zebulon and began to untie the ropes that bound Tanzy. Her ankles and wrists were raw from rope burns. Finally, he freed her and helped her to her feet. She fell against him. The days of being bound had left her muscles weak, and he lifted her into his arms and carried her toward the door. "Don't worry, you're safe now," he said fiercely. "And we're not waiting for any court or any Francis Scott Key. We'll be over the border and into Pennsylvania before they can get to us."

He'd reached the door when Tanzy screamed. Zebulon had gotten to his feet and was lurching for the brass candlestick. With Tanzy in his arms, Eli couldn't defend himself quickly enough and Zebulon brought the candlestick down on his head. Eli reeled back from the blow. Zebulon came at him again, hitting him on the temple. Stunned, Eli raised his hands, but Zebulon struck him once more and he crumpled.

Tanzy scrambled toward Zebulon and sank her teeth into his leg. Bellowing in anger, he kicked her aside. Tanzy screamed unendingly while Zebulon rained blows down on Eli until his face was a bloodied mass. "That for attacking a white man," Zebulon grunted. "And that!"

When Rebecca finally reached the house and managed to pull Zebulon off Eli, he had already bludgeoned him to death.

The death of Eli caused a great scandal in Washington, and sides were immediately formed. "Imagine, a nigger invading a white man's home and taking the law into his own hands!" said one camp of hardened southerners.

"It's murder, pure and simple," said the northern abolitionists.

In a cursory inquest, Zebulon claimed self-defense. That Eli had been caught on his property, carrying off his court-appointed slave, clearly put Zebulon in the right, and the court cleared him of any wrongdoing.

When Francis Scott Key finally returned to Washington, Rebecca's hopes sprang up. Eli was dead; nothing could be done about that, but at least Tanzy might now go free.

But Rebecca hadn't taken the mood of the capital into account. Though Key testified that he had indeed filed the papers to have Tanzy freed, he could offer no hard evidence except his word, for all his briefs had also been destroyed when Washington was burned.

Zebulon claimed it was all a plot cooked up by the abolitionists. "Key is a known sympathizer with the dastardly movement to free all slaves," he said.

Key's testimony was ruled as inadmissable, and as the year

ended and 1822 began, Tanzy consigned herself to a living death.

Rebecca went into the bedroom that Suzannah and Circumstance shared. The girls were playing with Bravo, exclaiming over this or that antic.

Rebecca watched them idly; then she was struck with the similarity between the color of Circumstance's and Bravo's eyes; they were almost the same shade of aquamarine. I wonder if Circumstance notices it, Rebecca wondered. She must, she's not a stupid girl and at sixteen she was remarkably adult.

"I've just received a letter from Elizabeth Kortright Monroe," Rebecca said to the girls. "She's asked me for tea."

"How exciting," Suzannah said. "What can she want?"

Rebecca held the notepaper to her lips and whistled. "I don't know, but with Mr. Monroe well into his second term, it would be uncomfortable to spend these last years in her continued war with Washington society."

"When are you to see her?" Suzannah asked.

"Tomorrow afternoon."

The following day, Rebecca put on a simple cambric dress with a high neckline and long sleeves. Whatever Mrs. Monroe's intent, Rebecca wanted to present herself in the best possible manner, including appropriate dress. "Besides," she said to Letitia, who was helping her dress, "I'm thirty-nine years old. Time for me to act like the demure matron."

Their eyes met in the mirror and they both burst out laughing. "Miss Rebecca, I was at the bedside when you was born, and if God sees fit, maybe you'll see me to my grave. So I knows you're forty-two."

"I'm forty-two to you," she said on a lilt, "but don't you ever dare tell anybody!" This was the first time that she had really laughed since all the tragedy struck, and in the middle of it all, her laughter turned to tears.

Letitia knelt beside her. "I knows, I knows, but you'll see— time, that's the only healing. When my boy died of the fever, it took so many years to get over. But then I had my other children, like you, and you've got to live for them."

Rebecca nodded and dried her eyes. "And by God, I'm going to get Tanzy freed if it's the last thing I do. If I get the chance, I'll speak to President Monroe about it."

Mrs. Monroe served tea in the refurbished Oval Room, all decorated in golds and with its stunning Louis XVI furniture that the Monroes had chosen.

Say what you will about the cold witch, Rebecca thought, she does have taste. There was an understated elegance about the woman, and lo! she wasn't a slave to fashion. She wore a white crocheted cap over her short dark hair, and her dark blue dress trimmed with white lace accentuated her refined looks. Elizabeth Kortright had been aristocratic by birth, and her father, even though he'd lost his fortune in the Revolutionary War by backing the British, had thought James Monroe beneath his daughter's station. Nevertheless, they'd married. Everything that Rebecca had ever heard about them indicated that it had been a true love match. Elizabeth had remained steadfast to her husband, and the wheel of fortune had elevated her to the position of First Lady of the land.

"My dear, we haven't seen you in the White House for ever so long," Mrs. Monroe began. "We've missed you."

"Then why didn't you invite me to your daughter's wedding?" Rebecca wanted to say, but bit back that retort. Instead, she said, "Well, as you doubtless know, we've both been busy with personal matters."

Elizabeth Monroe nodded, then said, "I'll be frank with you. I know that some of my social practices have angered the residents of Washington. I'd like to do something to rectify that. And since you've lived here all your life and know practically everybody, I'd certainly be open to any of your suggestions."

Rebecca experienced a tiny twinge of triumph. The First Lady of the land was making overtures to her! "I'm flattered that you think I may be of some small help. Of course, it will be minor, since you and you alone call the turn in Washington. That is traditionally the prerogative of the First Lady."

Mrs. Monroe nodded graciously and poured another cup of lapsang suchong tea for Rebecca. "Alas, there are certain things I cannot do; my health prevents me from the severe exertions of making and returning calls. The roads here in Washington are still so abysmal. The other day the President's carriage broke an axle as we were riding along Pennsylvania Avenue. Something must be done about these potholes."

Rebecca's mind worked with a number of ideas. Then she said, "It's been a number of years since you've officially reopened the White House. This might just be the time to make the people feel that the house has truly been returned to them. Americans are jealous of their White House—though of course it's yours during the time of your husband's tenure. The people have always considered it their second home. Would it be too tiring for you to declare a day of festivities? It's too late for Easter, but perhaps we could celebrate the Fourth of July?" Rebecca grew excited herself with the idea. "Some children's games in the morning on the lawn, followed by a high tea, which I'm sure the ladies of Washington will help you prepare, and then end the day with a grand reception."

Elizabeth Monroe looked bemused. "Yes, I think that's something that my daughter can easily undertake. Eliza's so good at that sort of thing."

Rebecca shook her head slowly. "Since you've been frank with me, then let me return the favor. It's your daughter's attitude that's caused much of the alienation. Being so versed in the courtly ways of the Continent, she's naturally more at home with that sort of behavior. But our men and women fought and died for their independence. They may be abrupt, and perhaps a little crude in their manners, but their hearts are good, and they're determined that no seeds of royalty infect their freedom. The people must feel that they're *part* of the White House, rather than that they are last-minute invited guests. Mrs. Monroe, you are the First Lady, and you must take charge of this yourself. If you think it will be too much for you, then invite Dolley Madison. If she attends, then all of Washington will follow. Nowhere in America is there a woman more loved."

Mrs. Monroe swallowed hard at this, but Rebecca pressed on. "You must also invite former Presidents Jefferson, and Adams, and Madison."

"Oh, they'll never attend."

"Probably not. But once it's known that they've been invited, it's bound to break down the barriers that have existed. In short, Mrs. Monroe, turn the American Palace back to the people."

"My instinct tells me that you're right," Elizabeth Monroe said. "This house can be very lonely when . . ." She interrupted her thought and said, "I'll start work on it this very day. One thing, though. I will not have Peggy O'Neale Timberlake in my house."

Rebecca shrugged. Peggy, the high-spirited daughter of an innkeeper in Washington, had gained an unsavory reputation for herself. She'd married a pursar named Timberlake, but since he spent long periods of time at sea, Peggy was rumored to be bestowing her favors on an assortment of legislators, including Senator John Eaton from Tennessee. Peggy was undeniably vivacious and witty, but Rebecca had never much cared for the girl; she was far too full of herself. Rebecca looked at Mrs. Monroe evenly. "As First Lady, it's your prerogative to invite whom you wish."

"May I count on you, then?" Mrs. Monroe asked.

"Absolutely," Rebecca said, as she rose to leave. "Oh, there's a small personal favor I'd like to ask, one that demands that justice be done, or I would not ask it." She told her about Tanzy.

"Naturally, we've been aware of it," Mrs. Monroe said, "and we're heartsick about it. Of course I'll speak to the President about it. But I must remind you of how hostile feelings are here in Washington."

"I know. But nothing ventured, nothing gained."

When Rebecca got back to the house in Georgetown she said to Suzannah, "There's to be a major event at the White House. Everybody will be there! We must get you looking your best. I want you to be particularly nice to the Van Ness boy, and to the grandson of Colonel Tayloe and—"

"Mother! You sound like you're trying to auction me off to the highest bidder!"

Rebecca started. "Of course I'm not, dear," she said with haste. Yet she knew that it had sounded uncomfortably like that. Rebecca also knew the reason for her feeling this way. The rise and fall of the Breech-Brand fortunes, brought about chiefly by Zebulon's excesses, had always unnerved her. She yearned for something more secure for Suzannah.

She smoothed back a wisp of Suzannah's hair. "There's no harm in being practical, now, is there? With the situation between me and your father so . . . tentative, to say the least, it wouldn't hurt for you to marry somebody who's financially secure. How old are you now?"

"Going on fifteen."

"A year's engagement, perhaps more; that would make you sixteen, or seventeen. That's the perfect age for marriage.

Childbearing is so much easier then. We'll make you a perfectly wonderful dress."

"What about Circumstance?" Suzannah asked. "I won't go unless she goes. And don't forget, we must do something about Tanzy."

"But of course," Rebecca said, and told her about Mrs. Monroe. "We must also corner some influential people that night—Henry Clay, John Calhoun, Daniel Webster, see if we can't sway some opinions. We all know that men think that they can exercise influence. Well; it's time to show them that women can do the same. If women had the vote, if women could sit on juries, this would never have happened to Tanzy."

Chapter 37

RESPONDING TO Elizabeth Monroe's invitation, Dolley Madison arrived in Washington three weeks later. She'd left James Madison at the estate in Montpelier, he hadn't been feeling well, and she didn't want to fatigue him. Dolley went immediately to her sister's house on H Street, which they'd recently purchased for the outrageously high sum of forty-five hundred dollars. As soon as she'd refreshed herself, Dolley went to pay her respects to Mrs. Monroe, and thereafter journeyed to Georgetown to see Rebecca.

At the sight of each other the two women burst into tears. They spent long hours in the sitting room and Rebecca recounted all that had happened. Dolley wept unashamedly, particularly at the description of Jeremy's death. At last she recovered. "We must honor the dead," she said, "but pay full attention to the living."

Suzannah came into the room with a tray laden with cookies and spun-sugar candies. "Letitia and I made you these sesame cakes and this lemonade."

Dolley blew her a kiss. Suzannah curtseyed and left the drawing room. "I've never see a young girl as beguiling as Suzannah," Dolley said. "Oh, my dear Rebecca, remember when we were young and our bodies fairly sang with such grace. Those dark eyes and that hair! Why, she has romance written all over her."

"She's inherited Zebulon's extraordinary looks, but without his disposition, thank the Lord. Though I'm afraid she's too easily led. I do so want her to marry well."

"You must let her choose, of course," Dolley said. "Surely there's somebody in Washington who'll catch her fancy. You'll never have to worry about Gunning, my dear. One can tell that he's your son. The same coloring, the same high spirits."

"And the same penchant for getting into trouble as his father. Already he's begun to make up to every serving wench. And he's so damned good looking that he has an easy time of it."

"Oh, I know what you mean," Dolley said, throwing up her hands. "I have the very same trouble with my Payne Todd. Mr. Madison has paid the boy's gambling debts, and his clothing debts, and bad checks and the like. He's been more than a father to my boy. But Payne Todd really has such a good heart, and a mother knows that he'll outgrow these youthful extravagances."

Since Payne Todd was already in his thirties, Rebecca thought it was a little late for that. Extraordinary how intuitive Dolley could be about other people's problems, but when it came to her own son, she was blind.

Then Letitia brought in Bravo. Dolley cuddled the boy; he took to her instantly, climbing all over her and grabbing at the ostrich plumes in her turban. Tears started to Dolley's eyes once more and she whispered to Rebecca, "Oh, my dear, he reminds me so much of one we've loved and lost . . . sometimes we wonder at the ways of the Lord. Who can ever know why things turn out as they do? But how fortunate you are, to have this child as proof of a love that God and nature sanctioned."

Just as Dolley made ready to leave, Circumstance came in. She'd been down at the Potomac drawing the plants, insects, and animals that teemed along the shoreline.

"But how you've grown!" Dolley exclaimed. "I left you here as a child, and now you're a young woman." She opened her arms, but Circumstance hung back. "Oh, come to me, don't break your poor old Aunt Dolley's heart."

Circumstance ran to her and rested her head on her chest. But even then Circumstance barely cried. Dolley was distressed at the girl's mood. But under the circumstances, how could she be otherwise?

"My dear Circumstance, I've come to Washington to attend the Monroes' reception," Dolley said. "And I've arranged for you to go with me."

She shook her head slowly. "How can anybody think of such a thing when Eli is dead, and Tanzy remains a prisoner? It's so unfair!"

"I know, Rebecca's told me. But that's why you and I must go, so we can *pounce* on anybody with influence. We must pounce, pounce, pounce, that's all these lawmakers understand. Don't worry—by the time we're finished, Tanzy will be a free woman."

"Do you really think so?" Circumstance asked.

"Yes, but only if we work at it. And that's why you must promise to come to the ball with us."

Circumstance flung herself into Dolley's arms. "Oh, I promise. Do you think we can do it, do you really?"

Surprisingly, the Fourth of July was quite pleasant. A quick breeze blew in from the Chesapeake, and it wasn't laden with the usual humid air. Dolley Madison conducted an egg-rolling contest on the White House lawn, an institution she'd established early in her years in the President's House, particularly during Easter.

By noon, huge pitchers of lemonade, and platters of seed cakes that had been baked in the new White House ovens, were set out on the lawn. The local tribes of the Algonquin and Susquehanna Indians had been invited to participate in the festivities, and a cry went up from the onlookers as the braves in their feathered headdresses pranced onto the lawn. With their drums beating and with ululating cries, they went into their ritual dances, brandishing their lances and tomahawks, much to the delight and fright of the watching children. Circumstance felt her blood quicken as she stared at them.

During the heat of the day, everybody retired to his own house. That evening, all of Washington put on its finery to attend the gala reception at the White House. Suzannah and Circumstance dressed; Suzannah, so excited with her new gown, turned this way and that in front of the mirror. She tied and retied the pink ribbons that ran through the neckline of the white organdy dress.

"You look wonderful," Circumstance said.

"Oh, and you do too," Suzannah said, staring at her cousin, who looked so different dressed in the fashion of the day. Her hair, which usually hung loose to her shoulders, had been bound in a bun on the back of her neck. It made her look years older. Suzannah had insisted that she take one of her good dresses, a pale green taffeta. But it somehow made her look sallow.

"It does fit you wonderfully well," Suzannah said encouragingly.

Circumstance smiled but said nothing; she felt uncomfortable in these binding clothes, and wished she hadn't promised to attend the ball. But she didn't want to hurt Suzannah's and Dolley's feelings, and so she resigned herself to having a dreadful time.

"Shall we go?" Suzannah asked, and called to Gunning, who was to escort them. Rebecca and Dolley had gone to the White House long before to help Mrs. Monroe with the arrangements.

Gunning used his whip liberally, and the horses got their carriage there posthaste. They drove in through the White House gates, got out of the carriage, and were dazzled by the huge lanterns blazing at the north entrance. The three of them started up the steps but suddenly Circumstance pulled back.

"You go ahead," she said to Suzannah and Gunning. "I must do something first."

"What?" Suzannah asked.

But Circumstance was already running across the lawn. Suzannah turned to follow her but Gunning grabbed her arm and swept her into the entrance.

"Oh, come on," Gunning said. "She's always been a little crazy anyway, and I don't want to miss a minute of this."

Circumstance fled the mansion with its candles and lanterns in the windows, and the liveried servants that greeted each guest. The ghost of her father seemed to linger over the house and the sadness in her had grown so unbearable that she had had to run. Drawn by some instinct, she found herself at her old cabin, the place where she'd spent so many happy years with Tanzy and her father.

Zebulon had inherited this also, but had barred and shuttered it. He'd refused to sell it; because of its proximity to the White House, he thought that one day soon the property would soar in value.

Circumstance pried aside one of the shutters and wiggled through the window into the main room. Her nose crinkled at the musty smell. She moved slowly through the dark space, touching familiar pieces of furniture that had meant so much to her.

Her eyes filled with tears with the realization that this life could never again be. Then she went into the small storeroom and rummaged through the trunk. Her fingers touched something that had drawn her here, drawn her like some secret talisman . . . something she'd forgotten even existed. But here it was, waiting for her, beckoning to her from the past.

"Yes, I will go to the White House," she whispered in the darkened room, "but not this way."

Without another thought she began to strip off her clothes, peeling away the yards of fabric and the boned stays and the undergarments and the frills and furbelows of dressmaking until she stood naked. She undid the pins that held her hair imprisoned, then raked her fingers through the sable locks until they hung free around the slender stalk of her neck.

She pressed her hands together, invoking all the spirits of wind, sea, and sky, praying to the memory of a mother she had never known save in dreams, praying to a father untimely torn from her. She stood motionless for some moments and then began to breathe deeply, feeling her body filling with strength and resolve. For what she was about to do could surely bring all of Washington down on her head. She knelt at the trunk, reached into it, and then began to dress.

Chapter 38

REBECCA STOOD in the candlelit East Room, surveying everything with satisfaction. White bursts of carnations and gardenias vied for attention with the magnolia and white tulips. The large Public Audience Chamber looked and smelled wonderful.

Dolley Madison bustled about, bestowing kind words on everybody and buttonholing legislators who might be able to help Tanzy. The women of Washington society had outdone themselves; gowns of pink and blues mingled with the yellow and greens of silks, taffetas, organdies, and cotton eyelet.

Rebecca had a curious thought; as the years had progressed, social functions in the White House had gone on later into the evening. Then she gaped as a woman entered the chamber, swiveling her head in a jerky way that signified she expected everybody to acknowledge her presence.

"My nerves!" Rebecca whispered to Dolley. "It's Elizabeth Connaught!"

"How wonderful that the good Lord released her from the prison of her madness," Dolley said.

Elizabeth Connaught walked directly to Mrs. Monroe, who was sitting against the far wall; Elizabeth made a deep curtsey, more in keeping with manners of thirty years before than with present-day greetings. In fact, dressed in her out-of-date salmon-pink crinolines, she looked slightly silly.

Rebecca couldn't get over how young Elizabeth looked. She had the face of an aging girl, if such a thing were possible. Elizabeth looked first at one woman and then another in their fashionable clothes. Her brow crinkled. "Yes, I'm out of time; but tomorrow—tomorrow I'll get some new clothes. I just had to attend this gala, to let everybody know that I was back in Washington. You see, I've been away—yes, away."

Devroe Connaught had come in with Elizabeth, and he stood at her side, pulling uncomfortably at his collar. He hadn't wanted to come, but Elizabeth had insisted. Since she now controlled the purse strings of the Connaught fortune, he danced to her tune. Then he caught sight of a lovely young girl across the room, with dark hair and eyes, and in a wonderful white cotton dress adorned with pink ribbons.

"Who is that?" Devroe asked his aunt.

She looked at the girl blankly and shook her head.

A woman standing nearby said to Devroe, "That's Suzannah Breech Brand, daughter of Rebecca and Zebulon Brand."

At the mention of their names, Devroe's thin handsome face hardened. Brand . . . the family responsible for all his misfortunes. "And the sins of the fathers shall be visited on the sons," he whispered.

"What, dear?" Elizabeth asked.

"Nothing, nothing at all." The seeds of a plan began to germinate in his mind . . . No, he wouldn't arrange to meet Suzannah this evening. He would just watch, the better to learn everything he could about her.

John Calhoun poured Rebecca a glass of punch. With as much tact as possible, she asked the southerner for his help regarding Tanzy. When he didn't respond, she changed the subject adroitly. "Looking at this room, one can understand why Monroe's term in office is being called the Era of Good Feeling."

The South Carolinian, considered one of the most astute politicians that America had produced, grumbled, "Call it what you will, but I'm reminded of what one of the French kings said: *'Après moi, le déluge!'* "

"Oh? You think there are stormy times ahead?"

"Without question," Calhoun said. "Why, we're building our nation on false premises. The Missouri Compromise is nothing but a stopgap measure. Mark my words, it will work against us."

"How so?" She knew that his was the voice the South listened to, a powerful voice to be taken seriously.

"We cannot allow the northern states to keep dictating their terms of economics and morality to us. By allowing the Negro slave to be counted as only three-fifths of a person in the representation of the states, the South has given away too much. They should be counted as a whole unit."

"But they're slaves," she said. "They don't vote."

"But they cost something to feed and to house and to clothe, and they're the responsibility of their loyal masters. Better for us to dissolve the Union right here and now than to persist in this abolitionist madness that will sooner or later lead the states to bloodshed."

"We're seeing men freeing themselves everywhere on this continent," she said, trying to keep her temper in check. "In Mexico and in South America, new governments have banned the traffic in slaves."

"Let other countries do as they like. It's the right of free white men to live in the society they choose, and the South has chosen slavery. The atmosphere is so hostile, I dare not do anything for your Tanzy. The issues are far greater than the life of one person. My sentiments are: The Union if possible, but freedom to choose first."

"I don't believe that," she said flatly. "No matter what compromises are struck, the Union must be preserved. It's the only chance that this nation has to achieve greatness. Look at Europe with all its squabbling countries—shall we degenerate into something like that?"

Calhoun didn't get a chance to answer her, for Suzannah appeared, her cheeks flushed with the adventure of her very first grown-up party. "Oh, Mother, this house looks so beautiful. The candles alone must have cost a small fortune. Mother, I was talking to Chief Justice Marshall about Tanzy when General Jackson came up to us, and he was with this wonderful second lieutenant who asked me to dance. Oh, may I? Please say I can."

Dolley Madison joined them just then and said, "I saw the young man. He's very handsome."

"Bring him to me and we'll see," Rebecca said. Suzannah ran off and Rebecca said to Dolley, "One can't be too careful these days, what with the riffraff that's flooding Washington. People with petitions or harebrained schemes—everybody with his own axe to grind."

"To say nothing of fortune hunters," Dolley said. "I can't tell you how many nights I lay awake fearful about Payne Todd."

Suzannah came back with a tall gangly soldier whose broad bony shoulders appeared to be sticking out of his dress uniform. "Mother, may I present Lieutenant Jonathan Albright?"

Rebecca's eyes narrowed as she searched the man's face. He was taller, broader, had filled out considerably and was no longer a youth, but he was still the same Jonathan Albright who'd been so damnably impossible at the battle of Fort McHenry!

"Why, look who it is!" Jonathan Albright exclaimed with genuine delight. "This your mother, Suzannah? We met seven—no, eight—years ago, didn't we, Mrs. Brand?"

Rebecca felt her color rising. "Thank you for asking my daughter to dance, Lieutenant Albright, but I'm afraid that she's not available this evening."

Jonathan reacted as if he'd been slapped.

Suzannah's hand flew to her mouth. "But mother—"

"That will be enough, Suzannah," she said.

Suzannah's eyes flashed momentarily, and she turned toward Jonathan, but Rebecca's hand clamped around her daughter's wrist.

"If you won't let me, then I'll ask Father," Suzannah said, freeing herself from her mother's grip.

"Your father?" she repeated, feeling a wave of apprehension. "Is he here?"

"Yes, talking to Henry Clay, right there." Suzannah pointed across the sweep of the room to her father's broad back.

And then a sight moved across Rebecca's vision that made her body go tense. Into the Public Audience Chamber came a creature from another place, another time. The crowd parted to let the apparition through. Women whispered behind their fans and one girl giggled inanely until her mother slapped her.

"Why it's Circumstance!" Suzannah exclaimed.

Rebecca clutched the bodice of her gown, unable to believe what she was seeing. It was Circumstance, and yet not.

She was wearing a garment of the palest doeskin, somewhere between buff and white in color, and it was clearly Indian. Fringes hung along the edges of the sleeves and from the hem of her skirt, making the dress appear to flow with her as she moved. The exotic costume only served to heighten Circumstance's own unusual appearance, accentuating her sable hair, the tawny complexion, and the slanted almond-shaped eyes. Only the color of the eyes, the startling blue inherited from her father, marked her as a Brand.

Suzannah rushed to her and embraced her, and then Rebecca led both girls away from the center of the room, where all eyes had been fastened on them.

"Your dress is beautiful," Suzannah exclaimed. "Where ever did you get it?"

"It belonged to my mother," Circumstance said. "My father told me that she made it as her wedding dress. When she died, it was the only thing that he kept." She said it loud enough so that Zebulon and a group of lawyers and legislators standing with him could hear.

A pall of embarrassment hung over the East Room. Nobody knew quite how to respond. "How could you do this?" Rebecca demanded. "How could you cause all this commotion? Don't you see what you've done? You've thrown down the gauntlet to all of Washington society."

Circumstance's posture grew even more erect, and her gaze didn't flinch from Rebecca's condemning look. She said softly, "I didn't do this to cause you any pain . . . but for all the years I can remember, the whispers have gone on behind my back. 'Half-breed,' 'bastard,' and worse. Now the world can see that I'm of mixed blood, and what's more, I'm proud of it."

"But that's not the way things are done in Washington," Rebecca objected. "I've lived in this city long enough to know that tact, diplomacy, discretion are the things that matter here."

"You give them lovely-sounding names," Circumstance said, "but my father would have called them hypocrisy, and deceit, and lies. And where has it gotten Tanzy? I am what I am, and must stand or fall on that. And no amount of boned stays or silken skirts will ever hide that in me. I am Circumstance Brand, and my mother was a Shoshone."

"And you are my dear cousin, whom I love," Suzannah exclaimed, slipping her hand into Circumstance's.

Gunning stormed over to them, stranded as they were in the corner of the room with a large space around them, as if they'd suddenly contracted a dread, communicable disease. "You've made me the laughingstock of all my friends!" Gunning exclaimed. "They're saying that none of them will ask either of you to dance. What do you think of that?"

"Oh, God, what next?" Rebecca said.

Then Wingate Grange strode across the room. He wore the uniform of a student of Georgetown University—white trousers, blue jacket, and red neckerchief around his throat. He bowed to Circumstance and said, "May I have the honor of this dance?"

"Wingate! I hardly recognized you in your uniform," she said.

"The school let us out for the festivities tonight." And with that, he swung her into a waltz as the band struck up.

In her total befuddlement Rebecca turned to say something to Dolley Madison. When she turned back to Suzannah, her daughter was gone. "Where's your sister?" she asked Gunning.

"I don't know. Wait a minute. There she is, with that tall lieutenant."

Rebecca saw her dancing merrily with Jonathan Albright. She made a move to stop them, but Dolley stayed her. "My dear, let them. If you forbid it you'll only throw them closer together. Anyway, I remember when your own father tried to stop you from seeing the man you wanted. And you stood up to him. Now, Suzannah *does* have your blood flowing in her veins, so can you expect anything less of her?"

Rebecca was so annoyed she couldn't think of anything to say. Rather than cross Dolley, she decided to let Suzannah have this one dance. But she'd make damned sure that Jonathan Albright never got close to her again!

On the dance floor, Wingate and Circumstance moved in rhythm to the music. He'd never been a very good dancer, but with Circumstance he somehow felt less awkward. Screwing his courage to the sticking point he said, "You look beautiful."

But Circumstance appeared not to have heard. "Do you feel it?" she asked. She threw her head back and her eyes reflected the light of a thousand candles.

"Feel what?" Wingate asked, spinning her around faster as the tempo of the music increased.

"I don't know exactly. But my father spoke of it many times. It's as though this house has a soul of its own . . . the stones hold a mystery that they cry out to all who'll listen. That this is a house dedicated to everything good and decent in the world."

"I heard him say that many times," Wingate said. "And yet . . ."

"Yes, I know—he died working on it. But knowing the way my father felt, he wouldn't have chosen any more glorious death. This is his legacy, to me, to the country. This house was his very life, and now it must be mine."

"What do you mean?" he asked. "Girls can't do construction, or—"

"No, no," she interrupted, her voice throbbing with excitement. "Father always wanted to keep a history of the house, a history of its architecture. I still have some renderings he did of the way the old rooms used to be. And now we have this new building. Don't you see? It could be a memorial for all the people of this land, as well as a memorial to my father."

"Circumstance, I don't like the sound of this. You've got to have a life of your own."

"One can have both," she said. "Doing honor to the past in no ways holds the future at bay. Oh, quickly, let's find James Hoban, I must tell him."

She broke off dancing and led Wingate around the room until they finally came upon Hoban. He was with his wife and their brood. When Circumstance explained her idea to the master architect, he beamed.

"Capital!" he said. "Your father talked about it often, but we were always so busy we never got around to it. And I've seen your drawings, my girl. You've inherited his gift. By all the saints, we'll leave the American people a legacy that they'll never forget!"

"Oh, Wingate, I'm so happy," Circumstance cried, and threw her arms around the startled young man's neck.

Since it was the first time she'd ever done that with such spontaneity, he put no further obstacles in her path. He had designs of his own this night, and said, "I must talk to you. I'm a student now, true, but in a few years I'll be a doctor— one of the best in the whole of the United States and Canada. Even though most doctors are frowned on, I hope that one day—"

She put her finger on his lips. "Don't say it, not tonight. I care for you more than anybody in the whole world, but it's too soon. If you forced me to answer now I would have to say no. Oh, please give me enough time for me to heal."

"I'll give you a lifetime," he murmured. "Because there's no other in the world for me. Now or ever."

Then Suzannah and her tall escort came to their side and introductions were made all around. Circumstance looked at Jonathan Albright and liked him immediately. She turned to Suzannah. "Careful, your mother's heading this way."

From across the eighty-foot-long room they saw Rebecca bearing down on them. "How does a body get out of this place?" Jonathan asked urgently.

Suzannah looked terrified of the thought, but Circumstance squeezed her arm and said to Jonathan, "If you go out this door, it will take you into the main entrance hall. From there you'll have access to all the other rooms. You can get lost in any one of them."

Jonathan took Suzannah's hand firmly. She hung back only for a second, and then went off with him, quickly leading him. They hurried through the entrance hall and into the State Dining Room. "We only have a moment," she said. "Mother knows this house like our own and she'll find us soon enough."

"If we only have a moment—" Jonathan Albright swept her into his arms and kissed her soundly on the mouth. When he released her, she slapped him. She turned away from him and he grabbed her arm. "Wait up now."

"Mother was right! What must you think I am to have taken such a liberty?" The tears welled in her eyes.

"I think you're the most adorable, beautiful creature that I've ever seen, and I'd cut off my arm rather than offend you. Though if it's all the same to you, not my shooting arm. Say you'll forgive me, or I'll throw myself from yonder window."

She smiled in spite of herself, because they were on the ground floor. But her distress was so evident that he dropped to his knee on the green baize carpet and clutched her hand. He looked up at her with his warm brown eyes. "If it's the last thing I do, I'll earn your forgiveness for something done so rashly. The moment I saw you I wanted to know you . . . and holding you on the dance floor I knew that I wanted to spend my life cherishing you, loving you. Suzannah, marry me."

Her mouth flew open with the audacity of the man, and she ripped her hand free and ran from the room. He called after her, "Meet me here tomorrow, two o'clock!"

Suzannah ran right into the arms of Devroe Connaught. He'd seen her and the lieutenant leave the East Room and had followed them here. "Ah, it's Suzannah Brand, isn't it?" His voice was as liquid as syrup. He took a silk handkerchief from his pocket and handed it to her. "Quickly now—your mother is on her way and she mustn't find that you've been crying."

Hesitantly, she took the handkerchief from him and dabbed at her eyes. And this was the way that Rebecca found them, talking quietly.

Rebecca rubbed her forehead, confused. Of all people, she hadn't expected to see Suzannah with Devroe Connaught.

"Hello, Mrs. Brand," Devroe said. "Suzannah and I were just saying what a wonderful day this has been. And it's been made all the more wonderful by her presence. If I may be so bold, by yours also. Really, you're two of the most stylish women in the entire palace."

Rebecca's immediate reaction was that Devroe's smoothness wasn't to be trusted. Yet as they talked, his attitude continued to be so charming, and his conversation so witty, that Rebecca's guard dropped somewhat. She even found herself laughing, and then experienced a glimmer of hope. This horrible feud with the Connaughts... how it had sapped them all of their energies. If only it could end! Could it be that with this new generation...?

While Devroe's attention focused on Suzannah, Rebecca studied him. The resemblance to his father was marked, though Devroe was far better looking. His face was sharp, with a thin straight prominent nose, and thin lips that always seemed to be glistening. Apparently he'd gotten over his Aunt Victoria's death, and had also resigned himself to the death of his father. For she knew that he was being seen everywhere in Washington, and was much sought after by hostesses for his dry wit and raffish charm. Not for a moment did Rebecca entertain the idea of his being a suitor for Suzannah, but she was so relieved to find her with Devroe rather than with that lout Albright that she found herself being perfectly civil to him.

"Look, they've started the fireworks," Devroe said.

The crowd streamed out of the East Room onto the lawn to watch the display. Cheers went up with each starburst of color, but nobody cheered louder than John Quincy and Louisa Adams and their three sons. The Adamses took particular pride in this occasion because it had been John Adams, Sr., who'd first suggested that America celebrate the Fourth of July as its birthday. The display ended with a rocket that went far higher than the others and then descended in an aerial fan of red, white, and blue. After the sustained applause, everybody went back into the East Room.

"Mrs. Brand, may I have the pleasure of escorting you and your daughter to the theater next week?" Devroe said. "I understand the traveling players are giving a wonderful performance of *King Lear*."

"Why, I'll have to check my calendar," Rebecca said, but knew perfectly well that she had nothing to do. "Perhaps we may be able to squeeze it in. Thank you very much." Then she took Suzannah's hand firmly. "Come along now, dear, we mustn't keep Dolley Madison waiting."

On the other side of the expanse of the East Room, Elizabeth Connaught, her pearl-handled fan fluttering, finally got up enough nerve to circle toward Zebulon. He was standing near one of the tall windows, in earnest conversation with John Quincy Adams.

"We must have nothing less than a continental policy for our country," Adams was saying.

"What in blazes do you mean by that?" Zebulon asked. He'd had more than a little to drink and he'd never liked the Adamses. Father and son tended to be as austere as monks, and neither of them really knew how to enjoy himself.

"The only restriction to our boundaries must be that which the Lord has seen fit to provide, the Atlantic and Pacific Oceans. That's why I insisted that our treaty with Spain spell that out clearly. We're in contention with England for the Oregon Territory, but I believe that our claim is stronger," Adams said.

"Pity we couldn't have annexed Canada, or Mexico," Zebulon said.

"Sir, I'm not talking about conquering other nations, but in claiming land that is basically uninhabited, or is settled by none save our own frontiersmen," Adams said.

Before Zebulon could answer, Elizabeth Connaught appeared at his side. He was so unnerved that he could barely speak. "Why, Elizabeth!" He turned to introduce her to Adams, but that worthy had seen her coming and had quickly slipped away.

Elizabeth laid her long, exquisite fingers on Zebulon's sleeve. "How exciting to see you again," she breathed huskily. "There's gray in your hair, and your eyes look a little weary, but I would have known you anywhere."

He almost laughed aloud at her feeble attempt at coquetry. Clearly, she'd been out of touch with the real world these past thirty years.

"I must see you," she said urgently. "We've so much to talk about, so much time's been wasted."

"That's not possible. You see, I'm married."

"I know all about that marriage," she said. "I've heard that you're separated—you living in Washington, Rebecca in

Georgetown. Besides, I was married once, and that didn't stop you."

"Elizabeth, please, that was years ago."

She looked at him slyly. "Oh, I see why you're acting this way. Because this is a public place and you're afraid people will talk. You're so right, darling; I'll meet you later."

"No," Zebulon said, but Elizabeth was already drifting away.

"The poor creature belongs in Bedlam," Zebulon said to himself, and then pushed Elizabeth and all the Connaughts from his mind. He saw Rebecca and Suzannah across the room and went to them. Rebecca was aloof and formal, but Suzannah flung her arms around her father's neck and whispered, "We've missed you so much. Oh, Father, please let Tanzy go, won't you?"

"Suzannah, mind your manners," he said, putting her at arm's length. "Don't meddle in affairs that don't concern you."

The corners of her lips twitched; she hung her head, crestfallen.

Zebulon turned to Rebecca. "You should know that the Brand patent has begun to bring in a very comfortable royalty. Enough so that we could all be living in style. Isn't it time that you thought about coming home? Both for your sake and the children's."

Rebecca stared at him; she knew him well enough to know that something was going on in his mind. He saw her discerning look and smiled.

"You see, I've been thinking of running for office—congressman from Virginia perhaps. Naturally, it would be easier if the voters thought of me a family man."

"I see," she said. "Well, you would have to let Tanzy go before I'd even consider it."

Zebulon hunched his shoulders, enjoying his moment of triumph. It made him want to toy with her all the more. He knew she was short of funds; though she managed the stone works with a tight hand, the recession was fast draining her. If it went on for another six months she faced the distinct possibility of being wiped out. Having suffered at her hands all these years, he took great delight in saying, "How ungenerous of you, my dear wife, to set conditions on my taking you back. Thank God we haven't yet reached the day when a wife can dictate terms to her husband."

She clenched her teeth to keep from creating a scene.

"Incidentally, it's come to my attention that you're having some trouble with business debts."

"Only because of your profligacy," she retorted.

"Nevertheless, I'm prepared to offer you a handsome sum for the stone works."

"Never! My father built that trade up. It was you who ran it into the ground before I salvaged it."

He shrugged, a sardonic smile on his lips. "Have it your own way. I'll pick it up for a tenth of the price when you go bankrupt."

Rebecca turned on her heel and left. Suzannah looked at her father in a new light. "I didn't believe you could be so cruel," she whispered. "Oh, Father, please, please, you must change before it's too late." And then she hurried after her mother.

Zebulon watched Suzannah weave her way through the crowd. "Rebecca's done a good job of alienating her from me," he muttered. "Well, mothers and daughters are like that, they stick together. But she'll never be able to turn Gunning's head."

Zebulon stayed on at the levee a bit longer, but soon became irritated with all the talk about Western versus Eastern money policies, and the constant jockeying for power among the supporters of John Quincy Adams, Andrew Jackson, Henry Clay, and William Crawford. Monroe's second term was only half over, yet each of these men had serious designs on the presidency.

Zebulon downed a last glass of Kentucky mash, then left the White House. "Politics be damned tonight," he grumbled. "I've got other things on my mind."

For all this foolish talk about freeing Tanzy had done nothing but inflame him all the more.

Chapter 39

ZEBULON STRODE along through the heavy summer night, swinging his walking stick and lopping off the magnolias from the flower-laden branches of the trees.

Fever hung in the humid air; many of the aged and infirm in Washington had succumbed already to the malarial contagions. One has to be of sound stock to survive in this pestilential city, he thought, and thanked the Lord who'd given him a treetrunk of a body and the strength of a bear.

"I'm fifty years old," he sang out to the night, "and I'll probably go on bedding women right onto my deathbed, just like old Benjamin Franklin!"

He passed the Octagon House. The Tayloes had come into town for the White House reception, and the windows were ablaze with lights. Then he came to his own house. Though substantial by most standards, it was modest in comparison to the Octagon House. But my fortunes are on the rise, he thought. If the royalties keep rolling in at this rate, I'll soon build the finest house in all Washington.

In this euphoric mood he arrived at his door. He sensed that he was being watched and whirled, his cane raised. "Who's there?"

Elizabeth Connaught drifted out of the shadowed shrubbery, her gown seeming to float with her in the moonlight.

"Oh damnation!" Zebulon swore under his breath.

Without a word she came to him. In the kind night light she looked like the girl he'd once lusted for—the luminous dark eyes smoldering with inner fires, the body so eager and insatiable, how they had once impassioned him.

But as she came closer, he saw that her skin was somewhat like a painted doll he'd once bought for Suzannah. Though time hadn't changed the facade, everything below the skin seemed to seethe with madness and corruption.

She put her arms around his neck and kissed him. With an oath he flung her to the ground. "Get out of here," he grunted. "Out, before I take the whip to you! And if I ever catch you here again—" He grabbed her arms and hustled her through the gate. "Out!"

She ran to her carriage across the street. Tears of confusion streamed from her eyes. She couldn't understand why he'd treated her so, and after all she'd risked for him! Her mind became a writhing mass of vengeful schemes. She knew about the scandal surrounding Zebulon and his slave. It was on everybody's lips. Somehow . . .

That night, in the flush of his triumph over Rebecca, Zebulon enjoyed himself hugely with Tanzy. He was so piqued by the seeming rejuvenation of his flagging powers that he returned to her quarters every night for the next week. Tanzy endured his bestiality; it left her with one wish only, to die. But the gods heeded neither her anguish nor her wish, and each passing day saw her grow more devoid of any will. This was her lot and there was to be no rest for her. She was sure that her spirit would dream of this demon long after she slept the blissful sleep.

Then one afternoon the door to her room cracked open and a strange woman wearing a large hat and garden gloves slipped inside. She was carrying an armful of flowers—anemones, cyclamen, and mimosa. She put her finger to her lips and whispered, "Here, I brought you these. This room is so dark and empty. It needs brightening."

Still carrying the flowers, Elizabeth Connaught busied herself, trying to find the perfect spot for them. She considered a small chest, discarded that notion, eyed an empty slopjar in the corner. Then she whirled and came at Tanzy.

Barely visible beneath the bouquet of flowers that Elizabeth carried, Tanzy caught a glimpse of pruning shears. She must have just been using them, for they were crusted with earth and Tanzy could smell the rich odor of manure on them.

Is she going to kill me? Tanzy wondered.

But Elizabeth Connaught stopped just short of the bound girl. She recoiled when she saw the cruel abrasions on Tanzy's ankles and wrists where the ropes held her bound. "I know your pain," she whispered, "for though he never tied me thus, he held me prisoner by other means." Then she buried her face in her hands, and the flowers and pruning shears fell from her fingers to the thin mattress. Without another word she disappeared from the room.

Tanzy stared at the shears lying just out of her grasp. She spent the next hour chivvying her body inch by inch along the bed, gradually drawing the shears to her until they were within grasp of her straining fingers. Zebulon usually came at dusk, and if he did appear this evening, she only had an hour or so at most.

She managed to grasp a blade of the shears and in her awkward position began sawing away at the ropes. For a time she considered sawing through the veins in her wrist if the ropes wouldn't give. But at last she managed to fray one strand enough to get a hand free, and after that it went more quickly. She had just finished freeing her ankles when she heard the heavy tread of footsteps descending the stairs.

Outside, the twilight had deepened to dusk. Within the room there'd be no light at all until he lit the candle. She assumed the position in which he'd tied her, the pruning shears hidden up the sleeve of her shift. The door opened, then closed, and Zebulon's presence filled the room. He grunted, and turned his back to light the candle. Slowly, she withdrew the shears from her sleeve just as the halo of light illuminated the corner where he stood. When he stripped off his jacket her body tensed, and as he struggled to get out of his trousers, Tanzy struck.

"For Eli!" she cried, and stabbed the blade at his heart.

But Zebulon jerked aside, managing to deflect the blow so that the blade sank into his shoulder. The force of it, though, sent him sprawling to the floor.

Tanzy sprang from the bed and made for the door. But she'd been tied in that position for so long that her legs felt watery.

She hauled herself up the stairs, fell, got up again and made it through the hallway of the house to the front door. But Zebulon had recovered and gave chase. He caught her just before she reached the street. The commotion had brought his other house slaves running.

"Help me!" Tanzy cried.

But the two old house slaves just stood there. They'd been in bondage so long that they didn't know what to do.

Zebulon dragged her back inside. "I'll see you hang for this," he said, as the blood welled from his wound.

Zebulon moved swiftly to exact justice for this outrage not only against himself, but against the entire structure of law and order. Tanzy was brought to trial within two weeks.

Despite the testimony of Rebecca and Circumstance, the jury found Tanzy guilty of attempted murder, and Judge Dothier pronounced, "I sentence you to be hanged by the neck until you are dead, and may God have mercy on your soul."

Suzannah, unable to bear this injustice, went to see her father. "If you would say something, ask for mercy, I'm sure—"

"Suzannah, this doesn't concern you," Zebulon said. His arm lay in a sling and he adjusted it to a more comfortable position. "An inch or so lower and her shears would have pierced my lungs. Don't you see? If we allow this sort of insurrection to go unchecked, we'll be murdered in our beds."

"But I've known her all my life," Suzannah whispered.

"Enough!" Zebulon commanded. He grimaced with pain as he heaved himself out of his chair. "I'm your father and I know best."

"It's not best!" she said, her heart fluttering with the recognition that this was the first time she'd ever crossed her father. "She's a decent woman, and if you hadn't—"

Zebulon slapped her face. His fingers left their welted imprint on her cheek. She stared at him for a moment, tears starting in her eyes, more in sorrow for the rift between them than in pain. Then she turned and slowly left the house.

Rebecca took up Rebel Thorne's pen with a cold fury, excoriating the laws that permitted such a miscarriage of justice. Though her articles might jeopardize Zebulon's reputation, and thus injure the children, she had no choice. This was Tanzy's life. "Is this woman less a human being because her skin is darker than yours?" she demanded. "Has she no rights in the eyes of man or God, debased and degraded in a sexual bondage not fit for an animal? And if she struck out in self-defense, is it less than any one of you would have done? Mercy! Where is our Christian mercy in all this?"

Though the Rebel Thorne articles brought tears to the eyes of many Washingtonians, they couldn't stem the rising tide of anti-Negro sentiment. In Charleston, South Carolina, a plot led by Denmark Vesey, a freed slave, had been unearthed. Extreme measures had been taken; one hundred and thirty-four Negroes were arrested and thirty-seven of them were hanged. Secretary of War John Calhoun had even sent Federal troops to the city to quell the expected rebellion, and though it hadn't materialized, the panic remained. In this hysterical atmosphere nothing could save Tanzy.

In a matter of weeks, Tanzy was taken from prison to a gallows set up in the public square in Georgetown. Rebecca, Circumstance, and Suzannah had come, believing, praying that there would be a last-minute reprieve. But then the trapdoor was sprung and her body turned slowly in the wind.

Circumstance just stared at Tanzy until they cut her body down. Suzannah sobbed uncontrollably.

"I don't know what you're crying about," Gunning said. He'd come to the execution with a gaggle of his friends. "She was just a nigger anyway, and she tried to kill Pa." But his braggadocio couldn't quite hide his own queasiness, and when his mother glared at him he shut up.

"We must fight," Rebecca said. "The only way Tanzy's death will have any meaning is if we don't forget, if we keep on fighting."

"But it's Papa that I can't understand," Suzannah said. "Why would he do such a thing?"

"It's impossible to tell what a man will do when he's suffered disappointments, and your father has suffered several in his life." Rebecca didn't add that most of them had been of his own making.

"But can God permit such a thing to happen?" Suzannah persisted. "Is there no terrible retribution to come down on all our heads?"

"The issue is greater than Tanzy or your father, or any single one of us," Rebecca said wearily. "I remember Thomas Jefferson once saying that the entire issue of slavery was like a firebell in the night, and I fear that we're beginning to hear the first alarms."

"I believe that I've got the ague," Zebulon groaned to Gunning. Gunning had come to visit his father and found him lying on the settee, shivering with feverish chills.

"I'll tell Mama," Gunning said, starting toward the door.

"No!" Zebulon called after him. He rose from the sofa but fell back again with the weakness. "Get Dr. Smith."

Gunning rode off and returned an hour later with the bumbling, fumbling doctor. He poked and pushed, peered into Zebulon's mouth, examined the color of his urine. "No doubt about it, you have a touch of Potomac fever." He prescribed quinine tablets. "You'll be up and about in a matter of days, I'll stake my reputation on it."

But Zebulon got progressively worse, and Gunning finally told Rebecca, "Mother, you must see him. I think he's very sick."

The last person in the world Rebecca wanted to see was Zebulon, but she did it for Gunning's sake. When she entered the house she found the drawing room in darkness. She went to open the curtains and Zebulon called weakly, "No, don't, I can't stand the light." He twisted on the bed and stared at her with eyes that seemed sunken in his skull.

"Dr. Smith says it's malaria, and that it'll soon pass," he said weakly.

"Dr. Smith is a fool," she said. "Gunning, go and get Wingate Grange. He knows more about medicine than anybody in Washington."

"But he's probably in the university now," he said.

"Then go and get him out of the classroom."

Wingate and Gunning returned two hours later. Wingate did a cursory examination of Zebulon. "You're right," he said to Rebecca. "It's not malaria." He turned to Zebulon. "When did you first begin to feel badly?"

"Oh, about a month or so ago. But I fought it off and didn't think any more of it. It's this damned stiffness in the back of my neck, that's what bothers me most, I can't seem to get comfortable."

Wingate ran his fingers over Zebulon's face. "Does that hurt?"

"Not so much hurt as feel stiff. Sometimes so stiff that it's hard for me to swallow food. I can't imagine what it is unless the fever's settled in my jaws."

Wingate poked Zebulon's abdominal muscles and found that they too were stiff. He took Rebecca out into the hallway. "If I'm right—and I pray that I'm not—we have a very sick man on our hands. Serious to the point of being fatal."

Rebecca stared at him. "But what can it be? Zebulon's always been in the most robust health."

"That's why he's still alive now," Wingate said. "Or else he would have been dead long ago. He's got lockjaw."

Rebecca's mouth fell open. "Oh, my God, no! But how?"

"The pruning shears he was stabbed with. They must have

had some fertilizer on them, horse manure or the like," Wingate said.

"What can we do?"

"Very little. I saw a man die of it from wounds gotten on the battlefield at New Orleans, so I know a little about it. Zebulon must have absolute quiet; the slightest noise, even wind stirring the curtains, will become excruciatingly painful to him. If the disease progresses, he'll find it difficult to eat at all. His jaw will become practically immobile, and all he'll be able to manage is soup."

"How ghastly!" she breathed, clutching her throat.

Despite everything that had happened between them, despite Zebulon's own unreasoned cruelty, he was still her husband, still the father of her children. Rebecca, Suzannah, and Gunning moved back into the house on New York Avenue. There they took turns caring for Zebulon. Rebecca left Bravo in the Georgetown house, with Letitia and Circumstance to care for the child. Though Rebecca missed Bravo sorely, there was no reason for him to be exposed to this horror. Wingate came to tend Zebulon whenever he could, and though other doctors had been consulted, all of them agreed with Wingate's diagnosis. Zebulon Brand had lockjaw, and only the direct intervention of the Lord could save him.

Each day Zebulon grew progressively worse. The stiffness in the back of his neck grew, as did that in his jaws until he could barely open his mouth. Then the corners of his mouth were drawn downwards and back and became fixed in that position. It gave his face a horrible look; all he could manage to eat was the thinnest of soups, which Letitia prepared and Gunning fed him for hours at a time, so long did it take for him to swallow.

Rebecca, exhausted from the endless vigil, spoke to Wingate one day when he came in from the university. "Things appear to be getting worse. Now he can't even swallow."

He nodded solemnly. "The muscles of the throat are now involved, and then the final step will be that the muscles in his abdomen will become totally knotted."

Zebulon cried out hoarsely and Wingate went to him. His arms and legs were in spasm, knotting with fierce pain, making him thrash about on the bed. First he would double forward, then backward, and once, when Gunning dropped a cup, the shock of it sent Zebulon into a cramp so severe that they could barely straighten him out.

"Can't you do something?" Gunning cried, hitting out at Wingate.

Wingate shook the boy off and gave Zebulon a dose of morphia. "It will relieve the pain, but it won't cure it. All we can do is pray."

Circumstance came to see Zebulon once, and stood staring at him. Her presence seemed to make him writhe all the more, and Gunning shouted, "Get out, get out, he can't stand the sight of you!"

As she left, Circumstance whispered to herself, "It's the hand of Tanzy reaching up from the grave, pulling him..."

The contractions became so severe that some of Zebulon's muscles tore, sending him into an anguish of screams that were muffled by his locked jaws. Then the paralysis struck his chest and his breathing became labored. Gunning couldn't stand the final throes and ran from the room, but Suzannah and Rebecca stood by his side until he gasped his last, his face a twisted, grimacing mask of death.

Mother and daughter stared at each other, remembering Suzannah's awful question about the Lord and retribution. But at this moment they could find no words, and they clung to each other, each locked in her own grief at the death of this man who'd been larger than life.

PART FOUR

Chapter 40

LETITIA SET the tea service down in front of Rebecca. "Made you some nice camomile tea and Sally Lunn cake," she said. "Now come on, you got to eat something."

"I've no strength to go on," Rebecca said. "I don't know how I've managed to get through these past two years."

"That's not up to you; that's for the Lord to say," Letitia scolded her. "And there's the children."

"Oh, they can get on without me very well, they're old enough," she said with a desultory shrug.

"Maybe Suzannah and Gunning is, but Bravo, he's only six. How you expect him to make his way in this world without a mother or father? You crazy or something?"

Rebecca looked out the half door and saw Bravo playing in the backyard on a hobby horse he'd nailed together. He was off in his own imagination, galloping across plains and mountains, fording rivers, conquering worlds.

Rebecca loved all her children; she had as strong a maternal instinct as any woman she knew, and this somehow surprised her. For she knew she never could be satisfied with only that. After all, were fathers only satisfied with being fathers?

She couldn't really say if she had a favorite amongst her children; it depended on her mood. When she needed the quietude of somebody generous and loving, then she turned to Suzannah; the girl was almost too gentle to cope with this world. Gunning provided a brand of breathless excitement. Spirited, impetuous, spoiled by his good looks and brutish charm, he demanded the most attention, calling to mind the old adage, "The squeaky wheel gets the oil." And then Bravo, the child she thought she would have loved the most. But he was already so independent that he sometimes infuriated her by reminding her of Jeremy's obstinacies.

Just then Bravo came running into the room. "My horse broke his leg. I need to fix it. String."

Letitia went to get it for him. Bravo looked longingly at the cakes and Rebecca handed him one. He took it, then pressed it to her lips. "You first," he said, smiling. She took a bite, then he did. He ran off when Letitia returned and gave him the string.

Rebecca looked up at Letitia. "You're right, of course. They are wonderful children, these Brands, but all of them need discipline and direction. If for nothing else, I've got to live for them."

Within a number of months Rebecca found additional interests when she was swept into the frenzy of the upcoming presidential election of 1824. For all practical purposes, the Federalist Party had ceased to exist after the successful conclusion of the War of 1812. And so there were now four candidates from the Democratic-Republican party running for the presidency.

Louisa Adams was enlisting the aid of prominent Washington women to support her husband, and this afternoon she had come to see Rebecca. Louisa said, "In my mind my husband is the man best able to lead this nation through the troubled times that lie ahead. I hope you feel the same way."

"What are our alternatives?" Rebecca asked. "We have William Crawford, who's a nice man, but the office requires something more than a nice man. In addition, he's suffering the effects of a severe stroke. Then there's Henry Clay; he's been running for the presidency since he first entered Congress. I don't trust Clay. I believe he covets the office not so much for the good of the nation as for the power it will bring him. He's a man wedded to power. One only has to hear him on the floor of the House to realize that."

Louisa Adams looked with surprise at Rebecca. "My dear, I had no idea that you were so politically astute."

"What woman in this entire city is given credit for any knowledge of the way government runs?" she asked. "Now as to your husband. I hope you don't mind my being frank, Mrs. Adams. He suffers from the same disorder as his father. They're both taciturn, often vain about their capabilities, and with little or no sense of humor about themselves."

Louisa Adams's pale fair coloring flushed and she rose to leave. But Rebecca stayed her. "You must let me finish, else you won't see the whole picture. On the plus side, John Quincy Adams is probably the most brilliant man in the government today. During his tenure as secretary of state, he's successfully negotiated the Rush-Bagot Treaty, which limits our arms with our Canadian neighbors; has gotten us the territory of Florida through the Adams-Onís Treaty; and has defined America's borders as extending from sea to sea."

Louisa Adams settled back in her chair. This knowledgeable woman could be a formidable enemy, or ally. She said quietly, "Then, of course, there's the doctrine that my husband wrote concerning the future of the Americas."

Rebecca nodded. "Unfortunately, the people of this country are at the moment so self-involved that they cannot understand its true significance. And since it's taken the name of the President, and is called the Monroe Doctrine, people tend to think that James Monroe is responsible for it. We both know that Monroe is an amiable man, well-intentioned, but without the brains to have formulated such a far-reaching and brilliant policy."

"It's so troublesome for a wife when she sees her husband passed over for credit that should be his."

"I remember when your mother-in-law told me the very same thing about John Adams," Rebecca said, smiling. "The nation lost a good woman when Abigail died. How long has it been?"

"Five—no, six years ago. And my father-in-law still hasn't gotten over it."

"Abigail said to me, 'Here my John was the principal patriot of our Revolution; in fact, it would be fair to say that there probably wouldn't have *been* a revolution without him! And yet it's George Washington who gets all the credit!' How it infuriated her. But of all her children, it was John Quincy who gave her the most joy. How pleased she would have been that he had the possibility of being President. But she certainly would have railed against his not getting credit for formulating the doctrine!"

During the preceding years, a number of nations in the North and South American continents had successfully fought for their freedom from the domination of Spain. Adams feared that the more conservative nations in Europe, which had formed a league, the Holy Alliance, to oppose such revolutionary movements, might try to help Spain win back her colonies.

Great Britain, queen of the seas, vigorously opposed such European intervention in the New World, fearing it would interrupt her trade with those lucrative markets. She suggested that the United States join her in a policy proclaiming a "hands off" posture. Both Thomas Jefferson and James Madison urged President Monroe to accept Great Britain's generous offer. But not Secretary of State John Quincy Adams.

Unique, feisty, and purely a product of America, Adams insisted, "It would be more candid to avow our principles explicitly to Russia and France, than to come in as a cock-boat in the wake of the British man-of-war."

Adams drafted a paper on the American position, and in 1823, Monroe had read it in an address to Congress. He warned, "Latin America is to be left alone; Russia, entrenched in Alaska, must not encroach southward on the Pacific Coast; . . . and the American continents, by the free and independent condition which they assume and maintain, are henceforth not to be considered as subjects for future colonization by any European power."

"In effect, what my husband is trying to achieve is the exclusion of any expansionist moves by any country other than the United States," Louisa said.

"That's his strongest selling point. He more than any other candidate sees the destiny of this country as it's manifested by its physical boundaries. Perhaps with the possible exception of Andrew Jackson, who is always so spoiling for a fight that he would invade *England* if given the chance!"

At the mention of Jackson's name, Louisa, a woman of delicate sensibilities, seemed to shrink. "Can you imagine Andrew Jackson living in the White House?" she murmured. "Why, you know we entertained him while he was in Washington and got to know him. The man is nearly illiterate, can't spell, has a facade of what passes for manners, but oh, that temper! You know he's already fought at least a dozen duels for one reason or another, but mostly over the honor of his wife. And killed two of those men! Well, say what you will, she *did* marry Jackson while she was married to another man."

Rebecca smiled, amused. She hadn't realized that Louisa Adams was that much of a fighter, and it pleased her. "Jackson in the White House is an awesome thought," Rebecca said. "There are many who say that the 'Napoleon of the Woods' would bring the wilderness back to Washington in more ways than one."

"Not too loud with those sentiments," Louisa said. "The capital seems to be rife with Jackson supporters."

"He won't be easily beaten. From the moment I met him

back in the summer of 1807, it was clear that he felt he was heeding the call of destiny, and everything he's done has brought him closer to the White House."

"What's to be done?" Louisa asked. "Can he be stopped?"

"Nobody ever knows how any election will turn out, but with four candidates, all of them may fail to win a majority of the electoral votes. If the contest is thrown into the House of Representatives, then the only way Jackson can be beaten is by a coalition of candidates."

After Louisa Adams left, Rebecca thought for a long time about the upcoming election. Something was happening in the nation, that was obvious enough; the entrenched men of property and wealth were losing ground before the middle and lower classes who'd gotten the vote. There was an element of uneasiness attached to the change, and further, she wondered whose side she was on. She remembered what Abigail Adams had told her more than twenty years ago, that one day American women would have the vote. How distant such a prospect seemed! She sighed, wondering if she would ever live to see that day.

As horrible as Zebulon's death had been, it did bring Rebecca a certain amount of financial security. The house on New York Avenue passed into her hands, and that, with the original Breech house in Georgetown and the cabin that Jeremy had owned, made her a woman of property. More important, the recession was gradually easing, the flurry of canal building and the opening up of the western territories had brought on a building boom, and the royalties from Jeremy's invention had increased. Rebecca divided the proceeds into two portions: one half went to the children, to be divided equally in four parts, for Suzannah, Gunning, Circumstance, and Bravo. She didn't want any of them to experience any of the deprivations that she had as a youngster. The other half she used as an investment fund, choosing those areas she thought might increase in value over the years. All the children, of course, would inherit that equally when she was gone.

"Certain property in Washington will increase," she told Gunning, trying to instruct him in some sense of business. "As the country grows, so must the capital. Your father said he wanted to build a dynasty, but since the Lord saw fit to take him away . . ."

"It wasn't the Lord, but a nigger, who killed him," Gunning said.

"Gunning, don't start that again; no good can come of it. What we need to do is build that dynasty for him. And you, as the oldest son, must take that responsibility."

"Yes, Mother darling," he said, kissing her on the forehead. "But must my responsibility begin this very minute? I promised my friends that I would meet them at the bowling green." And with that he was off.

She watched him from the window as he leapt onto his horse and cantered away. Like his father, Gunning was a superb rider, and rode his mount as though he might have been a prince. The combination of high coloring, and the physique of a Greek god made him irresistible to the young girls in Washington, and already he had something of a reputation.

"He'll grow out of it," Rebecca told Letitia. "It's only a question of youth, that's all."

"His father never growed out of it," Letitia said.

"Don't be impertinent."

"Don't rightly know what that means," Letitia said, "but you knows I'm right, and that's all I got to say on that matter."

Through Mr. Van Ness, the president of the city's largest bank, Rebecca made a series of investments.

"I cannot understand why you want to invest in something as silly as a gunsmith factory," Van Ness said as he looked over her choices. "We're not at war with anybody."

"Eli Whitney is a genius," she said, "and I've kept up an active correspondence with him all these years. He's built this factory in Connecticut. Jeremy told me that Whitney had an extraordinary turn of mind, making interchangeable parts for the manufacture of guns so that each gun wouldn't have to be painstakingly handcrafted. Now with the West opening up, and with the need to kill game, to say nothing of defense against the Indians, I think there's a future for Mr. Whitney. Of course, we pray that there will never be another war, but then people have been praying for that since time immemorial. Without too much success, I might add."

"All right then, I'll buy you some stock in his company," Van Ness said, "though it's against my better judgment."

"I think a thousand shares will do nicely," she said.

"I would suggest investing in some canal companies."

"That's a good thought, but I believe that those stocks have peaked," she said. "Too many people think as you and I do, and they've driven the price too high. But find out what you can about this car that runs along the tracks. You know the one I mean?"

"The one drawn by a horse?" Van Ness asked.

Rebecca nodded. "I think there's more than a novelty there. And if Robert Fulton's steam engine can power ships, they say that a similar engine can power this—ah, yes, the railroad, that's what they call it."

"Now on that one I must veto you, Mrs. Brand," Van Ness said. "Why, it's throwing good money away! Rivers and canals will be the principal means of transportation in this country for centuries. God himself has given us the rivers; how can man compete against that with puny tracks? And over the vast territory that this nation spans? Believe me, Mrs. Brand, you'd best leave it to the people with the expertise in handling money."

"I suppose you're right," she said. "Well, then, just indulge a woman's fancy, will you? I'm not saying I will invest; I just want to know more about it."

"I simply don't have that kind of time to waste," Van Ness said.

"I'll expect the information within a month," Rebecca said in a gentle tone. "If I don't have it on my desk by then, I'll assume you're no longer interested in handling the Breech-Brand account."

Van Ness turned beet-red, stood up, then gulped and said, "Of course you'll have the information if you want it."

Later that day Rebecca said to Letitia, "I've done what I can—secured the children's future, made some wise investments—and now I can die in peace."

"Miss Rebecca, from what I sees happening, 'pears to me that you're about ready to live again."

"No, I'm forty-five years old, and if the Lord called me tomorrow, I'd go to my reward thinking that I'd lived at least three lifetimes."

"Miss Rebecca, the Lord, he ain't ready for you yet! And that's all I got to say about that matter!" Letitia smothered her laughter in her apron, and though Rebecca was furious that her self-pitying mood wasn't being taken seriously, she also burst out laughing.

"What am I going to do with you?" she demanded, trying

to act stern. Then she sighed and stood up. "Here my mind's been so full of Tanzy, and I've been so busy writing about the injustice of slavery, that I've never even given you a thought."

Letitia shifted uneasily from leg to leg.

"Letitia, I've already made out my will, and in it I've freed you and Tadpole. But how unthinking of me to wait until I'm dead! As of this moment, I'm giving you your freedom."

Letitia's mouth fell open, and then tears started rolling down her cheeks, glistening on her ebony skin. "But Miss Rebecca, I been with you since you were a little baby. Where would I go? What would I do?"

"Anything you wanted. There's a whole world out there. You can do whatever you want."

Letitia buried her face in her apron and started to sob. Rebecca put her arms around her. "I should have done it long ago," she said. "I just didn't have the wit or the sensitivity. And I wish that something could be done about your other children to save them from a life of slavery."

But Letitia continued to sob.

"What's the matter now?"

"Oh, Miss Rebecca, couldn't I just go on working for you?"

"But of course, you silly goose, if that's what you want. Only now you'll be earning money for it, and you'll be a free woman."

Letitia slumped with relief. "Long as I can stay on here, then that's all right. And I thank you very much, and I thank you for my son too."

"Then it's settled. Now go fetch me some more writing paper. And some new goose quills. Hurry, there's lots to be done."

Letitia went out the door, mumbling under her breath, "'Pears that free or not, things stay about the same here, and maybe even a little worse."

Suddenly, Rebecca felt as if a great weight had been lifted from her shoulders, and she understood what Jeremy had experienced when he'd freed Tanzy and Eli.

But it was Letitia's attitude that had surprised her. Would other slaves have the same reaction to freedom?

Rebecca breathed deeply, drawing the air into her lungs. Somehow, in freeing Letitia, she'd freed part of herself.

Chapter 41

"CIRCUMSTANCE, LET'S get married," Wingate said. They were trudging along the path between Georgetown and Washington. There'd been a light snowfall earlier that day, and they left their tracks in the fresh snow. "I'll be finished with my studies very soon, and Dr. Smith said that I could apprentice to him. He's getting so old that I think he'll be my best patient."

Circumstance smiled but said nothing.

"It will be difficult at first," Wingate said, "but I know that one day people will come to take doctors seriously, and then I'll make a decent wage." He stopped in his tracks and put his hands on her shoulders. "Circumstance, I love you. I loved you from the very first moment I saw you."

She stared at him with eyes that seemed the same shade as the ice-blue surroundings. "If ever I marry it will be you," she said quietly. "And you've made me very happy by just asking."

"Then you agree?" he asked, his voice charged with happiness.

She shook her head hurriedly. "I'll never marry. I know in my heart that it's not for me. I couldn't do that to you—ruin your life. Why, what patient would come to you with a half-breed for a wife?"

"You're talking absolute rubbish," he said. He'd never before taken such a firm tone with her. "Where's the girl with the spirit I saw that night at the White House? You're only making your life worse than it has to be. If you dare people to treat you with contempt, naturally they will."

Caught off guard by his vehemence, she could only stare at him, wondering about this new Wingate Grange, one with such hidden strength.

"Circumstance, we don't have to stay in Washington," he said. "We can go west, to the frontier, where a man is judged on his own value rather than anything else."

"Now *you're* talking foolishly. Who's our frontiersman without parallel? Andrew Jackson, right? Yet he owns slaves. He defrauds Indians of their land and forces them to move farther and farther west to make room for more white settlers. The prejudice we'd encounter on the frontier would be worse."

On this issue he knew that she spoke the truth, but he couldn't let it rest there. He took her hands in his. "I'm not somebody who knows how to use words. I can only tell you what's in my heart. Without you, my life will never be anything but a half-life. I can see that you don't love me now, but that's all right. I have enough for the two of us. And I'll never give up until you love me as I love you."

She lowered her eyes and stared at the snow. "Please, Wingate, don't make this pain greater than I can bear. So much has happened, so many people I've loved have been taken from me . . . My spirit is like stone."

"I'm sorry, truly," he murmured. "And I won't mention it again. Not until you let me know that it's all right." Then he packed a fistful of snow into a ball and threw it up into the laden pine branches above them. A shower of flakes fell on them, coating their eyebrows and eyelashes.

"I see the world as through a prism," she said, staring through the crystalline snowflakes. "The forest, the sky, the land, it's all rainbowed. Oh, if only it could be this way all the time."

He slipped his arm around her waist and they walked on along the white path. She saw him to Georgetown University, then began the walk back home to Washington, where she'd moved with Rebecca and the rest of the family. She thought long and hard about what Wingate said, but couldn't bring herself to accept his offer. She felt that he was doing it out of pity rather than anything else. Besides, living in this stunned state, her own heart and body hadn't yet wakened to the full call of womanhood.

Her nights were filled with terrible dreams, of seeing her father falling . . . falling . . . while she stood helplessly by. But in her waking hours, she pushed all such thoughts from her mind and, numbed, rarely thought of the cryptic message he'd given her. The best she could do was to commit what he'd said, word for word, to her diary.

Circumstance retraced her steps, and for a brief span walked in Wingate's tracks, amazed at how her small feet disappeared into the impressions he'd made. He'd changed so much from the day she'd first met him, from a shy stripling to a young man, with wonderfully sensitive fingers that held a healing touch. If asked to describe him she would have had difficulty with his physical characteristics—tall, yes, and thin, with brown hair that curled and merry brown eyes—but all of those things were secondary to the glow that emanated from him, a glow of warmth and goodness.

Then her eyes picked out something that put her on the alert: another set of tracks. A man, somewhat lighter than Wingate, for the imprints in the snow weren't so deep. He was wearing a pair of boots that were quite new; impressions were crisp, no rounded edges on the heels.

The crepuscular light descended on the forest, turning the path and the snow-laden trees into an eerie blue, and though it was beautiful, the beauty was diminished by the danger she felt. Somebody had followed them. Who? And for what reason? Somebody was following her now.

She called out, "Who's there?" but was answered only by the trill of a freshet coursing its way through the snow. I've only another half a mile or so to go, she thought, and then I'll be in a more populated part of the District. She increased her pace, trying to outdistance the darkness that was gaining on her.

As she passed a tall oak, a hand reached from behind and grabbed her. Before she could turn and see who it was, a fist descended on the back of her head. She fought to keep her senses as she felt hands tearing at her clothes, but then she slipped down and down into a dark well.

A long while later Circumstance slowly surfaced to feel the cold wet nose of a fawn touching her face. Her head throbbed, and her body ached in a way she'd never experienced. A pale silver moon hung in the sky and played over the fields, turning them into silver. Then she realized what had happened. "Oh, no!" she screamed. "No!"

Her cry startled an owl high on a branch, and it took wing before her anguished call. She sat up, and in a frenzy, tried to wipe away the blood that had fallen in the snow, as if that could wipe away the deed. She had been raped.

She stumbled through the forest, to run to the constable, to Rebecca, to Suzannah, and tell them. But then she realized that though Rebecca and Suzannah would believe her, very few other people in Washington would. Everywhere in this city, one heard tales of the supposed wantonness of Indian maidens;

she'd heard them all the years of her growing up. She'd never understood these stories, for she felt no such thing in her blood. But the cruel jibes of her playmates, the sly glances and whispers of the Washington matrons, had helped set her apart from others. And if the news of what had happened to her became known, then these very same people would say that it had been her fault, that she'd brought it on herself.

"I mustn't say anything to anybody!"

With this crushing defeat on her, and the even more crushing prospect of what its consequences might be, she crept into the house. She went directly to her room, where she spent the night shivering in terror.

The following day Wingate came to see her but she pled that she wasn't feeling well and had Letitia send him away. She kept that up for an entire week, until finally one night Wingate hopped onto the shed roof that stood directly under her room and climbed through the windows. She bolted upright from her sleep, thinking that the intruder might be the same person who'd attacked her. She grabbed the firetongs she kept by her bedside.

He caught her arm and whispered, "Circumstance, it's me, Wingate."

Gradually, she stopped trembling.

"What is it?" he murmured. "Tell me, what's happened?"

With faltering words, and eyes averted, she told him. He listened, alternately consumed with compassion for her and with rage against her attacker. "And so you understand why I must never see you again," she finished. "What if I have a child? Then I'll have to go off by myself and bear the baby alone, make some sort of life for what's left of me."

He gripped her shoulders fiercely. "Do you think that love is so fragile that it can be stopped by something like this? For something that wasn't your fault? We'll marry as soon as we can find a justice of the peace."

"And what of the child?" she whispered.

"We don't know yet if you've conceived. And if by some chance you have, then we'll raise it with all the love we can. For it won't know its origins; it will only know the love it receives. And if it's your child, can it be anything but good and decent?"

"You would do this for me?" she said with a half-sob.

He crushed her to him and felt her warm tears on her cheek.

• • •

Circumstance and Wingate were married a few days later at a small ceremony attended by Suzannah, Letitia, Gunning, and Rebecca. James Hoban, though suffering severely from gout, made the trip in from Georgetown to give the bride away. Rebecca and Letitia did the best they could on such short notice and served a light wedding supper of Virginia quail stuffed with wild rice and Chesapeake Bay oysters, a sweet-potato soufflé, and a plum pudding with a hard sauce, a recipe that Rebecca had gotten from Thomas Jefferson.

"I would have invited as many guests as possible," she said to Circumstance, "but you didn't give me any time."

"Everybody that I care about is here, that's what's important. And thank you for all you've done for me."

Happiness simply beamed from Wingate. "And we're spending the honeymoon night in the new Indian Queen Hotel that the Baltimore chain's just built in Washington," he told Suzannah.

"No you're not," Rebecca said. She handed Circumstance a vellum packet. "This contains the deed to your father's house. When Zebulon died, the ownership passed to me. But your father built it with his own hands, and so it should be yours. Take it, and with it, a piece of my heart."

Circumstance threw her arms around Rebecca. "Oh, how wonderful!" she exclaimed. "Wingate, our very own house!"

"There's also some money due you from the royalties on your father's invention. Most of it is invested at the moment, but if you'd like I can have Mr. Van Ness sell off some of the stocks."

"Let the money stay there," Wingate said. "I'll be out of school in a few months and we'll manage till then."

Letitia came in with a huge basket overflowing with fried chicken, and fruit, and nuts, and puddings, and sweetmeats. "You'll find the house nice and cozy too," Letitia said. "Miss Rebecca and me been working on it since we found out. Fire laid out in the hearth and everything, and that's all I've got to say about that!" With a roll of her eyes at Wingate and a prolonged laugh, she left.

When Wingate and Circumstance arrived at the house they found that Letitia had been as good as her word. Everything looked scrubbed; the accumulation of cobwebs, ants, and dust that had collected during Zebulon's ownership had been swept away; and the place was as cozy as Circumstance ever remembered. Wingate lit the fire and they sat before it, leaning against each other.

"I never thought anybody could be this happy," he said.

Circumstance stared into the fire, lost in the consuming flames. At last she said, "I'm frightened. This awful thing that's happened to me, I'm so afraid that it will spoil it for you, and that I shan't be able to—" With a tiny cry she buried her face in his chest.

He stroked her hair, so anxious to protect her that he felt it as a palpable force in his entire being. "Don't worry, I'm as nervous as you are. You see..."

She lifted her head and glanced at him. "You've never been with a woman, have you?" she asked gently.

He shook his head. "Every time I tried...well, I just couldn't. Your father told me a few things, man to man, and that helped. Then when I met you, I knew there would never be another woman in my life, so why waste myself on someone unworthy of the way I felt?"

They talked for several hours, exploring, telling their most intimate fears, their deepest desires. Finally as the embers of the fire died, they crept into the bed stuffed high with pillows and a goose-down comforter. Letitia had also wrapped some heated bricks and placed them at the foot of the bed.

Wingate lay staring at the ceiling while Circumstance undressed under the covers. Then he slipped out of his own clothes. He leaned over, kissed her quickly, and said, "Goodnight, my wife."

Then he felt Circumstance's hand steal into his. Taking a deep breath he rolled toward her. He kissed her gently, for he knew no other way, nor did she. But somehow nature conspired to teach them all the secrets that lay dormant in their souls. And soon their bodies moved with a sure knowledge, and they found each other, warm and willing. She cried out once and he moved to withdraw, but she clasped his waist.

"It's all right," she whispered, "it's all right, my darling, come, be as one with me."

All through the night they made love, made love in ways that they'd never imagined, in ways as fresh as the time when the first man and the first woman had discovered each other. "I make you this promise," he said in the night-filled room.

"I will never do anything to hurt you, I shall cherish you above all others, for with you, I can dare to become anything."

"Then I will make you this promise," she murmured. "As long as I live, I shall remain faithful to your love. This I swear on the memory of my mother and father, and if I should fail in that vow, may the Great Spirit strike me down."

He barely heard her words, so lost was he in the wonder of her, so secure in his manhood. Gone all his fears, gone the doubts that had plagued him all the years of his youth. She was his, and together they had found strong sanctuary.

Chapter 42

"THIS DOESN'T bode well for our electoral system," Rebecca said to Henry Clay. They were standing in the lobby of the House of Representatives during a break in the voting.

"Would you see Andrew Jackson elected, then?" Clay asked.

"You know how hard I worked for Adams," she said irritably. "But there is something to be said for the will of the people."

"We are the people's representatives here," Clay said, "and as such, whomever we choose is really their choice."

"Save such sophistry for those not privy to the inner workings of Congress," she said. "You and I both know that of the four candidates, Jackson received the greatest number of votes, six hundred thousand, while Adams got only five hundred. Jackson also got ninety-two electoral votes, while Adams polled only eighty-four. Common sense clearly says that Jackson is preferred by more people. But through some flaw in the thinking of the Founding Fathers, he may be denied this election, and the presidency."

"He will if I have anything to do with it," Clay said. "The man is a despot. Have you forgotten that he invaded Florida and almost caused a war with Spain? Put the reins of government in that firebrand's hands and the country will be ruined. The Spaniards don't call him the 'Napoleon of the Woods' for nothing; if he were elected, he'd take the same route as that dictator. No, Rebecca, I'll fight to the last breath to defeat him!"

Oh, God, Clay's so boring when he starts getting dramatic, she thought. Hypnotized by the stentorian tones of his own voice, he was. He had missed his calling; he should have been an actor. And yet the gallery loved it, and he constantly played to the gallery. Sometimes the public can be a pack of fools, she thought.

"The fate of the nation hangs in the hands of the New York delegation," Clay was saying. "Martin Van Buren, the little worm, has so far convinced Stephen Van Rensselaer to hold fast for Jackson. But Van Rensselaer, who is a patroon, is much closer in refinement to Adams than he is to that frontier barbarian. Jackson is a killer! He's murdered at least two men who dared to question his wife's morals. Yet she's a convicted bigamist, and probably an adulteress. Shall we have a President who shoots anybody who disagrees with him or his wife?"

The Keeper of the Door announced that another ballot was about to be cast and Henry Clay hurried inside.

Rebecca went upstairs to the gallery and watched. All that Clay had said about Jackson was true, and she did have deep misgivings about the general. But if the will of the people was subverted, there was no telling where it would end.

On the floor of the House, Jacksonian Democrats were exhorting Van Rensselaer to remain firm for their man. The patroon, beside himself with doubt, cried out, "Oh merciful Lord, if only I knew your will!" Then he laid his hand down on his desk to ponder his choice. When he opened his eyes he saw a slip of paper, a ballot, lying on the floor. On it was written the name of John Quincy Adams. With a sigh he said, "That is the sign I've been waiting for!" When his turn came to vote, he switched to Adams. And so the sixth President of the United States was elected.

The Jackson forces were apoplectic, and the cry went up that their man had been cheated. But if they were angry then, a few days later it turned to a vitriolic hatred when Adams let it be known that he planned to name Henry Clay as his secretary of state, the position that had traditionally led to the presidency. "A corrupt bargain!" went the denunciation. "Clay sold his votes and his soul to Adams. Not since Judas Iscariot—" And so the cries resounded through the halls of government.

Rebecca and Gunning were in their drawing room playing chess, with Bravo watching and trying to learn, when the news reached them. Rebecca jumped up, knocking the chesspieces to the floor. "That is without doubt the stupidest, most damaging thing that Adams ever did!" she exclaimed. "All he's done is given Jackson and his cohorts the ammunition they need."

Letitia came running in with a copy of the *National Intelligencer* that headlined the news. Gunning scanned the pages. "People are saying that an unholy deal was made between the two men. Clay saw that he didn't have enough votes to win, so he threw his support to Adams, and in return Adams elevated him to the second most important position in the government."

"Those rumors are vicious and I don't want to hear them repeated in my house," Rebecca said. "Adams is difficult, but he's never been a party hack, which is more than most legislators can say. I'd stake my life on his honesty."

"Well then, you're one of the few people in Washington who feels that way," Gunning said. "The Jacksonians are out to get Adams. I'll wager that they don't give him a moment's peace while he's President."

Rebecca threw the chessmen back into their ivory box. She knew Gunning was right, but his obvious glee rankled her. Why does he always emphasize the mean aspects? she wondered. Was that a quality in her own nature that had become full-blown in his? "Pour me some sherry," she said. "This day has wearied me."

He brought her a cut-glass tumbler of the amber liquid and she remarked at how much like the color of his eyes it was. He sat beside her, legs sprawled on the settee, arm crooked carelessly behind his head. At fifteen he'd almost reached his full height, slightly under six feet, and his physique promised to be as magnificent as his father's had been. I bore you in my womb, she thought with a touch of pride. I helped fashion you in God's image.

"What would you like to do with your life?" she asked.

He raised his eyebrows. "I don't know. Take over the family business, I suppose. Or perhaps be a diplomat, or a congressman, or something. I must say, I like the life they lead; all sorts of extras come their way from people who want favors, and everybody toadies to them."

"They also have a great responsibility to chart the nation's course," she said.

"But of course, Mother," he said. "That's what makes it even more interesting. All that power—why, the President of the United States must feel something like God."

"I heard George Washington say that he'd rather be at home tending his farm. Jefferson called his tenure in the President's House a splendid misery. The elder John Adams said, 'I pray heaven to bestow the best of blessings on this house. May none but wise and honest men ever inhabit it.' Madison could never have kept his office without the help of Dolley. So you see, it's not as easy a job as you'd think. There are hidden shoals."

"I'd navigate them, you may be sure of that," he said.

"Would you consider a career in law, then?" she asked hopefully. "Most of our legislators have been trained in law."

"But George Washington was in the military. So is Jackson. That appeals to me more." Gunning took a dwarf gardenia from the bud vase and tucked it into the bodice of his mother's dress. "It's so like your skin," he said.

Her hand moved to her cheek and then dropped away. "Well, we'll talk about your schooling and your career some other time soon. Have you decided whom you're asking to the inaugural ball?"

He stood up, held an imaginary partner in his arms and danced around the room. "No matter whom I ask, you're to save the first and last dance for me!"

"Letitia, do you realize that by the end of this afternoon I will have seen five Presidents take up residence in Washington?" Rebecca said. "Adams, Jefferson, Madison, Monroe, and now John Quincy Adams. It hardly seems possible."

"I knows it, and it's a new dress every time," Letitia said, helping Rebecca into her clothes.

"What a pity that John Adams is too old to come to his son's inauguration. How proud he must be," Rebecca said as she pinched her cheeks. She never used rouge during the day, but a pinch or two helped bring the color to the surface, though with age she found she had to pinch harder.

"It's a cloudy day out there, and windy," Letitia said. "Best take your shawl and a parasol, case it rains."

Rebecca and Gunning stepped out into the chilly day. He'd agreed to escort her. "This promises to be the most impressive inauguration to date," she said. "People have been streaming into Washington for the past week. Every tavern and hotel is full, and I heard that by nine this morning, crowds were already clamoring at the doors of the Capitol."

"The whole thing is nothing more than a sideshow," Gunning said.

"You have such a generous opinion of our political system," she said with a frown. They proceeded by carriage to the Adamses' house on F Street. "I understand that the entire household has been up for two nights because Louisa took sick," Rebecca said. "Dr. Huntt is there right now tending to her. She's always had such a fragile constitution."

"So do we!" Gunning exclaimed, delighted with his pun. "The country, I mean."

At the Adams residence they waited patiently until eleven-thirty, when President Monroe's carriage arrived. Parading in front of the house were the militia and volunteer companies of the District, all in their full and distinct uniforms. The commotion was making the horses skittish and Gunning held them in tight rein, soothing them. At last John Quincy Adams appeared.

"How's the missus?" somebody in the crowd shouted, and Adams called back, "She's doing better, thank you, and sends you all her very best wishes."

The cavalry led the way to the Capitol, followed by Adams's carriage, then followed by President Monroe's, and a procession of citizens, winding up with many hundreds of people on foot. Several bands in out-of-tune cacophony hastened the assembly on its way.

As Adams and Monroe entered the Capitol, the Marine Corps band stationed in a line in front of the building saluted the men with spirited music. Gunning and Rebecca fought their way through the throng to the House of Representatives, but the crush was so great that Rebecca despaired of ever getting a seat. Then Henry Clay saw her and bribed one of his confederates to give his place to her.

"How gallant of you," Rebecca said.

"I have an ulterior motive, I must confess," Clay said.

"You?" she said. "I would never have believed it."

"The battle lines are already beginning to form, and we need all people of good will on Adams's side."

She glanced at him. "Is it that bad?"

"Worse," Clay said. "Jackson is furious, insists that fraud has been committed, and is hell-bent to make trouble."

Well, I can't exactly blame him, she thought.

At twenty minutes past noon, the marshals, with their blue scarves around their necks, entered the chamber, followed by the officers of both houses of Congress, and Adams. Minutes earlier, he'd seen Vice-President John C. Calhoun take his oath of office in the Senate. Directly behind them and still in his everpresent knee breeches and hose, came James Monroe with his wife Elizabeth and their family. A procession of black-robed Supreme Court Justices entered, looking very sober, though Chief Justice Marshall winked at Rebecca as he passed.

The judges were followed by Calhoun and then by many members of both the Senate and House.

"It's a wonder that somebody as plain and unassuming as John Quincy Adams ever served as our minister at foreign courts," Clay said. "It's a wonder they ever took him seriously."

"You only have to hear him speak to forget everything else but that mind," Rebecca said. She was annoyed with Clay for this swipe at Adams, but then Clay had always felt that he should have been President. She looked at Adams, who stood no more than five foot seven. He wore a plain black broadcloth suit with long trousers, made in America. He sat in the elevated Speaker's chair, and once silence prevailed in the galleries, he stood, and in a clear voice read a forty-minute speech in which he called for unity and asked for the people's help. At some points, applause rose from the assembly, but the cadre of Jackson supporters sat on their hands.

When Adams was finished, he stepped down to the clerk's table and took the oath of office from Chief Justice Marshall. Rebecca strained to hear the words, which in all of her inaugurations had never failed to thrill her. "I do solemnly swear that I will faithfully execute the office of the President of the United States, and will to the best of my ability preserve, protect, and defend the Constitution of the United States."

With those thirty-five fateful words, the power of the nation was peacefully handed down from one elected man to another. Without revolt, without bloodshed, without military coup... Rebecca marveled at the experiment in democracy—which, despite its flaws, seemed to be working.

Cheers rose from the gallery, followed by the booming of artillery outside. Then Rebecca started, for one of the first to congratulate Adams was General Andrew Jackson. "The man is canny," she said to Clay. "He's wise enough not to present the face of a sore loser."

The crowd streamed out of the Capitol and escorted President Adams back to his house. Despite her illness, Mrs. Adams made a game effort to receive all the well-wishers. Rebecca and some other ladies of Washington had volunteered to help with the crush of people.

"She looks so peaked, doesn't she?" Rebecca said to Gunning. "And the task of being a hostess in the White House can fell an ordinary mortal. I hope Louisa can survive it."

Then Devroe Connaught came up to her and kissed Rebecca's hand. "Ah, Mrs. Brand, how splendid to see you again. I hope we'll have the pleasure of seeing you and your family at the inaugural ball tonight."

"Why, yes," she said, "we all plan to attend."

"I say, young Gunning, I've just gotten these two wonderfully spirited Arabian stallions. Fastest animals I've ever encountered. Would you care to go riding with me some morning?"

"I would, yes indeed," Gunning said, flattered to be noticed by the richest man in the territory.

"I was sorry to hear about Elizabeth Connaught," Rebecca said. Shortly after Zebulon's death, Elizabeth had gone completely mad again, and had had to be confined to the plantation, where the doctors kept her under constant sedation. Devroe had reached his majority and had petitioned the courts for power of attorney. Since his aunt wasn't competent, that power had been granted. Devroe, for all practical purposes, now controlled the vast Connaught fortune in the United States.

Throughout the afternoon, President Adams continued to greet strangers and well-wishers with his usual cordiality. Later, he paid a formal call on former President and Mrs. Monroe at the White House, and after the exhausting day, returned home for dinner. Rebecca had stayed with Louisa Adams, clearing up the last of the mess created by the mob of people.

"I hope you're not going to ask Louisa to go to the ball," Rebecca said to Adams. "All this excitement has made her fever come back."

"I wouldn't think of having her leave this house," he said. "And if I had my way, I wouldn't go either. These social functions are such a damned nuisance."

"Well, the people demand it, so you've no alternative," Rebecca told him. "Now I must leave or I'll never be ready in time."

As Rebecca hurried back to her house, her mind was filled with thoughts of Devroe Connaught. Clearly, he was making a special effort to be nice to her and her children. Did he feel as she did, that it was time for this poisonous blood feud to be over? She hoped that was the case. Oddly enough, she found herself looking forward to seeing him this evening.

Chapter 43

A HOT bath with rosewater and oil relaxed Rebecca, and Letitia followed that with a gentle massage. "You know, as you get older and older, it takes longer and longer to tighten everything into presentable form," she told Letitia.

"I knows; I gave up tightening years ago. But I still gets invited to parties!"

For the festivities that night, Rebecca had chosen a navy-blue satin gown that helped disguise the fact that she no longer had a wasp waist. Strands of gray had begun to appear in her titian hair, but it wasn't unbecoming, for it only made her hair appear lighter. She'd recently purchased a necklace of amethysts and decided to wear it tonight.

"Suzannah, are you ready?" she called. Suzannah came into the room looking so lovely that Rebecca beamed. She wore a light-blue gown with a sash of paler blue that cinched her narrow waist. The ends of the sash hung almost to the hem of the voluminous skirt. Her dark hair was tied up with a pale blue ribbon.

"My dear, you do me proud," Rebecca said. On impulse, she took off the amethyst necklace and fastened it around Suzannah's neck.

"Oh, Mother, I couldn't," she protested. "They're yours—and anyway, they're far too grand for me."

"Nonsense," she said. "They're all wrong for my coloring and perfect for yours. And as for their being too grand—well, one day, my girl, you shall be covered in diamonds."

They embraced and then Rebecca said, "We'd better go. It's a damnable wet night out, and we're going to get soaked."

The horses slogged through the pouring rain that turned Pennsylvania Avenue into a quagmire. Carriages were stuck here and there with their miserable occupants, but Tadpole negotiated the road expertly. At last they reached Carusi's Saloon at the corner of Eleventh Street and Pennsylvania, and with shrieks of laughter at the rain, mother and daughter scooted into the building, and Gunning followed them.

In the spacious foyer, two crescent-shaped staircases led up
to the entrance hall. Two large fireplaces ablaze with logs
flanked the stairway and took the dampness and chill off the
dank night.

"I wish Circumstance and Wingate would have come with
us," Suzannah said.

"I don't," Gunning said. "They're always so serious; you'd
think that the two of them had it in their minds to save the
whole world. They're just not any fun."

"I offered to get them tickets," Rebecca said, "but they
wouldn't hear of it. Anyway, she hasn't been feeling very
well."

Once inside Carusi's, they ran into Devroe Connaught. He
was wearing an impeccably tailored violet-blue cutaway coat;
the sleeves had turned-up cuffs decorated with silver buttons
emblazoned with the Connaught insignia. His buff-colored vest
sported similar buttons, and the points of his high-collared shirt
were held in place by a blue cravat.

"I say, Connaught, that's an absolutely smashing suit,"
Gunning said. "I bet you didn't get that in Washington."

Devroe threw back his head and laughed, revealing small
white even teeth that looked like they were his first set. "It just
arrived from my tailors in Bond Street. Really, there's no city
but London for men's clothes. I'll give you his name."

"Would you?" Gunning said eagerly.

Devroe bowed to Suzannah. "May I have this first dance?"
he asked. Suzannah glanced at Rebecca, who nodded. They
went to the parquet floor, where the band began playing a reel.
Devroe had acclimated himself well to the American dances
and more than held his own.

"Suzannah, I'm a man of simple tastes and simple pleasures," he said. "I have very little of the guile that passes for
manners among the young men of our generation. In short, I
would like your permission to call on you."

As she hesitated for a moment, he said, "Of course, if you'd
prefer that I didn't . . ."

"Oh, no, I think it would be very nice," she said. This was
the very first serious caller she'd ever had and she blushed with
a combination of pleasure and embarrassment. Her head spun
as they danced, for Devroe filled her with compliments, both
obvious and subtle. Then he delivered her back to her mother
and went to get punch for them all.

"He's very attentive, isn't he?" Rebecca said. "Do you like him, Suzannah?"

"I don't know. He has ever such good manners, but sometimes I get the feeling that he's making fun of my ignorance."

"You know that we've had hard times with the Connaughts in the past," Rebecca said.

Gunning interrupted, "Isn't it time that we forgot all that? After all, Devroe didn't have anything to do with it."

"My sentiments exactly," Rebecca said. For a fanciful moment she thought, Suzannah Brand Connaught. Somehow the name had a ring to it . . . Suzannah would be the mistress of the vast Connaught estate and fortune. Come! You're being a silly middle-aged woman, she warned herself. It can never happen. Yet she couldn't dismiss the possibility from her mind.

When President Adams arrived at Carusi's, a great shout went up. But when General Andrew Jackson made his entrance, the crowd went wild.

"It's easy to see who the popular hero is," Devroe said. "Though I sense that he could be a dangerous man."

Rebecca nodded. "Despite his being all smiles this evening, Jackson can be vindictive. I doubt he'll ever forgive Clay or Adams for denying him this election."

The crush of people in the ballroom became greater and the conversation more animated, and the wine flowed. Senators and congressmen forgot old grudges; Daniel Webster was even seen talking to Vice-President Calhoun. Somewhere in the midst of all this Rebecca lost track of Suzannah.

"Have you seen my daughter?" she asked Devroe.

"I believe she's gone to the powder room," he said.

Suzannah had indeed gone there, but when she came out she was swept off her feet and carried into an anteroom. "Stop, put me down," she cried, unable to see who was carrying her.

Then she was deposited lightly and saw Jonathan Albright. "It was the only way I could get to see you alone," he said urgently. "Now wait, before you scream or run, hear me out. And then if you don't want to see me again, I'll just disappear out of your life forever, I promise."

She tried to get past him, but he blocked the door.

"I've offended you and I apologize from the bottom of my heart. Out where I come from on the Tennessee frontier, I guess a body just doesn't have time for all the niceties of civilization. He speaks his mind to the girl of his choice and she speaks her mind right back and that saves a lot of time all around, so they can get on with the important things—courting, marrying, raising a family."

"Why of all the impertinent—" Suzannah began, but Jonathan cut her off.

"I aim to marry you. Got to be fair and square about it, so you'll know my intentions. I'm working with General Jackson, been his aide for some years now. He's coming to Washington, yessirree—though next time it will be as President. And so I've got me a future cut out with Old Hickory, so he tells me. That means we won't go hungry."

"You're absolutely insane," she said, not knowing whether to laugh or scream.

"I swear, when you smile like that it's all I can do to keep from sweeping you off your feet and carrying you to the nearest minister. Incidentally, my folks are Episcopalian; yours too? That's good, then—not that I hold much for church-praying; but your Ma, like as not she'll want a big church wedding, I kind of see that in her eyes."

By this time Suzannah was giggling. "Really! And what are we going to name the first child?"

"I kind of favor Andrew, 'count of the general being so good to me, but if that doesn't suit you then choose your own. All I ask is that the baby look like you. Now I'll be in Washington for the next month, getting things squared away for the general. You'd make me the happiest man in the world if you'd let me call on you."

She shook her head vehemently. "I couldn't." A look of such pain flashed across his face that she touched his sleeve. "Oh, it's just that mother..."

"All right, then. I'll be going to the Capitol Building every day, talking to senators and the like. Meet me there? Two o'clock?"

She hesitated, and he said, *"Please."*

"I don't know," she said, confused. "Mother said...Oh, I don't know."

He stepped aside then and let her pass. She fled from the antechamber, stirred by a feeling that she'd never experienced before...something that Devroe Connaught hadn't wakened in her.

President Adams left the ball early, pleading his wife's illness, and there were many at the party who weren't sorry to see him go. The little Puritan, as he was called behind his back, was apt to be a dampener at any party.

Henry Clay looked at Rebecca with wine-sparkling eyes and said, "Why, I remember when Adams and I were in Ghent negotiating the treaty to end the Second War for Independence. We'd be up most of the night playing cards, or doing what any man would do in a foreign city known for its beautiful women. But not John Quincy. He was up at five every morning, lighting his own fire and writing in his confounded diary. And doing all this when we were getting ready to go to bed!" He slapped his leg and some legislators surrounding him joined him in laughter.

Rebecca removed Clay's arm from her shoulder and eyed him coldly. "Given the fact that American soldiers were dying at the very moment you were playing cards, I find your behavior less than exemplary."

"Oh, come, come, Rebecca," Clay said with a placating tone. "We were only having a little harmless fun." But her barb had hit the mark, and Clay said nothing further about Adams for the rest of the evening.

The ball continued, growing more raucous by the hour, and Rebecca got the sense that everybody was forcing himself to have a good time—as if the days ahead would have little of this revelry. "It's going to be a very difficult four years," she told Gunning, "and I pray that Adams will have the wisdom, tact, and fortitude to lead the nation."

"Where are you going?" Rebecca asked Suzannah the following afternoon.

"To see Circumstance."

"Will you be gone long?"

"An hour or two at the most."

"Devroe Connaught said he might call. I wouldn't want you to miss him."

"If he does come, make up some excuse for me, would you please?" Suzannah hurried out the door before Rebecca could protest.

She went directly to Circumstance's and found her working on sheafs of papers. Bills of lading, drawings on large sheets of paper, other drawings on scraps, accounts of wages paid to workers.

"What in the world are you doing?" she asked.

"Putting together all of father's notes on the President's House," Circumstance said. "He kept an account of almost everything, from the time he was first apprenticed to James Hoban, way back in 1792."

"I think it must have been wonderful to have lived then," Suzannah said. "To have known George Washington, and Thomas Jefferson—Mother says he was a devastatingly handsome man—Jefferson, I mean."

"Did you know that the White House used to be called the American Palace?" Circumstance asked.

"I remember mother once telling me that. Devroe Connaught says that our White House is the size of a gardener's cottage on some of the great English estates like Buckingham Palace, that has six hundred rooms. Or Versailles, which has *thousands* of rooms."

"But that's precisely why the White House was built to this modest scale," Circumstance retorted, "so that it would truly represent the home of a leader of a democracy, rather than the court of a monarch."

Then Circumstance stiffened with a twinge of pain.

"What's the matter?" Suzannah asked, alarmed.

"Nothing. It happens only if I'm on my feet too long."

"What does Wingate say?"

"I haven't told him."

"Well where is he? You may be sure that *I'm* going to tell him. The very idea!"

"He's out in the country making a house call." Circumstance sighed. "You know, the lot of a doctor isn't an easy one, especially one just starting out. Today, he'll get a shilling a mile for his trouble. And that's usually on account. But you know Wingate—he'd sing, be it feast or famine."

"Are you happy?" Suzannah asked tentatively.

"I never knew I could be this happy," she said. "Well, except for one thing."

"What?"

"Please don't tell anybody. I tell you because you're like my other self. I'm going to have a baby."

"But that's wonderful!"

Circumstance nodded. "However, I'm afraid that it will mean so much more responsibility for Wingate, and he's got so much on his mind already."

"Oh, I'll help you, I swear I will," Suzannah said, and hugged her cousin.

Circumstance didn't tell her about her fears...After the rape, she'd never resumed having her monthly cycles. Wingate said that often happened in cases of severe shock. But now she was sure she was pregnant, but she couldn't tell how far gone. She counted the weeks, praying that the birthdate would rule out the possibility of the child being the rapist's. How grim that might be for Wingate.

Dreamily, Suzannah asked, "How did you know when you were in love?"

"I didn't know. Until Wingate taught me."

Then Suzannah confided her secret about Jonathan Albright. "Mother wants me to pay attention to Devroe Connaught. I like him, but I feel so different when I'm with Jonathan. He makes me laugh, he makes me angry, I come away from every encounter with him feeling—alive. But I don't know what to do. Do you think I should meet him?"

"I can't advise you on that," Circumstance said. "You must honor your mother's wishes, of course. But first of all, honor what you yourself want to do. How else can one learn to be a woman?"

"I'm going to meet him," Suzannah said. "I am."

Chapter 44

"I KNEW you'd come!" Jonathan Albright intercepted Suzannah in the lobby of the House of Representatives.

"Then you must be awfully sure of yourself," she answered.

"You sounded just like your mother when you said that—just itching for a fight."

She tried unsuccessfully to repress her smile. "Really, you're incorrigible. I don't know why I came, I really don't."

"The important thing is that you did. Tell me, Suzannah, what can I do to make it right between your mother and me? We started out real bad, years ago at the battle at Baltimore. But why should she hold a grudge that long? I'm not a bad sort, honest."

"Mother's funny that way. Once she makes up her mind about something, it would take an earthquake to change it."

"Oh, well, let's not waste any more time talking about her." He looped his long arm over his shoulder and scratched his back.

"You are the scratchingest man I ever met," she said.

He quickly dropped his hands to his side. "Not used to this wool suit. Prefer my old buckskins, myself, but Senator John Eaton, who's handling Jackson's campaign here in Washington, thinks I ought to look like the rest of these dandified politicians."

All around them in the lobby of the House, petitioners were buttonholing congressmen and trying to get their special bills passed. Suzannah nodded her head in the direction of one such grouping. "Mother says that this whole thing is getting out of hand. These pressure tactics go on here in this lobby night and day. In fact, she says the whole exercise is becoming known as lobbying."

Jonathan nodded. "Been forced to do a little of it myself, and I hate it."

"Then why do it?"

"Because I'd do anything for the general. You know he didn't get a fair shake in the last election. Well, we don't aim to be defrauded twice. So we're doing our work damned well enough in advance to make a difference."

"I've got to admit that even mother thinks that the will of the people wasn't done."

"That's the first fair and decent thing I've heard from her yet," Jonathan said.

"Oh, she's wonderful, she really is," Suzannah said. "That's what makes it so difficult. If she were just a plain old simple mother, it would be easy not to heed her and go on my own way. But she does know so much."

"You've got your own life too, though, haven't you?" he asked softly.

"Of course. But you see, mother's had such terrible tragedy these past years. I couldn't do anything to add to her burden. You understand that, don't you?"

He threw up his hands, started to scratch again, and recovered with a grin. "I only understand that I lie awake every night, all night, and think of nothing but you. Suzannah, do you believe that people are somehow meant for each other?"

"I don't know. My cousin Circumstance says they are, but I never gave it much thought."

"Neither did I, until I met you. And now I'm suddenly a believer."

"But we hardly know each other," she said, trying to steer the conversation into a lighter vein. It was getting far too serious for her.

"People can spend a lifetime together and still not know each other," he said. "Seen it happen too many times not to know that for a fact. It doesn't depend on time; it depends on whether or not two souls touch—and mine touched yours the minute I saw you."

For some unknown reason that brought tears to her eyes. She shook her head and held up a trembling hand. "Oh, don't say such things, truly, or I shan't be able to think straight."

He gripped her hand and smiled at her, a smile so bright and infectious and winning that she had to smile back. Then they left the Capitol Building, descending the stairs to the base of Jenkin's Hill, and from there they strolled down to the banks of the Potomac. He cut a reed deftly with an odd-looking knife that had a double-edged blade.

"I've never seen anything like that knife before," she said. "It looks awesome."

"Friend of mine made this for me—invented it himself. Jim Bowie's his name."

She watched him as his strong fingers whittled the reed; he cut a number of holes along the stem, and then notched it near one end. He put it to his lips and piped a sweet woodland melody on it. It reminded her of open meadows, distant azure mountains, and the sound of a running stream; then it became intoxicating, and she imagined pointed-eared Pans gamboling in the bushes. Then in a quick change of pace Jonathan piped out "Oh Jackson's the Boy" with such verve that she applauded gleefully.

"Tell me about your folks," she said.

A look of sorrow came over his craggy features and his warm brown eyes lost their luster. "Dead, both of them. Killed in an Indian massacre in the Blue Ridge Mountains. That's when Aunt Rachel took me in."

"Rachel Jackson?"

He nodded. "Everybody down Nashville way calls her aunt. Finer, more God-fearing woman never drew breath. Must be a half-dozen of us that she's had under her roof. Orphans mostly. See, God never blessed the Jacksons with children of their own, so they just care for anybody needy who comes their way. As soon as I was old enough, I became a courier for Jackson, and I've been campaigning with him ever since. Florida, the Creek Wars . . . ."

She glanced at him, the pistols in his belt, the knife in its sheath. "Have you ever . . . ?"

"Killed anybody?" he finished. "Only when I had to, and even then I didn't much take to it. And when I see a man cut down, I think, What might he have growed into? You see, Suzannah, I'm getting on—twenty-six, almost. And so after this next election, I'm going to buy me a few hundred acres, start a family."

They watched a jeweled butterfly sipping nectar from a rubrum lily, its emerald wings moving slowly against the velvety petals of the flower. A second butterfly lit on the first, and the pairs of wings beat in tremulous synchronization.

"God made it beautiful, didn't He?" Jonathan said huskily. "Beautiful with butterflies, beautiful with people."

They stood together, their shoulders barely touching, yet feeling the energy and desire surging between them. "My cousin Circumstance says that butterflies are flying flowers."

"Flying flowers—I like that. Your cousin's a special friend for you, isn't she?"

Suzannah nodded. "Oh, yes, she's my very best friend in the world. I love her as if she was my own sister." She paused then added, "She likes you, she told me."

"Well, at least somebody in your family is on my side!"

Thereafter, Suzannah and Jonathan contrived to meet as often as they could. Some months he was off to various southern and western cities on errands of import for Jackson's campaign, getting commitments from political leaders on local levels. He was good at that; he spoke their plain and simple language and they trusted him. Jackson and the men supporting him—Eaton, Overton, and Van Buren—had an idea that a strong political party at the grass-roots level could prevent him from being denied the election a second time. More and more Americans were being given the vote, men mainly from the lower levels of society—farmers, laborers, new immigrants. They tended to gravitate more toward Jackson than to the remote and highly educated John Quincy Adams, so the Jackson forces encouraged the broadening of the voting franchise.

Suzannah found herself missing Jonathan when he was gone, and looking forward to his return. Not even the many diversions that Devroe Connaught planned could take her mind off the tall, muscular man, who smelled of burnished leather, fresh grasses, and a maleness that left her clutching her pillow at night. Behind her closed lids, she saw the jeweled wings of the butterflies in their mating dance.

On his last visit to Washington, Jonathan told Suzannah that he would soon return to Nashville, and most likely remain there until the election in 1828. "Gone for two years?" she exclaimed, and this thought threw her into a state of confusion.

Rebecca noticed the change in Suzannah, but short of attributing it to Devroe's attentions, didn't know quite what to make of it. Her daughter had grown even lovelier; a certain radiance in her intrigued the young hotbloods of Washington. And though she was overly polite to them, that only intrigued them all the more.

Rebecca took a fierce pride in her daughter, her kindness, her gift of making people feel at ease with themselves. But because of Suzannah's beauty, she also experienced a twinge of jealousy. There'd been a time when she herself was the belle of Washington.

"Ah, if only I knew then what I know now," Rebecca told Letitia.

"You'd have did the same thing anyway.," Letitia said. "Because you were the most devilment child I ever did see. Miss Suzannah, she's like an angel compared to you. Takes after her grandmother, she does."

"You know, ever since I freed you, you've gotten impossible."

"Don't rightly know about that. Made you some nice warm milk. Drink it and stay quiet. I don't like these dizzy spells you been having. Ought to see a doctor, but you never listens, and that's all I've got to say about that matter."

One day in the spring of 1826, Suzannah told her mother that she was going to Circumstance's to help her with the baby. Circumstance had given birth months before to a fine healthy boy with tow hair and the blue eyes of Jeremy Brand. With Wingate's approval and blessing, Circumstance had named the boy Jeremy Brand Grange. The birth had occurred almost a year after her marriage to Wingate, and so the child *had* to be his. The release from the fear that the baby might have been the rapist's offspring had turned Circumstance into a totally different person. She took to motherhood as a natural and revered task. Everywhere she went, she took the baby with her, strapped it to a cradleboard on her back. And though it raised quite a few eyebrows in sedate Washington, the baby never cried, always looked with wide-eyed interest at everything that passed before his vision, and grew up with superb posture.

But Circumstance still had a lurking fear that the man who'd attacked her might one day strike again. The fear became so potent that she took to carrying a knife, strapping it to her leg the way she remembered Tanzy had. If he dared touch her again, this time she would be ready, and she would strike to kill.

Circumstance wasn't far wrong in her fears, for the youth who'd attacked her, now grown to young manhood, was very much on the Washington scene. And as he watched Circumstance come and go every day, he remembered the first experience he'd had with her, and plotted for the moment when he could make it happen again.

Suzannah came into Circumstance's house with flowers she'd picked and a smoked ham. "Letitia sent this over."

"You seem melancholy," Circumstance said.

Suzannah gave a tiny shrug. "Jonathan will be leaving soon and wants me to go with him. But oh, I just don't know. If I even so much as mention his name in mother's hearing, she goes into a fit."

Suzannah picked up the baby and waltzed around the room with him. "Oh, he's so adorable, and he looks just like Uncle Jeremy, don't you think? And like Bravo when he was a baby."

Circumstance nodded, but didn't encourage this line of conversation. When she'd first noticed the resemblance between her son Jeremy and Bravo, she'd pondered it long and hard. In her sleep one night she'd had a slow revelation about it. Bravo was her father Jeremy's son. The more she saw him, the more convinced she became, and consequently, she developed a new wellspring of love for the boy. She told no one, not even Wingate, but committed the secret to her journal.

"Have you heard any further news of Presidents Jefferson and John Adams?" Suzannah asked.

"Only that they're still both very ill," Circumstance said.

"If only they can both live until this July Fourth," Suzannah said. "Wouldn't that be wonderful? That will be the fiftieth anniversary of the founding of our nation. I know that the whole country is praying for it."

"Wingate says that it's extraordinary that they've lived this long. John Adams is more than ninety, and Jefferson is in his eighties."

"Well, I shall keep praying for it; what a wonderful gift to the country that would be!"

While Suzannah was at Circumstance's, Devroe Connaught came calling at Rebecca's with an invitation for them to attend a musicale. Rebecca became so excited that she had to tell Suzannah right away.

"I believe that he's really interested in Suzannah," Rebecca said to Letitia as she put on her cloak. "Wouldn't that be wonderful?"

"Wouldn't," Letitia grumbled. "Don't like that man, never

have, never will, and I hope you're not going to force Miss Suzannah to marry with him. Can't trust a man with lips as thin as that. Talks funny too. Can't hardly understand him."

"Oh, be quiet," Rebecca said sharply. "And don't you go telling Suzannah any such thing, do you hear? Have Tadpole bring my carriage around." Then Rebecca reflected for a moment. "How old is your son now?"

"Forgets. High teens, most likely."

"Well, isn't he a little old to be called Tadpole?"

"Suppose you're right." She bit her finger. "What should we call him? He's long and skinny like a pole. But I think that we best call him Tad."

Rebecca called out into the yard, "Bravo, would you like to come with me? I'm going to Circumstance's."

"No, thank you, Mother, I'm building a war chariot," he said, and held up the pieces of a wooden wagon.

"That's the busiest child in all creation," Letitia said.

Rebecca drove over to Circumstance's. She was surprised when she didn't find her there. "Where's Suzannah?"

"She left just a few minutes ago," Circumstance said.

"Do you know where?"

Circumstance looked directly at Rebecca. She knew that she should have lied for her cousin, but she also knew that no good could ever come of that. Whatever the silken skeins of deceit, the entire web must sooner or later be torn asunder by the truth. "I believe that Suzannah went to the Capitol," she said quietly.

Rebecca frowned and shook her head. "That's not like her at all. I've never known her to have any interest in that den of thieves."

Rebecca drove over to the Capitol with a sense of unease. Suzannah had been acting strange these past few months. She parked the carriage and climbed the steps to the Capitol, lifting her skirts so that they wouldn't drag. Congress was in session and she heard the drone of voices every time the Keeper of the Door opened the chamber to admit anybody.

And then she saw them. Suzannah was standing against a column, her head thrown back in laughter, and Jonathan's body inclined toward hers in a posture of easy, intimate grace. The scene cut across Rebecca's heart . . . Jeremy had once stood that way with her . . .

Her taffeta skirts whispered angrily as she swept toward them. Then her fingers lashed out and knocked Jonathan's hand aside, and he almost fell against Suzannah. Rebecca's eyes glinted, as hard as yellow agates. "Is this the way you defy me?"

"Mother!" Suzannah exclaimed.

"Yes, Mother," she repeated icily. "Suzannah, need I remind you that you were raised a little better than this? Decent young ladies don't meet young men on the sly, certainly not young men of whom their parents disapprove."

Suzannah's eyes flashed angrily. "Mother, we're in a public place. And I'm almost nineteen, not exactly a child anymore. You yourself have been urging me to get married."

The color drained from Rebecca's face. "That will be enough, Suzannah. Now come with me."

"No."

Rebecca started, her lips twitching in anger. "If you force me, I'll call the constable and have this man arrested. You're still a minor, still legally under my jurisdiction. And as long as you are, you'll do as I say."

Jonathan grabbed Suzannah's hand. "Suzannah, can't you see? This is what she'll do to you for the rest of your life. Pat you on the head if you do what she wants, and threaten you if you don't. But she'll never allow you to be your own person. Suzannah, marry me—marry me right now."

Suzannah looked from her mother to Jonathan. The word was on her lips . . . Rebecca saw the determination in her daughter's eyes, and recognizing it for what it was, she fell into a dead faint.

Chapter 45

SUZANNAH SCREAMED and grabbed for her mother as she fell, but she slipped through her grasp. She knelt beside her. "She's unconscious," she said to Jonathan. "Help me, please."

"I swear, this woman has more ways to stop a person from living—" He scooped Rebecca into his arms and searched her face to see if she was actually in a faint. He was surprised when he couldn't find any sign of sham.

Jonathan placed Rebecca in the back of the carriage and then drove swiftly to the Brand house, where they put Rebecca to bed. She still hadn't regained consciousness; Suzannah, beside herself by now, sent Tadpole to fetch Wingate.

Smelling salts and cold compresses finally brought her around. Wingate did a thorough examination, bled her, gave her a mild sleeping potion, and left her to sleep it off. In the drawing room, he talked to Gunning and Suzannah. Jonathan leaned against the fireplace mantel, feeling uncomfortable and very much out of place.

"Your mother's always been a full-blooded woman," Wingate said quietly. "What happened today isn't very serious. Perhaps a small blood vessel burst; there's a sign of that in her eyes. But if she continues to be in a constantly agitated state, the condition could become serious. So for the next few months, keep her as quiet and calm as you can. I'll be back to see her again tomorrow morning."

After Wingate left, Suzannah took Jonathan aside. "You heard the doctor. I mustn't do anything to make her worse."

Jonathan clenched his jaw. "I'll be going back to Tennessee next week. I gave my word to the general. Suzannah, honey, I swear I'd give you the best life that any woman ever had. Don't mean in the ways of fancy frills and money and the like. I mean in the true ways that a man can do for a woman— caring, dependable, putting you above all others."

Tears welled to Suzannah's eyes and she placed a tentative hand on his arm. "I want that more than anything, Jonathan, but if I did run off with you, and something happened to Mother, I'd never forgive myself. Then what kind of life would we have? Let me stay here with her until she's better. We can write to each other. I'll be able to bring her around, I know I will. She's not a bad woman. You'll see."

"We're doing wrong, Suzannah. We're putting other people ahead of us, and it's going to bring us grief." Then with a final curt nod he left the house.

Within days after Jonathan Albright left Washington, Rebecca made a remarkably rapid recovery. "I'm getting old," she said to Letitia. "My body isn't serving me the way it used to. When she told me that she was going to Tennessee with that man, I guess it was just too much for me."

Letitia looked at her knowingly. "First time I ever knows you to use that fainting business to get your way."

Rebecca shook her head slowly. "I wish I could say that I'd arranged it. That I'd been one of those simpering, swooning females, but it's not the case. I knew somewhere in my soul that if she went off with him, I'd lose her. And I've lost so many people in the past few years that I couldn't bear it."

Rebecca blinked back her tears. Letitia looked at her somberly and then she said, "I don't know why, but this time I believes you, I do."

Every day for the next month Suzannah watched the mails, waiting for some message from Jonathan. He'd left in anger, and being so proud, he might never write. When no news arrived she confided her fears to Circumstance. "I think I've scared him off," she said wistfully. "Not that I blame him. After all, he wants a wife, not a mama's girl."

"You're being silly," Circumstance told her. "Have you any idea how long it takes a letter to get from Nashville to Washington? Weeks, maybe even months. You'll see—if he truly loves you, he'll write, and you'll work it out. Your mother will get used to the idea of your being with him. But Suzannah, you must tell her very carefully. Wingate says that she was truly ill, and could become ill again."

About six weeks after Jonathan left, Rebecca was at home doing the accounts when the postman came riding up on his mule with a letter. It was addressed to Suzannah, but she happened to be out that afternoon. Rebecca stared at the

crimped handwriting and noted the return address: Nashville,
Tennessee.

She felt the blood surge to her head and she had to sit down.
She took a spoonful of the elixir Wingate had prescribed, and
after several minutes the pounding in her head subsided. Then
she tucked the envelope in her dresser drawer, fully intending
to give it to Suzannah when she returned home.

But later that day Devroe came calling with wonderful plans
about a fishing trip on the Chesapeake, and the entire household
got very excited about that. "I don't recall the Connaughts ever
before entertaining in such a manner," Rebecca said. "It's set
such a tone for the capital."

Gunning ran upstairs to see to his boots and clothes; even
Suzannah's mood seemed to brighten. In all the excitement,
Rebecca somehow forgot about the letter. The following morning, it was even a little easier not to give it to her daughter.
Rebecca clasped her hands, and prayed. "Forgive me for what
I've done. But I must have her near me. I've lost too much
already, I can't risk losing her, too. Out there, there are Indians,
and disease, and no doctors anywhere. And the child's never
had a strong constitution."

Rebecca went to the post office and arranged to have all
mail delivered to the Breech-Brand business offices. That way,
as subsequent letters came in from Jonathan, she was able to
keep them from Suzannah. For the first months, the letters
arrived with disturbing frequency. She never read them; she
had no wish to know what had passed between her daughter
and Jonathan Albright. She wanted only for it to end. And then
as the seasons gave way one to the other, the letters gradually
tapered off.

Suzannah appeared to be peaked, and melancholy, and Rebecca ached for her daughter's pain. But how else could she
protect her? Also, she knew that her daughter had the resilience
of youth; whatever disappointments she was experiencing now,
she'd soon get over them.

For her own part, Suzannah had written two letters to Jonathan, and as was the household custom, gave them to Tad to
take to the post office. Rebecca intercepted these.

"Any letters that Miss Suzannah gives you, you're to bring
straight away to me," Rebecca told Tad. "If I find out that
you've mailed any of them, or that you've told her about this—
well, I'll just see that those bounty hunters get you. They'll

ship you off to one of those plantations in the Mississippi, where you'll die of fever and snakes!"

Disheartened and distraught at not having heard from Jonathan, Suzannah slowly began to respond to Devroe Connaught's attentions. And then one evening Rebecca rushed into her room.

"Oh, my dear, I've got the grandest news of all! Devroe's just invited us all away for a weekend! And you know that Devroe hasn't entertained anybody but family at the estate since Elizabeth Connaught's total collapse."

Suzannah stared at her mother through the reflection in her small vanity mirror. "Do you really think we ought to accept?"

Rebecca picked up a brush and began to rake it through the fall of Suzannah's lustrous brown hair.

"He told me that he simply wants us to see the house now that he's refurnished it. You know, he's even invited President and Louisa Adams that weekend, and they've accepted."

"Well, that's a surprise," Suzannah said, wincing under the tugging brush.

"Isn't it? Well, John Quincy Adams is independent, but not so independent that he can turn down the richest family in the territory. He has few enough friends in Washington as is. Just remember, dear, a lesson in life: money is power."

Suzannah caught her mother's hand. "You're hurting me."

Rebecca put the hairbrush down and kissed Suzannah's head. "Oh, I'm so terribly sorry."

"I'm still uncertain about the weekend. Wasn't there some dreadful talk about father and Elizabeth Connaught?" Suzannah asked. "I've heard rumors about it all my life."

"My dear, if every family held a grudge perpetrated in youth, soon there'd be nobody talking to each other in this District of Columbia. What Devroe is trying to do is the most civilized thing imaginable. The days of the tribal blood feud should be over. As far as I'm concerned, it's a thing of the past."

Dressed in their best clothes, and full of high excitement, the Brands set out one Friday in November, 1827, for the weekend at the Connaught estate. Suzannah, Rebecca, and Letitia sat in the carriage, with Suzannah at the reins. Gunning rode alongside on his chestnut stallion.

"I must confess that I wasn't exactly looking forward to

this," Suzannah said, "but the day is so beautiful, and the trees in such full color, that perhaps it won't be so bad after all."

"You're the silliest girl in all Washington," Gunning called to her. "There isn't one eligible female who wouldn't give a part of her dowry to be invited away by Devroe Connaught."

They passed through a cathedral arch of trees lining the road about a mile from the estate, and then Suzannah saw the plantation house, which had just become visible. Its proportions were impressive; a series of long low steps led up to a colonnaded porch that ran around all four sides of the house, and three-storied columns soared up to a Greek Revival roof. Liveried servants were waiting for them beneath the portico.

"There's more servants than we got luggage," Letitia whispered to Rebecca, who shushed her.

All the fuss made Suzannah vaguely uncomfortable, but not so Gunning, who took to it all as if he were to the manor born.

"Welcome," Devroe Connaught said in the great hallway, as he came down a curved staircase backlit by an enormous Palladian window. "You must be exhausted after the trip. I know how it fatigues me to make the journey from Washington."

Suzannah felt fine, but Gunning admitted that a bath and a tot of brandy might just be the thing to refresh him. Devroe led Suzannah to a large bedroom that overlooked the formal boxwood gardens, severely manicured in the English style. Through the gathering twilight haze she could make out the tiny city of Washington nestled in the cup of the Potomac basin, bounded by silver slashes of the river.

"It's very beautiful," she said.

He gazed at her, and it seemed to her that his face softened a bit. "Not nearly so beautiful as you," he murmured.

Before she had time to be embarrassed, he'd left.

She dressed for dinner, Letitia helping her on with a lavender off-the-shoulder gown that accentuated her dark eyes and hair. When Devroe came to escort her downstairs, he was visibly impressed. "I'd noticed that you had the type of skin that's used to give life back to the pearl," he said. "And so I've taken the liberty . . ." He fastened a rope of magnificently matched pearls around her neck. "These belonged to my Great-Aunt Victoria."

"Oh, but I couldn't," she whispered.

His thin pale eyebrows arched. "I intended for you to have

them as a token of my appreciation for your coming here this weekend. But if you feel compromised, then do me the honor of wearing them only for tonight. Pearls die unless they're given life by someone with skin like yours."

When Suzannah and Devroe came downstairs, Rebecca didn't miss the necklace around her daughter's throat. John Adams and Louisa arrived just in time for dinner. Louisa sat at Devroe's right, the place of honor; Devroe placed a premium on protocol. Rebecca sat on Devroe's left, and next to her, President Adams, then Suzannah. Gunning sat on Louisa Adams's right.

Dinner proved to be terribly formal. Unobtrusive liveried servants stood on either side of Rebecca, ready to attend to her slightest wish.

"This dinner is grander by far than any I've been able to give at the White House," President Adams said. "But then, you have the advantage of me, sir. You don't have to fight Congress daily for living appropriations. If the Congress had its way, the White House would be little more than a huge, empty barn."

During the fish course—a striped bass stuffed with crabmeat and topped with a delicate cream sauce—Rebecca said, "Mr. President, I'm sure we all offer you our deepest condolences on the death of your father, and though painful as it might be, the manner and timing of his passing was so fascinating that I'm sure this company would appreciate hearing it from you."

"Doesn't it concern Thomas Jefferson also?" Devroe asked. "I believe that I heard something of that nature last summer."

Louisa nodded. "Yes, and when you consider the events, it does seem extraordinary. John, do tell the tale."

John Quincy took a swallow of Madeira to clear his throat. "As most of you may know, my father and Thomas Jefferson were bitter political enemies. In fact, my father never remained in Washington to witness Jefferson's inauguration. But when Jefferson's term was up in 1809 and he left the White House, he wrote a letter to my father saying that they mustn't die before they'd explained themselves to each other. After all, they were two of the originators of our War for Independence. And so as the years passed, they engaged in a long letter exchange, talking about everything: the state of the Union, the state of the world. Their primary concern was what was best for the United States.

"Gradually, as may happen between men who are rivals but who nevertheless recognize the other's worth, they came first to appreciate and then to like each other. More years passed, and then they challenged each other to a contest: that they would both live to see the fiftieth anniversary of the signing of the Declaration of Independence—July 4, 1826."

"In 1825, my father's health had deteriorated to the point where we thought he must surely die; he was after all, in his nineties. Jefferson also had taken gravely ill. And yet the two men hung on, taking strength from their letters, literally willing each other to live to see the fiftieth-anniversary celebration.

"And then on that fateful morning, July 4, 1826, Thomas Jefferson lapsed into a coma. My father also barely clung to life. We knew that the end was near for him. Jefferson died around noon that day, and my father, who'd been slipping in and out of consciousness, said, 'Thank God that Jefferson still lives...' not knowing then that he'd already died. And then my father breathed his last. And so we lost, in that one day, two of the great men who were responsible for our battle for freedom."

An awed, respectful silence greeted this tale, and then Rebecca sighed, "Of the original Founding Fathers, only James Madison and James Monroe are left. And they're both ailing—so Dolley has written me from Montpelier. Well, we shan't see the likes of those men again."

Devroe rose from his chair. "A toast then, to the nation. One of the reasons I've asked you all here this weekend was to tell you that I've just applied for American citizenship. And I expect that very shortly I shall become, how do you say, naturalized?"

"But that's wonderful!" Rebecca said, beaming. She felt that another objection to his suit for Suzannah's hand had just been removed.

During the meat course, a paillard of veal garnished with parsley, President Adams expounded on the laws that he wanted Congress to pass. "We are seeing great things happening in the rest of the world. All over Europe, men of science, medicine, and philosophy are discovering secrets hitherto unknown. The universe is ready to reveal itself before our very eyes. And how awful it would be if the United States were not in the vanguard of that movement for knowledge. For this reason, I've asked Congress for funds for a national university."

"Wonderful," Rebecca said. "Your mother was always a strong advocate for compulsory public education."

"I've asked Congress to fund an astronomical observatory. Who knows what mysteries we shall unlock in the heavens? Perhaps even an inkling of God's plan."

"I doubt that Congress would admit that there was any plan save its own," Gunning said wryly, and everybody laughed.

"And most important for this nation, I've asked Congress for money for interstate roads that will connect the disparate parts of our far-flung nation and make us into a whole."

"Alas, Congress had neither the vision nor the inclination to support such programs. They call John a dreamer," Louisa said.

"But the day will come when Congress will have to act on these and related matters. Mark me well," Adams said.

When dessert was served, a frothy concoction of syllabub liberally laced with sherry, Devroe leaned toward President Adams. "Sir, what do you think of this man Sam Houston?"

"I've made his acquaintance," Adams said frostily. "An adventurer given to excesses and hyperbole. He's an intimate of Andrew Jackson's, of course. In fact, I believe that Jackson was instrumental in Houston's setting up a law practice in Nashville, isn't that correct?"

Devroe nodded. "Although Sam Houston has other interests—or as a soon-to-be-naturalized citizen would say, other fish to fry. He and a group of landowners and businessmen, including Jim Bowie, are trying to raise money to increase their holdings in Texas. You doubtless know that General Santa Ana of Mexico has responded favorably to American colonization of that vast Texas area, provided they swear allegiance to Mexico."

"And providing that they abolish slavery in the area," President Adams said. "Neither Jackson nor Houston looks favorably on that."

"Well, Houston's asked me to invest in that enterprise," Devroe said.

"And will you?" Rebecca asked.

"Probably not. I find those men highly erratic, and not good credit risks. We Connaughts prefer a more conservative approach to investments. Over the long term, they're much sounder." He paused, had a thought, and said, "Oh, and while my lawyer was in Nashville, a curious occurrence transpired between him and one of General Jackson's aides. Suzannah, I believe that it was somebody you knew."

Suzannah's heart suddenly started to thud erratically. "Who might that be?"

"A lieutenant named—umm, Jonathan something or other."

"Albright?" she asked weakly.

Rebecca's hands gripped the sides of her chair.

"That's it," Devroe said. "Lieutenant Jonathan Albright. He and his fiancée entertained my lawyer—or perhaps the woman was Albright's wife? Yes, I think that's the way it was. At any rate, I thought you might be interested in news of him."

Suzannah said gaily, "Oh, we haven't been in touch for more than a year now. But I certainly do wish him well in his new life."

Rebecca gradually released her grip on the chair. The conversation turned to other things. Suzannah kept a smile frozen on her face; she talked a little too loudly, laughed a little too often, and Rebecca ached for the pain that her child was bearing. Yet, Rebecca thought, Jonathan Albright hadn't wasted any time in getting married, so she'd been right after all.

President and Louisa Adams excused themselves while brandy and cigars were being served, claiming that they had to return to Washington. "Pressing affairs of state wait for me tomorrow," Adams said. "New efforts of Jackson and his cohorts to thwart the government, like their damnable Tariff of Abominations."

When the Adamses had gone, Devroe said, "He's clearly an intelligent man, but oh, what a dour disposition. Frankly, I feel more comfortable now that he's gone."

"Hear, hear!" Gunning said.

"You see, I've planned a little after-dinner entertainment for us. I've engaged a troup of traveling dancers for the evening. They're all the rage in Paris, and they're due to open in New York at the end of this year. I thought we might have a private preview. Toe dancers, they're called. I hope you'll find them amusing."

Gunning raised his brandy snifter and then with his intoxicating joie de vivre, called out, "Here's to you, Dev! I mean, a man couldn't ask for a better friend."

"You know, Mrs. Brand, the dancing master of this troupe caught a glimpse of you when you arrived and said that he thought he knew you."

"Me? How extraordinary! I have no recollection of any dancing master. What's his name?"

"I've forgotten—I'm so bad with names. But something very French. I confess I never can tell one of those foreign names from another."

A string quartet began to play behind an arras. Servants brought out candelabra and placed them strategically around the room, specifically lighting an area of the hardwood floor intended to act as a stage.

Then the curtain parted and with a precise pointed toe step, the dancing master appeared, preceded by the heavy scent of ambergris perfume. He wore black skin-tight hose that bunched unappealingly, a white bell-sleeved blouse, and a cummerbund pulled tightly around his paunch. Though he was close to sixty, his carefully applied maquillage made him appear younger. His haughty gaze swept the room, and then his eyes opened wide and fastened on Rebecca.

"Oh my nerves!" she exclaimed. "It's Audubert Ville-franche!"

Chapter 46

AUDUBERT VILLEFRANCHE tapped his staff on the floor and called out, *"Attendez, la danse!"*

Gunning's eyes popped as a trio of dancers tiptoed onto the stage. Their pink shoes had a flat section on the tip so that they could balance themselves on their toes. They wore pink bouffant skirts that came down to the floor, but when they stood en pointe, as they called it, and turned, their flaring skirts allowed Gunning to see clear up to their calves!

Gunning squirmed in his seat for the rest of the performance, so taken with one of the dancers that it was all he could do to keep from reaching out and grabbing her. She seemed to return his interest, for whenever she came out of a pirouette she flashed a ready smile at him.

Gunning clapped his hands red at the end of the performance. "I've never seen anything like it," he exclaimed eagerly. "What in the deuce do they call it?"

"Ballet," Devroe said. "They've just begun to develop it on the Continent. I don't predict an enormous future for it, but it does have its moments of amusement."

Then the dancing master approached the seated guests. "Ah, do my eyes deceive me? It is Rebecca Breech, is it not? But of course! The one true love of my life, have I not told you, *ma chère?"* he said to one of the dancers. "Permit me—this is my daughter, Véronique Villefranche."

Véronique made an elaborate bow and dropped her gaze demurely, just managing to catch Gunning's eye again as she did.

Audubert babbled on and on in a polyglot of English and French until Devroe finally snapped his fingers and dismissed him and the troupe. "How do you come to know such an odd fellow?" Devroe asked Rebecca.

She felt herself blushing. "Audubert and my father were once involved in a minor business venture. It came to naught, in part because of Audubert's obvious eccentricities."

"I shouldn't wonder," Devroe said with a lift of his eyebrow.

But Rebecca did wonder. To see Audubert now, reduced
to a dancing master, and with a daughter who was as saucy a
minx as Rebecca had ever seen . . . well, the wheel of fortune
certainly turned in strange and curious ways.

A short time later, when the women were about to go upstairs to retire, Suzannah started to take the pearl necklace off.
Devroe stopped her. "Will you wear them to bed this night?
It would give me great pleasure to think of them close to your
skin."

Suzannah flushed with the compliment, nodded, then went
upstairs with her mother. At the door to Suzannah's room,
Rebecca fingered the necklace. "I've seen these before," she
said softly.

"Really? Where?"

"A young Connaught girl named Marianne had them. When
your Uncle Jeremy was captured by the British, Marianne took
all the Connaught jewels and . . . well, never mind, we said that
the past should bury the past, and so be it."

Rebecca put her arm around Suzannah's shoulder. "I'm so
sorry that you had to hear about Jonathan this evening."

Suzannah gave a tiny shrug. "Well, you were right, Mother,
as always. I suppose it was nothing more than a fleeting flir-
tation for him."

"Suzannah, I don't want to influence you, but it should be
clear to anybody with eyes that Devroe has serious intentions.
Before you decide, just think of what it would mean. You'd
be mistress of this vast estate, of holdings in England, and New
Orleans, and wherever else the sure Connaught hand has gone.
I could die a happy woman knowing that you were secure."

"I'll think about it, Mother, I really will." Suzannah kissed
Rebecca goodnight and slowly got undressed. As she slipped
beneath the coverlet, the pearls lay heavy around her neck,
feeling more like a noose than a necklace.

In her room, Rebecca prepared her toilet. An unguent that
Letitia made up from the aloe plant for the tiny lines around
her eyes, a hundred strokes with the brush through the hair
whose titian hues were slowly giving way to silver.

Then the overwhelming odor of ambergris perfume wafted
its way into her room and she turned to see Audubert peeking
in at her from her door. He threw back his long hair with an
artless gesture and made for her.

She picked up a heavy silver picture frame and held it over

her head. "Audubert, if you take one more step toward me, I shall bring this crashing down on your head."

"But *ma chère,* we are all alone in this world. I have so much to tell you. The servants here told me of your tragedy. Rest your head on Audubert's shoulder and let him caress your cares away."

"If you're not out of this room by the time I count three, I shall scream this house down, and you'll be flogged by the master of this plantation."

Audubert beat a hasty retreat to the door. "I remember when your father and your Zebulon were only too anxious to involve me in your scheme to defraud the government by buying up its lots. You were not so proud then."

"Audubert, out!"

He left, muttering under his breath.

In the main drawing room, Devroe and Gunning sipped their brandy and engaged in a game of chess. You could tell a lot about a man by the way he played chess, Devroe thought. Gunning was rash, impetuous, audacious in his bravery. Devroe allowed his queen to be placed in jeopardy and Gunning pounced on it with his knight. "I'm afraid your strategies are far too brilliant for me tonight," Devroe said with a sigh, and refilled Gunning's snifter.

"I think you'll enjoy the foxhunt tomorrow," Devroe continued. "The hounds have been primed, they've been kept hungry, and I've ordered a steady, reliable mount for you. Pity, I'd planned for you to ride the Arabian, but I'm afraid that he's just too difficult for anybody to handle."

"Never saw a horse yet that I couldn't bring to rein," Gunning said.

"Oh, I'm sure of that. It's just that this stallion is a killer. Of course, if I ever could get him broken he'd be the best stud in my stable, and I'd be indebted to the man who did it."

"Leave it to me," Gunning said. Then with his head reeling slightly from the brandy, he said, "I don't suppose it would be possible to see that little dancer, would it?"

"Which one?"

"Véronique Villefranche. The one with the sweetest little heart-shaped face and the trimmest legs I've ever seen!"

"Ah, I see you're smitten," Devroe said. "But you'd have to be most circumspect. Her father is so insistent that she be a virgin when she marries that he practically keeps her locked in a chastity belt."

Gunning smiled broadly. "They all open if you've got the right key."

"I'll see what I can arrange."

"Really, Dev, I meant what I said before. A man couldn't have a better friend than you."

A quarter of an hour later, in the servants' quarters arranged for the dancing troupe, Véronique received a note from Devroe Connaught, along with a gold piece. "You shall have double this if you please my guest, Gunning Brand. In the summerhouse, as quickly as possible."

"Be careful," one of the other female dancers said to her. "These Americans—I hear that they're wild beasts in the bedroom."

"Nonsense," Véronique said as she arranged a spitcurl. "I have met half a dozen of them already, and when they're stroked properly, the raging beasts all turn into pussycats. Hah! What do these provincials know of *l'amour?*"

And with a toss of her skirts, Véronique went off to the summerhouse to meet Gunning. As she approached the rendezvous she saw a life-sized alabaster statue in the moonlight. It was a magnificent thing, carved muscles, arms akimbo, head erect—*Mon dieu!* erect like other parts of its body, she realized with a shock. Have these people no shame? she thought. Never in all of France had she seen anything like this, and Paris was supposed to be the wickedest of cities.

How then to describe how frightened she was, how shocked, how *scandalisée,* when she realized that it was no statue at all, but Gunning Brand. *"Mais, vous êtes fou!"* she cried. "Lunatic!" and turned to run.

But he caught her skirts. "Not a lunatic, only practical. Because I knew that if you did come, this is what you'd be coming for, so why waste time?"

He covered her face and mouth with kisses, his body rigid and insistent against hers. With fearful protests, Véronique allowed him to take a few small liberties. Then she played her trump card and burst into tears. Tears had always brought out the gallant side in men, and then usually a handsome sum of money to assuage her grief, usually without her having to do anything more.

But this young man was another matter! Not only did he know a great deal about women, not only was she aroused by his advances, but soon she found herself on the verge of being compromised. Finally, to save her most precious prize, Véronique performed in the manner which she'd learned could satisfy a man while at the same time preserving her chastity.

When the deed was done, she burst into tears again. But he was only moved enough to say, "More!" and once again she performed, this time with growing verve, for the young man was not only as beautiful as a God, but heroic in his ability. Véronique had an oblique, intrusive thought, that she had at last met her match.

"Best trick I ever saw," he exclaimed. "Why, it's like a whole new toy. Now, turn about's fair play." After a bit he mumbled, "All of this is fine for a diversion, and I'm pleased to learn it, but let me teach you about the main act."

But here Véronique stopped short, and pummeled him about the head with her tiny fists. *"Quelle horreur!"* she exclaimed. "They were right. You Americans are beasts!"

She fled back to her quarters, leaving him laughing, satyrlike in the moonlight. She bolted her door and flung herself on the bed, breathing heavily. He had kindled a fire in her. *"Formidable,"* she whispered. "What would it be like to be married to a man like that?" And in the wondering, she began to entertain the notion.

She had come with the ballet to tour America, to create a sensation and marry well, so that she and her poor father wouldn't have to drag their way continually from one end of the world to the other. Well, why not Gunning Brand? Though he wasn't rich—not like this Connaught man—he was rich enough by her standards. The mother, a shrewd and protective woman, would be difficult; but what mother wouldn't be difficult with a son like that to guard over? And she'd found him more stirring than any other man she'd cried for. "Véronique Villefranche Brand," she whispered into the darkened servants' quarters. "I could do worse."

The following morning, everybody was up early and dressed for the hunt. Both Rebecca and Suzannah had elected to ride with the hounds, and were smartly dressed in new outfits bought for the occasion. A sumptuous breakfast, in the best tradition of the English manor houses, was served. Gunning came in a little late, blinking his eyes from the effects of too much brandy, and the heady night of new lovemaking.

"I say, Devroe," he said, affecting Devroe's speech patterns, "I've taken the liberty of asking your groom to saddle up the Arabian."

"Absolutely not," Devroe said. "He's far too dangerous." He said it loud enough so that Rebecca overheard it.

When she discovered Gunning's intent, she pleaded with him not to try it—"Especially if Devroe says that the horse is dangerous."

"With all due respect," Gunning said, "I've never yet found a horse I couldn't master. Isn't that so, Mother?"

Rebecca had to admit that this was the truth, and even though Suzannah lent her voice, begging him not to, Gunning would have it no other way.

Devroe sighed. "Well, then," he said, "let me go down to the stables and see if I can't calm him."

He left and returned a few minutes later shaking his head. A few more times he tried lamely to persuade Gunning not to ride the Arabian, but to no avail.

With a blare of horns, the baying hounds were set loose, and then another call sounded and they were off.

Seated sidesaddle, Rebecca took the first leap over a stone fence easily, reveling in the exhilarating thrill of the chase. It wasn't so much a matter of running the fox to earth as it was of cornering Devroe. She felt he was going to ask Suzannah to marry him, felt it as only a mother could feel such a thing. The rushing wind was in her face, singing in her ears, the sinews of her mare gathering her muscles beneath her, and then vaulting the fence, and as the hedges and fences and rolling fields sped beneath the horse's hooves, Rebecca thought, My daughter will own all this! And there was a consummate pleasure in knowing that she, Rebecca Breech, had risen from being a lowly merchant's daughter, to the mother of the richest woman in the territory. Only in this glorious land could such a thing happen. It made all her miseries easier to bear, made her forget for a moment the tragedy of her one true love.

"You're fast!" Gunning shouted to the Arabian, "faster than any horse I've ever ridden." The stallion had a quick wiry body that could turn and plunge at the slightest provocation. A stone fence moved toward them and the stallion cleared it with a superb leap. Gunning's heart thrilled to the power of the animal beneath him, his knees gripped the sides of the horse tighter, until he seemed to merge with its flesh, becoming a centaur, at one with the beast.

But just over the next hurdle, as the horse landed and Gunning landed hard in the saddle, the stallion reared suddenly, almost throwing him. Only an involuntary reflex, ducking low over the horse's withers and keeping a short rein, saved him. But the stallion wouldn't be controlled, and leapt into the air on all fours, landed and kicked out with his hind legs. Gunning hit him again and again with his crop, tightened his hold on the reins, but the horse wouldn't respond and plunged about in an anguished rage.

The other hunters, seeing what was happening, wheeled from the chase and converged on Gunning. The Arabian threw himself onto the turf and tried to roll over on Gunning. Gunning leapt free, but his foot got caught in the stirrup and he was dragged a few feet. The Arabian struggled to get up, his mouth frothing at the bit, hooves pawing closer and closer to Gunning.

Rebecca screamed, then, leaning low from her own saddle, she managed to grab the Arabian's mane and yank back as hard as she could. With a shrill whinny, the stallion reared again and pulled Rebecca from her seat. She fell to the grass, but the diversion proved long enough for Gunning to finally free his boot from his stirrup.

Just at that moment, Devroe raced up, and galloping close to the Arabian, put a bullet through its head. Everybody stood there, ashen.

"We might have all been killed," Rebecca whispered.

"Oh, Mother, you do carry on," Gunning said with an attempt at humor, but he too was shaken.

They went back to the house, leaving Devroe with his prize dead stallion. No one saw him taking the murderous spiny burr out from under the Arabian's saddle.

Chapter 47

SHORTLY BEFORE they were to leave the Connaught estate, Rebecca and Letitia were in Rebecca's room, packing. There was a rap on the door and Devroe Connaught entered.

"Madam, might I have a few words with you? In private."

Rebecca dismissed Letitia, much to her annoyance. She'd known everything that had happened in the Breech and Brand families for more than fifty years, and she wasn't about to let some tight-lipped foreigner cut her out. She put her hands on her ample hips and stood there, as immovable as a mattress.

Rebecca glanced at her sharply, and grumbling, Letitia finally left.

"Really, servants in this country are so extraordinary," Devroe said. "In England, it would never *occur* to them to act in such a fashion. Madam Brand, under ordinary conditions I would have presented my petition to Mr. Brand, but since he's dead . . ."

Rebecca straightened, not daring to hope.

"I am asking for the hand of your daughter in marriage," he said. "I have every intention of making her the happiest of women. I must be frank with you. The Connaught men usually marry . . . women of their own station in life. But this is a new nation, one of enormous potential, and I'm persuaded that Suzannah is a girl of sterling qualities. And, of course, ah, chaste."

This last statement flustered Rebecca, but she kept her equanimity. "Why, I don't know quite what to say," she said, though she knew exactly, having rehearsed for this possibility for months. "Naturally, we're honored by your declaration. And you're entirely right, Suzannah is a girl of exceptional character. And, of course, chaste."

"Ah, I'm relieved at that. It is one of the Connaught traditions, that purity prevail from the marriage bed to the death-bed."

"Before I'd agree to such a marriage, I would have to be certain that my daughter would be accorded all the respect due

347

her station as your wife, and not relegated to the role of mere housekeeper and breeder of Connaught heirs."

Devroe flushed to the roots of his thinning hair. He'd made this proposal fully expecting that this woman would fall on her knees and kiss his boots, but instead *she* was making demands. The temerity! He managed to control his quavering voice. "You'll be happy to know that I'm totally in agreement with your point of view. Though the Connaughts are an ancient clan, even we are becoming more modern in our views concerning women. Rest assured, madam, your daughter will be in loving hands."

"Then there's only one more thing," she said. "I'm not a parent who forces her children to do anything against their wills, and so we must have Suzannah's consent. If she agrees, then the way is clear."

"I'll speak to her immediately," Devroe said, feeling somehow like a schoolboy who'd just passed a test. The daughter of a stone merchant speaking thus to a Connaught? Really, the world *had* been turned upside down! But you will pay, Madam Brand, Devroe thought as he bowed to her. You and your daughter will both pay dearly.

When Devroe presented his suit to Suzannah, she gazed at him with an expression so gentle that even he felt a trifle moved . . . in other circumstances, who knows but that he might have loved somebody like her. But his passion to avenge his father and the entire Connaught clan ran too deep.

"Devroe, I'm very flattered," Suzannah said. "But before we rush into anything we might regret, I think we should wait a year, get to know each other. Then if we're both of the same mind, the transition to marriage will have been made so much easier for us."

"Having declared my love for you, I cannot conceive why we would deny each other a year of bliss."

Suzannah bit her lip. "Call it a woman's whim, but I know that I wouldn't be comfortable without the time."

Recognizing that if he pressed her too hard he might easily lose her, he bowed and said, "As you wish, my dear Suzannah. A year it will be then—a year in which to make the Connaught estate suit your tastes, a year in which to anticipate all our future bliss."

He kissed her hand, and before she could withdraw it, placed a large square-cut emerald ring on her finger. "This will have to do until the simple gold band will bind us together for life."

Driving back to Washington in the carriage, Rebecca and Letitia couldn't keep their hands off the ring. "Biggest stone I ever did see," Letitia said. "All green with its fire."

"You're a very fortunate girl," Rebecca said. "Oh, I am so happy for you."

But later that night, when Letitia brought Suzannah her toddy, she found the girl in a state of high confusion.

"Devroe doesn't love me—a woman knows such a thing in her bones. Oh, he's perfectly pleasant, but what's really in his mind? I'm not a great heiress. I understand that the Van Ness girl is mad to marry him, and with her fortune, why wouldn't he choose her?"

"Because she doesn't have one good titty between the two of them. Besides, you're much prettier than her; you're the prettiest thing in all these parts."

"I feel like . . . something to be traded and sold," she whispered, and tears came to her eyes.

Letitia hugged her. "You don't have to marry any of them, not that Jonathan man who never wrote, not this here man either. Years ago I told your mother to listen to her heart, and I be telling you the same thing now. That's the only road to happiness—following your own heart."

But once the engagement was announced, wheels began to grind forward inexorably, and there seemed to be no way out. Engagement presents began to arrive at the Brand house, including an extravagantly expensive silver tea service from the Van Ness family, and a tole box painted with a picture of the White House, the standard present of President and Louisa Adams.

Rebecca set the wedding date for March 7, 1829, choosing that date because it was the first Saturday after the inauguration, whoever the President then might be. She reserved St. John's for the church ceremonies.

For Suzannah, spring sped by on swallow's wings. Her mother couldn't have been more generous with her trousseau, and seamstresses in Washington and Georgetown were kept sewing for months. She spent hours being fitted for a glorious

white silk wedding dress embroidered with Irish lace and
crusted with seed pearls.

"Mother, this is far too expensive for me," Suzannah said
as she turned before the mirror. "Whom are we trying to im-
press?"

"You don't understand," Rebecca said. "When I married,
it was a hasty affair, done in Chief Justice Marshall's basement
chambers, and in an ordinary everyday dress. Call me shame-
less if you like, but you're my only daughter, and I want this
to be the most glorious wedding that any daughter ever had!
Then one day, God willing, your daughter will marry in this
dress, and her daughter. Oh my darling Suzannah, let me have
my moment of joy."

When Rebecca wasn't busy with the wedding preparations,
she kept a wary eye on the presidential campaign; the elections
were to be held in November. Already the contest had become
bitter. The political group supporting John Quincy Adams
called themselves the National Republicans. Andrew Jackson
seized on the name Democrat, which seemed best to describe
his freewheeling, boisterous, western kind of electioneering.

One day, Gunning and Devroe went hunting on the Potomac
flats. The two men had shot more than a dozen wild geese as
they arrowed their way south. There were far too many fowl
for the Brand household, and on impulse, Rebecca decided to
take six of the birds over to Louisa Adams at the White House.
The Adamses didn't have the great fortune necessary to entertain lavishly at the White House, and Rebecca knew that they
would be grateful for the birds.

Letitia wrapped the fowl in the pages of the *National Intelligencer* and Rebecca, taking Bravo with her, strolled over
to the mansion. Bravo was nearly ten, and had a thatch of sun-
blond hair and intense, forthright blue eyes. He ran circles
around Rebecca as they walked; he chased a squirrel up one
of the poplar trees that President Jefferson had planted twenty-
five years before, which had since grown into stately shade
trees. Then he trailed after a visiting foreign dignitary from a
North African country, questioning him intensely about his
flowing robes, his curved saber, his cleft beard, and his turban,
until Rebecca called to him in exasperation.

When they got to the approaches of the White House, Bravo

climbed on top of the brick fence in front of the President's Palace, and the guard had to haul him off. Once inside the entrance hall, he wandered away from Rebecca, poking his head into the rooms, each one a new and different-colored world for him.

When Rebecca was announced, Louisa Adams came down from the family quarters on the second floor, and they went into the Green Room. Rebecca noticed immediately that Louisa had been crying. "What ever's the matter?"

Without a word, Louisa handed her a newspaper she'd been carrying. Rebecca's eyes opened wide as she read the scurrilous editorial. "This is absolutely shocking," she said. The article accused London-born Louisa of being an English spy. It went on to claim that John Quincy Adams had sold a white American girl into slavery to the Czar of Russia when he'd served at that court, and that the Adamses were royalists and wanted the monarchy back.

"The last is what hurts John the most," Louisa said. "Never did anybody take more pride in being American than John."

"It's utter rubbish," Rebecca said angrily. "We should be fighting this campaign on the important issues. Should we pass a protective tariff? What should our national policy be about land? Will we move forward with internal improvements to make the frontier more accessible, or will we allow our outposts to be overrun by Indians, or Spaniards, or British, or Russians? And what of the Bank of the United States? Is this indeed the best way to manage our fiscal policies?"

She paused for breath and Louisa said, "Oh, my dear, you mustn't excite yourself so. Remember your condition."

Rebecca clasped her hands and slowly regained her composure. "It's just that sometimes I get so angry. Instead of discussing the issues, all we do is assassinate the characters of the men who run for the highest office in the land. We've embarked on a campaign of personalities and slander, and woe to the political system if we continue so. And yet this is what the public wants, this is what sells newspapers. Why that's so, I cannot say."

Louisa nodded. "Do you know that there are at least half a dozen senators, and perhaps forty congressmen, who've refused to call on my husband? I ache for my John."

"And what an affront to the office of the presidency," Rebecca snapped. She riffled angrily through a stack of newspapers. "The chief culprit seems to be the *United States Telegraph.*"

The paper had once been the *Washington Gazette,* but had been purchased by John Eaton and turned into a Jackson organ. The paper immediately resurrected the charges that a "corrupt bargain" had been made in 1824 between Adams and Clay. The personal charges leveled against Adams and Louisa were so filthy as not to bear repeating in polite company.

One would think that Senator Eaton wouldn't be so free with his charges, Rebecca thought, not with the suspicions hanging over him. The talk was that he'd arranged for Peggy Timberlake's husband, John, to go off to sea again on the *Constitution,* so that Eaton could have Peggy all to himself. When Timberlake heard the tales about his wife and the senator, he supposedly drank himself to death. All the matrons of correct Washington society were now shunning Peggy. When Senator Eaton had asked Andrew Jackson what he should do about Peggy, Jackson said, "If you love Peggy Timberlake, then go and marry her and shut their mouths!" Rebecca thought, if Jackson's elected, then people like this will wield power and influence in Washington.

"There's only one way to handle this," Rebecca said, half to herself, half to Louisa. "The only effective weapon against scandal is truth. Sometimes the only way to fight fire is with a greater fire. But always the truth!"

Rebecca took her leave of Louisa Adams; halfway out of the White House door, she realized that she'd left Bravo behind. It took her some minutes to track him down. He was in the Cabinet Room, eyes aglow, staring at a huge map of the United States. "Some day, I will travel far and wide all across it," he said, his arm sweeping from sea to sea.

Rebecca's oil lamp burned far into the night as she pored through accounts of Andrew Jackson's life, and filled that in with her own trenchant recollections of the man.

"He is called a man of the people," Rebel Thorne began, "a true friend of the common man. Hah! Does the common man then own hundreds of acres of land in Tennessee? And does the common man own a host of slaves? True, he was born in a log cabin on the Carolina frontier, and was orphaned at an early age. We applaud his service as a messenger for our

Continental Army during the Revolutionary War, and also the
courage with which his men fought the Battle of New Orleans.

"But we do cry out for judgments in other matters, matters
grievous for the American people. Between the ages of twenty-
three and sixty, General Jackson has been involved in no less
than fourteen fights, duels, brawls, shootings, and cutting affairs! This man who wants to be President of the United States
has slashed, clawed, and killed various American citizens!
Shall we have a killer holding the highest office in the land?"

Rebecca sent a copy of her first article to the *National
Intelligencer,* and another copy to the men running the Adams
campaign. "Rebel Thorne is with us!" cried one exultant pol-
itician. "This article is to be the first of a series. Thorne suggests
that we collect these pieces and print them up as a pamphlet.
What ammunition that will give us. Now if we can just get
Jackson angry enough to challenge somebody to a duel—the
election will be ours!"

For the next two weeks Rebecca poured her heart out on
paper. On a personal level she genuinely liked Andrew Jackson,
thought him a man of magnetic charm. But she was absolutely
convinced that if he was elected, the country would be ruined
and the Union destroyed. It would be a government of the mob,
of the lowest man, and she would fight that with tooth and nail
and pen.

Rebecca pored over all the newspaper articles and editorials
concerning Jackson. Most of the material was familiar. Andrew
had met Rachel in a Nashville boarding house while she was
still married to her first husband, Lewis Robards. When Robards left Rachel, claiming that he was getting a divorce, Jackson and Rachel married. Thomas Arnold, a candidate for Congress from Tennessee, asserted, "Robards wanted a divorce
because he'd discovered Rachel and Andrew exchanging the
most delicious kisses! Further, Andrew and Rachel had taken
a trip to Natchez on Colonel Stark's flatboat and slept under
the same blanket!"

With an angry motion, Rebecca swept the newspapers off
her writing desk. She dipped her goosequill in the inkstand.
"I will not comment on the charges of adultery that have
plagued the Jacksons. Such gossip has nothing whatever to do
with the quality of the man's leadership. It is a matter of public
record that two years after the Jacksons married, Robards reappeared with the news that he'd never gotten a divorce, so Rachel

was legally a bigamist. Robards then gained a divorce from his
wife on the grounds of adultery. But Rachel and Andrew immediately remarried, and have remained so for decades, so we
know that their feelings for each other are profound.

"But what troubles me deeply is Jackson's attitude about
the gossip that's haunted him. For any man who dares speak
Rachel's name with less than the highest respect, Jackson has
kept his fists clenched, his knives sharpened, and his pistols
loaded.

"Do we see John Quincy Adams going around shooting
everybody who says anything nasty about his Louisa? If he
did, Washington would soon be devoid of any population at
all!

"Jackson's first big fight was with John Sevier, the Governor
of Tennessee back in 1803. They got into an argument on a
Nashville street; when Jackson mentioned his services to his
country, Sevier retorted, 'I know of no services that you have
rendered to your country except taking a trip to Natchez with
another man's wife.'

"'Great God, do you dare mention her sacred name?' Jackson shouted, drawing his pistol. Both men began firing away.
Fortunately, both men were intoxicated, their aim was bad,
and nobody was hurt. But suppose a Supreme Court judge or
a senator or congressman disagreed with Jackson while he was
President. Would that man be shot on the spot? Under such a
threat, how can any man hold an honest opinion? Everybody
around the President will be reduced to nodding and bobbing
fools, for to manifest any independent behavior might easily
get him a bullet in his brain. And where is Democracy then?

"In 1806, Charles Dickinson, a young dandy and the best
shot in Nashville, got into an argument with Jackson over the
outcome of a horse-racing wager. Heated words passed between
them and Dickinson profaned the sacred name of Rachel. Jackson instantly challenged him to a duel, and the two men met
across the Kentucky line.

"Eight paces were measured off. John Overton, the second,
called to the men, 'Are you ready?' Both answered yes, and
Overton yelled, 'Fire!'

"Dickinson raised his pistol, took true aim and fired, but
because of Jackson's loose coat, the bullet fractured a rib instead of piercing his heart. 'My God,' Dickinson exclaimed.
'Have I missed him?'

"Jackson then raised his own pistol, and squeezed the trigger. But the hammer stopped at half-cock. He pulled the hammer back deliberately again, and fired, and this time the bullet killed Dickinson. When asked if he had any regrets about killing this young man, Jackson said, 'I intended to kill him. I would have stood up long enough to kill him even if he had put a bullet through my brain.'

"That, good reader, from a man who wants your vote and your trust in becoming the President of the United States.

"In 1813, another fight, this time with Thomas Hart Benton, now our distinguished senator from Missouri. What if Jackson had killed him? We would have been deprived of this man's valuable services. In a country predicated on law, a man's recourse must be through the law. Anything less is anarchy, and that's what we'll have if Andrew Jackson, with his smoking pistols, is elected to the White House. My countrymen, think! Don't be misled by the supposed glamour of battlefield killings. Such things are best left to the battlefield. But the White House is a house of law, a house of reason; there is no room therein for demagoguery, no room for the law of *one* man and one man only, who will profane everything for which this country stands. Unite behind John Quincy Adams."

The Adams supporters gathered the material together from Rebel Thorne's articles and included it in a pamphlet entitled *Extract from the Catalogue of General Jackson's Youthful Indiscretions, Between the Ages of Twenty-Three and Sixty*.

Rebecca watched with growing unease as the campaign turned into the most vicious fight she'd ever witnessed. She hadn't intended it to be so; she'd only wanted to counter the charges against the Adamses. But the Pandora's box had been opened, and not even hope was left.

Chapter 48

THOUGH THE fire storm of the political campaign centered in Washington, the heat was felt in all parts of the country, and particularly in General Andrew Jackson's hometown, Nashville. The clapboard town of muddied streets, unpaved roads, and five thousand hardy souls was one of the last outposts of civilization at the vast reaches of the frontier. Beyond lay sparse, isolated farms, hostile Indians, and the unknown.

Jackson had made a fortune in Nashville, built a comfortable home, the Hermitage, there, and was considered a favorite son. Whenever the citizens saw a newspaper that happened to attack Jackson, they loaded their pistols; anybody who spoke ill of him was apt to be tarred and feathered and run out of town on a rail.

Jonathan Albright had spent the last two years working for the general's election. He exulted when the general was praised and ached when he was slandered. For example, everybody knew that Jackson had introduced the word "okay" into the language. It was from the original Cherokee word "oke," meaning "it is so." Jonathan knew that for a fact. But the Adams faction spread the lie that he was illiterate, and that O.K. was an abbreviation of his own spelling of "all correct," garbled to "orl korrect."

If the Adams supporters had confined themselves to that kind of attack it might not have been so bad, but one day Jonathan found Jackson slumped in a chair, tears streaming down his face. A newspaper lay open beside him. "They could not even let my poor mother rest peacefully in her grave," he whispered.

Jonathan read to himself, "General Jackson's mother was a common prostitute brought to this country by the British soldiers. She afterwards married a mulatto man, with whom she had several children, of which number, General Jackson is one."

"This is too much to be borne," Jonathan muttered.

"First my wife, now my mother!" Jackson exclaimed and

jumped to his feet. He snatched the paper from Jonathan's hands and ripped it to shreds. "By God, if ever I do get to Washington, John Adams had better beware, he and his hatchet men, like that Rebel Thorne."

As devoted as he was to Jackson, Jonathan had long since realized that this kind of life wasn't for him. Politicians spent most of their time either stabbing people in the back or keeping from being stabbed. He'd agreed to remain on with Jackson until after the election, maybe even accompany him to Washington if he won, though the pain of going to that fancy city might be too much for him. For in one of the newspapers that Jackson received regularly from the capital, he'd seen the announcement of Suzannah's engagement to Devroe Connaught.

The night he'd read it, he'd gone out and gotten rip-roaring drunk. Easterners, hah! She'd never even had the decency to answer his letters. How could he have been so wrong about her? Well, he told himself, she's settled for money, and that's all there was to it. "So what?" he'd shouted to the crowd. "She'd never be able to survive on the frontier anyway."

Yet her rejection had so injured him that he hadn't been able to take any other young lady seriously, though there were half a dozen who would have eagerly encouraged his attentions.

Election night in Nashville turned out to be an astonishing affair. The hickory pole, symbol of Jackson's popularity, was set up on every streetcorner, as it had been set up in most cities and towns in the nation.

A celebration was planned for that night, one that would include an ox being roasted and all the Bourbon mash a man could hold, ending with a torchlight parade that would weave up and down the streets. "Heaven help these wooden houses if one of the drunks gets careless," Jonathan said to Jackson.

"Better make sure to keep the fire brigade ready," Jackson ordered.

Jonathan took a jaded view of all this tomfoolery—hell, the general deserved to win on his own merits. But Jackson supporters like Sam Houston and John Eaton had gotten the ear of the general and convinced him that this was the surest way to gain widespread popular support.

"Hell, the people like a show, and we aim to give it to them," Houston said.

Rachel had come to Nashville for the election-night festivities; she was staying at the Nashville Inn, and Jonathan went to pay his respects. He found Jackson angrily pacing the floor of their room, his grizzled gray hair seeming to stand on end.

"By the Eternal, I've tried to protect her from all this scurrilous campaign muck, but when Rachel came to town to get some new clothes, she couldn't help but find out."

Then Rachel came into the room, her face swollen with tears. Though dowdy, some said even obese, Rachel was a kind and generous woman, with very little in the way of deceit about her. She'd shouldered Jackson's burdens for the forty years of their married life, and was proud that there had never been a harsh word between them.

She murmured to Jonathan, "My boy, the enemies of the general have dipped their arrows in wormwood and gall and sped them at me. I don't care so much for me, but they've disquieted him, and that they had no right to do. I found this pamphlet in the dressmaker's shop."

She handed it to Jonathan. He scanned the page. For the most part it rehashed old charges, but it ended with, "As for General Jackson's repeated insistence of his wife Rachel's purity, we can only wonder if the General doth protest too much."

Jonathan's heart sank as he looked at Rachel. Her health had seriously deteriorated these past months; the thought of having to move from the safety of the Hermitage to the White House had struck terror into her heart.

Rachel heaved herself into a rocking chair, wheezing for breath, her words coming out in gasps. "I shouldn't let it upset me so...but this afternoon, while I was being fitted...I overheard some of my so-called friends moaning that they would never be able to transform me from an illiterate pipe-smoking country woman into the First Lady, somebody who would be presentable to the society in Washington."

"I'm sorry that you had to overhear such stupid remarks," Jonathan said.

"I assure you that I would rather be a doorkeeper in the House of God than to live in that palace in Washington."

Jonathan knelt by her side and took her hand. "Don't you have another care about Washington. It's nothing but a small town anyway, with a lot of pretensions about its society. And from what I know about you, Aunt Rachel, you'll set the style in that city by virtue of your own goodness."

That seemed to reassure Rachel somewhat, and she dried

her eyes. Then she lit her pipe and offered it all around. She was sufficiently recovered by evening to take part in the huge election-night bonfire party, where throngs of people clasped hands and danced madly around the roaring blaze. The voting was done. Now it was a question of tallying the votes so that the people's will would be done.

When the votes were finally counted, what had been obvious to the Jackson camp became a reality for the rest of the nation.

"The general's won the election!" Jonathan shouted as he galloped through the streets of Nashville spreading the news.

Though the popular vote was close—648,000 to 508,000—Jackson had won an overwhelming number of electoral votes, 178 to 83.

Amid the general jubilation in the Jackson camp, only Rachel seemed depressed and crestfallen. "I have no other choice," she told her companion, Hannah. "I will have to be the First Lady of this land."

Jonathan, the Jacksons, and the rest of their household returned to the Hermitage, some twelve miles from Nashville. Servants and slaves began the tedious process of packing for the Jacksons' move to Washington.

"I'll be sad to leave here," Jonathan said to Ralph Earle, Jackson's closest friend and his official painter. They were coming from the plantation's outbuildings, trudging through the snow toward the Hermitage.

Earle nodded. "The Jacksons have made a home for us all."

The first small cabin that the Jacksons had built was made of rough-hewn logs with a shingled roof and two large fireplaces at the ends of the cabin. There the couple had lived while they cultivated cotton for the New Orleans market, working alongside and as hard as their few slaves. After many years they'd prospered, and Jackson built a two-story, red-brick structure, which Rachel surrounded with lovely gardens. Jackson had been so impressed with Mount Vernon that he planned to add a six-columned portico onto the front of the house.

"I know that Rachel is full of trepidations about going to Washington," Earle said. "Afraid that she won't do Andrew proud."

"What nonsense!" Jonathan exclaimed angrily as they walked into the gracious front hall of the Hermitage. An elegant

stairway curved up to the second floor. Argand whale-oil lamps
and candles cast their lovely muted glow throughout the spacious, high-ceilinged rooms.

"Aunt Rachel sets as good a table as any in Washington,"
Jonathan said. It wasn't uncommon for Rachel to be hostess
to forty or fifty people a day at the Hermitage, and fine French
china, rich cut glass, and damask napkins were a common
feature of the household. "Do you remember when General
Lafayette visited the Hermitage during his triumphal tour of
the country? Why, he said that he hadn't been in a finer home
anywhere!"

"Easy, lad," Ralph Earle murmured. "Rachel's coming
now."

"You'll see," Jonathan said under his breath. "Aunt Rachel
will surprise everybody in Washington, and they'll grow to
love her the way everybody does here."

On December 17, Rachel suddenly suffered a severe stroke,
leaving her with spasms of the muscles in her chest and left
shoulder, and a rapid, irregular heartbeat. The best doctors in
the area were summoned to the Hermitage.

To complicate matters, a chronic bronchial complaint had
finally been diagnosed as asthma. The doctors bled her three
times that day, while Jackson watched anxiously. After the last
bleeding, Rachel seemed to be resting easier.

The doctors finally went to sleep in a room adjoining
Rachel's, but Jackson sat by Rachel's bedside all night long.

When Jonathan offered to relieve him, Jackson waved him
away. "See to yourself, lad. This vigil is mine."

Rachel survived the crisis of the first day, seemed to get
better on the second. By the third, Jackson had propped her
up in a chair in front of the fireplace. Though she had difficulty
talking, the few people who were admitted to her sickroom
found her cheerful.

"She's going to get better, I know she is," Jackson said to
Jonathan, and in a tone that meant he would take God himself
to task if his prophecy wasn't fulfilled.

But on Sunday, December 22, Rachel came down with
pleurisy. The doctors poured hot drinks into her until she was
bathed in sweat. They said that her condition wasn't serious
and urged Jackson, for the sake of his own health, to get some
rest. Everybody went to bed, and the house grew quiet.

Jonathan lay in the room next to Rachel's, praying that they would get through this night. He heard Rachel get up twice, and looked in on her. With the help of Hannah, she'd gotten up and was sitting before the fire, smoking her pipe.

Jonathan tiptoed into the room. He watched the firelight play on her face, and the occasional tendril of smoke from her pipe. "Aunt Rachel, do you think it's wise for you to be smoking? Especially with your lungs congested and all?"

She seemed to look right through him. "It was a beautiful white gown. I would have looked pretty in it at the inaguration." Then she repeated in a distant voice, "I would rather be a doorkeeper in the House of God than live in that palace."

Jonathan turned to go, and then Rachel half rose from her chair and gave a strangled cry—"I'm fainting!"—and fell into the arms of Hannah.

Hannah's screams wakened the household. Jackson rushed in and helped Jonathan and Hannah lift Rachel onto the bed. The bed stood high off the floor to avoid drafts, and it was a struggle to get Rachel into it.

"Why are you crying, man?" Jackson demanded of Jonathan. "This isn't a time to be crying."

"Oh, General," Jonathan stammered.

Jackson stiffened. "She's not dead, she's not!"

Doctors Heiskell and Hogg hurried in and tried vainly to find her heartbeat. They shook their heads.

From the servants' quarters came shrieks and cries, and Jackson shouted, "She ain't dead! She's just fainted!—Bleed her," he ordered Heiskell.

Dr. Heiskell lanced Rachel's arm, but there was no flow of blood. "You see, when the heart stops pumping . . ."

"Try her temple," Jackson insisted.

The doctor did as he was ordered, but only two dark drops appeared on her deathly white skin. A table was brought in so she could be laid out, and Jackson said distractedly, "Spread four blankets on it, so if she comes to, she won't lie too hard on it."

Jonathan tried to lead Jackson away, but he refused to leave Rachel's side. "If she wakes up, she's got to know I'm here."

"General, you can't allow yourself to collapse. You've got a duty to perform," Jonathan said urgently.

Jackson blinked at him. "Millions of people voted for you," Jonathan went on, "voted for you as the savior of the poor, common man. Rachel is dead; there's nothing you can do about that. But you can save this country from the rich, heartless bankers who think only of lining their own pockets, save it from all those worthless thieves. General, you must pull yourself together. Otherwise you'll never make it to Washington."

Ten thousand people streamed into Nashville to attend the funeral of their Aunt Rachel. She was beloved by everybody in Davidson County. At the graveyard, Hannah flung herself into the open grave, and it was many minutes before she could be torn away.

"She was buried in her inaugural gown," Jackson whispered, "and she looked every inch the lady in it, didn't she, Jonathan."

Jonathan blinked at him through swimming eyes.

After the eulogy, Jackson looked into the bleak winter sky, his face ashen, his eyes as cold as death. He swallowed convulsively, trying to control his tears and the words that would not come. "I know it's unmanly to cry, but these tears are for her virtues. She has shed many tears for me."

Then he raised his voice and everybody in the graveyard heard him, "In the presence of this dear saint, I can and do forgive my enemies." Then his voice choked with fury. "But those vile wretches who have slandered her must look to God for mercy."

He began to tremble and would have fallen if not for Jonathan and John Adair—another veteran of the battle of New Orleans—who supported him under each arm. As they moved away from the gravesite Jackson whispered, "She was murdered—murdered by slanders that pierced her heart. May God Almighty forgive her murderers as I know she forgave them. I never can!"

Around the first of the year 1829, Jackson and his aides began the long journey to Washington. A steamboat, the *Pennsylvania,* departed from the Hermitage landing; the boat would take Jackson down the Cumberland River to the Ohio, then upstream to Pittsburgh. Then the party would travel overland to the capital.

As they departed, Jonathan Albright thought, I wouldn't want to be in the shoes of anybody who'd slandered him or Rachel. I surely wouldn't.

Chapter 49

WHEN REBECCA heard Gunning's footsteps clattering down the stairs, she hurried out to the hallway. "Gunning, would you please come in here? I want to talk to you."

"I can't, Mother. I'm late," he said, one hand on the door-knob.

"Where are you going?"

"First to see Devroe at the tailor's, and then off to meet Véronique Villefranche. She's been giving me French lessons, you know."

Rebecca's lips thinned. "You'd do well to stay away from that strumpet. She and her father are nothing more than a pair of fortune hunters."

"Well, then we've nothing to worry about there, have we? My allowance is so paltry she couldn't possibly be interested in me."

"In my day—"

"I know, I know, you were already earning bushels of money, and I'm nothing but a wastrel and a scoundrel and not worth my keep. Mother, I can't help it. I'm more like the grasshopper than the ant, would rather play than work, rather dance than sit at a desk counting figures, rather spark some sweet young thing than endlessly worry Washington politics."

"All right, then. I just wanted you to know that I've stopped your credit at the bank." She went back into the drawing room.

Gunning kicked the front door shut, and then with a huge suspirating sigh followed her into the drawing room. "Oh, Mother, can't we be reasonable about this?"

She waved a sheaf of bills and IOU notes under his nose. "Your bills and gambling debts are ruinous!"

"Well, I've been seeing an awful lot of Devroe. I can't let him pick up every check, now, can I? How would that look?"

"But don't you understand. Devroe has a vast inherited fortune. The Brands work for their daily bread. At least some of us do."

"I simply don't have a head for business. Am I to be shot because of that?"

"That's the least of it, Gunning. Your affairs with every tavern slut are legendary. And how many bastard children claim you as their father?" She flung the sheaf of bills down on the leather-topped Sheraton desk. "Not a day goes by that you don't bring some further disgrace down on the Brand name."

"Oh, Mother, do stop being so overly dramatic." Gunning sat on a gilt chair, making sure to keep from crushing the tails of his green velvet frock coat. He looked at her and smiled with his plaintive, beguiling smile.

But this day Rebecca wasn't having any of that. "There are times when I wonder how you could possibly be my son."

Gunning's chair fell over with a clatter as he bounded to his feet. He glared at his mother, his jaw jutting as he gritted his teeth. "There's no need to wonder about that, Mother, for you and I are very much alike. And the world isn't going to end because there are some bastard children wandering about. As you very well know."

He saw her start and he knew that he'd hit his mark. "Did you think that it was your secret only?" he asked softly.

"What secret? What are you talking about?"

"Oh, come on, Mother, you know very well what I'm talking about. Any fool has only to look at Bravo to know that he's not my father's son. The boy is Jeremy Brand's little bastard."

"How dare you!" she exclaimed, and moved to slap him. But he caught her wrist and held it. "Let me go! You're hurting me," she said, struggling.

"Not as much as you hurt me. Not as much as you hurt my father," he spat, and flung her arm aside. "And now you have the gall to lecture me about morals?" He'd worked himself into a temper, his face grew ruddy and his golden eyes flashed. "Extraordinary how easily parents judge their own children, how easily they forget their own transgressions. Why do you think that is, Mother? Are you all jealous of bygone days?"

Rebecca kneaded her arm, and then spoke from a deadly still center within her. "I've never been good at dissembling. I could deny everything, but then you and I would be no closer to understanding each other. And right now, that's what I want more than anything. My marriage to your father was over long before he left on his voyage. I tried any number of times before that to get a divorce, but he wouldn't give one to me. And then when we all thought him dead...well, you know the rest. Beyond that, I'll say no more, except that I've paid for my decision a hundred times. And though you may not believe me, I'm paying for it right now."

His half-smile stayed frozen on his full wide mouth; he'd expected tears and protestations, he'd expected to force her to a position where she would be more reasonable about his life. But her candor had robbed him of that. And more...he loved her; there was no one else like her in the entire world.

"Gunning, you're right, we are alike," she murmured. "Headstrong, willful, burning with some divine discontent that comes from I know not what. But I love you with all the feeling that a mother can bring to her child. And I know that you're making a mistake. Véronique Villefranche is an opportunist, and a girl of dubious morals. I'm sure she has an entire bag of tricks that she's used to intrigue you. But believe me, it's only for the moment. If a better catch comes along, she'll discard you."

"I've known her for months."

She brushed this aside. "But marriages aren't built on tricks. They're built on care and consideration and love."

"And, of course, you're the perfect person to lecture me about that, seeing how well you managed your own."

"Gunning, there's no reason to be cruel. My romantic life has been over for a long time, yours is just beginning. Don't be stupid about your choices just because you're angry with me. What I want for you is what every mother wants for her child—a rewarding life, one filled with happiness. And I can guarantee that you won't find that with Véronique."

"This conversation is becoming tedious," Gunning said. He moved toward the door of the drawing room.

"If you persist in seeing her, then I'll have no recourse but to cut off your allowance totally. You still haven't reached your majority, so under the terms of your father's will, that decision is mine. You must start to think about earning your keep. You're too old to be just lollygagging around this city, squandering your time and money at the racetrack and in the gaming halls. I'm not rich enough to support that."

"Exactly why I've just signed up with the President's guard," Gunning blurted. "Joined up three days ago. I'd hoped to spring the good news when I received my official commission—perhaps even make it a day of celebration for us all—but no, Mother, you were never one to wait, for anything."

His news stunned her. "The President's guard?" she repeated stupidly. "But that's not possible. There are requirements, applications to be made, recommendations from legislators, interviews."

"For other people, perhaps," Gunning said. "Not for me."

"But how did this happen?"

"I fell into conversation with one of Andrew Jackson's advance men. We hoisted a few drinks, then played poker. I beat him royally. He couldn't pay up, but he'd mentioned the President's guard to me. And so I bartered for his recommendation on my application. I tell you, Jackson's men are flooding the capital. And they're parceling out all sorts of government jobs, the way the church sells indulgences!"

"And you qualified?"

"All I had to do was show those army fools that I could ride and shoot, and you know I can do that better than anybody in this territory."

Rebecca pressed her fingers to her temples. She didn't know why she felt so uneasy about this entire prospect.

"Mother, you should see the new uniforms that Jackson's authorized. They're absolutely smashing. Blue and white, and lots of gold braid."

"Gunning, this isn't a game. There are great responsibilities that go with belonging to that army unit."

"Oh, I know. And the guard is so full of history. Remember? I was always intrigued with it. General Washington himself formed the guard. We assist in all the ceremonial functions, act as the President's personal honor guard. I can't wait!"

"Well, perhaps the discipline will knock some sense into you," she said. "But have a care. Andrew Jackson is a military man. From what I know of him, he'll brook no slovenly behavior, no dereliction of duties."

"I can't tell you how I'm looking forward to it. You know, I'm really not such a bad sort. I just haven't found my niche in life yet. But I think that the army might just be it. And Mother," he said, moving close to her and putting his hands on her shoulder, "I can promise you that I shall give it my very best effort. You'll be proud of me, you'll see."

She looked at him, so tall and straight and handsome, so

much wanting to please, and slowly her anger at him evaporated. "Well, congratulations. I'm delighted that you've finally taken a constructive step. You know I wish you all the luck in the world."

"Thank you, Mother. And now I really must go."

When Gunning had finally left, Rebecca slumped on the settee. It had taken all her composure not to collapse under Gunning's attack. She felt a deep well of sadness for herself, for him. She'd hurt him, unwittingly, and without malice aforethought. But how to explain that to a child?

And how would his knowledge about Bravo affect his behavior toward his brother? It all seemed like some endless, impenetrable maze.

But curiously, the most disturbing news of all was of his joining the President's guard. If Gunning thought that his duty with Jackson would be a lark, he was very much mistaken. The slightest infraction of the rules and Jackson would crush him. He'd been known to be uncompromisingly harsh; eight army men had deserted in Mobile, and Jackson had moved swiftly against them, court-martialing them and having them executed.

Another thought came to Rebecca, one that sent a shudder along her spine. What if Jackson ever discovered that she was Rebel Thorne? Without question, his vengeance would spill over to Gunning. Beset with these chilling thoughts, Rebecca's only consolation was Suzannah. Thank God she would soon be safely and happily married.

Chapter 50

REBECCA MOVED about her drawing room in an agitated state. The morning had been fraught with minor accidents; she'd pricked her thumb while sewing a peignoir for Suzannah's trousseau, then she'd dropped a Limoges plate that Dolley Madison had sent as a wedding gift.

"I have the same feeling as when the British invaded Washington," Rebecca said to Suzannah with a rueful little laugh. "The same sense of dread, that doomsday has come upon us."

"But Mother, be serious. Andrew Jackson is an American."

"There are many types of Americans, and contrary to public opinion, they aren't all equal. Jackson!" She uttered the name almost as an epithet. "Nobody seems to understand that we'll have a murderer living in the White House!"

Suzannah shook her head; she had no stomach for all her mother's carryings-on; with her wedding hard upon her, she had the distinct feeling that she was facing her own day of reckoning.

"An inauguration has always been a time of joy for Washington," Rebecca said. "But have you seen the state of the city? Everybody is in such despair. So many families that were permanent fixtures here—vanished. Even Henry Clay, who's been a familiar figure for more than twenty years—gone back to Kentucky, and out of fear of Jackson's wrath, most likely. Drawing rooms that held gay, laughing crowds, now stand dark and empty. Peggy O'Neale Timberlake's finally married John Eaton and now she thinks she's the queen of society. It's all so melancholy I can barely stand it."

"Mother, why in the world are you carrying on so? It's just the normal transition period."

Rebecca shook her head vehemently. "No, it's the end of an era, perhaps the end of our democracy as we know it. All we've labored to build up these long hard years will be snatched away from us by uncouth, grasping criminals. I hear that Jackson has even declared a personal vendetta against anybody who dared raise his voice against him. Reporters and pamphleteers, particularly."

"And why should that concern you?"

"No reason, no reason at all. Except that it's his devious method of stifling the freedom of speech guaranteed us in the Constitution."

"Mother, sit down and be still. You mustn't work yourself into a fit. Remember what Wingate said."

Rebecca took a deep breath and then kissed Suzannah on the forehead. "Every night when I say my prayers, I thank God that you're marrying Devroe. Whatever happens, it's less likely to touch a family as highly placed as the Connaughts. I can die in peace, knowing that you're secure."

Whatever fears Rebecca had about Washington turning into a deserted town began to disappear as the day of Jackson's arrival neared. One day at the general store she ran into Daniel Webster. Both were laying in provisions because of a sudden run on the food supply in Washington.

"I've never witnessed such a scene," Webster said, a grudging admiration in his voice. "You know that I was against Jackson, but people have come five hundred miles just to see him take the oath of office, and those I've spoken to seem to think that he's rescuing the country from some dreadful danger."

"Poppycock," Rebecca scoffed. "Frontiersmen, adventurers, confidence men, and a host of immigrants fresh from the seaports. And why have they descended on us? To reap the fortunes of war, that's why. Jackson's the victor and he's about to divide up the spoils. By the time he's finished, there won't be one Adams appointee left in office."

They went outside and watched the crowds of people streaming along Pennsylvania Avenue. Rebecca didn't see a familiar face anywhere, and every face she did see bore the look of defiance. "This is what it must have been like when the mob in Paris stormed the Bastille," she said. "Or when the barbarians overwhelmed Rome."

"Except that these are fellow Americans," Webster said, but Rebecca didn't seem to hear him.

Within days, the liquor supply of Washington, Alexandria, and Georgetown was exhausted. There wasn't a hotel room available anywhere; people were happy to sleep five and six to a bed, or on billiard tables, or on the floor. Men, women, and children camped out in the open fields, bearing the cold.

On February 12, 1829, a scant twenty days before the inauguration, President-elect Jackson arrived in Washington, and settled in Gadsby's Tavern. Upon learning of their hero's arrival, the mob immediately besieged him, pleading for job appointments. The crush became so unruly at Gadsby's that the disgruntled Washingtonians dubbed the hotel the Wigwam.

Jackson refused to pay the obligatory courtesy call on John Quincy Adams and took ads in the newspapers saying that he wouldn't go near him. "I cannot face a man who slandered my wife so, without the fear that I might resort to violence," he told the reporters.

When Adams heard this he insisted that he had never had anything to do with the articles. But Jackson retorted, "What difference? He probably had his hatchet man Rebel Thorne write them."

During his first day in Washington, Jonathan Albright resisted getting in touch with Suzannah. Why should he? She was already affianced, and according to the society page of the *National Intelligencer,* her wedding would be the social event of the season.

But his feet wouldn't heed his head, and one afternoon he found himself at the corner of Eighteenth Street and New York Avenue, staring like a tourist at the odd-shaped building that was the Octagon House, but really watching the Brand mansion across the street. A light snow began to fall.

He waited for almost an hour, but nobody entered or left, and finally he walked away, his shoulders dusted with flakes. He returned a second day, and after a long vigil, the door of the house finally opened. Out came Suzannah linked arm in arm with a sharp-faced priss got up in dandified clothes that must have cost a pretty penny. It made Jonathan all the more conscious of his own worn buckskins. As Suzannah's laughter echoed down the street, he jammed his hands in his pockets and stalked off.

He turned the corner and almost ran down the Brand maid. "Letitia?" he exclaimed.

"Ain't you—" she began, searching his face. "You is!" and hit at him with her canvas shopping bag. "What you doing here? You come to make trouble? The wedding is this coming Saturday. Don't you dare show your face till after; don't you dare!"

He gripped her arms, hearing in her words all that he needed to know. "She's not happy, is she? Why didn't she ever answer my letters?"

Letitia looked like she was about to expire. "She never *got* any letters! That's what turned her to that Devroe, 'specially when she heard you got yourself a new lady friend."

"That's a lie. There was never anybody but her!"

"You ain't married, then?"

"Of course not!"

"Oh my, oh mercy me, there's nothing but trouble ahead, I feels it in my bones."

"What should I do?"

"You asking me? Big strong brave *you* is asking *me?* You're the one who's fighting night and day with all them Indians, and killing bears and people and the like. Don't ask *me* what to do about a poor girl who's got her heart broken because she never heard from her man no matter what lies he says."

"You've got to tell her I'm here!"

"You want me dead? Miss Rebecca, she'd kill me if'n she knew I was just talking to you. And if you so much as came to the door, she'd kill you too."

"Will they be going to the inauguration?" he asked.

"More'n likely."

"Will you help me?"

"No. Miss Rebecca likely to have one of her fits, and her ghost would be on my head. You be too late anyway. Too many presents to give back, too many people got their invitations, church is all hired, and the ladies round town, they already been polishing and shining and sewing up what needs to be sewn."

"I'll ask you one question. Answer yes or no. And remember, the good Lord is listening to you. Is Suzannah really happy?"

"Best you go back to that Nashville and leave us alone," Letitia said, "and that's all I've got to say on that matter."

She tore free from his grasp and trundled down the street. When she reached the Brand house she turned back once as if to make sure that it had all really happened, and then she hurried inside.

Jonathan raced to Gadsby's Hotel, tried to get through the crush of petitioners to see General Jackson, then changed his mind. The fewer people who knew about this, the better. He had a moment's regret because he knew that this would mean the end of his career with the general. But Jonathan didn't care for Washington anyway. Not with all this backbiting, not with the fighting and clawing for power and position. And with Jackson in his deep despondency about Rachel's death, Jonathan thought that he wasn't exhibiting the most rational behavior. Perhaps it would change, but at the moment, the President-elect seemed determined to lead with a sword of vengeance.

Letitia said they'd be going to the inauguration, Jonathan thought. It will be crowded there. That would be his best moment to strike.

Chapter 51

"IT SEEMS entirely appropriate to me that this inauguration day should fall on Ash Wednesday," Rebecca said to Gunning, Suzannah, and Devroe as the Connaught carriage took them down Pennsylvania Avenue toward the Capitol.

"It is indeed a day for sackcloth and ashes," Devroe said. "I hear rumors that Jackson is determined to abandon the Bank of the United States. We'll have nothing but financial panic."

Suzannah stared out the window. "March fourth already, there's still snow on the ground, and not a sign of spring." She drew her stone-marten-lined cloak more tightly around her shoulders, but couldn't seem to dispel the chill in her bones.

"What do you think of old John Quincy not coming to the inauguration?" Gunning asked. "What a sore loser! His father didn't attend Jefferson's inauguration either, when he lost to him."

"What other recourse did John Quincy have?" Rebecca asked. "When Jackson refused to call on him, it was such a mark of indignity to both the President and the office that Adams had no choice."

"How old is Jackson now?" Devroe asked.

Rebecca did some quick figuring in her mind. "Sixty-one. And not in very good health. He's still carrying an old bullet in him, gotten in a duel with Thomas Hart Benton, I believe."

"Mother, you have more gossip at your fingertips than anybody I know," Suzannah said. "Where do you find out all these things?"

"Well, if Jackson is ill, and peppered with old gunshot wounds, then perhaps the good Lord will see fit to take him to his reward shortly," Devroe said.

"Then John Calhoun would become President," Gunning said.

Devroe nodded. "And that intelligent, worthy conservative would be a far more reasonable man to deal with."

"I hear that more than thirty thousand people have crowded into the District of Columbia," Gunning said. "I've never seen

373

such crowds in my life. Not even when you and I went to Philadelphia, Devroe."

Two hooting and hollering Kaintucks galloped by on their roans, and a glob of tobacco juice splatted on the door of Devroe's carriage. "Disgusting," he grimaced. "But I'm afraid that that's what Washington will be like in the next four years."

Gunning raised his whip to lash the horses. "I'll teach those hooligans a lesson!" he shouted.

"Gunning, stop!" Rebecca exclaimed. "I'm too old to have a carriage race along Pennsylvania Avenue. We'll only break an axle."

They managed to get close to the steps of the Capitol, where Gunning stopped the carriage. While they waited for Jackson to appear, Devroe told them of some of the honeymoon arrangements that he'd made. "We embark from Baltimore three days after the nuptials. Naturally, we'll have the best accommodations on the ship. In a month or so, we arrive in London, and I can't wait to show you that city. It is the most cosmopolitan of all cities in the world. Then to the Continent and Paris. Everybody should see Paris before he dies."

Devroe went on, weaving a trip of enchantment for the Brands, who sat there, eyes wide like children. But the scenario he had in mind for Suzannah was very different from the one he was mouthing. First she would slowly be made to realize why he'd really married her. And then when that full horror had seeped into her soul, she would have an unfortunate shipboard accident, probably in the English Channel. She would disappear in the sounding deeps, and he would return to the United States, a bereaved widower. Time enough then to take care of Gunning and Rebecca. Never had Devroe felt so consumed by a task, it gave his life shape and purpose, and called forth to the deep sense of justice in his soul. This family had been responsible for the ruination of many of the Connaughts, and now they would pay. Pay with their lives, for that was the only just measure. A pity about Suzannah; he'd even grown a bit fond of her. But fondness had no place in a scheme of such grand design.

"There he is!" Gunning exclaimed, pointing.

General Andrew Jackson came striding along. He wore a tall hat with a ten-inch mourning band, lest anybody forget. In deference to Rachel's memory, he'd banned a military escort, and the parade that had been planned. The citizens of

Baltimore had offered him a carriage made of hickory wood, but Jackson had refused that also.

"I prefer to walk to the Capitol," he'd said. "Just as Thomas Jefferson, another man of the people, did on his inauguration."

Jackson wore a suit of plain black cloth made from native-grown sheep, the fabric cut and sewn in Baltimore.

"If Jackson hadn't refused an honor guard, I'd be marching there alongside him," Gunning said. "Oh, well, the next parade."

Though Jackson had no formal escort, he hadn't had the heart to refuse a group of fifteen gallant old Revolutionary War soldiers who'd fought under George Washington, and so these venerable old men marched alongside him. A sharp breeze ruffled Jackson's shock of hair, which seemed to have grown even whiter since Rachel's death.

"He doesn't look so much the ogre as everyone's made out," Suzannah said. "In fact, he looks quite the gentleman."

"Don't you believe it for a moment," Rebecca said. "Give him the slightest excuse, and he'll draw his pistols to kill."

"He'll never get through that crowd at the steps," Gunning said.

An impenetrable mob of gaily dressed people jammed the East Portico and the grand steps leading to the Capitol Building. A ship's cable stretched across the bottom of the steps and kept the crowd away from the inaugural platform that had been erected for the ceremonies. Rebecca experienced a twinge of anguish when she remembered how Jeremy had built the first outdoor inaugural platform for President Monroe's swearing-in ceremonies.

Sure enough, Jackson couldn't get through the mob and had to climb over a parapet on the west side. He slipped into the building through the basement door. A roar as from a single throat rose from the crowd as Jackson stepped out onto the platform. He made a dignified bow, then raised his hand to still the crowd. It took several attempts before they quieted, and then Jackson began his inaugural address.

Rebecca strained to listen, her lips compressed. Jackson was offering nothing earth-shattering; in fact, his speech was marked by its blandness. "It has none of the brimstone and fire that we all expected," she said to Devroe. "So far, that's a blessing."

Jackson continued, "I approach the presidency with trembling reluctance. But my country has willed it, and I obey. The first concerns of my administration will be the liquidation of the national debt, a judicious tariff, and a just respect for states' rights."

"He threw that in as a sop to his Vice-President," Devroe said. "John Calhoun is a strict states' rights advocate, as anybody with any brains should be."

But when Jackson went on, he implied that he foresaw a strong clash between the states and the federal government. "Between the power granted to the general government and those reserved to the states and the people, it is to be regretted that no line can be obviously drawn, so that all shall understand its boundaries . . . This is a dilemma, and must be resolved by the good sense of the nation."

And then Jackson hinted at another source of possible trouble, and Rebecca stiffened.

"I intend to improve matters here in Washington. The task of reform will require particularly the correction of those abuses that have brought the patronage of the federal government into conflict with the freedom of elections."

"He means to turn the rascals in government bureaucracies out!" one doughty old warrior in the crowd shouted, and another cheer rose.

At last the speech was done. Then Jackson took the oath of office from Chief Justice Marshall, now looking old and somewhat feeble.

". . . preserve, protect, and defend the Constitution of the United States," Jackson finished. Then he kissed the Bible.

"It's done!" an old soldier cried. "He's President, thank God!"

Then the crowd surged forward. They broke through the barricade and rushed up the steps of the inaugural platform, eager to lay their hands on the President. They pulled and tore at him and Jackson fought his way slowly into the Capitol Building. He had to go down the long flight of steps to get to his waiting horse, and it took an interminable length of time, stopped as he was at every step by well-wishers.

Rebecca felt a pulse of fright for the uncontrollable power of these tens of thousands of adoring people.

At last Jonathan Albright and other of Jackson's aides managed to clear a passage for the President to his horse. He mounted, and with the crowd surging round, clutching at his stirrups, he rode toward the White House.

The crowd raced after him, in carriages, wagons, carts, and on foot. They were wearing hickory-nut necklaces, carrying hickory canes and hickory brooms, riding on horses with hickory-bark bridles. The crush of people carried Devroe Connaught's carriage along with it.

"We might as well go to the White House and see how Jackson handles this," Gunning said gleefully; this kind of tempestuousness had always brought out the celebrant in him.

"Jackson forever! Hurrah for Jackson!" came the shouts from the crowd. "I'll never forget this day as long as I live!" yelled an octogenarian from Missouri who'd made his very first trip to Washington. The mob took up the chant. "Jackson's President! The White House is ours! Jackson's President! On to the White House!"

Chapter 52

IN THE splendid and spacious East Room of the White House, Circumstance put down the final tray of cakes, ice cream, and orange punch on the groaning serving table. "There's enough food here to feed an army," she said to Wingate. "I hope it doesn't go to waste."

She and Wingate had been working since dawn with the rest of Andrew Jackson's family and staff to get the mansion ready for the open house after the inauguration. Jackson, true to his promise that this would be a government of the people, had invited absolutely *everybody* to the reception.

When Jackson first arrived in Washington, Wingate had gone to Gadsby's to pay his respects to the general. Wingate introduced Circumstance to him, and he'd immediately spotted her Indian blood. Living on the frontier, he had a nose for such things, and his face hardened. He made no bones about it; he'd always had a difficult time relating to Indians or those with Indian blood. Perhaps it was a consequence of his having lived in constant danger from Indian massacres, but it was a fact nevertheless.

Wingate, seeing the change in Jackson, quickly told him that Circumstance was Jeremy Brand's daughter, and somehow that managed to smooth Jackson's ruffled feathers. "Your father was a brave and a good man. At the battle of New Orleans, we owed a great deal to him. Any child of his is welcome in my house, and at any time."

"Thank you, General," Circumstance said. She too had seen the change in Jackson, and recognizing it for what it was, knew that she had to tread softly, carefully, to attain her ends. She hated doing it, but in this case the goal was more important than any false pride that she might have. "General, as you know, my father helped build the White House. Shortly before he died, he was compiling a record of this mansion, a history that could be left as a legacy to the people. Since his death, I've taken over the task."

"A legacy for the people?" Jackson repeated. "I like that

idea. I like it a great deal. And will you have a record also of the Presidents' wives?"

"Absolutely," Circumstance said. "And I was hoping that you would tell me all about Rachel Jackson. My father always spoke so highly of her."

"She was a saint," Jackson exclaimed. "Too good and too kind for this world." Jackson turned to one of his aides. "See to it that this young lady has access to the mansion whenever she likes. And give her any information that she needs."

"Thank you, General," Circumstance said.

Wingate was appalled at how exhausted and old the general looked. "General, with your leave, I'd like to prescribe something for you."

Jackson nodded wearily. "I'll do whatever you say, except I won't give up coffee or tobacco."

Wingate prescribed some bracing tonics, and within the three weeks the general had built up his strength to the point where he could walk to the Capitol for his inaguration.

President Jackson arrived first at the White House, but the mob wasn't far behind him. Without any thought for protocol—they'd never even heard of the word—they streamed through the gates, leaving waiting senators, congressmen, military leaders, Supreme Court Justices, and the leaders of Washington society in their wake.

Rebecca was shunted aside and separated from Suzannah, Gunning, and Devroe. Rebecca managed to get into the house by following close behind Congressman John Floyd of Virginia and his three-hundred-pound wife. Newly elected Congressman Davy Crockett in his coonskin cap greeted Rebecca and then was carried off by the crowd. Rebecca saw Peggy O'Neale Timberlake Eaton but was saved the embarrassment of having to acknowledge her when she was shunted aside by the crush of people.

"Suzannah! Suzannah!" Devroe called. "What in the deuce has happened to her?" he asked Gunning. Gunning shrugged. But, having just spied Véronique Villefranche and her father near the fireplace in the Oval Room, he left Devroe and made straight for them.

In the entrance hall, the crowd pushed and shoved, bunching up at the doors to each of the other rooms. The crowd outside pushed harder to get inside, the tens of thousands of people who had come for the inauguration, all now determined to get into the White House at once. A woman fell in the crush and screamed. A child was trampled. Glasses and china smashed to the floor, and one matron had her dress ripped from her back by the hickory rake of a passing farmer, and fell swooning into the Porter's Hall, where two drunkards had already collapsed.

When the press of people discovered that they couldn't all get a glimpse of President Jackson, they began to climb on chairs and sofas for a better view. Two riverboatmen hopped onto Dolley Madison's pier table and it collapsed with a crash under their weight. Springs broke, Mrs. Monroe's elegant damask furniture coverings were ripped, Bellangé masterpieces of chairs were reduced to kindling in a twinkling. Muddy boots slipped on vanilla ice cream and orange punch.

The crowd found its way upstairs to Jackson's private quarters, and a little girl jumped up and down on his sofa shrieking, "Mama, Mama! Just think, this sofa is one millionth part mine!"

Carried along in the crush of the crowd, Suzannah fought her way into the East Room. Since it was so large, she thought she might find a safe spot here, find some protection against the screaming mass of humanity. She caught sight of Andrew Jackson in the corner of the room, surrounded by aides.

And then she saw Jonathan. He was fighting his way to get to her. She recognized his scarecrow shoulders, the shock of unruly hair that wouldn't be tamed.

He reached her, and without a word, tried to lead her toward the door. A rollicking sailor came at them with a jug of whiskey, pressing the jug on them. Jonathan punched him in the gut and pushed by him. He got himself and Suzannah into the corner and stood with his back to the crowd, protecting her.

"I love you," he said.

"Don't. Please don't. Will you never cease breaking my heart?"

"I love you!" he repeated insistently.

"Then why didn't you ever write?"

"I did! At least a dozen times. But you never answered, and so I left off."

"But I never got any of them," she protested, at once not daring to believe him, yet feeling her pulse quicken as it did whenever she was in his presence. "I wrote to you also, but got no answer."

"How can this be?" he asked.

"I don't know. I gave them to the stableboy and—Mother!" he said with the sudden recognition. "But what of your wife?"

He looked at her blankly. "I'm as free a man as the day I left you here. Who told you such a tale?"

"Devroe Connaught."

"Your intended?" he asked, as a child at his feet began screaming. Jonathan picked the child off the floor and sent it on its way.

"Devroe said that his lawyer met you in Nashville with an attractive woman."

"Probably Emily Donelson—the wife of Jackson's nephew," he said. "Well, it's easy to see why Devroe would spread such a story about. Do you love him?"

"The wedding is set for this Saturday—three days off. All of the arrangements are made."

"Do you love him?"

"I don't know. I—when you didn't write, I thought that I might grow to love him. I—No! I don't love him."

He picked her up and tried to whirl her around, but they were bumped by the crush of people. "Come away with me," he said. "Come away right now."

Her hand flew to her mouth. "Oh, I couldn't. What of my family? What of Devroe? What of mother?"

"You saw what happened the last time you let her dictate to you. We would have been married for nearly three years by now, had I don't know how many children. Oh, my darling, I love you so much I feel as if the good Lord has opened my heart again."

He reached down and kissed her, and she gave herself up to the tall maleness of him, knowing in her heart that she would never love anybody the way she loved him. "What are we going to do?" she whispered when he released her. "How can I go? I don't have anything with me."

"Letitia's packed a few things for you. They're in my saddlebags."

"Letitia?" she asked, confused.

He nodded. "She's the only one with any sense in your whole household. She said to tell you, 'Listen to your heart.'"

"Oh, I don't know!"

He gripped her hands. "Suzannah, I've got two horses saddled and waiting just outside the White House grounds. It's your choice. You can either ride back to your mother and

Devroe Connaught, or you can take your chances with me. I can't give you any of the things that he can, with one important exception. I swear I'll love you like no other man can. Love you till the day I die. Will you come?"

"But where? Aren't you still working for President Jackson?"

"I am. And the general will be apoplectic when he finds out I've gone. But you're worth it. He did a few things for love in his day also."

"But mother and Devroe! They'll find us. I'm still not yet twenty-one. She can forcibly bring me back."

"I know, I thought of that already. And that's why we're leaving the United States. We're going to Texas to join up with a man named Stephen Austin. He's founded a colony of Americans there. Now I want you to know beforehand, there's not much of anything where I've bought some land, just a little mission called the Alamo. But we're going to Texas! And far away from the long arm of your mother."

"You mean go, right this very minute? Without telling her?"

"Absolutely! I'm not going to lose you again to her. She's a mighty strong woman, capable of doing just about everything to keep you with her. Suzannah, you've got to decide. Is it your life, or hers?"

At that moment, a cry went up from Andrew Jackson. The crowd had pressed so close to him that he was in danger of being crushed. "Leave him be, can't you see that he's ill?" Wingate shouted, but the pressing, surging people had one thought and one thought only, to touch their hero.

They forced Jackson against the wall, and he started to breathe in heaving gasps. "Over here, help! Before the general gets smothered!" Wingate shouted.

A band of Jackson's aides, including Ralph Earle, and John Eaton formed a ring around the President and pushed their way toward one of the tall windows in the East Room. Wingate shoved his elbow through the glass and then knocked out the entire frame. He helped the half-fainting President out of the window, and then down to the grass.

"Quick, get him back to Gadsby's," Wingate ordered, and a carriage was brought around. "We can lock the doors at the inn, and I can treat him there. I think he'll be all right."

Back in the East Room, Jonathan watched the delicate balance tremble and sway in Suzannah's eyes. Then she looked past him and the color drained from her face.

"What is it?" he asked, turning.

Then he saw Rebecca and Devroe heading toward them, Devroe flailing his riding crop about him and beating a path clear. His face was livid with anger, and Rebecca looked deathly pale.

"It's now or never," Jonathan said to Suzannah. "You've got another second or two at the most. What's it going to be?"

She slipped her hand into his and pulled him toward the window through which Jackson had escaped. She climbed out onto the sill. Jonathan vaulted out and onto the ground, and, reaching up, caught her as she dropped into his arms.

"Stop that man!" Rebecca screamed. "He's kidnapping my daughter!"

She and Devroe fought to get to the window, but the crowd closed around them again, and by the time they finally reached it they saw Suzannah and Jonathan galloping down Pennsylvania Avenue toward Georgetown and the west.

Rebecca appeared to be on the verge of fainting and her hand clutched at her throat. "I want him caught!" she said desperately.

"Consider it done," Devroe said. "My men and I will go after them. Don't worry, madam, they can't get very far. I have the fastest horses in these parts, and my dogs are the best trackers. We'll hunt him down, never fear."

"He forced her," Rebecca said. "You saw that yourself. And I want him hung!"

"To be sure," Devroe said curtly. "You may consider Jonathan Albright as good as dead."

"And there's no reason that the wedding can't take place as scheduled, is there?" Rebecca said, grasping at anything to hold her world together.

"No reason at all," he said. "Unless, of course, he has a chance to—well, you do remember the Connaught insistence on chaste brides."

The press of people became so unbearable that Rebecca moaned and struck out at them. But then some bright waiter had the idea of carrying what was left of the punchbowls out onto the lawn, and the greedy crowd followed after, swilling down the punch and gobbling the last of the cookies and cakes.

Rebecca stood in the empty shambles of the East Room. The grandest room in the American Palace had been torn to shreds by the mob. And as she looked around her, it seemed that everything she'd ever worked for, every dream she'd ever had—of a secure family, a decent, intelligent government—had been snatched from her.

Gunning, involved with a woman little better than a whore. Suzannah kidnapped. A government of law and order taken over by the mob. The American Palace reduced to a shambles. Even the President had had to flee for his life! How could the country possibly survive?

She felt the blood pounding in her head, felt herself grow dizzy with the onslaught of another attack. One more serious than anything she'd ever experienced. Has God ordained me to die at this lowest ebb of my life? she wondered. Is this my punishment for everything I've caused to happen?

And what will happen to my children . . . alone, defenseless.

"No, I can't, I won't die," she screamed inwardly. "I must save Suzannah!"

She pressed her hands to her temples, trying to contain the surging blood that threatened to overwhelm her. "I must live! I will!" she cried out, as the darkness engulfed her.

Selected Bibliography

Washington, D.C., and the White House

For a more complete bibliography on Washington and the White House, please see the listing in Book I of this series, *Bless This House*.

Adler, Bill, ed. *Washington: A Reader*. New York: Meredith Press, 1967.

Hurd, Charles. *The White House Story*. New York: Hawthorne Books, 1966.

Jensen, Amy La Follette. *The White House and Its Thirty-Two Families*. New York: McGraw-Hill, 1958.

Linton, Calvin D. *The Bicentennial Almanac*. New York: Thomas Nelson, 1975.

Sadler, Christine. *Children in the White House*. New York: Putnam, 1967.

Smith, Margaret Bayard. *The First Forty Years of Washington Society*. New York: Frederick Ungar, 1965.

Smith, Marie. *Entertaining in the White House*. Washington, D.C.: Acropolis Books, 1967.

Smith, Marie, and Louise Durbin. *White House Brides*. Washington, D.C.: Acropolis Books, 1966.

Tully, Andrew. *When They Burned the White House*. New York: Simon and Schuster, 1961.

Weisberger, Bernard A. *The District of Columbia*. New York: Time-Life Books, 1969.

Wolff, Perry. *A Tour of the White House with Mrs. John F. Kennedy*. New York: Doubleday, 1962.

New Orleans

Asbury, Herbert. *The French Quarter*. St. Simons Island, Ga.: Mockingbird Books, 1979.

Chase, John. *Frenchmen, Desire, Good Children*. New Orleans: Robert L. Crager & Co., 1960.

Dufour, Charles L. *Ten Flags in the Wind*. New York: Harper & Row, 1967.

Huber, Leonard V. *New Orleans: A Pictorial History*. New York: Bonanza Books, 1971.

Kane, Harnett T. *Queen New Orleans*. New York: Bonanza Books, 1949.

Stanforth, Deirdre. *Romantic New Orleans*. New York: Viking Press, 1977.

The Presidents and Their Homes

Barclay, Barbara. *Our Presidents*. Covina, Calif.: Classic Publications, 1977.

Boller, Paul F., Jr. *Presidential Anecdotes*. New York: Oxford, 1981.

Coke, Fletch. *Andrew Jackson's Hermitage*. Nashville: The Ladies' Hermitage Association, 1979.

Davis, Burke. *Old Hickory: A Life of Andrew Jackson*. New York: Dial, 1977.

Hunt-Jones, Conover: *Dolley and the Great Little Madison*. Washington, D.C.: American Institute of Architects Foundation, 1977.

Jones, Cranston. *Homes of the American Presidents*. New York: McGraw-Hill, 1962.

Madison, James. *James Madison in His Own Words*, 2 vols., ed. Merrill D. Peterson. New York: Newsweek, 1974.

Phillips, Leon. *That Eaton Woman*. Barre, Mass.: Barre/Westover, 1974.

Remini, Robert V. *Andrew Jackson and the Course of American Empire, 1767–1821*. New York: Harper & Row, 1977.

Remini, Robert V. *Andrew Jackson and the Course of American Freedom, 1822–1832*. New York: Harper & Row, 1981.

THE AMERICAN PALACE

As rich, as proud and fully as passionate as the
magnificent history on which it is based

FORGED IN FURY

by

Evan H. Rhodes

is the second in a monumental new series from
the pen of a major American novelist, telling
the story of our country's beginnings.

Watch for the third book in <u>The American
Palace</u> series,

coming next summer . . .

I love this country. I love its people, and I cherish its political form of government. When I began to work on *The American Palace* series, I naturally expected to be fascinated by Washington and its political intrigues, fascinated by the Presidents and their families who had occupied the White House—our American Palace. But what I discovered beggared any of my expectations.

Along with my research in Washington, I also set out across America and traveled more than ten thousand miles gathering material. In one such journey I followed the Lewis and Clark Expedition, by car, horseback, canoe, and foot. What I learned in my travels reaffirmed my belief in the basic goodness of our people.

My hope for this series is that it will effectively portray some of the magnificence of our heritage, and perhaps indicate an even greater magnificence in our future. I believe it can be ours if we but remain true to the dreams and aspirations of our forefathers.